ANCILLA

MASTER, TEACH ME

SERA MADDOX DRAKE

A Special Note to E-reader Users in 2026 and Beyond

A LARGE PLATFORM RECENTLY announced that it is rolling out a feature that enables its e-reader users to use enhanced AI functions. At a reader's request, books will be summarized by an embedded chatbot (without spoilers, supposedly, so you can catch up on your reading without being told how the story ends).

These e-reader users can also ask the chatbot to decipher the motives of characters, or just provide an opinion of what makes the characters and their relationships unique, or have "the book" (really, it's the chatbot) explain the significance of a scene, look for motifs, themes, and foreshadowing and other literary devices, and *voila!* There your answer is, right on the page for you, without your reading flow being disrupted! It's magic!

I can only say this: Please don't.

First, it's just plain lazy to get a bot to read and digest a book for you. "Brain rot" was Oxford University Press' word of 2024 for a reason. Hacks like this only make the problem worse.

Second, when I wrote this book, I meant it to be a highly personalized experience, but it's not the sort of highly personalized experience that an embedded bot can help a reader achieve. It took me eleven years of writing and editing to craft this first edition. If you opt to read the illustrated, revised edition, know that two more years of editing went into it.

Part of the process was spiritual. I meditated and prayed before writing each chapter. I wanted each chapter to embody the essence of a sephira on the Tree of Life, and I want you, the reader, to have the opportunity to receive insight as well.

A bot cannot help you with this. *Ancilla* is not meant to be easy on the reader. It's meant to crack an engaged reader open and let in light. You have to do the reading and reflection on your own.

The literary elements - themes, motifs, foreshadowing, characterization, structure, etc - are also better appreciated if they are not spoon-fed to a reader by a chatbot. Think of it as the difference between going to a restaurant and getting a chef-prepared, elegantly plated three-course lasagna dinner and nuking a frozen dinner in a microwave. In both cases, a meal is involved, and the meal will include lasagna, but one of these lasagna dinners is going to be far more satisfying and nourishing than the other.

Finally, as with all AI-assisted literature, the potential exists for plagiarism. I never consented to have a chatbot train itself on my writing. I also don't want anybody taking read-along summaries of my work and using those summaries to generate reviews of that work, or worse, generate characters or even entire stories that are just a regurgitation and rebranding of my intellectual property.

The technology may be available, but it is not a morally neutral sort of tech. It steals from me, and it ruins things for you. If that's "magic," then it's a malignant sort of magic. Please trust the magick of *Ancilla* instead, and surrender to the process. It involves a little more work, but you will receive a far better reward for your effort.

Content Warnings and Miscellaneous Notes

CONTENT WARNINGS

While the depictions of sexual activity in *Ancilla* are not exactly raunchy or smutty, nor are they the sole focus or even the primary focus of the book, this is still extremely sexually explicit material. The protagonist and her mentor/dom/soulmate do not make love behind closed doors, and they are BDSM edge players. *Adults only!*

The needles and blades used in the last few pages of the Gevurah chapter are potentially triggering to anybody afraid of sharp things or bloodplay. Also, the description of bloodplay might trigger people who fight an urge to self-harm.

There is a brief description of choking in the Netzach chapter; the Chokmah chapter has an Air working that involves breath control used as a method of vampirism, which might trigger memories or flashbacks of smothering for some readers. (*Dear readers, please do not do this at home. It's not safe*).

From what I have read online, it is common for descriptions of starvation or dieting to trigger people who have had eating disorders into relapse, so I should disclose that my protagonist spends more than half of the book starving due to food insecurity.

Chronic pain, vampiric starvation that closely mimics symptoms of clinical depression, and being generally emotionally overwhelmed make her contemplate suicide near the end of the book, and I have been warned that this could trigger some people who tend to self-harm.

There is discussion and depiction of homophobia because my protagonist is bisexual, and the book is set in the late 1980s to mid-1990s in rust belt Ohio. Anybody who is old enough to have survived that place and time knows how bad things were back then.

Beyond that... I'm sorry, but I have a hard time with content warnings because I haven't the foggiest idea what triggers people. Everyone is different. There are some things, some commonly encountered in real life, some not, that *I* find triggering. And to the best of my knowledge, there is no etiquette book for confused writers like me, so here I am, playing guessing games and hoping I don't cause somebody massive trauma just by writing words. If I have accidentally hit a trigger or a sore nerve or memory, put the book down, take a deep breath, do whatever you need to do to calm and ground yourself, and then, if you still want to keep reading, skim past the section that triggered you, and start reading again when you seem to have reached a safer part of the prose. Unfortunately, I can't come up with any advice more constructive than that, and I apologize from the bottom of my heart.

TRANSLATIONS

Translations of the Homeric Greek words "Magister" utters can be found in an appendix. I am not providing a similar page for the Latin phrases, because rough, loose, abbreviated translations are embedded in the chapters that make use of Latin quotes ("Binah" contains a short, rather famous one from Catullus; "Chesed" contains excerpts of the writings of Heloise and Abelard).

SOME GRATITUDE TO MY BETAS

Many, many thanks to my betas (especially Kirsten K, who midwifed key parts of the manuscript almost from its inception ten years ago, including sections that were not in her areas of interest or passion). You've done your best to stand in for the professional freelance editing I couldn't afford to use, and I am probably one of the most obnoxious writers ever. I snap at anyone who offers criticism, even when I need *and have solicited* criticism. I am thin-skinned and crotchety. I am stubborn. I never take the bad news of "this needs work" well, and I take "this needs to be changed or cut out" even worse. If it is any consolation, if you are reading this, I did take your suggestions to heart and I implemented them, which you will see if you read the book again. Thanks for putting up with me.

On Edge Play and BDSM In General

Ancilla is chock full of BDSM.

It's not that I have anything against vanilla *per se*, but it isn't the spice that I reach for first. Also, from a writing standpoint, I find that BDSM makes for interesting thought experiments.

BDSM stands for bondage, discipline, and sadomasochism. A number of non-fiction books have been written about it. Those who are curious would do worse than checking out the work of Lee Harrington, Dossie Easton, Catherine Liszt, Patrick Califia, and/or Jay Wiseman, to name a few. For something shorter than a book, Wikipedia is a solid enough place to start.

Like any hot pepper, BDSM can be used in small amounts to provide a little bit of extra heat or to bring out flavor, or the capsaicin level can be intensified to such a degree that the chili in the crock pot is asking for a visit from the local fire department.

It's not at all uncommon for otherwise vanilla couples to experiment a little in the kitchen and play around with a bit of spanking, light bondage, or creative role-play. The more intense things get, the less casual the kink, the less common.

This stands to reason if you think about it.

I'm not going to go into detail describing the various creative ways people can play with each other and find new and different things to do to spice up their lives. That would require me to write an entire book. I'd rather save that sort of writing for my fiction.

However, I do want to mention the existence of *edge play*. Please note that this is distinct from "edging," which refers to delaying orgasms for a protracted time.

Edge play is controversial in the BDSM community. Why? Because it might pass for RACK (risk-aware consensual kink) but it's only SSC (safe, sane, consensual) on a bare technicality.

We in the kink community put a great deal of stock in our alphabet soup, and our broth is full of SSC.

To be safe, play needs to be set up in such a way that actual harm and injury is unlikely to happen. Fun bruises and welts are one thing, but nobody likes a trip to the emergency room to treat ripped tendons.

Sanity is a bit more muddy and subjective, but basically it involves players discussing things well in advance of play and making sure trauma triggers are avoided, things do not get extreme to the point of being ridiculous, people do not make unrealistic demands of each other, and care is taken to approach things with a modicum of common sense.

I shouldn't even have to elaborate on what it means for love-games to be consensual, but I will, because in real life, there is unfortunately some confusion still about what consent entails. Enthusiastic consent is not just an "absence of no." People need to agree in advance to what they will be doing, they need to understand fully what the activity will entail, and they should check in frequently with each other to make sure they're still eager to keep doing it. If one person has temporarily given over power to another, it is especially important for the person in power to check frequently on the state of the person who has temporarily surrendered it. Safewords exist for a reason, and it's not just submissives who have the right to use a safeword.

Edge play pushes the limits of SSC on one or more of these points for the duration of play. Sometimes a person may agree to a temporary total power exchange, where no safeword will be honored and the dominant partner must be trusted with absolute control of the scene for the duration of play. Sometimes play may get very unsafe indeed - asphyxiation and other forms of breath play can cause permanent brain damage or even fatality, and while "choking" may be more popular these days than it used to be, that doesn't make it any more safe. Sometimes people may agree to play roles for a time in order to deliberately trigger traumatic memories and responses in an attempt to exorcise them or at least desensitize the person who has been coping with the trauma, which sounds like a great idea, except for the fact that sexual dominants are not trained therapists.

Edge play is controversial for a reason.

I write about edgy characters. Edge play makes for interesting thought experiments and interesting stories, and people who would dwell in the area marked HERE THERE BE DRAGONS if there was a map drawn make interesting characters. In real life, however, I will now urge people to exercise discretion, move at a pace that is comfortable, and keep the principles of SSC in mind. I would be surprised if many of you want to be characters in my tales. Some situations are better stories than realities.

REGARDING MATTERS OF CULTURAL SENSITIVITY

THIS NOVEL CONTAINS MATTER that is potentially offensive to members of some oppressed/colonized populations.

Some conservative Catholics may also find the content matter offensive.

Western esotericism is part of this story's bones. The protagonist starts her journey of personal and spiritual growth questioning her sedevacantist Catholic upbringing (more on this later) and dabbling in whatever New Age philosophies she finds. The man who eventually becomes her lover, meanwhile, is a magus who studies the philosophies and systems of Aleister Crowley, Thelema, and the Hermetic Order of the Golden Dawn.

Anyone who knows anything about the history of the Hermetic Order of the Golden Dawn and/or Thelema knows that those esoteric systems were cobbled together from a mishmash of looted mystical ideas from other cultures. The Kabbalah used by these orders has very little to do with Jewish Kabbalism, but were it not for Judaism, there would of course be no Kabbalah at all. Also appropriated wholesale by the Hermetic Order of the Golden Dawn and by the A∴A∴ only to be altered to the point of being barely distinguishable: meditation, yoga, Tantrism, alchemy, and elements of religious belief.

The world was their cafeteria, if by "world" you meant "anywhere the British East India Company set foot."

Does this mean anyone who believes in the principles of Thelema or sincerely strives for enlightenment within the belief system of the Hermetic Order of the Golden Dawn, including "Magister," my protagonist's mentor/dom/soulmate, is inherently wrong? No. It means there are some devout believers who follow inherently flawed systems. The same could be said of the believers of mainstream world religions. (And I say this as a believer myself, since I am a convert to Islam. God is perfect, but we humans are not. We get stuff wrong... so very, *very* wrong).

Since Western esotericism is built into this book, so is colonialism. There is no way around this. Because of the nature of their spiritual beliefs and practices, my characters loot and pillage cultures that have been oppressed by the West.

In the prologue (aka "Beginning") my protagonist dabbles in what she and a friend-with-benefits call "Tantra." It's not really Tantra. But they think it is, and they see nothing wrong with helping themselves to it. I have been told by a Desi reader that this is not only an inaccurate representation of Tantra, but it's also a profound offense to Hindu people. (It's probably equally offensive to Buddhist people, since Buddhist Tantrism is also a thing).

References to what the characters call "kundalini" appear in the "Tiphareth" chapter and the "Kether" chapter. This, too, is potentially offensive to Hindu and Buddhist believers, as is the sacred marriage "Magister" and "ancilla" bind themselves into.

Martial arts references pop up from time to time in this book as well, along with discussions of manipulating *ch'i*. This, too, is a form of cultural appropriation. Kung fu, aikido, and other martial arts were "borrowed" and made popular in the West many decades ago. Although I did my best to be respectful in my treatment of various martial arts principles and concepts, that does not change the fact that these are not originally Western arts.

The Hermetic Order of the Golden Dawn's version of the Kabbalah has structured the book to the point where each chapter is themed on a sephira of the Tree of Life. The lessons imparted by the chapters correspond to the sephiroth. There is an Afterword about this, but for now I will just say that this is not Jewish Kabbalah, it's Golden Dawn Kabbalah. I felt more comfortable stealing from the Hermetic Order of the Golden Dawn, a society of mostly male, mostly rich, occasionally deeply anti-Semitic dilettantes that was founded in the Victorian era, than I did from the original source. My Kabbalistic references, and their origin, may be triggering to Jewish people.

Finally, Catholic people may look at the practices and beliefs of my protagonist's parents and say, "That's not us. You're misrepresenting us." My protagonist's parents are not mainstream Roman Catholics - they're sedevacantists, people who believe that the Papal Seat has been *vacant* since Pope John XXIII enacted the Vatican II reforms. This is a reactionary schismatic sect, and sedevacantism is classified as a heresy. Its most famous adherent is Mel Gibson. The vast majority of Roman Catholics do not hold such strict beliefs, nor are they much like my protagonist's parents.

CONTENTS

DEDICATIONS

Fixed it for you, James. Better late than never. You're welcome.

For my Teasing Georgia muse, for my wonderful and long-suffering husband, and for my Beloved.

I have saluted my opponent, and I have honored the ones that inspired me. Now I lay on.

BEGINNING

INTRODUCTIONS ARE POLITE, so let's start here.

(Don't worry, this early bit won't take very long. We'll get to the more exotic fare soon enough, I promise).

I was playing in the backyard of a neighbor. I was maybe ten or eleven years old at the time.

My companion was a five-year-old who had started following me around whenever she saw me – I have no idea why my actual peers avoided having anything to do with me, whereas children much younger followed me around as if I were the Pied Piper, but that seemed to be the case, and I wasn't really in a position to object. It kept me from getting too lonely, and later, it turned into some paid babysitting jobs, which meant I could buy more books than what I could purchase with just the tiny allowance my parents kept me on. When I was still in lower school, though, it was more of a trade: I got somebody to play with who didn't bully me, and the parents tolerated or even welcomed my presence in return because they got free, unofficial babysitting, and time to themselves.

So, at any rate, I was in the girl's backyard by the jungle gym, as some of the other kids on the street, including her big sister, played soccer in another part of the yard.

Most of us hadn't bothered to change out of our school uniforms yet.

The girl who attended the more distant country day school had the best uniform, I thought: She had a dark blue blazer with a crest on it, a coordinating striped rep tie and pleated navy skirt, and a white dress shirt that had a really cute collar. Her knee socks blended in with the uniform perfectly, and the whole effect was very well put together. I thought she looked like one of the characters from The Facts of Life, only her uniform was blue, not red.

Meanwhile, I wore what the other three older kids were wearing, which was the plaid skirt and white dress shirt of the lower school that was only a few blocks away. Our plaid wasn't that different from the plaid of the nearby country day school. We had to wear saddle shoes, though, and their students did not. The saddle shoes were almost impossible to find unless you bought them from a store that had an arrangement with the school. We hated wearing them. We thought they were ugly and uncomfortable.

The kids I attended school with who were playing soccer had bagged their uniform shoes and kept on the cleats they'd worn for soccer practice. Why they felt a need to keep playing soccer with their neighbors after they'd just finished two sweaty hours of soccer practice with their classmates on our school's athletic field, I had no idea.

Nobody in my neighborhood went to a public school.

Since the others were busy kicking a ball around the yard, the only people near the jungle gym were me and the little girl. I was sitting on a swing, trying to read The Martian Chronicles. *I'd just discovered Ray Bradbury. I'd already read* Dandelion Wine *and* Something Wicked This Way Comes, *and I couldn't get enough.*

The little girl wanted to go across the monkey bars hand over hand, but every time she tried to do it, she crumpled under her own fear. She looked like she was close to tears from frustration.

I probably wasn't going to have peace and quiet enough to do any reading, anyway.

"Would you like some help?" I asked.

She looked up, dubious, and nodded. I was her favorite Pied Piper. She'd ask me for help.

I lifted her arms high again and hoisted her so that her hands could once again grasp the first bar. "Hold on tight. I'm going to let go," I said, remembering what my swim instructor said when she was teaching me how to tread water in the deep part of the pool.

The girl's eyes widened.

"I'll be right here," I said. "I won't let you fall." I slowly let her go but kept my hands about an inch away from her trunk. "See? I'm right here."

She nodded.

I stepped back by about a foot. "Now grab the next bar with your right hand. That one," I said, tapping her hand, realizing that I didn't want to make her think hard about anything right now, including which hand was her right and which hand was her left. "I'm right here. See? Here are my hands. They're right here. I won't let you fall. I promise."

With eyes as big as dinner plates, she let go of the bar and grabbed the next one.

"That's it. Now do the same thing with your other hand. Forward, now. I'm right here."

Eventually, we got across the entire set of monkey bars that way. When she fell into my arms after the last bar, I put her down on the ground, and she shrieked, "I did it! I did it!" and started jumping around, unable to contain herself.

I smiled and went back to reading.

The soccer game in the other part of the yard continued unabated.

FOR THE MOST PART, *though, my playmates were not children of any age – not peers, not the little toddlers and preschoolers that always seemed to be attaching themselves to me and trailing in my wake. They weren't even really playmates. Adults liked me better than other children did. When I played, I played alone. When I socialized with grownups, it was just talk, unless we were playing board games or otherwise doing something formal.*

I've always liked board games. I think I got into the habit of playing board games because of my father. We were very close, then – when I was young. He was the one who taught me to play chess.

He started with checkers. When I could beat him fair and square at checkers, he said, then he would buy me a chess set. It took me almost a year to win my first game of checkers, but when I did, he was as good as his word, and that was how, at the age of five, I became the owner of a beautiful chess board made of polished wood, with matching pieces carved to look like medieval foot soldiers, nobles, and courtiers. And then he used it to teach me chess. By the time I was six years old, I had learned all the gambits he knew, and I had even managed to beat him three times.

He never let me win. He didn't believe in coddling. With my father, you either beat him on your own, or he beat you at the game he played with you, and that was that. It's a great way to teach a child the game of chess if you see the child has an aptitude, and you want to nurture it. He might have seen in me the potential to be a chess master, and had I not discovered Barbie dolls on my seventh birthday, I might very well have gone in that direction.

Oh, well.

He also taught me how to dance. He taught me the fox trot, the box step, the waltz, even the jitterbug. I forgot how to dance when I got older because I had no occasion to use my dancing skills, but when I was little, we used to dance around the marble entryway of our house, laughing, circling the fountain like whirling leaves.

Before I was born, he said, he used to dance with my mother; but that was in the past. Her health was not robust. Her joints hurt her, and she always seemed to have a headache. She took to her bed once a month for several days with what I eventually found out were heavy periods that not only doubled her over with pain but actually drained her so heavily that she took iron pills that had been prescribed for anemia. She had help in the house on the weekdays, and when she was up and around, mostly she just sat in her chair in the television room and crocheted lace or sewed, or if it was winter and the trees had lost their leaves, giving us an unobstructed view of the river, she would gaze out the window at the barges that could sometimes be seen. Her dancing days were over.

On our piano were framed pictures, including one with her dancing with my father at their wedding. She looked like a completely different person in that photograph. My father just looked like a younger version of himself. Thin, like me. Red-headed, like me. Dapper in white tie. Smiling at his lovely, elegant new bride.

He used to read to me – Winnie the Pooh and Heidi and the fairy tales of Hans Christian Andersen, when I was very young indeed, and of course, stories from the Bible when we said prayers at bedtime; but as soon as I seemed old enough

to appreciate stronger fare, he would read to me stories from Edith Hamilton's
Mythology *and tales of King Arthur from Malory.*

The more questionable stuff, such as how Zeus begat practically everybody in
Greek myth and legend in practically every form imaginable or unimaginable, or
how Mordred was conceived when Arthur had a tryst with his own sister, he skipped
over, but I got quite a healthy dose of tales of chivalry and adventure. He also read to
me from The Song of Roland, *and other medieval tales, and from* The Chronicles
of Narnia.

He was a history teacher at the upper school that was a part of the school con-
sortium whose lower school I attended. Different campus, but same school – as
I gathered from reading old yearbooks and news clippings, there used to be four
separate private schools that merged into a sort of educational cooperative, and the
campus of the former upper school used to be located on the campus of what became
the location of the lower and middle school I was enrolled in.

I was at that school because that was where my father had taught for years, and
we had a discount on the tuition because of it, not that we needed it, since most
of our family income came not from my father's meager salary, but from interest
on inherited investments. (I'm sure there are many private schools that pay their
teachers almost the same salary that could be expected by a tenured professor at a
college or university, but the school that I attended and that employed my father
was not one of those schools. But really, who teaches history for the money?)

Having his only child be a precocious and lonely young girl meant that he could
share his love of the age of faith and chivalry with a captive audience, with his history
lessons falling on eager ears. How could I not love Arthur and Merlin, Percival and
Gawain, Lancelot and Galahad? They became more real to me than my classmates.
They were kinder and more interesting.

My father believed in chivalry. I believe he fancied himself, in his more senti-
mental moments, to be the scion of some ancient noble family or other, and given
the family tree, his self-perception may very well have had some basis in reality,
although genealogy is ultimately a self-flattering game of Six Degrees of Separation,
because anybody can be related – related legitimately! – to a rich, noble, or famous

person by enough marriage lines traced. Still, nobility seemed to be important to him, and that is probably more important than any actual noble blood, whether real or imagined.

Noblesse oblige, *he would say, as if we were in fact noble, and thus required to act like the lords and ladies we secretly were; and while I am not so certain today that he completely managed to live up to his ideals, I think it would be fair to say that he probably* tried *to live up to them.*

I BECAME PART OF my small church's choir after I was confirmed. The choir consisted of one bass, two tenors, one alto, and three sopranos. I was the designated alto. Technically, I was also a soprano, but I had a wide vocal range, and the choir needed altos, so an alto I was.

That September it was as hot as July. Our church hadn't yet bought its two central air units for the sanctuary and parish hall (the units were eventually nicknamed Paul and Silas because they were nested in a protective barred metal cage that looked vaguely like a jail) so the only relief from the heat came from open windows, and from several electric floor fans that did little real cooling. I was roasting in my vestments. More than anything, I wanted to sit down in the pew to rest, but that was out of the question because the choir stalls were up front near the altar, and on display to the rest of the congregation.

Noblesse oblige.

It was some time shortly after the consecration of the Host that I succumbed to the heat and, I think, the incense and the candle smoke, and lost consciousness.

When I came to, I was lying on the cool, tiled floor of the refectory, with wet cloths on my forehead and wrists. Church was still going on, so the only people there were my mother and father. I had no idea who carried me downstairs to the parish hall, or how. It couldn't have been my mother. She wasn't strong enough.

"I should have been allowed to sit down," I grumbled.

To which my father said, "Can the priest, who is wearing even hotter clothing than you are, and far more of it, sit down? He has an obligation to celebrate the Mass, no matter what. And you, as long as you are in the choir, seen by all members of the congregation, have an obligation to behave as a chorister. That means showing up for rehearsals, even when you have more interesting things to do, such as reading that new science fiction book you just bought; it also means kneeling or standing to sing when you would rather be sitting down comfortably, and remaining in your place even when you want to be elsewhere, such as a cool, air-conditioned room, because you are setting an example for all who behold you. You are in a leadership position, whether you are aware of it or not, and a leader must follow stricter rules than everybody else, to earn the respect of those who follow. Nobility imposes obligation."

In other words, it was my fault that I fainted.

He did try to live by his creed of leading by example. He tried to give back to the community what he might take from it as a member of the taking class, albeit in what I would consider very minor ways – giving food and other charitable gifts to the impoverished, volunteering in a soup kitchen on Thanksgiving morning and afternoon, taking part in community litter clean-up and tree plantings and Neighborhood Watch patrols.

And of course, he tried to lead by example in the way he felt was the most important of all, namely, doing his best to live in an upright and moral way, at least as he saw it. He put more energy into doing that than he did into any kind of community service.

We have since had our differences, which I will go into, and there were many, but I would be lying to myself if I did not admit that of all the teachers who were my friends and role models when I was a child, he was my favorite, and I probably do take after him in many ways.

THAT WAS MY CHILDHOOD, then. Wealthy? Yes. Sheltered? Yes. Lonely, absolutely yes. But it was hardly something I should call unhappy.

Even when I was bullied by classmates who were better at sports or, I guess, at simply talking to each other than I was (and for all I know, they probably bullied each other as well, over other minor things that made good excuses for bullying) I would not call my childhood a bad one. I think for the most part I was probably happy.

I had what I wanted. I had a never-ending supply of books to read, teachers whom I generally impressed and beguiled into making me their pet, and a life free of want. I might have been unhappier had I been more desperate to make friends my own age and to fit in with my peers, but I was not very interested in that. Or so I told myself.

And then came adolescence.

My parents pulled me out of the school I'd attended since I was four years old and put me in a private Catholic school for girls.

They were a little concerned that the school's required religious curriculum, post-Vatican II that it was, would give me liberal ideas and corrupt me away from what was supposed to be a very straight and narrow path, but my father considered it inappropriate, due to conflict of interest, to be one of my school-teachers, and he would have taught my history classes had I gone on to the upper school in my academic consortium.

Also, the upper school, like the lower schools and the middle school, was coed. My parents had moral sensibilities straight out of the Victorian era and considered it unseemly for a girl of my age to be in classes with boys. I would have been more than happy to go to a boarding school in New England like the one my father attended when he was my age, but I was the only child, and my mother said she would miss me too much if I was sent up to boarding school somewhere, so a local private school for girls it was. The only single-sex high schools in our city were all Catholic.

It wasn't a bad change. Without boys present, gym class was suddenly a lot less embarrassing. Even better, for some reason, I have no idea why, the bullying stopped. I still wasn't even remotely popular, but being ignored was a step above being bullied.

The new school, furthermore, had something that my former school did not: philosophy classes. All the philosophy classes were taught by a genial old priest whose shadow I worshiped the instant I heard him talk.

My new school was in one of those experimental open-air buildings that had been so popular in the late sixties and early seventies – they were called "open-air" despite being indoors because there were almost no interior walls or classrooms for the most part (the wing that housed the noisy and messy areas, such as the music rooms, the gymnasium, the art studios, the theatre, and the home economics lab, was an exception, as was the perpetually chemical-scented wing that housed the darkroom and the science laboratories). The whole idea was to encourage students to learn to concentrate carefully on their own classroom teachers and tune out any background noises. Some students floundered and wound up going elsewhere; I never really had a problem with it. Either you sink or you swim, in that kind of environment, and I was a swimmer.

One time, though, I found my attention wandering during Latin class, and directly behind me happened to be the most amazing lecture I had ever heard.

"According to Plato – and, by extension, Socrates, whom Plato uses as his authorial mouthpiece – the vast majority of human beings are like prisoners in a cave, chained facing a wall, and unable to turn their heads to see anything other than that wall and whatever shadows get reflected onto it," I heard a teacher's voice saying.

Curious, I turned my head enough to see the classroom behind me. The teacher was a short, apple-cheeked, somewhat rotund man wearing a clerical collar and black shirt over neatly pressed blue jeans.

For me, it was love at first sight. Love of Plato? Love of the priest who was teaching the philosophy class? I would not have been able to answer that question then, and I doubt I would be able to answer it now.

Like the proverbial prisoners in the cave, I could not turn my head any more than I already had, but I could tune out my Latin teacher and listen to the lecture that was going on behind me.

"So, what happens when one of the prisoners somehow manages to free himself?

"First, the prisoner will behold things in the cave itself as they are, rather than mistaking the shadows dancing on the wall for reality.

"Of course, increasing knowledge begets yet more curiosity, and the former prisoner will eventually leave the cave, and emerge, blinking, into the blinding light of day. He will begin to grow accustomed to the sight of this strange new world.

"And first, he will see the shadows of things best, and things as they are reflected in water, until he can look around him and see the objects themselves; then he will gaze upon the light of the moon and the stars. Finally, he will be able to behold the sun; and he will, as Plato puts it, 'contemplate him as he is.' This, then, is enlightenment.

"Enlightenment confers a certain responsibility, according to Plato. The enlightened philosopher is called to be a teacher; the philosopher must attempt to share enlightenment, you see, although often the gift of enlightenment will be unwanted by the prisoners who still define their lives by the shadows they see flickering on the wall.

"Nevertheless, knowledge must at least be made available to those others who would seek it, no matter if it causes a certain amount of discomfort by shaking the status quo. It's about seeking heaven, in a sense; the quest for ultimate truth is the quest for union with God, even in the face of society's lack of understanding, even in the face of social opprobrium and utter loneliness.

"Plato calls God 'the sun,' but I think we can all agree that this must be allegorical – Plato was not a sun worshipper. It was the truth he was after. 'The prison-house is the world of sight, the light of the fire is the sun, and you will not misapprehend me if you interpret the journey upwards to be the ascent of the soul...'

"And there you have it. We must look away from the world of phenomena and direct our eyes to the sublime."

It was then that my Latin teacher managed to break into my trance of concentration. She had been calling on me to read and translate aloud a certain passage from the Aeneid for some time, and this was the third time she had called my name.

"I'm sorry. I got distracted. There was a really interesting class behind me. They were talking about Plato."

"Well, at least you were paying attention to the classics, although you're supposed to be studying Roman literature right now, not Greek," she said, her mouth quirking with amusement. "Now, kindly translate Virgil for the rest of us."

Of course, as I was to find out later, it didn't really matter how well I did in school, or how well-read I was, at least not to my parents. Appearances were everything.

THE OTHER CHANGE THAT came with adolescence, and this, alas, brought problems enough to cause me trouble, was that I discovered sex. Or maybe it would be more accurate to say that sex discovered me. I was unaware. I was so ignorant that you, who read these memories I have committed to paper, will probably want to laugh... Or maybe cry. I don't know.

See through my eyes.

I STAND NAKED IN my boyfriend's bedroom, my gawky teenage body shivering in the air-conditioned chill. The cold is making my nipples stick out from what little I have of breasts. Or maybe it's my nervousness making them do that.

I never thought it would happen, but somehow, I found a kindred spirit.

We met several months ago through a school musical. My high school's thespian society was putting on a production of *Scrooge*, which had a few large choral numbers, and since I was in the chorus and the vocal ensemble, I got dragooned into the production as an extra, along with the rest of the chorus and vocal ensemble.

We were collaborating with one of the local all-male Catholic high schools to get a supply of tenors and basses to fill out the cast and to obtain male actors for the appropriate roles – Ebenezer Scrooge, Bob Cratchit, et cetera. My boyfriend was the Ghost of Christmas Future.

I met him backstage. He was reading Tolkien.

My parents aren't happy about me dating anyone, but they're tolerating it for now ("He seems harmless enough," my mother had muttered after I got back from our first date – I'd introduced him to my parents before going out with him to see the latest Star Trek movie, in which Kirk and Spock steal a spaceship to go down to Earth and save the whales, and the less said about the small talk we tried to make for the duration of the introduction, the better) and somehow we've managed.

I have a very early curfew – ten o'clock, well before my bedtime – but there are ways around curfews.

One way to spend plenty of time with him is to set up afternoon dates. After we had several months of library dates, and closely monitored study dates at my house, it convinced my parents that I could be trusted to actually *study* on a study date, so I am now allowed to study at his house on occasion. During the summer, when we don't have school, we mostly just read science fiction books, or play Talisman. His mother is downstairs the whole time, so it's not like my parents need to worry about our dates being unchaperoned.

We still haven't worked up the nerve to kiss each other yet. Isn't that funny? We've been dating for months, and we decided today to play doctor because I'd never played doctor as a child, and neither had he, and we found out that apparently that's something nearly every kid does, and we've missed out on a large part of childhood, so here I am, naked.

Although we still haven't even kissed.

We have at least established that my temperature is 99.1 degrees ("Well within normal range") and that I have a pulse. Also, that my amber eyes are a clear indication of a rare recessive gene trait, although it doesn't seem to mean anything other than that I have weird eyes, which I kind of already knew.

He bends down to put his ear up against my chest to listen to my heart.

"Sorry. I don't have a stethoscope," he says, his voice an octave higher than usual. "Heart seems fine. Nice, strong heartbeat."

His hair tickles my chest.

"I need to test your reflexes, now," he says. "Could you sit on the bed and cross your knees?"

He doesn't have a rubber mallet, so we decide to use one of my Dr Scholl's sandals as a substitute.

My left foot flies in the air.

"Ow."

"Sorry," he mumbles. "Your shoe is heavy. I didn't hurt your knee too much, did I?"

"No."

"Good. Okay. And you have good reflexes. Um." He blushes. "Could you open your legs?"

"Why?"

"I need to check you."

"*Why?*"

"Because... because that's just how it's done. Doesn't your doctor do a complete examination when you have your physical every year?"

"No."

"Huh. Mine does. Um. You're not... bleeding, are you? Like, wearing a tampon?" He blushes even harder.

"No! Mom says I'll lose my virginity if I use a tampon. And anyway, I'm not having my period. I just had it, remember?"

"How can you lose your virginity to a *tampon?* That's not even possible."

I blush.

"I promise, I won't try anything. I just want this to be done the right way."

Oh, God. He's going to be the first person to get a good look at me since I was a baby, or at least since I was eleven years old, and he's going to think I'm horribly, horribly ugly, because I'm not normal.

I had a friend in sixth grade who told me this. She was one of the few friends I ever had. She was as unpopular as I was because everyone said she was a lesbian, also that she had lice (she did *not* have lice) so we wound up always eating lunch together and eventually, we had sleepovers, and one night we were up late playing

Clue after watching Saturday Night Live, a show that would have given my parents conniption fits if they'd known I watched it, and we were both naked because we'd been playing Truth or Dare and one thing led to another, so there we were playing Clue naked, and out of the blue she looked at me and said "You have a penis." (She'd also tried to kiss me, earlier, which I'd found confusing). But anyway, we were friends. Friends don't lie to each other, do they?

"Please don't hate me," I say, as I cringe and open my legs.

He blinks. "Why on earth would I hate you?"

"Because. Because I have a penis. My best friend said so. She saw me."

"What? No, you don't."

"I *do.*"

"I got a good look at you when you took your clothes off, actually. You don't." He grins. "Trust me. I'm a doctor, remember?"

"But why don't I look like... I thought I was supposed to have a hole there."

He sighs. "No, no, no. I mean, I've never seen a naked girl up close, except for you, but I know that's not always what girls look like externally. I've seen pictures. In magazines." He blushes again. "Haven't you had sex ed? My high school required it as part of ninth-grade health class."

"I was embarrassed. I got an F."

"Oh. Hmm. Well, that explains things, I guess... Would you. Can I. Um. This would be easier if I could point and use my fingers. Um... Could I?"

I nod. I'm blushing harder than ever, now.

"So, okay. This is what I remember from my health class. I'll put it together with some of the, um, pictures I've seen. The diagrams they give us in sex ed class are kind of crap. So. This is your vagina. You absolutely do not have a penis. We don't look anything alike. I mean, if you really want, I could show you, so you have some basis for comparison – no, no, better not. Anyway. These folds of skin here," he says, his face red as a plum as he quickly runs the tip of his finger along the portion of my anatomy he's referencing, "that look kind of like curtains, only they stick out, these are part of your vagina. They're called your labia. Labia minora. They come in all different shapes and sizes, from what I've read. And sometimes they sort of dangle outside, rather than staying tucked neatly behind the outer labia, because for some girls they extend past – um, are you okay?"

I'm gasping. God, it feels good when he's touching me there. It feels much better than when I touch myself there, even when I'm rubbing myself to get off.

I'm also probably blushing harder than he is. He's my *boyfriend*. And he's touching me.

"I'm okay."

"Good. Okay, this part right here at the top? Sort of peeking out from behind that little bit of skin, when I lift it? That is a clitoris. Also, like your labia minora, not a penis..."

"...*Oh!*"

"You okay?"

"I'm okay," I gasp. I'm definitely okay, now. I'm more than okay.

"Gosh, you turn red all over when you blush... Oh." He notices that I'm still panting a little. He gulps. "Sorry. I didn't mean to... I was just trying to get things right. So, anyway. You're healthy. And I can safely say you're a girl. Nothing extra there. I'm not sure what your friend was going on about. Maybe she was trying to play a trick on you?"

I'm normal, after all?

"*It's a miracle!*" I cry out, and then I start laughing. "Thank you! Thank you!"

After I have my clothes back on, we cuddle together on the bed, reading our books – he's reading something called *A Fish Dinner in Memison*, I'm reading *The Mists of Avalon* because I can't take it home. My father would want to borrow it because it's Arthurian stuff, and if he read it, he would absolutely freak out at the Goddess worship and the Druidism and the sex.

It's probably just as well he doesn't know about my boyfriend's large collection of *Advanced Dungeons and Dragons* modules, and the gaming we've done, alternating who gets to be the player and who is the dungeon master, or the back issues of *Dragon* magazine, which has this really funny comic strip about gamers who are so stupid that they think gazebos are monsters – all that's Satanic, according to my parents.

Or about the Heinlein novels, either. Thanks to my reading about Valentine Michael Smith and Lazarus Long, both of whom seemed to live very happy lives, without hurting anybody, despite doing things differently from the way my parents taught me life ought to be lived, I have decided that monogamy is just an exotic rainforest wood, and nothing I particularly need to have as a fixture in my home, once I am grown up and have a place of my own.

My boyfriend then asks me, "Wait, how could you think you have a penis if you've been having periods, and you don't want to insert a tampon?"

"Can't a person have both?"

"Oh. Hmm. Probably yes. But you don't."

We go back to reading.

A little after that, he gives me my very first kiss, and I have my second orgasm that day, and learn that I have something called a "hair trigger."

I WAS STUPID. I wrote about liking being kissed in my diary, which I had thought was stashed in a safe hiding place. The aide found it and took it to my mother.

I didn't mention the circumstances of the kiss when I wrote about it, but the very fact that I had allowed my boyfriend to kiss me was enough for my parents. They made me break up with him. He was no longer "harmless enough." Neither was I. I spent my senior year grounded.

My father made me do evening prayers with him every night as if I were a child again, and he made me leave the church choir because I was no longer someone to be looked up to. I didn't understand why my being seen in church wearing choir robes and singing hymns at Mass should suddenly be a shameful thing, nor did the choir director, who had no idea what was going on behind the scenes and begged my father to let me stay in the choir, because I was still the only alto, but my father was adamant.

Actual sexual experience, due to a number of different factors, didn't happen until I was in college on a partial academic scholarship that my parents were too proud of to make me turn down (and I was glad to be several hundred miles away, on the other side of the state – by then I wanted nothing to do with my parents' rules. I think I must have been the only freshman in my dorm who didn't cry from homesickness on my first night away from home).

By then I had acquired a different boyfriend, who I'd met when he sat next to me in my Rationalism and Empiricism class and struck up a conversation about Pascal's wager. And yes. By then I knew it was possible to do more with my body than just kiss.

HIS MOUTH IS WARM and moist against my genitals, his tongue doing insane, almost unbelievable things to me until I fall over the edge into orgasm, screaming out in pleasure and need.

He's been at this for a while tonight.

Months, really; we've been groping and mouthing each other for months, while I've wrestled with the demons of my childhood religious indoctrination, banging my head against the concrete wall of my boyfriend's dorm room until he begged me to stop before I hurt myself, crying myself to sleep in his arms after every make-out session, or at least trying to cry, for what passionate joy could I have if I did not pay a price in guilt afterward?

It has finally reached the point where I no longer care if I burn in hell for having sex before marriage. I've already been seen naked, all of me, including all the parts normally covered by underwear, and I've had all those parts touched, as deeply as fingers can reach inside; that means I'm not a virgin, by some definitions anyway, right?

So, it's too late for me.

And I want to, so badly. I want him, he wants me. I'm pretty sure I love him. He's told me he loves me. What more do I need? Maybe we'll marry later, maybe not, but we've been fumbling at each other for all the last semester and the beginning of this one, now, and I don't want to wait any longer than he does.

The orgasms he's given me tonight haven't satisfied me, any more than they have before. They've only left me hungry for something more.

"Now," I moan. "Tonight. Now."

"You're sure?"

"Yes."

He gets up and takes a condom out of his drawer, one that came in a discreet brown paper bag from the campus health center. He struggles with it for a few seconds, but eventually manages to get it on his member – it seems to be fairly goof-proof, really – and reaches for me.

He's warming me with his fingers, caressing me, entering me, gently stretching me, making me burn again until I'm practically engulfed by my need. I don't know how he can be so patient. He's been waiting so long for me, an eternity of unfulfilled desire, all because of my wavering and fear.

He climbs on top of me. I open my thighs for him and guide him into me with my hand.

And instantly my world is blazing agony.

I collapse onto the floor of his dorm room into a fetal ball. Blood is gushing out of me. It's not a period. It's not that kind of blood. There's too much of it. The pain stabs me; I clutch my abdomen, keening, trying to shove everything back, to make it stop.

"Are you all right? Do I need to take you to the emergency room?"

I'm pretty sure it wasn't supposed to be like this. I know I don't want to go to the hospital, though. My parents would see the bill, get scared, and ask questions, and if they find out I'm not a virgin any longer, I don't know what they'll do to me. Nothing good.

At the very least I'm pretty sure they'll pull me out of college. I don't want to leave college – this is the first place I've ever really been happy and made friends. I'm picking all my own classes and my professors and classes are all great; and I'm in a medieval reenactment club and a gaming club and a classics club and a chorus. I'm enrolling in an introduction to bagpiping class. I'm going to be initiated into a sorority soon. Oh, God, I don't want to have to give all of this up...

"No, I think this is normal," I reply, still crumpled in a fetal ball, trying not to whimper. "I've read about it in romance novels. I'll be fine. Can I have a towel?"

In RETROSPECT, *I* DO *know that it's not normal to have an experience right out of* The Bell Jar.

(Even in The Bell Jar, *it wasn't normal. Since that sort of profuse bleeding was supposed to be a "once in a million occurrence," I have to wonder if maybe Plath drew on her own personal experience when she wrote about the aftermath of cherry popping. Surely that was too weird for her to have just made up. Did she also think about turkey necks the whole time, too, then, the way her self-modeled protagonist did? That must have been unfortunate).*

Hymens are thin outer membranes, part of the labia, rather like half-open sheer curtains at windows, not internal blood bladders that sit inside the vaginal walls, acting as gate guardians that somehow allow fingers and tongues and tampons to enter, but not penises, and should some cock manage to bypass security, they perforce self-destruct to create a fatal distraction that stops coitus from happening.

All my research tells me that one's first experience of sexual intercourse is not supposed to cause near-hemorrhaging, indeed, if there has been adequate foreplay and plenty of lubrication and stretching, the hymen may not bleed at all – it may just part as it is stretched. Which was certainly the case with me. I couldn't have had a gentler, more attentive first love. And yet, there it was: I experienced awful pain upon first being entered, and I bled like a stuck pig.

More proof that I am a freak.

At any rate, I survived. I even somehow recovered without getting any real medical attention. I wish I could say the same thing about the relationship, but I can't.

One reason things didn't work out was that I discovered girls soon after I discovered sex, but that was only one contributing factor. There were many, many others, foremost of which could be summed up by saying that attraction does not always coincide with compatibility. Forget the old saying. Amor, eheu, non omnia vincit.

SHE IS SO WARM in my arms. We have been dancing around each other, finding excuses to sit together, so that our skin touches; to put our heads on each other's shoulders; to give each other back rubs. We hold hands, then trail our fingertips along each other's palms and forearms when we break apart...

I've never wanted anybody so badly.

"What if we're damned?" she asks me, her voice trembling. "What if the whole reason we're so attracted to each other is that our faith is being tempted?"

"Do you really think God would be that cruel?"

"No..."

We silence our words and thoughts with kisses.

She has a long-distance boyfriend who is in the army. Her boyfriend does not know about me, or about the fact that his girlfriend is starting to realize that she likes other women more than she likes men.

She wants to come out of the closet and break up with him in person, rather than through a letter or over the telephone, and I wish I had the strength to wait for her until after the fact, but he won't be visiting her for many weeks, and we only have so much time before spring is over and with it, the school year, and we are tired, so tired of waiting.

What if we never have each other? I have no more strength to hold out against this need, nor does she. It is done.

All the desperate love poetry we've written to each other has ended here, in this dusty storage room in the attic of the art building, while our sorority sisters play volleyball on the quad outside, heedless of what is going on in here.

I went through Rush Week for the experience, and the free food; I pledged the sorority on a whim because it had a reputation for being the straight arrow geek Hellenic organization on campus (average GPA: 3.91; during the lip synch competition last Greek Week, they lip-synched to Handel's "Hallelujah Chorus" from the *Messiah*; good grief, half the sisters, including the woman in my arms, who was my sorority Big Sister, were members of the town medieval reenactment group, just like I was, having discovered the meetings that were held on our college campus; and they were also gamers, and they wanted to initiate me because I seemed open to learning how to play Dungeons and Dragons, and they needed a rogue to round out their adventuring party. Where were they, all my life? Oh, God, what if they find out about us and expel us? No, I can't think about this now) and a part of me wanted to belong to a group, just wanted to *belong*, and maybe being an only child made the idea of having a group of sisters seem somehow so exotic that how could it not be everything I ever wanted?

And then I met her, and it was clear to the both of us, given the passing of enough time, that we wanted to be so much more to each other than just sisters.

If her parents find out, they will disown her. If my parents find out, they will disown me. Hell. If my parents find out, it will probably *destroy* them.

But now we are here, stealing kisses from each other; stealing gasps and sighs. Her skin is so soft. Her breath is so sweet. She's moaning into me as I kiss her, melting her skin against mine. Trembling, I reach for one of her breasts.

I didn't know this ecstasy was even possible.

Desire shakes us like thunder.

THAT WAS IN MID-APRIL. Two weeks later came the spring formal. If you are wondering how much religious angst, self-recrimination, second-guessing, and general worrying a sedevacantist Catholic and an Apostolic Pentecostal can produce when coming out of the closet to each other and falling in love, or maybe, if we are being honest with each other, in an infatuation so overwhelming and hopeless that it seems virtually indistinguishable from love, the answer is: A lot.

None of that was enough to stop us from succumbing to desire, of course.

A cynical part of me even wonders if maybe the guilt and existential torment added spice. Few things, after all, are tastier than forbidden fruit. If that was the case, the hot sauce had a very limited shelf life. Before the school year was out, I had gone sort of generically Unitarian, bordering on Emersonian transcendentalism, with occasional moments of "what the hell can we even know about all this, anyway?" and a heavy dose of New Age; and my girlfriend, meanwhile, eventually converted to Wicca after she ignored her resolution to stay completely in the closet and poured her heart out to one of the townies, a motherly sort of schoolteacher who, like us, was a member of the local medieval reenactment group. A motherly schoolteacher whom she wound up seducing, many months later. It's funny how things work out, isn't it?

SHE LIES ON HER bed, naked. I was the one who undressed her. Her long, dark hair and tiny frame take my breath away. I've never seen anyone like her. I've studied the nude female form in works of art – statues, nude paintings, that sort of thing, I took an art history course this year – but nothing prepared me for her. She is radiant.

Her formal dress, a confection made of navy blue and white striped taffeta and ruffles, lies crumpled on the floor. My long yellow vintage granny gown, with the square neckline and lace and seed pearls that made me think I was Juliet Capulet the first time I tried it on, lies on top of it in coital abandon, a single filmy cotton sleeve nudged into a wrinkly crevasse of navy satin. The dresses seem surer of themselves than we are.

I swallow past the lump in my throat to kiss her lips. When her mouth opens and her tongue darts out to meet mine, I taste the blackberry wine we've each had a glass of.

One of us is trembling. I don't even know which one of us it is.

I want every inch of her. Her ears. Her dark walnut hair, which smells like flowery shampoo. Her eyes. Her cheeks. Her throat, oh, her throat, which feels like rich, smooth silk.

I resolve to kiss her everywhere no matter how long it takes.

Her musk blends with the vanilla scent emanating from the lit candle that sits on her dresser.

"My lady," I whisper as I kiss her hand, one reverent kiss, then another and another until I am covering her in a flurry. When I work my way up her arm until I finally reach a small and perfectly pointed breast, she moans, and the gasp she makes when I take her nipple in my mouth lances my heart.

The candle flickers and makes wild dancing shadows on the wall.

She has small feet, almost dainty. I bend down on my knees to worship them before working my way up her legs. Her skin, by candlelight, is a perfect shade of ivory, aside from the areas where the shadows dance; and soft, so soft.

Thighs like white satin.

Lips ripe as berries, and the juice as sweet.

A moan like a dove's cry.

Oh, my lady. Let me fill the night with your cries. I want to hear nothing else. I want my ears to be filled with your beauty.

Then came May, and with May, spring finals, and the end of the semester. We had a private graduation celebration of our own, beautiful, wretched, passionate, ecstatic, and above all, awkward.

"You want me to what?"

"Tie me up."

I blink. "Okay... Um. Why?

She looks at me shyly with one eye, dark hair in curtains around her face, while her lazy eye stares off in the distance somewhere. I always found that trait fascinating, although she says it's more a nuisance than anything else – only being able to use one eye means she has no three-dimensional vision, so her depth perception is nonexistent, and she's made clumsiness into a form of ballet.

"I think it would be fun."

Oh, well, in that case, why not.

I look around the room. I don't see anything that would be very useful for this. Her bags are already packed – graduation is tomorrow, and she leaves immediately thereafter – no doubt she has scarves or a bathrobe with a tie or something I could use, but I'd have to rummage through her bags to find them, and I don't want to have to make her repack all her belongings.

I'm wearing a pair of purple argyle socks that go up over my knees; maybe they'll do, although all things considered, I'd better keep them away from her face. Maybe if I tie one around each ankle, on the metal frame of the standard-issue dorm bed? It will stretch my socks out something wicked, but they're only acrylic, so they'll probably shrink back after a wash or two. I hope.

Perplexedly, I get to work tying my girlfriend's ankles to the metal bedframe with a sock. I don't see where the "fun" enters in, but maybe she knows something I don't.

On the other hand, she is on the bed, and so am I, and that's nothing to be displeased about. I lie down next to her and take her into my arms as best I can. As always, everything about her is sweet, from her freshly shampooed hair to her skin to her breath, which tastes of peaches when I kiss her. The dining halls served peach pie as a dessert option tonight.

Her lips are so perfectly shaped that I find myself running my finger over them, around and around, and she giggles and lunges for my finger with her teeth. I pull back.

"Uh-uh," I murmur. "No biting. Not allowed."

Her breath quickens.

What on earth? All I said was, "No biting."

"What are you thinking about?" I whisper, almost afraid to hear the answer.

"You," she replies.

Well. That's gratifying. I kiss her and take my time before surfacing. Her increasingly ragged breath urges me on.

"Naked. I'm naked, too."

That's even better, and it's what I was longing for tonight, anyway. "I think that can be arranged," I say, and strip my clothes off slowly, one article at a time, doing my best to caress myself with my blouse and jeans as I remove them. She watches me with hungry eyes. I start to remove her clothing next, although I realize when I get to her trousers and underwear, that I won't be able to completely remove them because I tied her ankles to the bed with my socks. I can only push them down as far as I can get them to go.

Her body stretches before me in the evening half-light. Tonight is the last night I'll be able to see her before the school year starts up again in the fall, at the very earliest, and I gaze at her fixedly, trying to memorize her every curve and muscle.

"And there are whips and chains in the room."

Wait. Stop. What? What would I possibly do with – My mind boggles. Clearly, her imagination is a little more fertile than mine.

"All I have is myself," I reply, and cover her mouth with mine before she has a chance to say something else that will confuse me even more.

Some intuition, though, tells me to reach down between her legs. She is soaking wet, and within seconds, she shudders and cries out.

That was all it took to make her come?

I think for a moment, then lean onto her body, pinning her shoulder underneath mine while I bend around to bring my mouth to her ear. I don't move my hand. "Maybe you'd better tell me what you want in a little more detail," I whisper. "I'm not quite sure I caught all that."

Her breath catches again, and she starts to buck against me.

I don't get much sleep. I learn a great many odd and baffling things about the contents of her imagination, though.

THAT WAS MY FRESHMAN year as an undergraduate, and at the end of it, my girlfriend went away to Vermont for the summer to share an apartment with

another one of the graduating sorority sisters. Meanwhile, I let myself get dragged back home to my parents, because I didn't know what else I could do with myself.

We wrote letters every day – desperate letters, letters that we carefully intercepted before anybody else could see the mail. We wrote each other poetry. We sent each other little tokens of our affection: locks of hair, pretty flowers we crushed and dried and inserted into cards; poetry, more poetry. Oh, the poems we wrote.

And we talked endlessly on the telephone. Every day I would take a long walk to a phone booth in the little public park that sat on the corner of a shopping district in my neighborhood, and call her collect because I didn't have an endless supply of quarters; and we would sigh hopelessly at each other, telling each other all the things we wished we were doing to each other, which, in retrospect, weren't all that extensive, but they were much desired nonetheless.

Had she been there for me to hold, I would have happily died in her arms.

When school started up again, she went to graduate school at a large state university about an hour away from me to the north, and we tried to keep things going, but what long-distance relationship can possibly survive when neither partner has any way of visiting the other? Neither of us had cars – she did not exactly come from a moneyed background, although she was by no means poor, and my parents did not believe in feeding me with a silver spoon, for all that our family had wealth. What I wanted, I had to earn, and I had yet to find a job that would pay me enough to let me afford a car of my own.

Meanwhile, although she didn't talk about it much until the very end of our relationship, she was starting to see other women. My place was not secure.

It didn't take either of us long to slide from indoctrinated chastity to bouquets of lovers, and that should surprise no one. Ever see a kid with sudden freedom and an allowance to spend let loose in a candy store after years of being forced to live on nothing but macrobiotic health food?

We still wrote and called each other, trying to keep things alive despite the impossibility of the situation; I even took a Greyhound bus to see her a few times, a trip that took several hours each way, because the bus did not travel a direct route, but rather made a circuit through two major cities, laying over in one of them for an hour before winding back to the town my girlfriend's university was located in.

All this cost money, and eventually, that had some terrible consequences for me, because I hadn't been as discreet as I thought I'd been.

A clean break probably would have been wiser, but I was young, and I was foolish, and I was driven by the noisy demands of my passions rather than the clear advice of my rational mind. Also, just maybe, I was following the dictates of my inner calling, even then. My fall from grace did, after all, get me onto the path on which I sought truth; had things continued to be easy and my life sheltered, I would not have become who I am now. Perhaps I engineered my own fall without letting myself know it.

At any rate, that was summer.

After summer came my sophomore year, which I at least got to attend half of before losing my family name, my funds, and my right to attend classes in the white brick buildings of my college campus; and a couple of incidents stand out that, I think, shaped me significantly as well, although at the time they seemed rather minor.

One involved something that transpired between me and a fellow member of the college concert choir.

I'M VISITING ONE OF the friends I met in chorus. He's a baritone, and part of the college's Conservatory of Music, majoring in conducting and composition. He's also an artist. The walls of his dorm room are covered with pictures he's drawn, and bits of sheet music, as well as the usual posters dorm rooms get decorated in.

He has a single room. It's not much larger than a walk-in butler's pantry, but still, it's a *single*. Lucky him. He's a senior, and seniors get top priority in the room draw – that, and there are more single dorm rooms available for male students than there are for female students, which seems remarkably unfair.

I keep finding myself gravitating toward him. We can talk for hours about philosophy, about art and music.

We spend a lot of time these days talking about how impossibly harsh our choral director is – he makes us spend several hours a day in special sessions with our respective sections to work on the Bach motet we're studying (*Singet dem Herrn*, BWV 225, which according to my friend is one of the most diffi-cult-to-perform pieces of Baroque era choral music in existence) in addition to the two hours every other afternoon that we spend in chorus, and often we practice while being barked at by an irritable terrier of a director for not having memorized our music to his satisfaction.

The director obviously loves music, and he possibly even loves teaching music, and we're stretching our voices and learning an astonishing amount of informa-tion from him about how to use our throats and lungs, and how to blend well together, and about the composers we study; but none of this matters, because he is a holy terror.

That's what my friend thinks, anyway.

I kind of have a crush on the director. I love the way his face lights up when he's conducting. I haven't mentioned this, though. It doesn't seem quite right to confess to being hot for teacher when we're in the middle of complaining about the teacher in question.

"I don't see why I have to have my part memorized now," my friend says. "The first concert won't be for another month and a half. And I have to finish the rough draft of my opera before the end of this semester if I'm going to stage it for my senior independent study project... Maybe I'll drop out. Chorus is only a quarter of a credit."

"Well, it is kind of easier to nail the counterpoint if you don't have to look down at the notes to remember what you have to sing."

"No, it's not. If anything, it's harder, given that we're still just learning the first movement. It's not like the second and fourth movements, those we got down pat within a week. The first movement is a *beast*. And unlike *you*, I can sight-read my music easily. Wait, why are you taking his side?"

"I'm not."

"Yes, you are."

"Don't drop out. We need you. Most of the other people in your section are first-year students. Without you, they'll be all out of tune."

The song on the Siouxsie and the Banshees CD changes from "Ornaments of Gold" to "Turn to Stone."

"And here's the thinly disguised sex song."

"No, it's about spirit channeling and magic," I argue. I've managed to learn about the existence of such things thanks to an anthropology class I signed up for: an upper-class course called, appropriately enough, Magic, Witchcraft, and Religion.

Apparently, some things I read about in science fiction and fantasy books have some basis in real-world belief. No doubt I'll have a flaming argument with my parents when they see my report card and see what courses I've been taking this semester, but I'll cross that bridge when I come to it. I was only allowed into the course, sophomore that I was, because I am in the honors program.

My friend is in my class, too. We seem to be in a lot of the same classes together this semester.

"Sex."

I sigh. "She's doing a religious ritual to invoke a god. When she's singing 'ferry me down,' she's singing about the path to the underworld. She's singing about Charon's ferry."

"Flesh turning to alabaster? All that stone imagery?" He laughs. "Sex."

"Fine. Spirit channeling *and* sex. The Great Rite."

"I'm pretty sure it's just sex."

He reaches across me to turn off the stereo. Our hands brush. There is a pregnant pause. There have been a lot of those lately. I don't know why – well, I do, but it's nothing I've wanted to acknowledge to myself. I look away; I am afraid, somehow, of meeting his eyes.

He clears his throat. "Want to work on meditation exercises?"

Yet another thing we have in common is meditation.

That, and awkward silences.

"Yeah. We probably should. It's been a few days; we've been getting lax. Let's sit *zazen* for a while."

Also, we have to find a way to fill the time that doesn't involve paying attention to a growing attraction to each other that neither of us wants to confront.

We sit in traditional postures – I am jealous of his ability to sit for long periods of time in lotus, for the best I can manage is that of the student pose, my feet and legs bent under me in a modified kneeling position – and try to clear our minds while staring straight ahead. The point of *zazen* is that it teaches you to let your emotions and sensations wash over you like water, flowing past you, until all is gone and all you remain focused on is the still, empty point of quiet within your soul.

At least, that's the theory. We probably shouldn't have taken positions facing each other.

Several minutes of predictable awkwardness pass before we give up. I don't know who moves toward the other first, but we are drawn together like magnets, and we can't stop ourselves from touching. His fingertips brush my jaw, my throat.

"We could try meditating while doing this," he whispers raggedly. I am dubious – it seems to me that conditions are not very good for concentration – but he takes me by the hands, pressing his palms to mine. "Let's try concentrating on each other this time."

"That's not Zen, is it?"

"No, I read about it in a book on Western tantrism."

Oh, so we're going to cross the streams, then.

This is an interesting development. I'm focusing on him, on his warm flesh, on the increasing sweatiness of our hands as they press together, and it feels electric. We have *become* electricity, our desire arcing lightning, flaring before us. His mouth has met mine now – there is no way to stop this, might as well stop a summer thunderstorm – our lips barely touching, his tongue teases out and flicks across my lips, and I lean to crush my mouth to his, to devour him and entrap him in my arms but he holds me back, whispering about focus. I focus. I focus on him, rather than on the sudden violent passion that is threatening to overwhelm me.

Slower, then. I need to be slower. All right. I will see what slower does.

I am once more aware of him, awareness as sharp as a blade, as fine as a ribbon, a thread. I trail my fingertips along his arms, listening to him gasp with sudden pleasure, and bizarrely I feel fire under his skin, in lines along his veins, or maybe it's his nerve endings – it feels like some kind of searing pathway, if I close my eyes, I can almost see it. Entrancing. Beautiful. I've never seen anything like it. I massage the fiery path and feel it burn.

He puts his hands at the base of my spine, near the small of my back, making slow circles, pulling fire from the caldera of molten need between my legs, up into the small of my back, along my spine, and it sears my chest and chokes in my throat and threatens to pour out of my now blind eyes; I feel him on my skin, through my skin, and it's all I can do to remain in my meditative posture – as his hands rise, so does the heat. A stream of lava is within me, flowing up me.

"Ooh. Feel that? It's *Kundalini*," he whispers.

It seems to be like the fire I've seen in the tracings of sensation I felt in his arms, and I reach around him to place my fingertips on his spine, to see if I can call up more fire. I want to play with it. I want to see what I can do with it. My hands tingle madly. My head buzzes. I'm drunk, even though I've had nothing to drink, and I feel his drunkenness too, and I want him to get more drunk, so I reach. I reach with my hands, I reach with my mouth, my kisses, his kisses invading, my kisses invading, burning –

It explodes in a concussion of light. I can't see anything but him and me and the desire we have wound together in braids of crackling fire; we fall onto the floor clutching at each other, mouths fused, our pelvises grinding at each other. There are too many clothes in the way, so we tear them off. Hunger. Need. He's engulfing me with it. I'm trying to drown him with waves of fire as he drives into me, splitting me, and as I start to feel the beginnings of spasm take us both, I reach out with myself and drink him in, his moaning breath as he kisses me and crushes my mouth, his sudden ecstasy, and everything else he has that burns. Oh, delicious.

Stars. Burning and dancing in space. We are burning and closing in and we are mad swarming particles consuming each other and we are the explosion, the end, the beginning, light too bright to comprehend, transfixed –

And then it is done, and we lie panting on the floor, too heavy and amazed to move.

After a long, long while, he rasps, "Sex. The song is about sex."

"It's about *magic.*"

He lifts himself on one arm and gazes down at me. I couldn't break away from his eyes even if I wanted to, at this point; and I don't want to. His eyes seem too beautiful. Why would I want to stop staring at a sharply cloudless sky? "Red-headed witch." He grins.

"You did mean that in a nice way, right?"

"Oh, yes. Yes, yes, yes." He kisses me. My lips tingle; I wrap my arms around his neck and gently pull him down on top of me again.

That. Magic was what just happened. Magic. The universe spins above me, dizzying me, and I am lost in the whirl.

THAT WAS HOW I discovered magick. I discovered something else, arguably another form of magick, a couple of months later, shortly before the beginning of winter break; although at the time I had no idea how to contextualize it. Silly me.

IT'S DARK, SO I flick on the lights.

The padded walls and floor of the wrestling room have an acrid under-smell of perspiration, the result of years of bodies writhing, straining, and sweating in a struggle for victory – mastery of techniques, dominance over opponents. No matter how well or how often the room gets scrubbed and sterilized, it will always smell faintly of sweat.

Above us, I can hear shouts, thumping noises, and the occasional muffled whistle tweet – the wrestling room is beneath a basketball court, and there is apparently a game going on. Probably just intramural, or we'd have heard more about it. Or maybe it's a class. I've never really paid much attention to the sports schedule.

"Oh, good," he says, "we have the place to ourselves for a while."

My sparring partner is built along my lines: tall and gawky. He's even taller than I am, which is saying a lot. Most people stop growing before they are old enough to enter college, but not I. I gained two inches in my freshman year alone and going by the way my clothing fits (or, more accurately, doesn't fit) I'm *still* gaining. I'm taller than most men; I tower over other women. But he's taller.

He's also thin, although it's more of a lean and wiry kind of thin than a "feed me, I'm starving" kind of thin. When we fight together, we probably look like storks trying to do interpretive dance.

The only thing the wrestling room needs to be perfect would be unbreakable mirrors along one or two of the walls. It would be much easier to practice *kata* if I could see my body's reflection and correct any errors before they get entrenched. Maybe one of these days someone will invent a padded, shatterproof, non-warping mirror specifically for use in martial arts training.

We decide to warm up with some *tai ch'i* forms first.

As we run through our *tao lu* and universal breathing, I can't help but notice that my partner is cute, in a gangly, fluid sort of way.

He's watching me.

"Yes?"

"Your stance is a little off," he says. "Try copying me."

I watch him and see how my stance is different from his, and copy his somewhat wider foot spread and more upright position. My natural tendency is to lean back a little bit more, but I can see right away how his posture works better. It feels more stable. Even better, it enables flow, something I hadn't noticed before when practicing in class because, of course, I'd been doing it wrong until now.

We finish several rounds of *tao lu*, and then it's time to fight.

This is the whole reason we decided to get into the wrestling room two hours early by signing for it in advance. We both need practice – myself more than he does. There are some people for whom physical motions like ballet, fencing, mock armored combat, and East Asian martial arts come easily and naturally, who learn the required motions quickly and retain the motions in their muscle memory.

I'm not one of them.

I am a slow learner. Once I have something down, I'm generally quite good at it, but it takes a lot of repetition and practice before I reach that point, and because the *Tai Ch'i + Kung Fu* class only meets once per week, I'm doing badly at it. The instructor has been giving me A's for effort, but I am so bad that I didn't even compete when there was a local competition with the townies that my other class members took part in. I want to change that. I hate being bad at things. It's embarrassing.

It would be nice to earn a belt.

Yes. It's true. I don't even have a belt. I'm that awkward at it.

We've squared off. As usual, there is tension regarding who is going to be the attacker and who will take defense. We really should talk about this sort of thing ahead of time. Finally, I decide to take the offensive, and so I throw a punch. He blocks it easily.

I'm not fast enough.

I feint and come at him again. At least this time I make contact.

"Put your breath into it like the instructor tells us to," he advises me. Jerk. He's not even breathing hard. "Like this."

At least I'm good at blocking.

"Good block. Can I show you how I'm punching?"

I sigh. "I think you'll have to."

He moves behind me until we're only about an inch separated and mirrors my horse stance. I try not to think about the overtones of this. I can feel him through the air; he radiates heat in a way I find almost bizarre, because the heat is dancing in waves. When he takes my wrists and holds them by my abdomen, his hands tingle.

"Like this," he says, putting my hands into fists, chambering them, and going through a few rounds of punching like we do in class, only a lot slower than the instructor does it. "Breathe out. There. Breathe in. Chamber. Punch out. Exhale."

The air is moving with my hands and breath.

"Let's try again," he says softly against my ear.

I'm almost disappointed; I was beginning to like the feel of his body behind mine, and his hands on mine. However, I still feel the air. I feel the flow. This is something I never felt in class. It makes me giddy. I throw another punch, harder and faster than I thought possible, and the contact is immediate and raw.

He doubles over.

Oops.

"I'm sorry," I squeak. "Are you all right?"

He laughs. "That," he says, "that was perfect." And he immediately kicks out and topples me onto the ground.

From below, I sweep out with my own foot. Contact. He goes down and lands gratifyingly hard. It would probably hurt if the floors weren't thickly padded.

"Gotcha."

I'm smirking. I can't help it.

And then he's on top of me, flattening me with his weight, and I'm flailing out with my feet and struggling to get my arms free because he has them pinned. I can lift myself, but that's about it – I can't get the kind of leverage I want. No arms. I thrash and almost manage to wriggle free, but he grinds against me with his pelvis, which keeps me from wriggling out from under him, and we freeze for what feels like an infinitely long period, staring red-faced at each other, unable to look away from each other's eyes as his body betrays his aroused state. A mewing noise escapes my lips before I can stop myself from making it.

I can either kiss him, or I can pretend this isn't happening.

I start to writhe, trying to free myself, and ignore the taut, stretched feeling of my own need as I pump against him, lifting him off the ground, rolling out and away. I get back into stance.

We wait. Awkwardness thick enough to cut with a knife.

Finally, he says, "Fighting. Back to sparring... Okay. We can do this. So. Something I've noticed. You're not very comfortable being the attacker when you fight, are you?"

He's right. I'm not.

"You need to come at me," he says, shaking his head. "Come on. Practice makes perfect."

If I don't attack, he won't move; we can either crouch here, wasting time, or we can fight and train. I leap at him with a cry that is as much a form of attack as the leap itself, punching out with my leg.

Which he catches and uses to flip me onto the ground again. "Weak offense," he says.

I snarl and yank him down by the ankle. If the only way I fight well is when I'm flat on the floor, fine, I'll fight him down here. He falls, cursing, and I'm on top of him, grabbing him by the hair and holding him down, slamming him down as he tries to rise, and it feels *good*, so very, very right; I give in to the need I feel and take his mouth and we kiss, our tongues dueling, and I push him, every time he tries to rise I push him.

Meanwhile, he's harder than ever. It's time for the sweatpants to get shoved out of the way.

I smile down at him.

And then we resume our battle. Just because we're having sex doesn't mean we're done fighting.

Sweat and desire. His straining to free himself and seize control maddens me, and I yell as I force him back down by his arms and shoulders and impale myself on him. All I know now is craving, a driving hunger that has made him not just a sparring partner, nor even a lover, but prey, helpless against me. *My* prey.

Several minutes of violent wrestling and another orgasm later, I collapse on him; he bucks his hips under me furiously until he too cries out, his body arching and racked until at last he groans and presses his head into the mat we've been bruising.

"Good offense," he gasps at last. "Your follow-through is improving."

I nod against him. I don't know what to say. I don't know what to think.

The door starts to open.

"Don't come in," we both yell.

THAT WAS BACK WHEN I could still be easily embarrassed. I was even more embarrassed when I found out he had a bit of a reputation himself and had made it obvious that he'd been planning for some time to try me out. To the rest of the world, I was just another one of his conquests.

Silly if you think about it – why should anyone be embarrassed about people knowing whether they'd just had sex? Sex is nothing to be ashamed of. Provided all parties consent to it, it is essentially an innocent act, no matter how or where or why it is conducted.

I was so naïve when I was young. Fortunately, I divested myself of that naivete as soon as I had the chance to do so.

See through my eyes.

The Magus

The man standing next to me in the Classic Literature section of the book-store has interesting taste. Surreptitiously, I'll look up every now and then to see what else is in his stack of books; I can't see all the titles, but from what I can tell, it's an eclectic mix of occult philosophy, poetry, history, and something I can't quite make out. Some kind of fiction, maybe. Given the section we're both browsing, that seems to be a reasonable assumption to make.

He's also very good-looking, for an older man. Hair dark sable, with strands of silver – a shade of brown so dark that it's almost black. On second glance, maybe it *is* black. I can't tell in this lighting. Nice wool dress trousers, silk shirt, both slightly rumpled, both in dark hues. Slender – unusually so – I suspect he has muscle, but of the wiry sort. Pale skin, a bit on the olive side. Almost my height, so he's tall. I'd say he's probably about six feet one or so, maybe six-two.

There's something compelling about his hands, although I can't for the life of me say exactly what. Maybe it's because of the way they're held still, but seem full of pent-up energy. Maybe it's the fascinating way they're gnarled and lined. I look at his hands and think of the grove of birches that was on the lawn in front of my college library.

He's interesting.

His books look interesting, too.

Heck with it.

"You buy books the way I do – in bulk," I say to him. "What have you got so far?" It's been a long while since I've been able to buy my books rather than just read them in the store while soaking in the bookstore ambiance, but I don't feel like talking about that.

Without a word, he holds out his books for me to see. Books on the Golden Dawn; the complete poems of William Butler Yeats – all right, I saw those earlier. A rather outdated text on the supposed religion of the Etruscans written by Charles Godfrey Leland. Saw that. Then I see the titles I didn't catch earlier. An issue of *Gnosis*. An issue of *Yellow Silk*. Nice. Umberto Eco's *Semiotics and the Philosophy of Language*. Jung's *Red Book*. Some paperback with a plain yellow cover and the title in understated black lettering; the author appears to be French. So does the book's title, which means whatever the book is he's reading, it's in the original French, unless it was written in English, in which case he's reading a French translation for whatever reason. The first scenario seems the more plausible one. Hmm. *Histoire* translates as "story," if I remember correctly from my very rusty lower-school French classes. It's fiction. Other than that, I've no idea what it is, and I can't puzzle it out.

At the bottom of his pile are a couple of Julia Child cookbooks.

"You cook?"

"It's one of my hobbies."

He has an accent. I can't place it, though. His voice is too quiet. The only thing I can determine is that it's not Midwestern, so he's possibly not from around here.

I want to hear him talk more. It's not just that I'm hoping I might be able to place the accent if I listen to it more. It's also the fact that his hushed voice is warm and velvety and seductive. It needs to be on a recording. (Ideally, that recording would be a romance novel).

Cute. Unusual voice. Multilingual. Broad taste in reading, including some stuff I've heard of or read, and some stuff I've never heard of that looks like I might want to hear of it at some point in the indefinite near future… and he cooks? *Very* interesting.

"Leland's not considered very reliable," I remark. "He had a pronounced tendency to embellish or to just make things up. His writings are classics, as far as the Western mystery tradition is concerned, but they're not good primary resources for mythological or anthropological research."

I'm so good at making polite small talk that I amaze myself.

"True. Of course, Aleister Crowley made up more than half of what he wrote, but he's a classic in his own way, as well." He's so quiet. Shy, or just reserved? I can't tell.

"Haven't read him yet. He's on my get-around-to list, though."

Silence.

"You like poetry?"

"Yes. Although I'm also reading Yeats as part of my study of the philosophy of the Hermetic Order of the Golden Dawn."

"Oh."

More silence.

"Where did you find the magazines and the books? I've never seen these in the New Age section." His selections look way too esoteric for a little shopping mall bookstore like this one.

"I put them on order."

Our hands brush as I hand him back his books.

I think I just made him blush.

Shy. Definitely shy.

I've spotted him again. Funny how I'd never noticed him here before, given how I practically live in the downtown library when I'm not selling magazines – a part-time telemarketing job that I hate, because no matter how good I am at it, I'm always afraid one bad week will get me fired. Also, faking being an outgoing "people person" is exhausting, especially since they have me assigned to a day shift right now, which means I also have to fake being a "morning person," and no amount of free coffee seems to completely do the trick for that.

It could be I've never spotted him here because I don't usually use the reference section. Most of what I read is in circulation even when it's not fiction. Today, though, I'm looking for books and journals on archaeology related to the Trojan War. Rereading Lattimore's translation of the *Iliad* made me curious, and of course, I couldn't let the subject rest once it had lodged itself in my mind (well, reading it completely for the first time, really. Like many books I was assigned for courses, while I was taking the honors tutorial on Bronze Age Greece I couldn't bring myself to read the assigned material from cover to cover, and only skimmed it, only to rediscover it later when I had more time on my hands and when the reading was not compulsory). Translations of the *Iliad* and the *Odyssey* are in circulation, of course, as are some books on ancient history, including a couple that focus exclusively on the Trojan War, but aside from a coffee table book by Michael Grant that seems to be the book form of a PBS miniseries, there's nothing on archaeology in circulation. So now I'm here.

He's one of the reference librarians.

I walk up to the desk. "I don't know how to find the journals Manfred Korfmann published his findings in. Could you help me, please?"

"I can check the print index. You'll have better luck finding those in the university library, though. What we have on classical civilization and archaeology is extremely basic. If you like, we could order some materials through interlibrary loan... But I think you should use the classical collection at the university library. It's well-stocked, plus they currently have an exhibition of documents on loan from the Blegen Center archives, including excavation records from the Palace of Nestor and some of Carl Blegen's original papers. They also have some first-edition Schliemanns. You'd love it."

And then his face lights up.

"*You again!*"

"Me again."

We act quietly flustered at each other, including some obligatory awkward conversational pauses.

Finally, I blurt out, "Want to go out on a date with me?"

Another awkward pause.

He smiles. "All right. Yes."

This more than makes up for my not having found the journals I was looking for.

WE SAT IN THE cloud club section of the university auditorium for a traveling repertory company's performance of *Die Zauberflöte*. What we miss in a close-up view we gain in good acoustics, which is just as well because neither a telemarketer nor a librarian can easily afford the more expensive seats. This, I think, had to have been as perfect a first date as one could get. A bonus is that I have established that he likes opera. Most of my acquaintances think my love of opera is insane, or at least a sign of some deeper character disturbance.

"I thought Monostatos was a bit much. So was the Queen of the Night, for that matter."

"You should have seen the libretto before Mozart edited it," he replies.

"It was *worse*? How could you get much worse than an evil, lustful Moor saying his blackness made him ugly, so he wanted to rape and kidnap the pretty white girl who wouldn't be interested in an ugly guy like him, which sounds like the plot of *Birth of a Nation* only too early and wrong setting, and a malicious queen with too much power telling her daughter that she'll disown her if she doesn't subjugate the hero, and oh, yeah, an occult brotherhood admonishing the hero and his sidekick to avoid women if they want to be enlightened?"

"It was worse. Rather in the same way *The Taming of the Shrew* was far more misogynistic before Shakespeare wrote his own version of the play, and *The Merchant of Venice* was even more anti-Semitic when it was *Il Pecorone*."

"Oh, well, at least the music was good," I say with a sigh as we climb the stairs to his apartment. I like the street his apartment building is on. It's a quiet residential cul-de-sac on the west side of town, without many other houses or other buildings on it. His section of the street is right across from a cemetery, and there are lots of trees, so the overall effect is almost park-like.

"That it was." He unlocks the door and lets me in.

I AM NOW PERCHED on his couch, drinking peppermint tea and feeling the unseasonably warm, cherry blossom-scented breeze that blows through the open window. I take in details of his apartment while he bustles in the kitchen – I'm failing dismally to be subtle about it, but he's in the kitchen, so that's all right, I guess. The living room decorations consist of bookshelves. All the shelves are used for books. Some shelves are double stacked, including all the shelves on a bookcase that appears to be dedicated to science fiction and fantasy trade paperbacks. I wonder if he would loan out his books if I asked nicely.

There's a magazine called *Prometheus*, lying on top of the issue of *Gnosis* and the issue of *Yellow Silk*. It seems to be a literary magazine of some kind. It looks interesting.

I pick it up off the table – which is really an ornately carved chest – and flip it open at random.

On the left page is a poem. On the right is an exquisitely rendered drawing of a bound and gagged woman. The placement of the ropes is elaborate enough that it makes me squint and turn my head, trying to figure out how everything was set up. In real life, it would be a sculpture with rope. My eyes flick left; the poem – which is beautifully written – seems to go along with the art. As I turn the pages, I notice a distinct and recurring theme to them.

Of course, it would be just this moment that he emerges from the kitchen carrying a tray of freshly baked chocolate chip cookies.

The awkward silence between us this time is very awkward indeed.

"Very artistically done," I say at last. No, I am not blushing. And I'm not stammering. That is not a stammer. Not at all.

He puts the tray of cookies down on a side table. In a quiet and careful voice, he replies, "That's the literary journal of the oldest BDSM society in North America."

"Oh."

There's a literary journal?

"Have you read the poetry of Swinburne?" I finally ask. "Some of his poems combined eroticism and pain."

"I'm quite fond of Swinburne," he replies.

"Same here," I murmur, willing my mug of tea to calm my hands, which are shaking. "It's amazing the things you can find in libraries."

My eyes lift and wander back to his shelves. Aside from the bookcase devoted to speculative fiction, there is also a stack of history and archaeology books – heavy on prehistory, early Near Eastern and Egyptian history, and classical Greece and Rome – and two cases contain texts on philosophy and comparative religion. A tall case in the corner nearest the couch is crammed with occult lore of various backgrounds.

One shelf at eye level has several books on Tantra and ceremonial sex magick. It also has a couple of non-occult-related texts relating to different activities also starting with the letters "S" and "M," which, while not mystical and esoteric, are nevertheless fairly mysterious, at least to me.

"You filed them with your occult books?"

"Yes."

Silence again. These silences are getting painfully tense.

I swallow past the dryness in my throat. "Why?"

"Because they go together. It's not unheard of; for instance, Gerald Gardner and Aleister Crowley were both notorious for it, each in their own way. Also, if you get into the histories and philosophies of various parts of Asia, you'll find a strong note of mystical asceticism."

"And you?" Stupid voice. Stop croaking.

"I follow an established Western mystery tradition, but there are some things that I make up as I go along."

I look down as I sip my peppermint tea. It's gone cold.

The quiet of the room descends again. My heart rattles against my chest. I breathe deeply and try to think about nothing, to let my feelings flow past and away, as they do when I sit *zazen*. I listen to myself breathe. I make my breathing slow and calm until the quiet of the room no longer hurts.

I'm extremely surprised that my reaction is so violent. There really is no reason for me to be shaken by the mere mention of sexual kinks in a conversation, or by their portrayal in written and visual art. It's not like I only just now found out such things existed. Of course, the man whose living room couch I am sitting on seems rather more involved in such matters than any other love interest I've had so far. No doubt that has something to do with it, although it once again raises the question of why I am trembling from nervous excitement. Why be nervous? That's silly...

Oh.

Not quite meeting me in the eyes, he asks in a small voice, "Do you still find me attractive?"

I put down the tea and rise from the couch. I walk over to where he is standing, put his face between my hands, and pull him close to me until his lips are touching mine.

"Yes," I whisper against his mouth, and as he reaches for me and encircles me with his arms, the room's silence becomes a heat I can almost touch.

I TURNED TWENTY-ONE TODAY. We didn't have enough money to go out to eat, and there were not enough ingredients in the larder to bake any kind of dessert from scratch, so we are sharing some packaged cupcakes we got from a convenience store in lieu of traditional birthday cake.

We've been seeing each other for several weeks now. I hesitate to call it "dating," or to call him my "boyfriend," because he's twice my age, and "dating" and "boyfriends" seem inappropriately adolescent as ways to describe an affair with him – and it is an affair. We aren't boyfriend and girlfriend, going steady and making plans to attend the prom. We're lovers.

He gave me a birthday present: a rare used hardback copy of the poems of Emily Dickinson. It's an antique first edition – maybe not of the poems themselves, but certainly of that particular anthology, which was printed in the very early part of this century. And it's in mint condition. This is probably the reason my "birthday cake" consists of plastic-wrapped snack food. I'll take the book over cake any day, though, especially when part of my present involves his reading aloud to me.

Wild nights, wild nights,
were I with thee,
Wild nights should be
our luxury –

He punctuates the verses with kisses: my forehead, my cheeks, my hair, my neck. My lips. My lips are burning under his. He has such soft, warm lips, to take my breath away.

Futile the winds
to the heart in port –
Done with the compass,
done with the chart –

Time to screw my courage to the sticking point.

I lean back into his embrace, and interrupt him by whispering in his ear, "Master, teach me."

His breath stops, and I feel his body suddenly become as tense as a bowstring. Any more tense and he'll be jumping out of his skin.

"*What?*"

"I know what you want. And I know what I want. Master, teach me."

He groans quietly and closes his eyes. He's closing them against himself, I think. That can't be very effective.

"You don't know what you're asking."

"I ransacked your personal library on our last few dates, remember? Then there was that little game of Twenty Questions we played last night. Good heavens. I know what I'm asking."

"Do you have any idea what kind of effect you're having on me?"

"Yes. Yes, I do. I know because I can see you. Silly. I can reach out and feel you, too, where you're threatening to burst out of your pants. Master, teach me. I want to apprentice myself."

I can feel him trembling. Am I trembling too? I must be. My voice is. But all I feel is him.

"Is this something you really want, or do you just want to learn how to be a dominant?" Shaking. God, he's shaking. His raw need rips through me. "You did mention your former girlfriend wanting you to play the dominant. I can advise you without actually asking anything of you if that's the case. Or is this about that conversation we had a while back about studying magic –"

"If I only wanted advice, I'd ask for advice. I don't just want advice. I want *you*. Master, teach me." I take a deep breath.

Silence falls.

"I want that very badly," he says at last.

"I'm yours for the taking. Please. Take me."

The room is still. Too still. The very air is holding its breath.

"Please."

The only one trembling now is me.

He seizes my wrists in one of his hands and pins them to the futon, behind my head. My nose decides now, of all times, to itch, and I try to scratch it, but of course, I can't, because he's pinning me down. I can't get loose. I had no idea he had this much strength. He's only slightly built, but he has me caught. He's unbuttoning me with his other hand, freeing my breasts, and he squeezes my nipple until it is hard, and I moan with desire, arching against him, nearly lifting him off the futon with me as I do so.

"We need to negotiate. Is there anything you absolutely do not want to do?"

"I don't know."

"Of course. Rather silly of me to ask, if you don't know what my specific quirks might be. I probably have you at something of a disadvantage, as well." He smiles. "Should I stop?"

"Oh, no. Please don't stop..."

He's teasing my nipple with his fingers, kissing and nibbling my neck, and licking around my ear in slow, careful circles, making me cry out and writhe and buck up against him. I am made of fire and need. Such little things – of course, he's kissed me and used his fingers to pleasure me before, and done other things as well, leading to the usual denouement, but somehow it was never like this. What is this? Being pinned down makes everything different? That doesn't make sense; I've been pinned down in martial arts, many times, and never responded this wildly, not even when it turned me on. His personality, maybe? Something he's doing? I am being consumed. I had no idea it would feel this way. So delirious. Oh, so beautiful.

Raggedly, he asks, "What do you dream about doing?"

That's harder to answer than it might initially sound. The things he's doing to me almost make me forget how to speak; I just want to moan. I find it oddly comforting that he's struggling to keep his composure as well. Let us both be consumed by the same fire. "Um. I've never actually been tied up before, myself, although my last girlfriend had me tie her up once. The end result was a bit awkward. I told you about that. I saw a riding crop in a novelty store in the mall that looked really interesting. I get turned on thinking about Vulcan mind melds."

He stares at me incredulously. "Vulcan mind melds?"

"They're romantic."

"Hmm. Unfortunately, I don't think I can help you out with the Vulcan mind meld thing." He takes his free hand, wraps it around my jaw, and presses his mouth to mine. Now my mouth is as trapped as my arms are; he opens me and devours me with his tongue. Meanwhile, his body is still pressing itself on mine, grinding into mine. He's hard – incredibly so. It feels good. I start to moan.

"First lesson: you do not speak until I give you leave. You do not cry out. You do not moan."

Rats.

"Noise releases energy; I want you to keep your energy inside until I ask for it." He takes his hand off my jaw and, moving aside slightly, reaches down under my leggings and underwear to rub his fingers against me. I'm soaked. I almost whimper, but I have to stay quiet. Not being able to make noise hurts. I feel my hips rocking of their own accord.

"Be still."

Now *that* was not even remotely fair.

His fingers continue to play with my nether lips as he works off my clothes, rubbing wet cotton back and forth against my genitals as he pulls my panties down. I can't move. I can't moan. Throat aching, I gasp desperately on the edge of orgasm.

"Open your legs."

I do my best to comply. It's not difficult; I am burning up with my own need. At some point he must have removed some of his own garments; I never even noticed, and for some reason, I find that eerily disorienting.

He still has me by the wrists.

"Wider."

No, no, I can't scream when he enters me, I can't. I can't move. I have to contain this. I bite my lip, trying not to make noise.

His mouth on my mouth, his lips on my lips. "Mine," he gasps. His free hand is in my hair, holding me fast. "Mine, now. Mine." Suddenly he yanks me back, hard, and I feel his teeth wrap around my exposed throat. Biting. He moves down, down all along my neck, covering me with bites, seizing my skin, pulling on it as if he could suck my soul from out of my flesh.

And then he pulls his teeth away; and a completely different part of him, equally hard, finds its mark.

"*Mine.*"

Driving into me, violently; the futon is soaked with the juices of my desire, the sweat pouring from me as I strain to avoid crying out in ecstasy, avoid wrapping my legs around him to move things to my own pace. Too much –

He bends down and murmurs into my ear, "I am going to kiss you again. When you need to scream, scream into my mouth. Give your scream to me."

His voice is shaking.

It doesn't take me long; within seconds, I am screaming. I am also writhing, bucking, thrusting madly against him as my orgasm overwhelms both of us.

"I NEED TO GRAB a couple of things. Wait right there, please. Don't move."

Right. I'm not going anywhere.

He is only gone for a couple of moments – it's not exactly a large apartment – and when he returns, he has some unfamiliar items in his hands. They're black and leathery. I stare in fascination; my imaginary idea of being "tied up" has so far been limited to things like scarves and curtain ropes, because those things are a normal part of my daily life, whereas articles made of black-dyed leather are not. The smell of the leather is intoxicating. It's not a shoe store smell at all. It's sharper. It's almost narcotic. It goes up into my nostrils when I breathe, down through my lungs, and out places to which I never expected lungs to have any connection.

"Hold out your wrists."

I hold them out obligingly. I want to see what these things are and how they work.

They're a pair of leather manacles, cushioned and lined with some kind of velvety soft fabric, adjusted with holes and buckles, shiny silvery things that look as attractive to my perverted magpie eyes as the leather itself. He uses the tightest setting.

Then he puts my wrists over my head and affixes them to something that goes click. It appears to be a clip, attached to a chain, attached to an eye bolt screwed into the futon frame. I had no idea that it was even there. How interesting.

"Your wrists are almost too thin for these to properly restrain you." He looks down at me with a concerned expression. "I've always noticed you were slender, of course, but goodness, that's thin. Are you getting enough to eat?"

"Yes."

"Hmm."

The other black, leathery thing is a riding crop.

"Riding crops are very versatile," he says, as he settles into a kneeling position and picks up the crop. "You'll want to have one of your own eventually. The one you saw in the mall – if it was the same store I'm thinking of – was cheap and shoddy and would not have been good for much other than show; you'll want something a little more high-end if you want to use it as a whip. The cheap version you saw will also be hard to clean because it's braided suede, and whatever soap or other cleaner you use on it will tend to get lodged in the braided parts – another strike against it."

My voice is an octave higher than normal when I ask, "So, what do you do with it?" I hadn't intended on that. Oops.

Sangfroid apparently isn't one of my more reliable virtues when I'm facing a riding crop.

"Attend." He takes the handled end and thrusts it gently under my chin, forcing my head back. "Many people find this a little intimidating, especially when they are immobilized or otherwise helpless, possibly because of the threat of the riding crop itself being used."

"Um. Yes, I can see that."

"Your voice is shaking. Did you know that? By the way, I remind you that you are to be silent and still until I give you leave when you are receiving lessons. From now on, be quiet, please. Another use for the riding crop: you can gently stroke a slave's nerve endings to provoke arousal. If you are knowledgeable of such things as pressure points and nerve paths, the effect can be quite explosive. Different people, of course, can have different sensitive spots. I haven't had a chance to find all of yours yet; in time, I imagine I will."

Do I get to return the favor? I wonder. Practice makes perfect, after all...
The possibility intrigues me. Then thought ceases as he pushes the flap of
the crop gently behind my ear and trails it along my jawline, down to my
collarbone. Then down and around my breasts, circling my nipples, first one,
then the other. Then back again. Up and down, until he strokes my cheek
with the shaft and places its length against my lips. There it rests. Eventually,
I figure out that I'm supposed to kiss it, so I press my lips against the leather,
imagining that I am kissing not an inanimate object, but flesh. The crop is
an extension of my lover now, and I kiss it fervently.

"Good," he says, and once again the shaft moves along my cheek until
the flap is again stroking my skin, moving down to trace the outlines of my
breasts, small circles that spiral in until he is rubbing my nipples back and
forth with the leather. He gives my left one a light smack. I gasp and force
myself to hold still. I want to groan; I want to sway into the motion of the
strokes. But that is forbidden to me.

He trails the flap down my abdomen slowly until it is hovering between
my legs, stroking my clitoris, rubbing up against my labia with the shaft end,
back and forth in a massaging motion until I feel a cry building at the bottom
of my throat, escaping my mouth as a faint, high-pitched keening despite my
best efforts to remain silent. He taps me on my clit, and I gulp. It wasn't even
a very hard tap, it didn't hurt me at all, and yet suddenly I am terrified.

"Shh, now," he murmurs, leaning down to touch my cheek. "I've got you.
Are you all right? You may nod or shake your head."

I nod.

"Is this still what you want?" He caresses my face with his free hand.

I nod again.

He leans over, covers my lips with his, my body with his body, and my
world becomes stable again. It had been shaking, or I had been shaking, but
I hadn't even fully noticed until I felt his flesh against mine, reassuring me
with its warmth. I relax into him as he grounds me with kisses and heat.

Don't stop. Please, don't stop.

"I'm here," he says, and he buries me under his weight. His lips are so soft, his breath so delicious. We sigh into each other as our tongues duel.

When he pulls away, I notice he is slightly breathless. I, on the other hand, am oddly full of energy.

"Let us continue. Various parts of the riding crop can be used on the genitals, in various ways, depending on whether your slave is male or female, and on whether that person is into pain. Not all submissives have a masochistic streak; not all dominants are sadists. If your objective is to produce pleasure that does not involve pain, you might try using the handle for penetration... Hold still, please. And I remind you again, do not make any noise. I want you to keep your sounds, and energy, inside." He would have to illustrate that one. "Until I say otherwise." Of course, he tells me this as he proceeds to do everything possible to make me writhe and cry out.

Pressure, little nudges. Oh, God.

It's very difficult to keep still and silent when the head of his riding crop is pushing at some of my more sensitive areas. I glare at him. So far, that's still acceptable.

"Consider this honing your willpower; you'll need it when you're the dominant. Willpower is important when your submissive asks you to stop doing something, and you don't want to stop, but have to stop anyway. That is what the social contract demands. Scene etiquette requires consent, even when you are perpetuating the illusion of non-consent. Speaking of which, since many submissives like to have you pretend that they are being forced to submit, they may scream 'no,' or 'stop,' or 'mercy,' or something like that, without meaning it literally, which is one reason why safewords are important. A safeword is a word that all parties agree on that means 'I really do mean stop.' The other major reason safewords get used is that dominants are as human as the next person and are as likely as anyone else to get carried away in the heat of the moment if things get very intense; a safeword sounds a bit incongruous and is more likely than 'no' or 'stop' to get an impassioned dominant's attention and halt the activity, should that be necessary. What would you like to be yours? You have leave to answer."

I think. I try to think, anyway. Martial arts. "*Mate,*" I reply, a bit unsteadily, partly because what he's still doing with the head of the riding crop (good grief, he never even paused. *Not once*) is nothing I want to associate with the word "stop."

"That would work well," he muses. "I studied *aikido* some years ago, also *ninjutsu* and a couple of other martial arts; hearing the word *mate* would make me stop automatically. It's almost Pavlovian. When not given leave to speak or make noise, meanwhile, please pound three times with your fist, or flex your hand three times, or grunt three times in succession. I will be watching for it. When you are in a position of power over someone, you should do the same. It does not have to be the three thumps or grunts, of course; it can be anything the two of you agree on. Are you getting all that?"

I nod yes.

The handle of the crop continues to push against me with an impatient sort of stiffness and weight. I gasp, choking on the screams of pleasure I'm holding inside. So close.

"Good. Roll over."

He hasn't moved the head of the riding crop yet. It's still shoved inside me. Rolling over proves interesting; the fact that I can't use my arms doesn't help much, either. I hope I look cute when I'm flopping around like a fish and humping myself on the head of a crop.

Unfortunately, he stops what he's doing before I can come again and pulls the crop handle out. The loop of the wrist strap trails, teasing me, and brushes my thigh on its way out, leaving me covered with the evidence of my need.

The near edge of orgasm hurts me like a knife.

"There are two other standard uses for a riding crop," he says, wiping the crop handle off with his shirt tail. "One is rather obvious. And today happens to be your birthday. You're twenty-one today, yes? Let's round it up to thirty and give you a few to grow on. It builds character. Would you like that?"

"I don't know. Maybe. There's only one way to find out."

"Yes, that's very true."

He slowly trails the tip of the riding crop down my back until it reaches my buttocks, caressing me with the shaft in slow circles until the crop rests in perfect alignment with what I suspect is the only part of my posterior to have anything resembling curves.

He lets it hover there for one long moment before he lays into me.

I don't scream. I don't grunt, flex my hand, or tap out, either.

HE LIES ON TOP of my back. It doesn't hurt as much as it could. Part of this might be distraction; his hand is underneath me, working the wet spot between my legs. It might also be more accurate to say that yes, it does rather hurt to have him draping himself on top of my backside, given my injuries, which are not major but are just raw enough to sting, but what he's doing to me is distracting enough that I don't really care that it stings to have him lying on top of welts.

And no, I still can't make noise.

He has hardened again. I suppose that shouldn't come as a surprise.

"I will not repeat the experience if you didn't enjoy it; you did say, however, that you were interested in riding crops. Was that... welcome? Or was it too much?" He has that shy sound in his voice again. I think I like it at least as much as the steel that came out tonight. "You have leave to speak."

I smile, although he probably can't see me do it. "Oh, don't worry. It was welcome."

"The other standard use for a riding crop is as a gag," he says as he rises from his position on my back. "Open your mouth. Good. Bite down."

Now he's gagging me? Why not before? Oh, right. Energy.

"Do not make noise. You may, however, move. Lift, please."

He slips a pillow underneath my hips as I rest my weight on my elbows and knees to raise myself. Then he leans down to whisper in my ear, and I feel his hand slide between my legs. God, I'm gushing.

"Ride my fingers."

He has them inside me now – I'm not sure how many – more than two, less than five – I think. Maybe. Maybe he does have all five of them in there. I can feel his knuckles against the bones of my pelvis. Pressure, fullness, my nerves stretched like tightrope. One of his fingers gently massages my clitoris. His thumb? Maybe. No, that's not anatomically possible, is it? I can't tell. For all I know, he might be using both hands. I'm wet enough that the sensation of being stuffed gives me no discomfort, only pleasure. I rock, I rock, and I am drowned in wave after wave of orgasm. Dear God, keep doing that, whatever it is. I'll ask you what and how later. Not now. Oh.

Want to scream. Can't.

Arching back. Biting down; pushing hard against the hand inside me. So good, I want this forever. I don't want it to end. Ever.

When my body relaxes, and I collapse in a heap on the pillow, he says, "Open your legs again. You closed them."

I was expecting him to immediately slide inside me and take me the way he did before, but instead, I feel his fingers, which are still covered with the juice of my orgasms, sliding up into the smaller orifice between my buttocks. Lubricating me. I hope he's gentle. The last time I tried this with a boyfriend, it was somewhat awkward and painful. What he's doing with his fingers is certainly nice enough. It almost seems a shame for him to stop.

When he slides into me, I find myself biting down on the riding crop, but not because of any kind of pain. He's very good at what he's doing. Astonishingly good. I didn't know it could feel *this* pleasurable. I want so badly to make noise. To move.

Maybe he won't notice if I twitch my hips against him just a little.

Ever so slightly, he groans.

I wonder if I can also get away with making a few small noises. Just little moans. Surely little moans would be all right?

Gasping, he reaches for me with his other hand, the one he did not use to lubricate me, and I do my best to entwine my fingers around his.

Then he shudders and lets out a loud sigh as he spends himself, collapsing on top of me.

His weight is warm and good. Breath hot against my skin. Kisses on my neck and cheeks; he can't quite reach my lips.

"Happy birthday," he says.

He leans in to kiss me on the cheek; I rub my nose against the pillow, because I'm itching again, and his kiss lands on my ear.

"I presume I can talk now?"

I hear him smiling, although I can't see it from this position. "Yes."

"My wrists are starting to get uncomfortable. Could you please let me out, now?"

"Oh. Of course. Sorry." He does.

It occurs to me that I also desperately need to use the bathroom, both to empty my bladder and to clean off; I stumble in that direction, knees wobbly from exhaustion and pleasure, and when I return, it's his turn to use the various facilities.

I burrow myself into his arms when he lies back down beside me.

"Was that what you were looking for?"

"It was what was necessary. I look forward to learning more. That, and... yes. Yes, it was." I pause, not quite sure how to phrase all the words and feelings that are rolling in me like large waves. "Thank you, Master." That wasn't coached. It did, however, seem the polite thing to say.

"Hold me," he whispers. "Hold me."

Rowing in Heaven, ah, the sea; might I but moor tonight in thee.

MALKUTH

THE BLINDS ARE DOWN, and the curtains drawn over the windows, so that neighbors and casual passers-by will not get an eyeful. We are in the living room because this is the room that has the most open floor space. It's also where he keeps his altar and his ritual supplies. They store easily enough when not in use; he keeps most of them in the carved ornamental chest that doubles as a coffee table and an altar. Tonight, he has some of the supplies laid out on top of it. A chalice filled with water; a dish with salt in it; a long, slender dagger made of what appears to be bronze; two lit candles; a long wooden rod of some kind.

Some of the supplies have already been used to cast the circle around us. Tonight, the circle is designated as a space for lessons.

Shadows flicker and dance on the walls from the candlelight. There is no other light, although there are enough candles that either one of us could read a book without straining our eyes. Just.

"You are, I believe, familiar with these concepts already," he says, "but reviewing them will be helpful. We will work together better in a cast circle if our perspectives, and thus our energies, are in absolute synchrony. Attend."

I am naked and sitting straight-backed on my knees in the classic student posture that I had been using for years to practice Zen meditation. There isn't much difference between meditating and actively listening to *Magister* in that regard (that being the formal title we have settled on; it was also decided that the best description of my role, incorporating all aspects as an apprentice, student, temple servant, and sexual submissive, would not be *discipula* but the more general term *ancilla*). Except, of course, I never sat *zazen* while nude.

He is also nude tonight. This has not always been the case – the act of wearing clothes when one's student or servant is naked carries its own semiotic power, and so far, when he's taken me into his bedroom for instruction, he's made it a practice to keep me naked and himself at least somewhat clothed – but tonight we are going to do magickal work, and there is raw honesty in nudity. This, too, is a departure from his usual habit; he usually does his magickal work while wearing ritual clothing. Tonight, however, he is bringing me into the circle formally for the first time. Tonight, this one time, therefore, we are both in the world as we originally entered it.

"The first element I intend to work with is Air, which is associated with the east and the light of dawn; with ideas, beginnings, and the mind. Before we act, we think. In the beginning, there is *Logos*." He takes the bronze dagger from the altar. "My tradition uses a dagger to represent Air. Most of the Western mystery traditions use a blade of some kind. High ceremonial magick uses a very specific kind of wand for Air, and a sword for Fire, perhaps because trees, which provide wood for wands and staves, get blown around in the wind, and blades, meanwhile, are forged in fire; but I think the symbolism in my own tradition makes just as much sense. Wood can be set on fire, and the metal of a blade can conduct heat or cold depending on the temperature of the air, and it cuts through the air on the way to its destination. Furthermore, the metal blade is hard and keen, as is the focused will. Blades are therefore Air. That is how I learned magick, and that is how I am used to doing things."

He thrusts the tip of the dagger against the soft, hollow spot of flesh just under my chin. Reflexively, I start to look down.

"I wouldn't," he says mildly. "It's extremely sharp. Look up instead."

I look up.

"It would be better to run onto this blade than to cast or use the circle in fear," he intones. I recognize the phrase from one of my independent readings in the occult. This isn't the exact phrase; he's using a variation. I can't remember which tradition makes use of it. Possibly my memory lapse is due to the sharp tip of a dagger biting into my flesh. "How do you serve? You may speak."

Think. "In perfect love and perfect trust," I reply, my voice mostly managing to avoid rising into the squeak range.

"Good focus. That was what I was looking for." He pauses. "Also, the trust, of course. Rise."

I don't really have a choice in the matter; the blade is pushing up hard against me, lifting me. If I don't rise with it, I'm going to get a worse cut than the minor, tickling nick I gave myself while trying to look down when I should have been looking up. I rise, and follow him slowly across the room, led by knifepoint.

Candlelit shadows jump crazily in our wake.

He's led me to the couch. "Stand," he says, "and bend over, supporting yourself on the back of the couch. Arms out. Good."

I knew this was coming.

"The next element is Fire, which I have reason to believe is your primary element, which means your training will be rather more difficult than it might be were you primarily of Air, Water, or Earth. It's not an easy or gentle element to work with. It represents the southern direction, desire, passion, action, heat, raw energy, and courage; if Air is the will, Fire is the imperative. You will recall that I talked about it being represented by wands, although a branch of Western ceremonial magick uses a sword instead. Either way, the meaning conveyed by the symbolic instrument is the same. I have a staff that I use in my solitary rituals, one I constructed and painted myself, which is standing in the corner of the room, but it isn't appropriate for what we will do here." From the corner of my eye, I see him taking the rod from the altar. I turn my head to get a better look at it. It's a long pale slender stick, has a red handle, and appears to be about three feet in length. "I've never used this particular wand before, for ritual use or for anything else. Nor will I after our tutoring sessions end. It will be yours, and you will most certainly have earned it. I remind you that you do not have leave to cry out, nor do you have leave to move from your position until I say otherwise. This tool is a little harder, and a little harder to bear, than others we've worked with so far. I thought it best to warn you. Brace yourself."

I feel the slight breeze before I hear the whooshing sound of the cane, and then fire lands across my thighs. I gasp. It's all I can do to keep from yelling, and while I don't move out of position, I flinch hard.

"Courage," he says, and then the blows rain down.

I can't scream. I can't jerk away or dance in place. But I can cry; he hasn't said anything about that, and eventually, despite my efforts to stifle them, sobs come up my throat, and I am choking on them, and tears are pouring out of me in torrents.

It stops. In the sudden quiet, I notice that I am shaking and covered with sweat; I wonder how long I have been this way. I feel him coming up behind me, and then his arms are around me and he has his hands on my sweating breasts and body; he kisses me on the neck, and as I start to melt into him, his kisses turn to nips and then the deep, possessive bites I love, making me gasp. His hand reaches down between my legs. It's harder not to moan than it was to avoid screaming.

At least he seems to be in a similar state. I can feel his erection poking me in the back.

"Courage," he whispers, and pulls away just as I am on the verge of orgasm.

I hear him picking up the cane again.

"Have courage," he says, a little more loudly, and it is all I can do to obey.

I AM COLLAPSED ON the couch, unable to move. I haven't been secured. There is no need. I am too exhausted, and in too much hurt, to even think of getting up.

My nerves are on fire.

Perhaps that was the point all along. We were, after all, working with Fire.

He crouches next to me, stroking my hair; a cool washcloth sits on my forehead. I can't read the look in his eyes, but he seems to be struggling to say something. I wish I knew what.

"Water," he says at last. "Water is the element associated with the west, the setting sun, and thus with death and dying. It is also the element most closely linked to submission and surrender. It stands for emotion, intuition, dreams, visions, and certain forms of healing; it is represented by a chalice or a grail in all the traditions that I know of, including mine." As he bends over to kiss me, I can see from his shaking arms that he, too, is exhausted. "Water is a common symbol for the divine feminine. Open your legs for me. And remember that you are still in the middle of a learning session, and I have not yet given you leave to use your voice."

The couch upholstery scrapes my skin raw as I comply; I wince.

His hand finds the cleft between my legs; he parts my lips with his fingers and covers me with his mouth, and as he laps me gently with his tongue I am lost, trying to remember to not use my voice. Over. And over. I can't stop. I can't scream. My pleasure screams for me, my body convulsing in a rictus of sensation until I sink into the couch, faint and gasping from *petit mors*.

And then he surfaces and plunges himself into me.

"Earth," he says, in the shortest instructional lecture he has ever made, and that is all he says about Earth. But he is obviously near the end of his energy. And that is all he needs to say about Earth, anyway. We both know what Earth is for; we also know what grounding is, and we know what the common ways are to ground power. This is one of the more classic grounding methods.

I tap him lightly on the hand.

"Yes?"

I whisper, barely audibly, "May I..."

"Yes."

And I wrap my legs around his hips and strain with him, moaning with pleasure, and my moans soon become cries, and parched, he covers my mouth with his to drink them in.

WE DOZED OFF ON the couch for a bit but eventually woke up enough to blow out the candles and relocate ourselves to the bedroom and the futon (one of us limping more than the other) where we lay in a tangle, legs and arms and hair and breath all entwined, kissing each other slowly, languorously.

"One more thing," he says at last. "This is a purely temporary arrangement, as it is a finite apprenticeship; I will therefore not be giving you a collar or any permanent marks of ownership. I only consider those appropriate when there is a lasting commitment. However, I would like you to always wear something of mine while you are under me, some kind of token or favor to remind you of me. That is, if you feel comfortable doing so. I don't want to impose." He strokes my cheek. "Is there anything you might particularly like? You are, after all, the one who is going to be wearing it."

For some reason, this makes me glow as if it were something romantic.

"No, of course I don't mind." I think for a moment. He probably can't afford jewelry on his meager salary. Jewelry has rather serious overtones anyway, even when the jewelry in question is not a ring. Not many options here. "How about a scarf?" I reply at last. "They're discreet enough."

He nods, gets a thoughtful look, then gets up, stumbles to the bureau, and digs around. The scarf he brings out is a large square made of fine black silk. "I'll find something else to put my tarot deck in," he says. "This seems very you; when you asked for a scarf, my tarot cloth came to mind. Black. Of course. I can't think of anything more symbolically appropriate. Give me your right wrist, please."

I hold out my wrist, and he winds the scarf around it, tying it neatly at the ends.

And lies next to me again, and is soon asleep, cradling my wrist and its scarf in his arms. He could almost be a young boy sleeping with a cherished teddy bear.

I look at him and wonder. Eventually, sleep takes me, too.

HE DROVE ME HOME shortly before going to work, dropping me off at my door. I'm used to it now. It took me a little while; I don't like other people to see my apartment, which is a converted attic above a duplex home, and now that it's almost summer, I *really* don't want visitors, because I have no air conditioner, and I can't imagine anyone wanting to stay for even a few minutes in the heat. It's too stifling. I do have a floor fan and a window fan, but they can only do so much.

For one hundred eighty-five per month, you get what you pay for.

If either of my downstairs neighbors moves out, I'm going to take over before the newly vacant apartment even has a chance to be advertised in the classifieds. I don't know what I'll do with that much space, given that both apartments below me are two-bedroom apartments; and I'll have to pay more in rent, of course. Having an apartment with more windows would be nice, though, as would having a kitchen that's equipped with more than just a hot plate, a microwave oven, a toaster oven, and a cube-sized refrigerator. I suppose I'll just have to bite the bullet and look for a roommate.

Another pleasant thing about moving downstairs would be the knowledge that my new dwelling would be legal to inhabit. The reason this attic I'm renting now is so cheap is that it isn't zoned for residence. That's also why the lease is month-by-month, whereas the two regular apartments downstairs have year-long leases.

As I climb the dogleg back stairs from the ground floor to the attic, the heat presses against me, clinging to me until I stagger and have to stop and pant for breath. I'll get used to it in a few minutes. It could be worse. It probably will be worse in a week or two.

I have a few hours to kill until I have to catch the bus. Finally, they transferred me to an evening shift – and the days are long enough that I won't have to walk home in the dark when I get off at my bus stop on the way back. Later in the year, getting home from work is going to be scarier, because I'll have to walk on several blocks of dark side streets, but I'll deal with that when the time comes. It could be worse. The neighborhood I'm in is at least half populated by college students who wanted something within walking distance of the university but couldn't afford student housing. Or at least, that's the case about half a mile or so north. Students don't seem to want to live here on my section of the street. I'm not sure why. It's run-down, and it's noisy on the weekends, but it's not awful. A few blocks away is the street that runs by the county jail. That neighborhood's rougher than this one. No students would ever want to live there, even though it's a little closer to the university than the community here.

On my way to lying down on the mattress I use as my bed, I grab a box of store-brand cornflakes. I'll eat them dry. I have no milk right now, and I won't be able to shop for food until next payday. I make a note to get the toasted oat cereal next time in case I go without milk again. The box of cornflakes is larger, but toasted oats are more filling and easier to eat dry.

I also grab the copy of *Wuthering Heights* that I took out of the library. It's interesting how much more fun it is to read literary classics on my own than it is to read them because I was assigned the book as part of an English class. It's nice to not be compelled. Or maybe I just appreciate my assignments more now that I no longer have access to them. I'm reading the Cliff's Notes to the books, as well. They're the next best thing to a lecture or a discussion, and I'm not even being graded on my work. It's an interesting change of pace from my usual fare of science fiction and fantasy novels.

Especially this one. Catherine and Heathcliff are complete jerks. I can't wait to see what they'll do to each other and their hapless relatives next. The Kate Bush song makes their story sound so very romantic; it lies by omission. These two are not a romantic couple. They're an evening soap opera waiting for a scriptwriter.

When I first moved up here with the girlfriend I was seeing at the time, we signed the lease for this apartment because it was a place that we could get on short notice, without needing a massive deposit. (I had met her through the campus gaming group and the campus Lambda Society, which, like the medieval reenactment club, were also open to townies, including former-students-become-townies like me. As it turned out, we had almost nothing in common except gaming and sapphistry; but we were both women, we were both unattached, and we happened). We moved to this city because she had been hired as a grocery store cashier here; she had interviewed for the out-of-town position because she wanted to be closer geographically to her grandmother, who was getting on in years and needed a little help. The only problem with getting employed immediately at a job that is an hour away from where you live is that you have to move right away. So we moved. New jobs, new apartment. And yes, a toaster oven was involved. One can't set up lesbian house without a toaster oven. It is known.

The timing couldn't have been better. After the next-door neighbor caught a brief glimpse of me and my new girlfriend through my apartment window before we pulled down the shade and turned off the lights, he'd taken to standing at his window, directly opposite from the one he saw us through, with a shotgun in his arms. Through the window, he could see that all I had was an efficiency apartment and that there was only one bed: a double mattress, the mattress that we wound up taking up here to the new place when we moved. It had gotten to the point where I was avoiding my own apartment and we were spending almost all our time at hers, just to avoid being shot. It was not at all an easy walk to and from the fast-food restaurant where I worked stocking the salad bar and washing dishes, but at least she didn't have neighbors pointing shotguns at her.

The new job and the new apartment in the new city outlasted the relationship. My girlfriend met a man shortly after we settled in here, and that was that.

It happens.

From what I've read, it happens a lot.

Unfortunately, what I've read also says that I am just as likely as my ex to leave a girlfriend for a man the instant a man shows up in my life, because I'm bisexual and therefore not really "womyn-identified," whatever that means, and so I shouldn't be surprised or hurt if my bisexual girlfriend abandons me for a guy, since I'd do the same to her, and really, oughtn't I be looking for couples to date, so that I could be truly satisfied, and not have to inflict myself on proper lesbians when I'm just going to break their hearts with my inherent faithlessness anyway?

Needless to say, I find that advice less than helpful.

The drunks are yelling more loudly, now; I hear the sound of glass shattering. I hope somebody with a telephone line calls the police soon before things get really out of hand.

When we were first settling in, the noises on our block used to keep us awake. Neither my girlfriend nor I had yet grown accustomed to sleeping through yelling, loud music, and other disturbances. We'd been spoiled by living in a small college town on a street that was well away from both the main drag and the college itself. (It took her less time to acclimate to our new surroundings, though than it took me; she had been raised here and was coming back, so none of this was new to her).

One night I had been startled to hear a chainsaw. "It's three in the morning. Isn't it unsafe to chop down trees? Is that even allowed?"

My girlfriend gave me an odd look. "That's not a chainsaw. It's a machine gun."

Oh.

This is why I don't go out much unless it's to catch the bus to work, buy food, or go to the library.

I'm used to it now. Really, I am.

Four more hours until my shift in the call center starts. If I soak one of my tee shirts with water, the evaporation might keep me cool for the time I need to kill. I get up, strip off my clothes, wet down a large tee shirt that I wear when I sleep, and flop back onto my mattress. If I pretend hard enough, the air blowing on me from the floor fan will transform into the wind blowing across the moors. I will enjoy Cathy and Heathcliff behaving badly better if I can sit on the moor to watch them.

YESOD

FLAT ON MY BACK. Tied down in the spread-eagle position again. Working on grounding and centering, and focusing energy, again. Grounding my energy involves associating it with a sensation of being secure, which, for some reason, means being secured, and no doubt figuring out the link between being *secure* and being *secured* will be a great moment of *satori* for me; centering involves me trying to concentrate and hold my meditative focus while he finds ways to distract me.

We do this a lot.

Today's variation involved infinitely delayed orgasm – mine, of course. It's been a good three hours. He'll do something with his hands or tongue or with some item pulled out from his dresser drawer of doom that almost gets me coming, and then he stops just as I show signs of an impending climax. Worse, I have to help him do this. Now that my face and upper chest are stuck in what would ordinarily be a purely temporary state of crimson flush, I've been given leave to say "edge" whenever I get close to orgasm so that he knows when to pause what he's doing to prevent me from climaxing. If I catch myself starting to orgasm before he notices or I warn him, and I let myself, there will be penalties, and I don't feel like dealing with them today.

I've lost count of the number of times he's pulled this now. I'm on the edge of screaming, but it's from frustration rather than pleasure, and of course I can't do that, either, because this is energy work, and I am under silence.

I'm almost tempted to ask myself if this is all worth it and if I really want to be here.

But that's just the frustration talking.

I know I am more than a bundle of frustrated nerve endings. I am a soul, a soul that has a body, not the other way around. I am trying to hear my soul around the din of anguished nerves.

November. The path in the nature preserve near my house is mucky from fallen leaves, and wet with freezing rain. A wind blows against me. I shiver in the chill.

I am here because I like to hear the wind make the trees talk.

Bare branches brush the mist and sky.

My down parka is too short to allow me to sit down without soaking my jeans, so I take it off and spread it over the wet leaves that lie at the foot of the old oak tree. Maybe if I think warm thoughts, I won't get hypothermia. I think about fire and sunlight and miserably hot summer days as I sit on top of my parka.

At some point, I stop feeling the cold.

Branches sway back and forth. Wind and rain kiss me sharply. Grey sky leans on me like a lover. I breathe clouds and stare into a half-dark murk. I imagine myself dissolving into the mist and rain.

I am alone. I feel like I ought to be miserable and lonely, but I'm not – I am just alone, now, as nearly always. I am myself, alone, sitting at the foot of a large tree, with no company but the woods and the rain.

This is how I spend my weekend afternoons.

My peers spend their weekends going to the football and basketball games held by boys' high schools, the masculine analogs to our own school for girls; or they go to parties, drinking beer and wine coolers they've managed to scavenge, and get trashed; or they shop and hang out in malls; or talk endlessly on the phone to each other. Some have boyfriends. Some manage to play around with their boyfriends, though probably stopping just short of anything that could result in an embarrassing pregnancy and expulsion from school.

I meditate in the woods and talk with trees. I am sixteen, and I have so little in common with my classmates and, for that matter, with my own family, now, that I sometimes wonder if I am an alien.

I raise my gloved hand to clutch the silver unicorn pendant that hangs at my throat and feel cold throb at me like a pulse of lightning where the unicorn's hooves and horn have pierced the yarn of my glove.

As I start to give myself up to the late autumn cold, the trees shed their bark and become light. Forks of light grow down through my body and entwine with old roots. My hair pulses in unison with the glowing, swaying branches; and the rain that kisses and slaps my cheek, and the wind that drives it, are divine fire.

Love, says the fire. Love.

Love all.

Be in love with all. Be love. Be.

I say yes because there is no other answer to this imperative

and I am love and the trees are love and the wind and rain and mud and cold are love and my parents and teachers and classmates are love and all the people of the Earth are love and the crow that flies cawing across the sky is love and we are all one. We are One and we forget, only to remember ourselves in Love

and the world is afire and I rise, pulsing with hot light, feeling the embrace of wind and hearing the whisperings of trees.

BENT OVER THE COUCH. The hum of the air conditioner does not quite cover the sound of the riding crop slicing through the air or the crack of impact on my flesh. My grunts, which I am failing to hold in, are threatening to turn into whimpers. The temptation to jerk away is strong. I maintain my position and reassert my silence. It isn't just discipline that holds me fast; it's pride, and mixed in with the pride, a good deal of pigheadedness. I'm pretty sure *Magister* knows this and uses it as ruthlessly as he uses every other part of me.

I don't want to be a disappointment. I desperately, desperately want him to be pleased with me.

My raw skin protests, but I ignore it.

I am steel, being heated in the flame and hammered on the anvil. I will be strong.

My mother reads my diary passage aloud: "We finally did it. After months and months of fumbling and talking about it, we finally did it. We finally kissed each other. I had no idea it was like this. I'm so happy. I know I'm a real girl now. My lips are still tingling."

The aide found my diary when she was cleaning my room, read the passage, and handed it over to my mother. I'm not sure how the aide, who attends the same church we do, and who my parents hired as a mutually beneficial favor because she needed work and my mother needed assistance with her daily activities, found it; I've been very careful about hiding it. My diary's latest hiding place was under my bed in a box of unsorted papers and old school workbooks. It must have taken her a long time to ferret it out. From now on, I'll have to keep the diary in my locker at school. Or maybe I could stash it behind the carriage house or the pool cabana.

My father cuffs me across the cheek – not very hard, the humiliation hurts worse than the slap – and bellows, "How dare you abuse our trust this way? You let a boy touch you? What's next? You're a slut! You're a whore!"

My purity is everything. If I lose it, I will be nothing but soiled, ruined goods, and nobody decent will want to marry me. I have been foolish. Weak. A sinner. I have shamed the family...

He rages on and on in this vein, while I cower. Of course, I'm cowering. What else would I be expected to do? I can't stand up to them.

My mother starts crying.

If only this would stop.

It never used to be this way. My father and I used to be so close. He called me the apple of his eye, once. He never used to scream at me. He used to be proud of me. He used to play chess with me, and Monopoly, and Risk. He used to read to me. We used to talk together about the Middle Ages. We went to museums together. We brunched together after Mass on the days that my mother could not go to church because she was too sick to get out of bed. On the rare days that she was healthy, we all went out to eat together.

Then I started growing. My peers, from what little I've gleaned from listening in on the edge of their conversations, seem to merely be in the process of growing up. I'm growing away. I don't know how to stop it from happening, or even if I should stop it from happening. I probably don't have a choice in the matter. I almost wish I'd been born to different parents because my own parents seem to be not at all happy with the daughter they got stuck with. I can't help being myself, nor can I stop loving who I love, and it was so good to finally find a boy – to find someone, anyone – with whom I had things in common, and it felt so good to kiss him, once we got past our nervousness.

I no longer agree with my parents about everything anymore. Kissing before marriage, for instance, is something I disagree with them on. I see nothing wrong with kissing. I want my lips to be kissed.

"You are grounded until further notice," he says at last. "And starting tonight, you will do an hour of evening prayer and Bible study with me before bedtime. You will have nothing more to do with this boy who took advantage of you, and you will not have any further contact with boys until we say otherwise, since you obviously cannot be trusted to control yourself." He sighs. "I'm very disappointed in you."

In a year I will go away to college, somewhere, assuming they will let me.

It won't be soon enough.

I'm SITTING AT A carrel in the university library in the religion section on the second floor, a stack of books shoved to the side in a pile. The *Zohar* – several books of it. Isaac Luria. A medieval treatise on golems that he doesn't have a personal copy of, which is why I'm doing my work here. My weekly readings usually include at least one obscure work that I can't find on his bookshelves and have to look up elsewhere. Plotinus, who doesn't seem to fit into this assignment on the movements and the evolution of the soul at all, but maybe I'm missing something; then again, maybe not. He's given me unrelated tangential readings before as a way of keeping me on my toes. If I don't notice that the readings are unrelated, then I'm not paying attention. Then again, sometimes the seemingly unrelated readings are related to the study material after all, and if I don't catch that, I'm not paying attention. The bottom line is that I need to read everything thoroughly and think about it or meditate on it.

Then I have to write him an essay, which I read aloud so that my findings can be critiqued – or, as some other, less thick-skinned people might call it, torn apart to the very stuffing. It's a learning experience. Builds character. No, really, it does. On rare occasions, I'm able to conduct study in an area of esoteric philosophy which I happen to already know fairly well, and in those instances, the grilling session turns into a real debate.

He seems to like that even better, interestingly enough.

He started giving me assignments after I told him I missed being in college. Like every other aspect of my training, the assignments are difficult – they're more difficult than some of the assignments I was given for my philosophy classes after I declared my major and started taking upper-level courses.

I think it's one of the sweetest things he's ever done for me.

"She's four years older than you are; she's a graduate student, while you're only a sophomore. You let her take advantage of you? I don't understand." I was expecting him to scream at me, the way he did when he found out I'd kissed my boyfriend, but he has yet to scream. He's so quiet I can barely hear his voice. His face is crestfallen. This is so much worse than screaming.

"If it was my idea, how could she be the one taking advantage of me?"

My mother is crying too hard to talk. At least she hasn't run to the bathroom to throw up again.

"Don't you know how horrible a sin this is? It's worse than murder. How could we have failed you so badly in teaching you right from wrong? You say you love her. You say this was your idea. You might not care about your own soul, but don't you care about hers?"

I swallow. Hard. I am not going to start crying in front of them. Not now. "Dad, I gave up Christianity for Lent. Your argument doesn't mean anything to me."

"When did that happen? Was abandoning your faith her idea, too?"

Actually, yes, it was, sort of, in an indirect kind of way, although I was already questioning it by the time she had her faith crisis and wound up giving up her Christian beliefs as part of the angst attack I had to talk her through. That was a long night. But that's nothing that needs to be discussed with my parents.

They found my long-distance phone bill, which, like all other campus communication, got sent to my home address during school vacations, before I could intercept the mail. Of course, they opened the bill. They said it was their responsibility to pay my college bills. They wanted to know why there were all those long-distance charges to a certain college town in the northeast part of the state, which my girlfriend happened to be living in because that was the location of her grad school. I can hide the truth, but I can't tell lies. (My now ex-girlfriend, actually; we broke things off a week before I went home for the Christmas holidays. Not that that's any of my parents' business, either).

And so, I was outed.

"You need help," my father says, and my mother nods tearfully. "We can get you therapy. It's not too late. We were probably blessed by God to have found out about this situation as early as we did."

Eventually, they give me an ultimatum. I can go through professional deprogramming – then, once I am back home, I can undergo spiritual guidance from our parish priest, while they keep me under house arrest, with constant monitoring; or I can leave and never come home or consider myself part of the family again.

If I allow them to take me under their control, they may eventually send me to the local public university and let me graduate. If not, they will mourn me as one dead, and that will be that. Either way, I won't get to attend the private college I've been enrolled in anymore, since it's several hundred miles away and puts me out of their reach, away from their control and their watchful eyes. I won't be able to afford the tuition payments on my own, since my partial scholarship only covers half the tuition, and I have no income of my own. However, the deprogramming option at least lets me stay in their good graces. Sort of. And it lets me have a chance of eventually getting back into college, albeit a public university that has a reputation for taking any student that breathes and probably won't be nearly challenging enough for me. Better gut classes at an undemanding, noncompetitive public university than no college at all. There isn't really much of a choice if I care about my own interests.

I start packing a bag.

I hope I can hang out at the Greyhound station overnight until I can arrange transportation to my dorm to collect the few things I can't bear to leave behind. I'd rather not spend the night on the streets. It's January.

NAKED, I SIT ON my knees on the living room floor, in my student posture. The air-conditioned chill in here is making me shiver, and I am starting to get a stiff neck from looking up at him. He isn't cold at all; he's wearing one of his nice silk shirts and a pair of charcoal grey pressed trousers, which is what he was wearing when he got off work. I'm severely jealous. The goose pimples on my arms won't go away. Other parts of me are sticking out from the chilled air, as well, and I have a sinking suspicion that this means I won't be able to cover up. There is too much aesthetic appeal in my being kept cold. I hope he warms me up soon, anyway, one way or another.

"I have a somewhat unusual request this time," he tells me. "Well. Perhaps not that unusual."

I indicate that I'm listening. I have learned how to be very eloquent with my eyes.

"I would like you to pleasure yourself in front of me."

He wants me to do it now, on the spot, with no foreplay or any kind of lead-in or mood-setting? I give him what I hope is an extremely quizzical look.

"It's not so much that I'm curious to see if you embarrass easily, although there is certainly a small element of that. Mostly it's that I want to see what the best way is to bring you to a climax. You know your body better than I do. I can't think of a more efficient way of finding how to pleasure you than watching you do it to yourself. I want to see if you do things differently from me when you touch yourself, from the way that I do it when I touch you, and if so, how; I might learn something new. I'm sorry it didn't occur to me to ask this of you earlier. I should have brought it up months ago when we first started seeing each other. Please forgive my thoughtlessness." He looks at me apologetically. "I want to make you happy."

I don't think he has anything to worry about on that count; he's always been able to give me so much pleasure that "happy" seems a paltry way to describe the afterglow.

Well.

Ordinarily, by myself, I don't bother with foreplay; I just wet my finger and start playing with my clitoris. It occurs to me, however, that he might appreciate a bit more of a show; and really, why not? Perhaps getting to business with no prelude, and getting it over with so that I can move on to more important things, is a less satisfying way to achieve an orgasm than something that involves teasing other parts.

I lie down on the couch, on my back, and trail my left hand up to cup my breast, taking the nipple between my fingertips and rolling it gently as I slowly work my other hand downward, caressing my skin as I go. I'm not very wet. My fingertips are cold, however, and the sensation is interesting.

Much more interesting, though, is the thought of *Magister* pleasuring me with his tongue, and that has me soaked in no time. I've always gotten off more on using my fantasies and memories to augment what I do with my fingers than I have on sensation alone. Pure sensation doesn't really do it for me. Imagining *Magister's* mouth, and the feel of his skin, I slide my finger down to wet it in my vaginal juices before going back to rubbing my clitoris. It's a different sort of feeling from the sensation of using just my saliva as lubricant, and if I'm extremely aroused and using a finger to get off, it feels better. There's less friction. More of my sensitive areas get touched that way, as well.

My breath grows ragged. My legs tremble.

I no longer feel cold.

After a while, I barely notice what I'm doing to myself. The dream is all, and it consumes me.

When I imagine him rising from me and taking me, imagine him biting my shoulder, hard, as hard as his thrusts as he pushes himself deep into me, I cry out.

"What are you thinking about?" he asks. "You may speak."

"You. Your cock inside me. You're biting me. You're drawing blood. Oh, God." I'm gasping. I'm not that close to orgasm, yet, but I feel a need to make noise that I've never felt before while doing this. It feels so much better to masturbate for him than it does to just do it for myself. Maybe that's because when I'm alone, it isn't really erotic at all – it's just a physical release, like trying to trigger a stuck sneeze. But this is different.

After a while, he asks, "Would you like me to take over from here?"

"Kiss me," I groan. "Please. Please kiss me. I need you. I want your mouth on mine. I want to taste you. I want to feel you in me. You set me on fire when you kiss me. Please."

He kneels and bends over me, leaning on my shoulder, careful to avoid obstructing the movement of my right arm as he embraces me. His mouth on mine is warm. Such soft lips. It feels so good to be held and kissed when I'm using my hand to pleasure myself; I never imagined how good it would feel. His hand, too, is warm when he reaches for my other breast and takes the nipple between his thumb and forefinger. He squeezes hard, slowly building pressure until I see stars, and I moan. *Oh, yes. Yes, I want that. Don't stop, don't stop*. His fingers squeeze ever more tightly.

I wince.

"Too much?"

"No. Yes. I don't know. Maybe. Please, please don't let go..."

"There, now. I've got you." The pressure ceases, although he is still holding me by the nipple, his hand cupping my breast. "Are you still thinking about me biting you? Making love to you? Taking you deep and hard?"

"Yes..."

"And you feel so good like that, underneath me, hot, wet, rising to meet me, taking me into you. Listen to me, now. I'm going to bite you here, on the chest. Hard." He kisses the top of my chest, indicating the intended target, sucking gently. Kiss marks the spot. When his kiss becomes a nip, I moan. "You liked that, didn't you? I believe you did. Good. I'm going to bite you and slide my fingers inside you – why, you're *drenched*. No, you don't need to stop what you're doing. Keep pleasuring yourself. That's it. I'm just helping you along. Oh. You're so beautiful like this." He pumps me gently with his fingers. Then his mouth is on my flesh, hot and urgent, opened wide, and his teeth sink in, and it hurts. It hurts so beautifully. The pain is sharp enough to make me gasp – but inside it is a gift, like a flower made of fire, and I tingle as the blossoming flames lick at me.

His fingers fill me, push against me, each gentle thrust going in just a tiny bit deeper than the last one. My walls are stretching. Hardness of bone. I'll be on his hand soon. I can feel the back of it, bumping against my fingers as I rub. The sensation of my own fingers on my clitoris is intense now, much more intense than it had ever felt when it was just me getting off by myself. The bottom of his hand is warm under me as I slide against him. Push through the ring of fire, push past. There, I'm on him. Warm, warm, I don't want this to end...

And then I am coming, and eventually, he rises, his hand slipping out slightly as he meets my mouth, and he covers my mouth with his kiss as, still riding the tips of four fingers, I cry out my pleasure for him to drink in.

His mouth tastes coppery.

"I DON'T KNOW HOW to make you happy anymore," my boyfriend sighs. "You just don't seem to be all here. Your head is always somewhere else, even when we're making love. Do you still love me?"

It's been three months since I gave him my virginity, and we're already on the verge of breaking up. Three months ago, I had been picking china patterns in my mind. It did occur to me, eventually, that sex and even true love are not always indications that a romantic relationship will last forever, that there is more to a mating of true minds than romantic feelings and passionate sparks, but I hadn't known it would end like this.

"I love you. Very much."

"But I can't make you happy."

I look down. He's right.

"What do I need to do?"

"I don't know," I reply sadly. "I don't know what's wrong. I just know something is missing."

And it's over – not with a bang, but a whimper.

HE'S FINALLY LETTING ME climax. He's still not letting me make any noise. Fire rips through me. I'm flying out of my head. I can't tell if it feels good or if it hurts.

My fingernails scream as they scratch the sheets.

HOD

A WARM SEPTEMBER SUN streams through the kitchen window. It's finally cool enough that we can turn off the air conditioning without broiling ourselves alive, so we have the windows open. Of course, the weather this time of year is fickle, so tomorrow we might well be broiling again. Alternatively, we might get a hard frost and wake up shivering.

I'm in the middle of one of my essay assignments. My books and papers take up a large part of the kitchen table – basically, whatever part of the table is not already occupied by food. Stacking the spare notebook paper, folders, pens, and other miscellaneous supplies in a wooden garden carry-all I found stuffed in the back of the coat closet helped to tame my mess somewhat, but the books still have a tendency to sprawl when I write, because I'm cross-referencing them, and it's a pain to keep them in a neat little stack if I have to be constantly pulling them out to look for quotes.

This time, he has me reading Campbell's writings on the Hero's Journey, a pop psychology book by someone called Maureen Murdock, some of Jung's writings on the Shadow archetype, and Gerald Gardner.

What a combination.

I have to take some responsibility for the selection – he has me reading the authors to come up with background material for a new initiation ritual. Ritual magick hasn't been something I've taken to. I found out the hard way when trying to conduct a ritual that while I make a decent temple assistant when he needs help boosting his concentration and power, my own talents are not so inclined. I work better on a path without much ritual at all, feeling delicate awareness of currents around me, while spontaneously focusing my power to push those currents around. That's how I clean a sacred space. Focusing on actual ascent is even more chaotic, and it only happens when I meditate.

Except when sometimes, now, it doesn't.

We were hoping ritual would give me enough structure that my search for gnosis would use a path for regular enlightenments, but unfortunately, the details become too interesting in themselves for me to remember what it was that I was trying to accomplish in the first place.

In keeping with this, he suggested creating an initiation ritual of the "make it up as you go along" variety, rather than something scripted in his esoteric tradition.

"Of course, it's not working for you," he mused. "My tradition is fraternal. There are women in it, but Florence Farr and Mina Bergson and goddess imagery notwithstanding, the rituals were still written in the nineteenth century by men, and mostly for other men. You're not a man. Dig hard enough and you'll find some criticism of the rituals, saying that they're oversimplified and sexist whenever feminine energy is concerned. Too polarized, in all the wrong ways. The women who find them useful and do well in the tradition probably have more polarized extremes of masculine and feminine energy than you do, and all of it conventional. Your animus and anima are differently shaped. Might as well ask you to fit a Procrustean bed."

It made more sense, he said, to devise a home-brewed initiation ritual that I would find more personally meaningful and more suited to the raw and chaotic way I work energy, and I agreed. It's only common sense. If his tradition doesn't suit me well, why use its established rituals?

Everything points to the necessity of my finding, or blazing, my own path.

Everything also points to the need for an initiation of some kind. It can only be an initiation. Initiations are not just once-in-a-lifetime occurrences; they're ways to acknowledge transitions, achieve purification, and clear away obstacles.

That's exactly what I need at this moment. I have been searching for my higher Self, that part of me that goes beyond my petty short-term awareness and connects to, and embodies, a wisdom that is divine. I lose my attention often when meditating, though, something that never used to be a problem, and when I try to work with energy currents, things feel sluggish, for lack of a better description. It feels like there is a barrier in my way that I need to break through if I'm going to continue in my studies. I just can't break it using the scripts that are available, because they mean nothing to me personally. There wouldn't be any point.

Hence the research and the increased workload.

Unfortunately, not all of the new material seems relevant to my needs.

"None of the myths Gardner's second-degree initiation ritual borrows from have anything remotely resembling a romance in them," I gripe. "And if they had, we'd call it pathological, given the dynamics. Inanna and Ereshkigal? Incest is the least of the problems with that pairing. Hades and Kore? Don't even get me started. The idea of making Kore fall in love with the Lord of the Dead as part of becoming Persephone is just ridiculous. That would never happen in real life. If the legend was based on the typical marriage transactions of Bronze Age Greece, the kidnapping probably mimicked the aftermath of an arranged marriage between a teenage bride and someone three times her age. Depending on what part of the Hellenic world inspired the legend, there might even have been a mock kidnapping as part of the ceremony. Or a real abduction. Bridal consent utterly optional. I doubt whatever Hades was feeling for Kore could remotely be called love, for that matter. People who are in love don't kidnap and rape their loved ones. They send them flowers, maybe sing romantic ballads outside their windows, or compose poetry to them. Kore and Hades are just not a romantic pairing. So why do the parts played by the High Priest and High Priestess have to be so schmoopy? It doesn't come across as romantic; it comes across as fake. The realm of the dead is no place for schmoopiness. If Gardner wrote this himself, he's not much of a writer. 'I feel the pangs of love.' No, doofus, you feel the pangs of a flogger hitting you on the back, or you would, anyway, if your High Priest was hitting you with any kind of force, which he isn't. Why not just have a whip made of bunny fur, if you and your co-celebrant are in it for a little mild titillation before enacting the Great Rite? Also, why is it so important for the High Priestess of a coven to be young? I can see why it would be important for the purposes of this specific ritual – Death and the Maiden, and all that. But saying the coven head needs to step down when she reaches some kind of age-linked expiration date, as if she was a carton of milk about to spoil? That's not very nice to crones, now, is it? Funny, there's no such requirement for the High Priest that he be young, either. Gardner's being ageist *and* sexist. Heterosexist, too, for that matter. Charming. No, don't worry, I won't write that into the essay."

He raises an eyebrow.

"Well, probably not."

I put down the book I'm citing and gather up the dishes from dinner. He says I don't have to do the washing-up – it's his apartment, not mine – but I feel like doing it as a favor. It's a small act I can perform for him. If I've been spending so much time over here, now, that I habitually leave my homework on his kitchen table rather than doing the assignments at home or in the university library from where many of the books come, then I might as well contribute a little more to the upkeep of the place.

I'VE BEEN RE-READING SOME of the anthropological papers compiled in my old *Magic, Witchcraft, and Religion* textbook (the textbook that gave the class I took its name). I started doing it on my own. Purely my own idea. It wasn't on my weekly assigned book list.

Call it a hunch, or call it a nagging suspicion based on half-remembered classroom discussions from years ago. Probably both would fit.

"I know part of why none of the initiation rituals of the Western esoteric traditions move me," I say. "They're not hard enough."

"How so?"

"Shamanic initiation rituals and tribal rite-of-passage rituals – initiations in cultures that see the world of the spirit as crucial to human survival, not just as something mystical to dabble in – are life and death struggles. They're terrifying. The initiate never chooses to be a shaman, according to Mircea Eliade, any more than the initiate chooses to be an adult. Life chooses the initiate. It forces itself. To ignore the spirit realm is to doom oneself. People with shamanic potential often have unbearable migraines, or seizure disorders, or come down with an illness that threatens to kill them, and I think if it wasn't for that unbearable stimulus, they would not choose to become shamans at all. Why? Because the initiation rite is so brutal. They know, at least in a general sort of way, that the *becoming* will be terrible. Nobody wants it. Nobody sane could ever want it.

"And the initiate actually has to fight to get something of worth: his or her membership in the tribe, communion with the spirit world, whatever. The stakes are higher, too. Failure doesn't just generally mean go back and study some more; it means death or banishment – and banishment is practically the same thing as a death sentence, in a harsh climate like Siberia – or it means loss of sanity. No offense to your tradition," I add hastily, "you're obviously not a rich dilettante like so many of the Symbolists and Decadents in the Golden Dawn were, or Crowley's disciples for that matter, but I'm pretty sure a man of the upper classes in nineteenth or early twentieth century London would have approached an esoteric initiation a little differently from the way a Siberian mystic would have done it. Or the way a young Masai warrior would have approached initiation into his tribe. The perspective would simply not be the same."

"You feel you have more in common with a member of an aboriginal tribe?"

"Yes. I have no idea why. I know my background would give me far more in common with an Edwardian dandy, but I just can't work within their systems."

"Shamanic magic is a bit rawer and more intuitive – instinct-based," he muses, "which would certainly be compatible with your instinct toward the more chaotic forms of energy work. It also deals more directly with the underworld, including the world of dreaming. Do you feel called to dreams?"

"More like they call to me."

He gets a thoughtful look on his face.

I'VE BEEN REVIEWING ANTHROPOLOGICAL texts on rite-of-passage rituals for the past two weeks, now that the focus is on shamanic magic in pre-literate cultures. He also has me keeping a dream journal, to better remember my dreams and look for symbolic messages, and to get accustomed to working with my dream states so that I might attempt familiarizing myself with the Underworld via lucid dreaming.

On top of that, he has me reading the *Epic of Gilgamesh* in conjunction with related myths surrounding Inanna's descent into the realm of death, along with the Homeric Hymn to Demeter, Orphic hymns, and articles on the greater and lesser rites at Eleusis. My complaints about the second-degree and third-degree rituals of Gardnerian Wicca appear to have inspired him to direct me to Gerald Gardner's original source material.

He's also assigned me *more* Joseph Campbell, *more* Jung, *more* Eliade, and both the Tibetan and Egyptian iterations of the *Book of the Dead*.

As if all that isn't enough, in addition to my occult readings, he's picked now, of all times, to have me commence a study of erotica beyond what I've already read in *Yellow Silk*. He wants me to be familiar with the classics. The short stories of Anais Nin; *The Story of O*; *Justine*. He wants this done *now*, despite my lack of a personal time machine to help me stay on top of my studies.

The latter text was underwhelming, and would have been underwhelming even if I'd done more than just skim it to get it read in time to write my weekly essay.

"Sade has a nicely vicious sense of ironic humor," I complain, "but otherwise, yuck. It's like reading Ayn Rand, only with more sex, and the sex scenes aren't even written well. And comparing Sade to Ayn Rand is no compliment, whether you're talking about his philosophical outlook or otherwise. Libertine, libertarian, whatever, they're both just sociopaths who glorify predators, think might makes right, and can't edit to save their lives. *Juliette* was about a thousand pages too long. Was Sade being paid by the word?"

"Truly ironic, when you consider that in most of his work, he advocates a sort of radical communism that relies on the abolition of privacy and private property. Not very libertarian, that."

"*What?*"

"Reread the material, please. And yes. He was paid by the word. He had debts to pay. Lots of them... He is considered a classic writer, for all his many faults. The French made him part of their literary canon."

"Why? For heaven's sake, *why?*"

"I don't know. It might be that they ignore his pornographic works and concentrate on the larger body of literary criticism, historical research, and philosophical discourse that he left behind – most of which has yet to be translated from French into English – but given how writers like Georges Bataille and publishers like Maurice Girodias and Jacques Pauvert were clearly more influenced by the pornography than by the non-pornographic writings, I find it unlikely. That's an interesting question. I don't have an answer for it, though."

"Maybe the French are more perverted than the rest of us?"

"Hah! No, I don't think that's it. Actually, if any world civilization could be awarded a distinction as being more perverse than others, I'd give the prize to Japan, or maybe to India. Remind me to show you some of my art history books sometime. Anyway, something you may want to consider when you reread Justine is the theme of violating conventional ideas of virtue. When Sade wrote his books, libertinage was reviled not just because murder, rape, theft, et cetera were objectively bad things, but also because these crimes were a violation of Christian morality, as was atheism, as was the radical free-thinking that was part of the libertine philosophy. Left-hand path tantra likewise requires its adherents to deliberately violate cultural norms. Radical independence combined with the shock of committing taboo acts is a path to transcendence and enlightenment. It's not an end unto itself. What we two do here is consensual, and therefore, in my opinion, not a wrongness, but it does violate convention. To certain sectors of society, we who fly in the face of sexual convention are monstrous. You know this from personal experience. Consider the power that can come from monstrosity. It can release you."

To be honest, I haven't exactly been overwhelmed by the *Story of O*, either. It's certainly got an artistic beauty to it, and parts of it made me shudder from arousal just because of the subject matter and the imagery, but there isn't a single likable character in the entire book, except maybe for a couple of minor characters in the section on Samois. There are some religious overtones to the work that make the protagonist's sexual submission and gradual metamorphosis seem at times like spiritual asceticism, rather than just like the sexual martyrdom that it is, which is interesting, but the further the plot moves, the more selfish and callous O appears. I can't identify with her, although I can't exactly find myself cheering when she gets violated by the men she loves, either. I almost wonder if Pauline Reage partly wrote the book to say that men are jerks, women like jerks, and meanwhile, women are bitches who deserve what they get. That's not exactly erotic, as far as themes go.

Certain passages are not only beautifully written, but are also intense to the point of bordering on terrifying; I'll give the author that much. She knew her craft. It is inherently scary to see O utterly lose herself in her submission, to see her body and her very life taken over without her so much as protesting, let alone resisting. Something about the inevitable march of events in her story makes the "I don't want to live without you" ending seem horrible and real, rather than cliched. A lesser writer could probably not have pulled that off.

Still, this is supposedly the best erotic novel ever written? Who decides these things?

And why am I being given an extra study load of erotica as assigned reading now, of all times?

"*Magister*? What have the erotic stories you've been assigning me as reading to do with Greek mythology, and with shamanic initiation rituals and traditional rites of passage?" I ask in confusion.

"Two things," he replies. "First has more to do with your sexually charged personal energy than with tribal initiation rituals, although some shamanic rituals, as you will have seen in your readings, do have a sexual element, especially if the initiate's future duties will have much to do with blessing a hunt, or with encouraging the growth of plants. Your power has a raw current of sex to it, even when put to completely nonsexual purposes; I've never seen anything quite like it. You're unusual. I think any kind of initiation for you would have to incorporate that and honor it somehow. The second reason is that the stories you've been reading haven't just been about sex. They've also been about death. In case you hadn't noticed, in most of the readings I've assigned, the protagonist dies or comes very near to dying. You want to do this the traditional way? Well, then. Somehow or other, death is going to have to be involved."

I look at him, wide-eyed.

"No, it does not have to be a literal, physical death. But a part of you is going to die. I've been doing some research on tribal rituals, too, because I don't want to make a total hash of this, and the materials I've read have been clear on that matter. You need to be prepared for it. Initiation is a sort of rebirth, and to be reborn, the initiate must first die. Before recreation comes the necessary destruction. The initiation rituals of the various Western esoteric traditions likewise involve death somehow, as well as a certain amount of symbolic suffering – you've seen that in your readings – but it's considerably more obvious when you study the more primitive initiations and rites of passage. Civilization takes the edge off. If you want to go directly to the source of magickal initiations, we'll need to put the sharp edge back. The ordeal needs to be genuine."

Oh.

What have I got myself into?

"Are you sure you want to go through with it?" he asks gently.

I nod.

"There's still plenty of time to back out, if you change your mind and decide to try another path. Assuming you want to time the ritual with Halloween, Samhain, or whatever you like to call the traditional day of the dead that's coming up, we have several weeks to go."

I go back to reading.

He takes his earplugs out and looks up, frowning, from the sheet of paper he's been working on. It's the first time this morning that I've seen his face; whatever he's been writing has kept him preoccupied. I'm glad to see him surface. He's been spending so much time in his reading that it's almost like he's not there, except during the times that have been formally blocked out for instructing me. I'm even starting to get jealous of his books and projects because they see more of him than I do now, which is ridiculous of me. It's not like I'm not buried in books and projects of my own, as deeply as he is if not even more so.

"This is important," he tells me as he walks across the room to me, his voice quietly intense. "We still haven't had a formal discussion about limits. So far, I've taken the view that if you didn't like what I was doing and wanted me to stop, you'd use your safeword, and that would be an end of it, aside from discussing the matter later to hammer down what to avoid doing in the future, or to see if maybe a different approach would work better. Now I actually need to know, exactly and specifically, what is acceptable to do to you, and what is absolutely *unacceptable*. I've been working on a ritual outline. For the duration of your initiation, your safeword is going to be temporarily suspended, so I'm going to have to assume that anything you do not inform me of in advance as forbidden is something you are willing to tolerate if not necessarily enjoy. And it *will* be unpleasant."

Um.

He hands me a spare pen from his pocket, along with a blank sheet of paper. "Get to work," he says.

My mind is as blank as the paper before me, but I start thinking anyway.

I hear his footstep creak the noisy floorboard that hides beneath the living room rug. I think I also hear him mutter, "I don't like this," but I might be mistaken about that. His voice is quieter than that creak. The building is old. It has quirks.

WE'RE DOING GREEK TONIGHT because that's what he felt like preparing. Feta cheese, sliced cherry tomatoes, chopped salad greens, and kalamata olives, sprinkled with ladolemono dressing; spanakopitas; chilled dolmathes; moussaka, the sweet tomato sauce used in its preparation leaving an aftertaste of basil and cinnamon; baklava for dessert. Accompanying this is white wine, a dry, crisp Moscofilero from the Peloponnese (according to the label that I read, since I am not a wine expert enough to be able to identify wine by taste alone). He's made everything from scratch except for the phyllo dough used in the spanakopitas and the baklava; he bought the sheets of dough pre-made in the frozen food aisle of the local grocery store. This is his idea of being lazy. The grape leaves came from wild vines that grew by the banks of a local stream. I helped him gather them.

I love it when he cooks.

"I think I might have overcooked a little," he says at last, "but that's all right, it just means there will be leftovers. Here, have some more moussaka. You're staring at it as if it's the Holy Grail. Are you sure you're getting enough to eat at home?"

"Yes," I lie, and go back to attacking my food.

Some time later I feel his eyes watching me and look up from the second helping of baklava I've been nibbling at.

"Yes, *Magister*?"

"I'm ready for dessert."

"It *was* very good baklava. Wait, I thought you already had some."

"I wasn't referring to the baklava," he says with a smile. "Come to bed."

I shiver with anticipation.

BRAHMS' *FIRST SYMPHONY* PLAYS on the portable CD player as, legs splayed and shackled to the futon frame, I strain underneath *Magister*. Every time he bites me on the neck, I shudder, and pull at the manacles that pin my wrists together above my head. When he comes up to devour my mouth, his kiss tastes like wine and spice.

We're not doing lessons or magickal work tonight, so I have my voice back.

"Can you please reposition my wrists?" I ask. "I want to be able to hold you."

"Later. I'd like to keep you fully stretched, for the time being."

He gets up from the futon to rummage in the dresser drawer, eventually pulling up a silvery-looking chain with little black things on the ends of it.

"What's that?"

"Something I hadn't got around to trying out on you yet."

He drapes the chain across my chest and starts fiddling with one of the ends of the chain. I feel it slide onto my left nipple; then he tightens it. He proceeds to do the same thing to my right nipple.

"These are, as you can see, adjustable. They're also a relatively innocuous iteration, as far as nipple clamps go. They have to be screwed manually to be tightened. There's a Japanese style, called clover clamps, that start out tight and get increasingly tighter every time the chain is tugged. Those can be quite nasty. There's also a form of clamps that look like a pair of hairpins that drape over the nipples and are adjusted by sliding an ornament up and down their length; those are very pretty, and they look like easy enough jewelry to wear, but they're tighter than they appear."

"Let me guess. You have a pair of those, too."

I catch him smirking. "I have one of everything. Now then. Let's see how you handle these ones."

He pulls gently. It feels odd; I can't tell if it hurts, feels good, or just feels like pressure. I squint down at them.

"Not much of a response. Hmm. I think these could be tightened some-what."

This time, after he twists the little adjusters, it hurts, making me gasp and wince.

"Ah. You noticed that. I think we'll go with that setting. Other side, then..."

He bends down to resume ravishing my mouth with his. Although he's supported himself on his arms, his bare chest brushes lightly against mine anyway. I cringe. The music picks that precise moment to hit a crescendo, one of many, and bizarrely, I feel the sound vibrate through the chain. It's beautiful. It hurts. It's some of the most painful beauty I've ever heard.

"Well," he says after he surfaces, "that's interesting. Your chain seems to be resonating with a certain note in the music... The look on your face is quite charming. I wonder what you'll look like if I use something else to make the chain vibrate."

This time, when he returns after fishing through the dresser drawer, he has something I recognize and am familiar with. It's vaguely phallic-shaped, made of plastic, and runs on batteries. The high setting is loud enough, and strong enough, to wake the dead. I am told that this is unusual for this type of vibrator, so the vibrator is a curiosity of sorts. When it's inside me at just the right angle, it gets me off within minutes. When it's placed externally, it either tickles me unpleasantly or makes me grimace in pain and shrink away reflexively, depending on the location.

He almost never uses the low setting, since he has other vibrators for that.

I look at him, aghast. I feel myself going bug-eyed. *Oh, no. Please, no. That's just evil. Don't do that.*

"No? Have I reached a limit?"

I gulp.

"This is the first time I've put clamps on you. Maybe I should save vibration play using the clamps for another night. You seem anxious."

I'm so glad he doesn't put it on the chain. I don't think I could handle that. He's wearing an amused look. Surely that's enough for me to endure, without the additional torment of wildly vibrating clamps. I have yet to get used to his grin. For the most part, I find his presence profoundly comforting, a source of absolute security and peace, even when I am burning up with arousal and need, even when I am trying not to cringe from blows he gives me with his hands or his horsewhip or a cane or some other implement of destruction, but that smile of his is unsettling. Sometimes I wonder if he practices it in front of a mirror to make sure it achieves maximum effect.

The vibrator plunges into me, a hard plastic presence; I cry out, trying to work it in deeper. Its loud hum blends with the sound of the music coming from the CD player.

The chain, and its clamps, still oscillate in time with the music.

Around my gasps, moans, and grunts, I hear him say, "I should warn you, they hurt more coming off than they did getting put on, when your circulation comes back."

THE CLAMPS ARE OFF. My nipples are giant, throbbing bruises. My nether regions are a giant, throbbing plain of orgasm from his plowing me. My throat is throbbing, because I have been screaming around a rag he stuffed in my mouth to muffle me, when it became obvious that I was going to make enough noise to disturb the neighbors. I so seldom get to scream like that. It feels positively luxurious to scream, now.

The gag is out. I'm done screaming. I think.

"I want to hold you in my arms, now," I rasp. "Could you reposition me? Please?"

"I think I can manage something," he says as he unhooks the manacles from the eyebolt.

I wrap myself around him, and find his mouth and take it in mine. I want to memorize his lips. I want to devour them. I want to keep them on me forever, if this moment can last forever. I want to always taste his wine-and-cinnamon breath. I want to feel the warmth of his skin under my arms forever, the swollen hardness of his cock forever, as I rock my hips under him. I want this now to be forever mine. Even the soreness in my nipples, and between my legs, even that soreness is something I want to keep. I thrust myself against him, struggling, needing another release.

Eventually, he pulls away to undo my ankle restraints one by one.

"Roll over," he says.

Soon I feel his fingers massage the lubricating oil inside me, and then I feel him enter me from behind, slowly and carefully, and we begin to rock back and forth together, and I am on fire, moaning my need into the bed coverings. But I have managed to grab his forearms. I am still holding him.

THE LIGHT OF THE setting sun falling on his freshly washed, naked flesh makes him glow golden. His repose is a breathtakingly beautiful thing. He looks like an ancient and forgotten god, the futon mattress we lie on his altar; I have a sudden irrational desire to wind garlands of ivy and grapes around his head and along his body in tribute, to worship him. I reach out my hand and gently stroke his cheek, his hair, tracing the black and silver strands with my fingertips.

He opens his eyes and smiles sleepily at me.

"May I have your wrist for a minute?" I ask.

Silently, he hands out his wrist.

I untie the scarf that I've been wearing around my wrist for weeks and re-wrap it, this time securing it around both our wrists. "This is how I want to sleep. I want to be bound to you. Do you mind?"

He smiles again, kisses my wrist where it is bound to his, and reaches for me with his free arm. I slide up against him as if we could somehow melt together, and listen to his breathing as it becomes slow and heavy.

"I love you," I whisper, surprised at my words, but realizing the absolute truth of them as I utter them. "I love you. I love you..."

NETZACH

THE MAPLES HAVE SHED their leaves. Bright yellow windfall clumps on pavement and lawns, a defiant contrast to the gloom of the afternoon sky. As I walk from the bus stop down the street, a cold, light rain begins to fall. I pull my coat closer to my body.

His apartment, which is part of what used to be a large, sprawling house before it was divided into separate units, is at the end of the street. Some of the other people in it have turned on their entrance lights, the way many of the houses on this street have, for the trick-or-treaters. He isn't passing out candy this year. His paycheck didn't stretch far enough to allow for both candy and rent. Maybe after tonight, when the candy goes on clearance, it will be another story. We do both like chocolate.

I reach the apartment building, enter, and walk up a flight of stairs to his door. A single ear of corn hangs from it as decoration.

HE LOOKS AT ME thoughtfully. "It's interesting," he says. "There's something about you – some kind of inner presence. You have a certain untouchable, virginal quality about you."

"Really? After all this?" I smile. "I don't see how that's possible. I think the only part of me that's still inviolate is my left nostril."

"No, no, you know that's not what I mean. I refer to your self-containment." He pauses. "You're unusually self-possessed. Also, you also seem to have a sort of regenerative tendency. I've noticed that you always grow yourself back, somehow, should an event happen in your life that cuts you down – losing your family, losing your ability to attend college, losing your wealth – nothing has ever broken you. It's a very good quality to have. I think we'll be glad of that tonight."

If he's trying to cheer me up, it's not working.

"Do you still want to do this?"

"It's not a matter of want. I still *need* to do this. You know that."

I smile nervously, pick a few seeds out of the sliced pomegranate that sits on the kitchen table, pop them in my mouth, and go back to my reading, of which there has continued to be a ridiculous amount. It's all been related to the initiation I'll be going through tonight. He wants me to be well-prepared. It seems like every week's reading list was longer than the one from the week before it.

I've even helped him write the ceremony. Well, I helped him write some of it, namely, the parts of it that aren't meant to surprise me – which would be less than half of it. What I did contribute, though, was important in its own way.

I remind myself of extremely common elements of rite-of-passage rituals and shamanic and magickal initiations that won't be part of tonight's experience because they were among the things I specifically listed as personally unacceptable when I gave him an inventory of my absolute limits: Mutilation, either performed on myself by myself, or by my initiator. Prolonged fasting. Poison ingestion, to trigger hallucinations, purge impurity, or simply to test endurance. Burial alive. I'll be spared all these things. I could almost say I'm getting off easy tonight.

Making me complicit in the terms of my ordeal was critical. I know this. I cannot go through with this without having crafted my explicit consent well in advance.

Terror and dread are meant to be part of the experience, too. He had me suggest possible material that he could add that I found frightening. Who better to know the measure of my own Shadow than myself?

Bastard.

WE'VE PUSHED FURNITURE ASIDE in the living room to provide extra space, and he has me cast circle to seal and consecrate the area we will use.

When it's just him, or when I'm only helping, he goes through an elaborate spoken ritual that involves calling the archangels, using formal language, and he has specific postures that get used, a ritual robe that he sewed himself by hand, and other details that help him focus.

My own methods are simpler. I cleanse the area using my hands to pantomime scouring, and I put a bit of frankincense on the brazier, mostly just because I've always liked the smell of frankincense, ever since I was a child. Then I draw the circle by walking it, stopping at each compass corner point to imagine the element it corresponds to and to summon that element in. I must be silent when I do this. I found that being under imposed silence while working with energies made silence one of my primary tools for focus, and we both agreed that if it worked for me, I should continue doing things the way I did them.

In silence, I use my raw will to seal the circle, and then I face him.

"Open up, doorman, open up. I am all alone and I want to come in."

"Who are you?" *Magister* intones, using the words we scripted.

"I am myself. I seek entrance to the Underworld."

"Then come."

I approach him and take a deep breath. I am wearing special clothing tonight: a shift made of white silk gauze, cinched at the waist with a long, glittering scarf; a veil covering my head, made of the same gauzy material as my shift; a copper circlet set with a smooth oval of lapis lazuli. The circlet came from a catalog of occult books and accessories; I assembled the rest by hand from fabric I got at a local fabric store. It cost me about half my weekly paycheck. I'll be cutting my daily ration of ramen and canned peaches in half for a long while after this.

And of course, I'm wearing the black scarf on my right wrist.

He removes them all.

"What is this?" I ask.

"Be satisfied, seeker, a divine power of the Underworld has been fulfilled. You must not speak out against the rites of the Underworld. The Seven Gates are barred against you, seeker."

"I would enter."

"Those who would enter must surrender. If you would pass, you must lose your pride. On your knees."

I drop.

"Why are you here?" he asks, then nudges my left thigh with his foot. "Legs open," he murmurs.

That last part wasn't in the script.

"I crave wisdom," I reply; my mouth sticks on the ritual words.

"Do you?" His voice is soft and gently remote. "Then pass the gates, but know this: for as long as you are in the Underworld, you belong not to yourself, but to the Underworld, and the laws of the Underworld are absolute. I will have your sight, now." He takes a blindfold from the altar – it is dark, and silky like the scarf I wear for him, but it seems to have some kind of decoration on it, tassels, maybe; no, feathers, they're feathers – and ties it around my eyes. "I will have your voice, your throat, and your mouth. They are no longer your own. Open," he says, and I feel his fingers on my lips, gently but firmly prying my mouth open. "You will stay this way until I say otherwise. Your mouth is mine." Then I hear a movement of fabric, and his hand is on the back of my head, and it's not his fingers that I have in my mouth anymore, and for a time the only sounds in the room are the sounds of my tongue, my jaw, and his increasingly hoarse breathing. He keeps his hand in my hair, moving me with him, and it's all I can do to breathe, myself. After what feels like an eternity, he finally spends himself in my mouth and relaxes his grip.

He doesn't completely release me, though. He caresses me for a moment, then moves behind me to sit at my back, and wraps his arms around me. I lean into his embrace, hungry for reassurance even though I know it won't be there.

"If you would gain the wisdom of the Underworld, your resolve must be weighed, and not found lacking," he murmurs in my ear. It occurs to me that he has never once raised his voice to me, not in all the months that I have been his partner. "I would weigh your resolve."

And then that arm that is wrapped so gently around me moves ever so slightly, and his fingertips trail to a place just under my collarbone, and he grabs and twists.

I'm in so much pain that I forget how to scream. I writhe, gasping.

When he releases me, it's all I can do to keep from crumpling on the floor.

He takes a deep breath. "Are you sure that you still *need* to go through with this?" he asks.

I wish I wasn't. I don't know quite what he has in store for me, because everything after the circle casting was drawn up in sketchy terms only, but it's not going to be pretty – descents into Hell rarely are – and it's only going to be safe, sane, and consensual by a bare technicality.

We have already established, though, that while I don't want to go through with it, I do absolutely need to go through with it. There is no way around it. Even my uncertainty is an indication that my studies have reached a mental block, and the only way around that is to break through that block via initiation.

"Yes," I hear myself reply.

"Very well. *Alea iacta est.*" A long silence follows. I think his voice is shaking. It's probably my imagination. "Please forgive me for what is to come," he whispers, and gets up.

I hear a rustling and a clinking from the general direction of the altar. When he comes back, I feel his fingers against my nipples, hardening them, and then a sharp, pinching bite. These clamps don't screw on. They don't need to. Compared to what he just did to the nerve endings under my collarbone, the sensation is almost bearable, but not by much.

"I didn't say you could close your thighs," he says, forcing them open again with his hands. "Also, I'm not done adorning you, yet." There's a steely quality to his voice, now; most often these days, when he's doing things to me, his voice reminds me of a particularly luxurious and decadent velvet, but not now. "Because you have willingly entered the Underworld, and become its captive and its property, you will wear this for as long as you remain here." I feel something go around my neck. It's wide and heavy, and it smells like leather. He fastens it in back, slips a finger underneath – it's loose enough for that, so, loose enough for me to breathe and swallow, I suppose – and gives it an experimental tug from the front. There must be a ring there.

And then I feel a hood descend over my head. A hood, or a mask. It, too, is heavy, and from it I feel a cloak of feathers brushing my shoulders. The air has become stale around me.

"You may be a seeker of mysteries, but you are in the realm of Death now, and nobody returns from this place of darkness. This is called the House of Darkness for good reason, and whoever enters here, magistrate or warrior, king or shepherd, milkmaid or goddess, can never return. Whoever enters this house has no more need of light. Dust will be your bread and mud will be your meat. Your dress will be a cloak of feathers. The Gates are already bolted behind you, my lady." He slides his hands under the hood and places his fingers on my neck, above the collar, knuckles brushing my ears. There is an odd pressure against my eardrums. It feels like something wants to explode out of my head; I begin to tremble. "This is the last, the Seventh, Gate: you forfeit your will. There are no safewords in the Underworld. You are mine, and I will use you as I see fit."

And then he does something sudden and sharp with his fingers that pushes in and squeezes at my neck, and agony seizes me, and I am taken by stars and nausea, and the world goes black as I fade out of consciousness.

I WAKE UP IN the recovery position – prone, feet elevated, head turned to the side – and decide, based on the taste in my mouth, that I managed to escape vomiting. As soon as I regain consciousness, however, he pulls me up and, after taking a few experimental steps to see if I can walk, leads me across the room by my collar and stretches me over the couch. My nipples, already throbbing in pain from the clamps he hasn't yet taken off, become fire when they brush against the upholstery.

He's done something with cords to keep me in place. They're tight and uncomfortable.

Something lands hard on my back, a heavy spray of braided leather cords. And does not stop.

I whimper against the cushions.

He's flipped me over on the couch, rearranging me so that I'm facing up. The cords are back on, only now they're not just holding me in place, they're holding me taut. My arms feel like they want to wrench out of their sockets, but he has a pillow placed under my hips, supporting my weight. Somewhat. My body still wants to slide down, and my arms are on fire. I'm still fighting to breathe under the hood, too, which only makes it worse. Somehow, impossibly, he has managed to crucify me in a legs-splayed position on the couch. I gasp for breath that never quite seems to give me any actual air.

His hand reaches between my legs and seizes me, making me cry out. "This, too, belongs to me," he says flatly, as he releases me, and soon the blows rain down on me again.

When I start to sob, he puts a wadded scarf in my mouth.

Help me. Somebody, please help me.

HE'S UNTIED THE CORDS and removed the hood and collar and the clamps – I screamed at that, but my mouth was still gagged and not much noise escaped – and I'm on the floor, and I can breathe again, just, and he's driving into me with all his might. He's splitting me into pieces. My spine is on fire. Everything below my waist hurts, everywhere. From somewhere outside of myself, I can hear myself weeping.

He stops. I feel his sweat dripping onto my skin.

"This is mine," he says, and there is no velvet in his voice at all. There is no comfort for me to reach. I can't even find him. The only thing there is cold steel. "You are mine. And this is no place for the living. *Ancilla*, your life is mine."

And his hands are about my throat.

I don't have enough air to scream.

My heart fights. There is a pain in my ears, which are threatening to pop. My ears and my head are full of pain. Against it, I am helpless.

Blackness.

I'm lying on the couch. There is a cool, wet cloth on my head, which is free, and open to the air again. There is another wet cloth at my lips, moistening them. I bite at it and suck the water from it. His hand is on my shoulders. It is shaking.

"Meditate," he says softly.

He leans his head against mine.

I meditate.

LATER IN THE NIGHT, I awaken from the exhausted slumber I slid into sometime during my meditations, and he grounds the energy of the circle for me, and we go to bed, where he has his first aid kit waiting. He insists on carrying me. I want to walk, but then, maybe his assessment of my ability to walk, or lack thereof, is a sound one. I don't know how he manages to do it so smoothly, given that we're roughly the same size; he must be stronger than he looks. I burrow my face into his shoulder, too tired to cry.

MORNING. OUR BODIES SCRAPE against the sheets. His hands and lips are soft, so soft. We cling to each other, proving to ourselves with every kiss, every brush of slow, tentative fingertips that we remember how to be gentle with each other. That there is still tenderness possible between us. Eventually, he takes me, and I moan into his mouth as he kisses me. I'm sore, but I don't care. We roll like clouds, and I ride him, tossed by a wind of need.

"*Livomai pou se pligosa, sinkhorese me. Oh, eromene, se philo, se philo,*" he gasps. "*Se philo. Se philo...*" Over and over, until he cries out and arches his body against the rays of the morning sun. "*Se philo!*"

The light reveals the glistening track of a single tear escaping his eye and creeping down his temple.

Tiphareth

I'm staring at his eyes, because they are stars, and I'd somehow missed that before. They mesmerize me with their light.

Shining. Dancing. Full of the fire of eons.

"...Come back. Can you hear me? *Attend. Come back.*" He grabs my chin and holds me fast. "Can you hear me now?"

I flash agreement with my eyes. He's used the language of instruction, so I neither speak nor move.

I can't hear anything but him now, now that he is touching me. My entire being is attuned to him. Nothing outside us exists. His hand on my chin is a promise of ecstasy. I want more. I don't want to let him go. Ever. I feel his being pulsing under his skin, and sense the passions he bottles up so well that he can't even speak them aloud; and a terrible, consuming guilt when he looks at me. I sense the pain of swollen hand joints, reacting badly to the cold, damp weather outside. He never told me his hands hurt him. Why didn't he say anything? I can comfort him; I can take it away. I know this, I know it as surely as I know the air I breathe. I reach for his hands, covering them with mine, and absorb his pain into myself, letting it soak me; then *push*, flooding the areas of pain with warmth and healing love until they are permanently washed away.

The act arouses me. I want him to touch me more, and harder. I ache to be claimed.

"...*Attend!*" he shouts. And then he sighs. "Sorry. Did not mean to yell... I think I might have demolished barriers that only needed a door to be cut into them. Your energy is a bit messed up. I am very sorry for this, my *ancilla*. I doubt it will be permanent, but let's see if we can't help repair the damage and get you back to the land of the living rather earlier."

I let my eyes convey assent. Anything.

"Let's work on grounding and centering. I think more meditation work would be useful now, too. It will help you find enough of yourself to rebuild your walls. They need to come back up; they're as much a part of you as anything else, and they seem to have been built largely of your will, and your will is... out on holiday, much farther than it has gone in the past." Almost inaudibly, he adds, "Part of your soul is wandering. The ancient Egyptians called it the *akh*. The name doesn't really matter, I suppose."

He *hurts*. I can't bear his hurt. I take him in my arms and kiss his mouth until the stars shoot up between us and surround us and we entwine and become a column of fire. "Know this. Know me. Know that I love you. Now." I place my forehead gently against his and feel him in his entirety, feel him opening ever so slightly until his emotions flood me and I gulp them down in a torrent.

He gasps as fire and flood consume us. We dance together in stars, now, a sea of stars.

"Take me," I sigh. "Use me. I know you need it. I feel you. I feel your need. It's all right; I'm yours. I'm yours as long as you need me. I'm yours forever." Desire melts me from within. My flesh dissolves like wax. His hands are the only thing holding me together. Beautiful. He is so beautiful; how can he not see it? Melting, I'm melting. He burns. I dissolve.

He is the first one of us to break the contact.

"We have to rebuild your walls," he says sadly. "Awakening without being able to control your energies is a very good way to permanently lose your sanity. This isn't quite you speaking. Come with me. Let's ground the energy, since you'll be useless for anything until we do; and we will work later." He takes my hand, leading me to the bedroom. I follow. Anything.

He is gentle as he undresses me, nudges me down, and arranges me on the bed. "*Se agapo*," he murmurs, his voice trembling as he takes me. "*Se agapo. Se agapo, se philo, s'ero, eromene.*" With each slow and careful thrust, he whispers into my ear, my flesh. "*Se agapo. Anistaso.*" His mouth finds mine. His hand is on my forehead, soothing me on the painful place just above and between my eyes. "*S'ero. O, eromene, se agapo, se philo, s'ero, anistaso. Se agapo, se philo...*"

His need transfixes me.

An overwhelming of light.

WHEN HE FINISHES, I am shaking and weak from climaxing. He strokes my hair.

"*Enupniazomai, eromene*, sleep and heal. Dream of wholeness. Dream of rebuilding. Find yourself again. *Gnothi sauton. O eromene se agapo se philo...*"

His voice holds me close and entrances me. I sleep.

HIS ARMS ARE AROUND me. I am warm and secure. The room is dark; it is nighttime.

My stomach is an empty cavern.

"Hungry," I whisper.

He kisses me on the forehead and lets me go. I feel him leave me, and soon sounds of food preparation emanate from the kitchen.

In time, he returns with a bowl of something warm and steaming. It smells like chicken broth.

"Eat," he says, and hands me a spoon.

I try to sit up on my own and fail. He helps me up, and I find myself attacking a stew made with rice, a great many large chunks of chicken meat simmered in its own broth, egg drops, and chopped garlic. I taste lemon juice, ginger, onions, and pepper in the broth.

I am too tired to ask for a second helping, despite still being hungry, and I let my head fall onto his chest.

And then I begin to cry.

"Sleep, my *eromene*," he says, stroking my hair. "*Hypnotte*."

I sleep.

His repeated murmurs haunt me, dancing ahead of me in my dreams like will-o-the-wisps. *Se agapo, se philo, s'ero, s'ero, eromene...*

It's still dark when I awaken again. I've had dreams of suffocating, sealed alive in a tomb. It's too dark. I weep uncontrollably. There is so much dark.

His arms tighten around me.

"I can't breathe," I sob.

"Hush. You're breathing right now. You are strong," he tells me. "*Anapnei, eromene*. Breathe in life."

"The rocks are too sharp..."

"You are strong. You are finding your way."

His hand strokes me back to sleep.

In dreams, I climb. And climb. And climb. My hands are shredded to ribbons.

Surfacing through grey haze. I am missing something. I need to find it. There's only one problem: I don't know what I am looking for. I start to look around me, but something, some winged voice I hear inside me, says, *No. What you seek is not there.* I open my mouth, and it fills with water, and I am sucked below waves of grey.

I will drown if I do not find the thing I have lost.

Falling down through the waters. Through the cold.

Swim. I must remember how to swim. Frantically, I undulate, and my undulation becomes a speeding flight through waters as I am sucked out and away.

And then I remember. I remember my Self.

I swim toward a circle of light that dances before me, showing me the way.

A PALE RAY OF early morning light falls through the window. My eyes focus. His eyes are already open, and they are watching me. They no longer dazzle me with stars.

They are just his eyes: grey, worried.

I reach for him; it doesn't take long to get him hard. I have to undo and work off his trousers, however, because he is fully clothed. A part of me wonders idly when he put on his regular clothes.

"*Eromene...*"

"Hush. This is what I want. I'm not just responding to you." I grab his hand and place it between my legs. "Feel me. Feel that? I want you. Now. I want you *now*. Take me now."

He teases me.

I groan, riding his fingers, and seize him by the shoulders, pinning him to the futon. "No more waiting. *Now*, dammit."

"Ah. You're getting pushy," he says, and smiles. "A good indication of will. Welcome back."

And then neither of us cares for words.

IT'S HARD FOR TWO people to work simultaneously in the small kitchen, but that's all right, because he's insisting on making food for me while I rest. I can't object to it strenuously. I'm still so tired that the very act of walking from the bedroom to the living room is a chore. It's all I can do to sit on the couch.

Besides, he's *cooking*.

In the background, I can hear his stereo, which he has tuned to the local public radio station. They're playing some kind of instrumental Baroque-era piece, something in which violin strings predominate. It's not mathematical enough to be Bach, at least not Johann Sebastian. It's not brutal enough to be Leclair, and it's definitely not Vivaldi. Odds would indicate Telemann, who seems to have never stopped composing even for sleep or food, going by his output. My instincts want to go with either Geminiani or Corelli, though. I flip a mental coin, heads for Geminiani, tails for Corelli, and get heads. Geminiani it is. It's a very wild guess, though, because I'm shaky when it comes to Baroque composers, outside of Bach and Vivaldi, who I imagine being, respectively, to the Baroque era what Led Zeppelin and Rush were to seventies album rock. Their styles are too distinctive to be mistakenly attributed to anyone else; and people not particularly interested in the genre would be tempted, not without reason, to say that every single song by its respective artist sounded like all the others written by the same artist.

At any rate, given that the radio is playing actual music rather than NPR news reports, it must be somewhat late in the morning.

I look out the window. The trees have lost their leaves.

"Um. *Magister*? What day is it?"

He comes into the room and hands me a plate with an omelet on it. "Tuesday."

Tuesday. The last day I remember clearly, without hallucination, was Thursday – the last day of October. Trick-or-treaters. Falling leaves. Pome-granate seeds. Descent.

I look around. I am not in the Underworld. The living room is only the living room. I must remember that.

"You've been with me this whole time, haven't you? Don't you have to go to work?"

"Leave you? Like that? *Eromene*..." He stops and composes himself. It seems to take some effort for him to do so, I notice. "My *ancilla*, quite aside from the dubious ethics of abandoning one's submissive when she is falling to pieces, I don't think I could have left you. You needed me. I was there." He frowns. "I had several vacation days saved up, so I used them. I still have a few left. That, at least, is something that doesn't need worrying about."

I probably don't have a job anymore, though. I don't have a salaried, stable, full-time career as a librarian. I'm a part-time telemarketer with no clout, and even though I am reasonably good at what I do, I am expendable. Finding a similar position somewhere else won't pose too many problems – this is one field that's always hiring, because the vast majority of people either quit in disgust, or they get fired within days because they can't make quota. I'm looking at a hiatus no matter what, though. I will probably need several days to job hunt unless I get lucky on my first day of pounding the pavement, and then there will be a dry spell while I wait for my first paycheck. I think gloomily about paying bills. If I'm going to make next month's rent, I'll have to skimp on groceries. I was already skimping on groceries before this. I'm not sure how much more I *can* skimp. I suppose I could simply not buy groceries for a few weeks... Oh, hell. November's rent. I still have to pay this month's rent. It's overdue now, so I'm going to have to pay an extra fifty dollars. I hadn't planned on being gone for longer than the weekend. I hope my landlord doesn't think I've just skipped out on him. Really, if I'd handled this like the responsible adult I'm supposed to be, I would have written my landlord the rent check and given it to him before leaving the apartment on Friday. This crisis was preventable. I'm going to have to call him to make arrangements as soon as I've finished breakfast.

I attack my omelet, gorging myself on egg and cheese and mushrooms. I'd better eat my fill now. When I go back home – assuming I still have a home – and start job hunting, I won't be seeing much food in my refrigerator.

HE HAS ME DOING martial arts again. Specifically, *tai ch'i*. This is to help me balance my energy. It's been a couple of years; I'm rusty. He had to help me with my forms until my body once again worked out the feeling of flow and started going through them automatically.

In the morning, when we are awake enough, by the grace of coffee, to keep our eyes open, we perform *tai ch'i* forms in the living room, with the furniture pushed far back to allow us room. We push hands and perform universal breathing; then, side by side, we go through our *tao lu.*

I sense him moving gracefully beside me. It feels good.

"What did you do to your arms?" he asks.

I look down. Fingers of red run up my forearms. I have no idea what they are, or how long I've had them, but as soon as I notice them, they start to itch. My spine also itches; I reach behind myself to scratch it.

He turns me around and runs his fingers up my spine.

The itching increases. I hiss between my teeth.

He lifts my shirt and tuts. "Like a bolt of lightning. Well. That's not good." Pensively, he runs his hand back down my spine and places the palm of his hand on the small of my back, low, near the tailbone. "Here. Have you been hurting?"

He's not referring to bruises or welts from the whipping he gave me.

I nod.

"I think we've managed to burn your energy channels. They're raw. Oh, *eromene.* I'm sorry. I didn't mean to do that. I think it is safe to say that while accomplishing its purpose, your initiation ritual went horribly right." He sighs, and massages my lower back with his hands, which are full of warmth.

I hadn't realized how badly my back hurt until he stopped it from hurting. I groan and lean into him, draping my head over his shoulder. His hands work at me, and eventually, the simple rapture of a sudden lack of pain becomes an entirely different ecstasy that runs up me from a place somewhat below my lower back.

"You're moving around a good deal more energy than you used to; you seem to be having some trouble acclimating to it. I think we need to work more on grounding."

I grind up against him. I like the sound of that.

AFTER NOTICING MY RESTLESSNESS, *Magister* decided to give me another reading assignment, one that would require me to go for a longish walk so that I could see the university library downtown. His apartment is within two or three miles of the university, if you take the most direct route. He lives in a midtown section of the city's west side that's mostly inhabited by instructors and non-tenured professors, administrative staff and their families, and a handful of the more successful bohemian types. The walk downtown has a couple of rough blocks near the hospital, but they're safe enough to walk through during the daytime. Just don't walk there after dark.

Once I arrive on campus, I make my way to the library. I'm not sure why he specifically has me using the university library, because what books aren't on his personal shelves could very easily be found in the local branch of the public library that's only a few blocks from his apartment. I suspect he just wanted to give me a few extra blocks to walk, for extra exercise.

I'm studying art history this week: occult and pagan themes in the work of Sandro Botticelli and other artists of the Italian Renaissance, along with some side reading on Marsilio Ficino, who influenced Botticelli's views on love and the soul's journey. It's not a very rigorous assignment.

In between looking up various scholarly opinions on *La Primavera* and the *Birth of Venus*, I get interested enough in the classical influences on his earlier work that I decide to start pulling out books on the art of ancient Greece and Rome. Pictures of frescoes, busts, statues, and mosaics beckon. Looking up art history is a lot like being a kid and drooling over the wares displayed in the window of a candy store. Well, for me, it is, anyway.

One of the books flips open to a full-page illustration of a calyx krater decorated with a picture of an older male cradling the lanky body of a younger one. He's looking at the youth in his arms tenderly; the youth's body curls in, as if to embrace. The lines are fluid and beautiful.

The caption reads *Erastes and eromenos.* Lover and beloved.

My hands shake as I gently place the book back onto the reading table.

He called me *eromene.*

He loves me.

It's not so much a revelation as it is a confirmation of something I already knew, knew in my very flesh and nerves and bones; even had I not been recently overwhelmed with an onslaught of his emotion, due to my inability to tune out his presence, I think I had already intuited something to that effect. Little hints, here and there; I can't think really when I started noticing, but I did notice.

It's another thing to see it in print, however, in words as bold as red paint on black.

He called me beloved.

He called me back to life by weaving a spell out of his own love.

He loves me.

I WALK BACK TO his apartment in a daze. When he answers his door I throw my arms around him, pressing my face into the top of his shoulder, which smells like the essential oils of sandalwood and cedar that he likes to wear. I think I will always think of him now whenever I catch a whiff of cedar or sandalwood. His neck is warm and soft and sweet under my lips.

"You called me beloved," I murmur. "When you called me *eromene.* You love me. You're in love with me."

"Yes."

"Oh, my *Erastes.* Oh, my love…"

With one free hand, he shuts the door, and then we are bound together again by our desire, and we heed nothing else.

MOVING WITH HIM ON top of the sheets. Our hands move. Our mouths move. Our hips rock in unison. Driving deeper. Gasping. We wrestle together, our bodies slick with sweat. His weight holds me fast; I strain against him, lifting off the futon as my hips buck violently. Our usual dance: it never gets old. I want more, more, and my orgasm is lightning as I impale myself on him, crying out my delight. Then we strain together again. Neither of us is finished yet.

I feel a hand closing about my wrists, dragging them above my head, and moan in pleasure. At last. This. Yes.

"I must confess, I quite like the times when I do not have you under silence," he says softly in my ear. "I love to make you cry out. You have a very musical voice."

"I do?"

"Yes. You do." He strokes down my neck and shoulders with his fingertips, causing me to moan and writhe again, and takes hold of my left nipple. His fingers begin to squeeze. A smile plays about his lips. "Sing for me."

Gevurah

I don't have many monthly bills to pay. To be exact, I have three.

Even the three I have are too many.

Rent takes precedence over everything else, of course, and I managed to pay it. I needn't have worried about keeping the apartment. My landlord was perfectly happy to accept my explanation of having had a longer weekend than I had expected, which, given that it meant an extra fifty dollars for him, should have come as no surprise to me.

In fact, as things turned out, my immediate downstairs neighbors had vacated their apartment while I was gone, so I moved into it; I wish I hadn't, even though it was a necessity. My new living arrangements are too large and too expensive. The landlord also made me put down a deposit when I signed the lease. What am I going to do with a two-bedroom apartment? I grit my teeth and put a notice up on the bulletin board in the university student center, and a card on the notice wall of the supermarket, because those options were free, and free is all I can afford, but so far there have been no takers, and really, besides my not liking to share my space with other people, I can't imagine anybody wanting to live with me, either. Especially not here. There are worse places to live, but there are also much better places.

The alternative to moving downstairs would have been eviction from an illegal apartment, though. It was only a matter of time.

My landlord was even kind enough to waive the first month's rent on the new apartment. I therefore must only come up with the deposit, plus the late fee of fifty dollars. Paying a late fee on a waived month of rent strikes me as being more like a discounted first month's rent, or possibly like massive unfairness, but whatever he chooses to call it, I have to pay it. The main problem is that I still can't really afford the move or an increase in my monthly rent, especially since I moved in the same month that I ordered occult supplies from a catalog to make ritual garb for an initiation.

Magister would no doubt have reimbursed me for that had I made mention of just how badly the expense hurt me. So, I haven't mentioned it.

It's my other two bills I'm having a hard time with, since the apartment itself has now been paid for until December. If I pay my gas bill, I get to keep my heat and hot water, and I can use the stove in the kitchen; on the other hand, if I pay the electric bill, I get to keep my lights, and the refrigerator stays on. Now that it's finally turning cold outside, a functioning refrigerator isn't strictly necessary, especially since I don't have very much food that needs refrigeration, but lights are another matter.

I decide that the lights are more important than central heating or a functioning stove, now that it's getting dark early, and the sun rises later in the day. I need to be able to find my clothes and see myself in them when I dress for work. I do have a flashlight, but the batteries are dead, and I can't afford to replace them.

More importantly, I need to keep my alarm clock functioning. It's the only clock I have, and it runs on electricity. I need it to make sure I wake up and catch the bus on time if I want to keep my job. I could buy a wind-up clock or a battery-operated travel alarm, but that, like new batteries for my flashlight, or candles and matches for that matter, would require spare funds that I don't have, because I need what little spare change I have for bus fare.

My new job working for the local newspaper is close enough that I can walk to it, the same way I can walk to the university from my apartment, but there is no way I'm walking home from work after dark, not in this neighborhood. I'm working a split shift, nine in the morning until one, several hours off, then five to nine at night, which means it will be dark when I get off work. I can spend my spare afternoon hours in the library. It's only a few blocks away from the call center. But I can't sleep there overnight. The university's nearby student center isn't open around the clock, either. I'm the right age to be a student and probably still look vaguely collegiate, and if necessary, could crash on a couch on campus and pass convincingly for an exhausted student taking a nap, but I can't do that when the student center is closed for the evening. I have to go home at night. That means taking the bus, which means I need to hang onto what spare change I have. Each trip costs eighty-five cents.

I have a coat and warm clothing to layer, and I have an electric blanket to hide under, so I don't think I'll freeze if the heat gets turned off for a while. In a few weeks, if I need heat and can't afford to pay my gas bill with a late fee and a new deposit, I can always buy a space heater. The space heater will cost less than the gas bill would. I only need to keep my bedroom warm, anyway; I don't really use the rest of the apartment. I'll still have to do without hot water, but I can sponge bathe when I'm at home, and take my actual soaking baths at *Magister's* place. At least I don't have to pay for my own running water.

I realize I'll also have to do my laundry at his place for a while. I've been hand-washing my dirty laundry in the bathtub and letting it drip dry to avoid spending quarters I don't have on the washer and dryer downstairs, but I can't imagine doing this in cold water in the middle of the winter, and I certainly won't have quarters to spare on machine-washing my laundry in the near future if I've already had to choose between the convenience of machine-washing my laundry and the convenience of having enough money to cover my bills during these next few weeks. I hope he doesn't mind.

THIRD DAY ON THE job, and I've managed to get my name on the Top Ten Sellers board. It's on the Welcome, New Employees! board as well, so if job security here is based on name recognition, that's a very good thing. Of course, job security isn't really based on name recognition. It's based on sales. I'll need to keep mine up.

This shouldn't pose too much of a problem. Newspaper subscriptions are a very easy thing to sell, and the call center that takes up the entire fifth floor of the downtown building the newspaper uses just switched from manually dialed phones to a computerized auto dialer network, which makes it much easier to reach enough people that consistently hitting quota is possible. I tried one job on the northeast side of town selling magazines, like I had been doing at the last call center I worked at, and I only lasted a day there due to the old-fashioned telephones. They said I sounded great, and that I would probably be one of the best sales representatives in the room if only I could work the phones more quickly, but I couldn't, so that position didn't work out. Apparently, I need a computerized system to do my dialing for me if high sales volume is a job requirement.

Working for the local newspaper company has its advantages. I get free newspapers. I also get to sell a product that everyone seems to want, at least, compared to the magazine bundles I used to sell (If you subscribe to these four hunting and sporting magazines for five years, sir, a portion of your purchase will be donated to a cancer charity! And just think of all the money you save compared to buying these off the rack every month!) Yes, rejections are still a part of the job, but they don't seem to be as rude, or as frequent, at least not from what I've noticed so far. Maybe I just need to give the job more time. And at least I won't have to wait too long to be paid. Like most telemarketing positions, this one has a weekly paycheck. It will take until after my ninety-day probationary period for me to see the commissions from my sales, for some reason I didn't quite understand when going through my orientation, but at least I won't have to wait too long for my hourly wages, which are a whole dollar above minimum.

The pay is a bit low and slow for this line of work, which might explain why the turnover is high here. There's a large call center north of here that pays twice the hourly wage that the newspaper pays, plus a high commission, and it's on a major bus line, but it's owned by fundamentalist Christians and the job involves fundraising and push polling for right-wing politicians and causes. Scratch that.

I do wish the piped-in office music here in the call center wasn't as automatic as the number dialing. For the most part, it's inoffensive pop music, selected for us in the hopes of inspiring us with peppy, upbeat tunes, and I like it well enough, but there is little variety. After a while, all the male vocalists start to sound like Lionel Richie or Michael Bolton, and all the female vocalists like Amy Grant or Paula Abdul. Certain songs come up more often than others, too. I have decided that there is a special room in Hell reserved for overly motivational sales managers, and in that room, "I Wanna Be Rich" plays on a nonstop loop. Then the ranks of damned managers will see just how motivated they really are when they are forced to hear that song, while they wait for the people they are calling to pick up the phone.

I don't see what being rich has to do with being filled with love, peace, and happiness, anyway. Being rich just pays the bills. I might have had love when I was rich, but peace and happiness? No, I didn't have those. Good grief, what stupid lyrics.

MY STOMACH GROWLS AT me. I ignore it. It's growled since I woke up this morning, and it can keep growling until suppertime, which is at four; because when you can only eat one meal per day, if the meal is too early, you get hungry hours before it's time for bed, and if the meal is too late, you get faint halfway through the day. I have no extra food for additional meals. Growling is therefore pointless. Sooner or later, my stomach will figure that out.

I wish today wasn't the day I have the morning shift off to keep me from reaching forty hours and qualifying for full-time status. Work keeps me too busy to think about food. Also, there's plenty of free coffee at work, and I can calm my stomach down with coffee, especially if I dump in lots of powdered creamer.

My checkbook is on the floor beside my mattress. As I reach for it, I see a cockroach scurry past. It doesn't scurry fast enough; my checkbook lands hard, and I grind it against the roach for good measure. This produces a satisfying crunch. Beware, cockroach, I am the hammer of doom.

The landlord won't call an exterminator. He thinks it costs too much money, and maybe he's right; even if he were to exterminate through the entire building, we'd probably just get invaded soon after by cockroaches from the building next door. He'd be spending all his profit on exterminator fees. It's easier for him to just tell us to buy roach motels. I've scattered Borax around the perimeter of my apartment, and I have a can of roach spray; and every couple of weeks or so, the landlord comes and sprays with something industrial, which drives the roaches downstairs. They then establish themselves down in the first-floor apartment, and the downstairs neighbor complains, and the landlord sprays, driving them back up here again. These must be some of the healthiest, most in-shape cockroaches in existence. If there was a roach Olympics held, these roaches would win gold medals in track and field sports.

They used to disgust me. They don't anymore. What would be the point?

My stomach growls again, more loudly this time. Shut up, stomach.

Eventually, the growling becomes a gnawing, a horribly empty and hollow sort of ache. But if I eat my slice of bread and peanut butter now, I'll get hungry in the middle of my calling shift, and I won't be able to concentrate, which will hurt my sales, which will lose me my new job. I've only been there a week and a half, now, and that's not long enough to cut me the slack I need to have an off day due to hunger pains.

Clearly, I have to do something.

There's a stack of notebook paper that I bought for seventy-nine cents to use for my weekly essay assignments. I still have plenty of paper. One sheet won't make a huge difference.

It takes a while to chew it and swallow it, but I manage, and as luck would have it, it does stop the growling. It might not be very nutritious, but it gets the job done. No more pain in my belly, well, not as much; the void is filled. And it's fiber. Fiber is supposed to be healthy, right?

There are only a few days left until I get my first paycheck. It will be minuscule, because I was hired near the end of the pay period, so only worked one day out of the week, but after another week, the money will start coming in, and the commissions from my subscription sales will be added a few weeks after that, once I officially get out of my probationary period, assuming I make quota, which I generally do. If things get really bad, I can always force myself to sell my plasma again. Hopefully, things won't come to that, because I don't like having a needle jabbed into my vein and hooked up to a machine that I have to feed. The one time I did it, I had to keep my eyes shut the whole time, and even though my eyes were shut, I knew the needle was *there*.

The fifteen dollars from selling plasma, though, can buy enough ramen, generic toasted oats, bread, peanut butter, and canned fruit to last for two weeks, if I'm careful enough stretching the food. Most of that food won't need to be cooked. Only the ramen poses a problem. I can't use the stove if the gas has been shut off, so I'll have to eat the ramen dry. Maybe my landlord would let me grab the electric hot plate and toaster oven from the old attic apartment? Then I could get rice and dried lentils and boxed macaroni and cheese and some other cheap things that would also be warm and stick to my ribs, in a way dry ramen and peanut butter sandwiches on cold bread do not.

I can survive this for a few weeks. It could be worse. At least I'll eat well on the weekends, when I visit *Magister*. And today is Wednesday, so I only have to wait a couple more days until I can eat better.

The mind is its own place and in itself, can make a Heaven of Hell, a Hell of Heaven. I of all people should know this by now. I am not going to mourn my fall. It was a fortunate fall. I chose my own path. Freedom is better than wealth. I have myself, now. I gave up my family and my life of ease, and in return, I kept my integrity. It was a more than fair trade.

I don't even miss my family. No, really, I don't. I don't remember what it felt like to love them, or if I ever really loved them at all. Isn't that funny? It's strange how things work out, sometimes. When I think back to the times I hugged my mother and told her I loved her, or the times I won an academic prize and made my father proud of me, it's like watching an old movie without any sound. There's no context, and everything seems vague and distant and a little confusing. It doesn't seem like something from the world I actually live in. I don't feel emotion watching the memories. College is a black-and-white movie. My girlfriend – both my girlfriends – they're in the past, too, on hazy slides and jumpy movie reels that fall off the spool and need putting back together if they're to be watched at all. My sorority sisters are dusty albums (in the end, my first girlfriend and I didn't have to worry about being kicked out of the sorority. "We want you to know that no matter what, *you're still sisters*," our sorority said. They even used some of the sorority's funds to help me get the off-campus efficiency apartment after I got disowned. They let me attend sorority events for as long as I lived nearby. But we lost touch after I moved here, an hour away, with no transportation, and that ended the sisterhood, for me).

Everything is in the past. The past is dead. The past is in books and old photographs and dilapidated reels of celluloid.

Several minutes go by.

I am not crying. My eyes are just making tears. Stupid eyes.

After a while, I put my mouth to the pillow I buried my face in, and suck my tears. Maybe they will ease my hunger pains. It's worth a try.

OUR FIRST REAL DATE in months – he took me to see *The Addams Family*, which just came out this weekend. I am enthralled. This is perfect, absolutely perfect.

We are snuggled up against each other, at least, as far as we are able to around the armrests. I wish they were the kind that could be lifted out of the way, but the seats, while well-cushioned, lack certain conveniences and comforts, movable armrests being one of them. We press as close together as we can, though.

A large tub of buttered popcorn sits between us. I've been gorging myself on it.

So, Gomez was a desperate, howling demon in the night when he was making love to Morticia, was he?

"I wonder if I could make you howl like a demon?" I murmur.

"I think I'll leave you wondering on that count," he replies.

I nestle in closer; he tries to wrap his arm around me, but it doesn't work very well around the seats, so we settle for bumping up against each other. I stroke his shoulder with my right hand, brushing my face against my wrist so that I can feel the black silk scarf he gave me caress my cheek. The favor of his love.

Next weekend is Thanksgiving. Four days of weekend, rather than two. Four whole days of food. Roast turkey. He's having me handle the turkey, although he's doing all the side dishes. He says roast fowl is a fairly easy dish to learn cooking technique from. I'm a little nervous about the possibility of botching the main course of our holiday dinner, but my mouth waters at the thought of eating turkey.

Gomez is fencing with Tully now. I've always wanted to learn how to fence.

Magister reaches into the bucket, fishes out a couple of pieces of popcorn, and holds them to my lips. I nibble the proffered popcorn and then suck the butter from his fingers. Slowly, I run the tip of my tongue along the tip of his index finger, then take the finger into my mouth and fellate it. I hear his breath quicken, and I smile.

We scream with laughter at Wednesday's expression as she electrocutes her brother, and at what she thought their little "game" ought to be called. The people sitting immediately next to us give us strange looks and seem to shrink away from us. That might be the wisest course of action, all things considered.

Now Gomez has Fester in a headlock and chokehold. Fester is pleading for mercy.

He apparently forgot the secret "password."

"Uh oh! Bad thing to forget!" I mutter. Password? *Safeword* is what Gomez and Fester are talking about here, and we both know it.

We snicker.

How can the people in the theater not get it? Are they blind?

They must be blind.

We clutch at each other, alternately howling with laughter and wiping tears of mirth from our faces. The jokes in this movie really only make sense if you're a complete pervert. Otherwise, they're just gratuitously weird.

The movie is about *us*.

WHEN WE EXIT THE theatre, making our way to his car, a blast of cold air hits us. Earlier this week, the relatively pleasant mid-November weather gave way to a cold snap from the north. Weirdness and rapid change are typical weather for this part of the state. We're just close enough to the lake to experience a lake effect in all seasons that are not summer. There's even snow on the ground now, although I don't know how long it will last since we haven't had many hard frosts yet. I wrap my coat around myself more tightly in a vain effort to warm myself up.

The instant we're inside the car, he has his arms around me in a crushing embrace. His lips are hot against mine.

"*Cara mia,*" he murmurs with a smile.

"*Mon Sauvage.*"

Talking suddenly seems pointless.

Eventually, he surfaces for air and gets the ignition started, and the car is warm enough by the time we're on the way home that I can unbutton my coat.

Soon he has his right hand undoing the buttons of my blouse, reaching underneath to stroke my breasts until I'm panting and writhing and arching my back. I cry out from anticipation when he slides his hand under the waistband of my leggings. I don't want to wait. I can't wait. He works me gently with his fingers. I shudder and rock up against him, begging for more.

I don't have to see his smile to feel it. It permeates the interior of the car like the evidence of desire.

Lights flickering, the noise of rushing air. Other cars pass by us occasionally. No doubt anyone bothering to look in our general direction would get an eyeful.

At some point it becomes clear that he's taking the scenic route home; the drive to the movie theatre didn't take more than ten or fifteen minutes, and we've been driving for longer than that. Also, the road we used to take to the theatre was not wooded and twisty, the way the road we are on now is, and the lights and noises of passing cars stopped intruding on us a while ago. I wonder where we are. Then I stop wondering, or caring.

He pulls over onto the shoulder.

"You're close, aren't you?"

"Yes. Don't stop, please don't stop..."

"I don't intend to stop. Ride my fingers."

After several minutes of grinding against his hand, I come, let out a strangled scream, and collapse back onto my seat, gasping for breath.

He bends over, wraps his arm around me, and tries to pull me toward him, but the space between the bucket seats has other ideas, so we clamber into the back seat to nestle together, where we sit, curled into each other's arms, watching the windows fog, watching the fog frost over, reaching for each other's warmth.

"*Se philo*," he whispers, brushing the top of my head with his lips.

I start to doze off.

"Bother," he says, then. "I needed you on edge for our next lesson. I should have restrained myself when you begged for an orgasm. It's a good thing you don't have much of a refractory period."

HE IS AS GOOD as his word, as always; when he turns into our parking lot, I am more than ready for another round in bed – or on the living room couch, or on the entryway floor – but the lesson he wants to conduct does not make use of any of those places.

"The conditions are perfect right now for energy work," he says. "Not only do we have a nice large full moon to work with, but the weather right now is quite bracing."

I suppose bracing is one word for it. Also, I'm so horny that if he were to ask me to mount myself on a nearby bush and ride it, I might very well do just that. Damn him. He's too clever with his fingers by half.

He takes me by the hand and leads me to the denuded thicket of honeysuckle, mulberry bushes, and scrub trees that grow at the back of the parking lot. Through the bushes a way, and then we are in a little wood that sits on a vacant land plot. It's been for sale for as long as I've been visiting *Magister's* apartment, but nobody wants to buy it, probably because it's too far away from the main road where there are stores and restaurants and other businesses, plus it's across the street from a cemetery and for some reason nobody wants to build a house and live across the street from a cemetery. We could almost have our own private park, it's so secluded. Go too much farther, and there are railroad tracks and an electrical station. He'd better not be thinking of tying me to either of those places.

"Here, this is perfect," he says. "A very good spot. Strip. You may keep your shoes on to protect your feet."

I look incredulously at him. There is snow on the ground, and an icy wind is still blowing. He must have lost his mind.

"I shouldn't need to ask you a second time, *ancilla*," he remarks quietly, steel creeping into his voice.

I slowly begin to remove my clothes.

"Also, I remind you that you are under silence, as we are doing work and I am about to instruct you. There. Hold your arms out from your sides, please. I need to use them for a minute."

This will leave my ribcage exposed to the cold; also, for that matter, my arms. I comply, shivering as I do so.

He pulls some cords out from the pockets of his overcoat and takes off his gloves.

Nuts. He is absolutely nuts.

As he's tying me to the branches of honeysuckle bushes and young maple trees, he leans against me and says softly into my ear, "You will meditate on the element of Fire. Summon Fire." His lips and tongue are hot against my ear as he wraps his arms around my torso and pulls me forward, lifting me to grind my pelvis up against his. The rocking movements make the branches I'm now more or less hanging from sway back and forth. He kisses my mouth. He's so warm.

Some dark instinct takes hold of me; I use my breath to suck his, feeling his warmth and life start to fill me. The taste is exhilarating.

He breaks away, though, leaving me cold once more. "Interesting," he gasps, a peculiar look on his face. "Although it really shouldn't surprise me. Not exactly what I was looking for, but... interesting." He fishes around in another coat pocket and pulls out something that glitters and clinks. "Hold still, please. Shivering makes this more difficult. These aren't the Japanese clamps, so I need to screw them on to get them onto your nipples."

That chain is freezing cold. I hiss between my teeth and dance on tiptoe.

The wind gusts.

He circles around behind me; I hear him rustling in the undergrowth, and then the sound of snapping twigs and branches. Somehow, he manages to sidle up behind me. He wraps an arm around me, leans in, and murmurs, "Let's try this again. I did not ask you to suck my heat, my life, and my energy away from me. I asked you to meditate on the element of Fire, and to summon Fire. I will help to some degree, but the bulk of the effort must be yours." His hand, which is still bare, reaches down between my legs and finds wetness. I start to whimper but catch myself. I want to do more – moan, cry out, rock my hips to ride his fingers, plead – but of course, I can't. Into my ear, he says, "And when you show signs of having summoned sufficient Fire to warm yourself, I will take you."

He pulls away.

Then I find out what the noise of snapping branches was all about.

I grind my teeth. Meditate on Fire. Through this. Right.

On the other hand, at least he is managing to warm me up a little as he circles around me, slashing at my legs and back with the improvised switch.

I've done this before. Admittedly, I wasn't naked, tied to scrub brush in a snowy thicket, and getting thrashed at the time, but I've done it. This is just a little bit more advanced. I can do this.

I think of sun, and warm beaches, and hot muggy July afternoons. I think of bonfires and volcanoes. I think of *Magister's* kisses. I think of all these things entering my body, filling me with power and heat. I see myself in my mind's eye, a torch blazing in the night.

I don't even notice when the snow around us has melted, when he stops lashing at me with the stick, when the air becomes permeated with mist. I don't notice when he unzips his trousers; I only feel him when he crouches before me and drives himself up into me, and his hand is at my head, grabbing me tightly by the hair, and he's kissing me and I'm moaning into his mouth and then screaming as pleasure takes me, and him along with me. I can't hold it in. It's pouring out of me in crackling torrents. Branches rattle back and forth, pinned to my arms.

Eventually, we collapse against each other, spent.

As he starts to unwind the cords that held me by my aching arms to the brush, he remarks, "That is a five-foot radius of melted snow. Look. You did that. Not I. All I did was give you a little extra energy and encouragement. You, my *ancilla*, did that."

I look. The thicket is full of mud and dense fog and is entirely devoid of snow.

That was me?

That was me.

I didn't even know that what I just did was possible.

ROASTING A TURKEY IS surprisingly easy. I'd always thought it involved staying up all night to slow-roast the bird in the oven, basting every hour on the hour to keep it from getting dried out, which is what I remembered my grandmother doing prior to our family gatherings; but apparently, all I need to do is follow a recipe, and "following a recipe" involves putting the thawed bird in the roasting pan, covering it with foil, setting the oven for 325 degrees, and then letting it sit in the oven for an amount of time calculated by multiplying the weight of the bird by a certain number of minutes. There's even a little embedded plastic pop-up timer in the turkey that indicates when the bird is fully cooked and safe to eat.

All this is right there on the turkey's label if the cook doesn't happen to have a cookbook handy as a reference.

That's it.

Gosh.

"If you want to get creative with flavoring," *Magister* says, "think about what tastes good with turkey, and you can put it in a sauce at the bottom of the pan. Every so often, use the turkey baster to squirt the sauce on top of and inside of the turkey. There's really no need to be intimidated by the thought of making a marinade from scratch."

I think.

"Wine?"

"That sounds good," he agrees. "I've already used the pinot noir for the cranberries, but there's an extra bottle of chardonnay you could use for the marinade if you want. Turkey's the sort of meat that would go just as well with white as it would with red."

In the end, I wind up adding some random green herbs, butter, Hungarian paprika, and a little chopped garlic and onion from the plastic storage containers in the refrigerator to the wine I've used as a base, and pouring honey on top – the honey, he says, not only brings out the flavor of the turkey, but it turns the turkey a nice golden brown on the outside when it roasts.

And the turkey goes in the oven.

"I did it!" I exclaim. "I prep cooked a turkey!" I feel absurdly pleased with myself.

"Cooking, and feeding other people, is as much a form of magick as any other act of love," he replies, kissing me on the cheek, then moving to my mouth.

He embraces me. I feel a hand glide under my shirt, and I sigh as he cups my breast, brushing my nipple with his fingers.

"More..."

"Later, I think. I still have food to make."

His hand moves down and lingers for a while on my torso. He presses in. I wince. My ribs have been sensitive lately. I'm not sure why.

We exchange places. The kitchen only has room for one cook at a time, and it's his turn to play with raw ingredients.

I take up a place on the living room couch and start reading. He has me studying Plato, Aristotle, Nietzsche's *The Birth of Tragedy*, and Robert Pirsig's *Zen and the Art of Motorcycle Maintenance*. Aristotle is obviously the odd one out here. I'm pretty sure the message for this week has something to do with altered states of consciousness – *There are two paths possible on the quest for gnosis: Classical and Romantic. The former is rational, and exact, and were every aspiring magus aligned with the Temple of Apollo, this would seem the most logical way to achieve self-perfection and wisdom. However, let us not assume that the rational path is the path best traveled. For deep magick is hidden in a stranger place, that being the ivy and grapevine-bound bower of Dionysos. Some seekers of wisdom are given the gift of Romantic sickness, and for them, the only way to access it is through destruction and change. For them, magic is madness*, I write.

That's assuming this week's lesson has something to do with altered states of consciousness, the rational versus the irrational, and the need to get out of one's own head when doing energy work, but I won't know for sure until I finish all the material, even though I've already read most of the assigned books at least once before.

Given that the readings are well in my bailiwick, consisting of stuff I read in college for my philosophy classes (except for Pirsig, whom I read in high school, and Nietzsche, who I had never got around to studying – my knowledge of existentialism is embarrassingly sketchy) it looks like the next oral critique of my essay will turn into one of our long rhetorical debates. I find myself getting excited.

I'm still reading when he takes my turkey out of the oven to carve it, and to put it on the kitchen table (which we're using as a buffet) along with all the other Thanksgiving dishes he's pulled out – there must be at least fifteen of them. Vegetables. Casseroles. Pies. Quiches. We could feed everyone living in this apartment building, were our neighbors to descend on us.

He's working on a salad right now made of chopped figs, spinach and mint leaves (*Mint!* Where on earth did he find *mint* in November?), pomegranate seeds, and nuts, that will probably taste as beautiful as it looks, as will a boozy cranberry tart that he made on the stovetop with an entire bottle of pinot noir, after chopping the contents of an entire two-pound bag of cranberries in half and soaking them overnight in Armagnac, but what has my mouth positively watering is a loaf of white bread. There's a dish of cinnamon honey butter to spread on it, but I could eat the bread by itself. There is something almost visceral about the smell of fresh, hot bread. Bread. Just bread.

He made a good half of this stuff from scratch yesterday and the days before, cooking throughout the day and storing the dishes one at a time in the refrigerator to reheat this morning. And yes, there is still Chardonnay. He was not wrong when he described the bottle I used up on making turkey marinade as his extra Chardonnay. So, we have that to drink with our meal.

There will be leftovers for days.

It's so good to be able to have Thanksgiving dinner with somebody again.

We pile food onto our plates and eat in the living room because there's no space for us to sit at the kitchen table. The stereo plays Mozart softly in the background.

My stomach growls. I attack my dinner with desperate abandon.

He gets a pained look on his face.

"What is it?" I ask.

There is a moment of awkward silence. Finally, he answers, "You're obviously starving. I'm not blind; this isn't the first time I've seen you eat like you'll never get another meal again, and I've noticed you losing weight over the course of the past couple of weeks or so. And you can't afford to lose weight; you never had much padding to begin with. I hate to ask this, because you seem to be rather sensitive about your situation, but I don't think you have an eating disorder – are you having a problem affording groceries?"

I shrug.

"No. *Stop that*. Starvation is not something to just shrug off." He puts his plate of food down and reaches under my shirt again. "Here, look: you're getting dangerously thin. This is not acceptable. *Mens sana in corpore sano*. You need to be healthy to keep up your studies; hunger ruins concentration. It also makes you more susceptible to pain and lowers your endurance, which I have reason to find objectionable. When did you stop eating?"

"When I lost my job. In a few weeks, I should start seeing the commissions added to my hourly at my new job."

"Meanwhile, you starve? No, that's not right. Come to think of it, you weren't eating all that well even before then, were you? It would explain a few things. Your ribs, for instance. I take it you don't know where the nearest food pantries are?"

"Food pantries? But those are for people who have *nothing*. I can't take a needy person's food away. That wouldn't be right."

He stares at me. I don't think I've ever seen him dumbfounded before.

"And anyway, I remember my parents donating lots of canned goods and boxes of spaghetti to food pantries when I was a kid. I don't have any way to cook that kind of stuff right now. My stove isn't working."

He sighs. "My *eromene*, I know you will not accept financial assistance, but would you at least let me raid my cabinets and refrigerator and give you food? Please? I don't want to order you to take home food and eat more regularly – in case you haven't noticed, I really don't like ordering you to do anything outside of the context of the bedroom, or the closed circle, because I don't feel it is appropriate to order you about in other aspects of your life when you aren't my slave, and don't wear my collar, and haven't consented to that level of power exchange – but I can ask."

I don't want to be a kept woman. I don't want charity, either. I don't like this. I don't know why, but for some reason, I see a difference between eating what he cooks for me and accepting the raw materials of groceries.

"Please. It hurts me to see you hunger."

He would have to point that out.

I relent.

THE STORES DOWNTOWN ALL have their Christmas displays up, and the potted sidewalk trees are strung with lights: white, blue, red, and green. We're window shopping. It's only two more weeks until Yule, and I have no idea what to get him for a present.

More specifically, I don't know which book would be perfect for him. I'm hoping something good will leap into my hands when I next visit a used bookstore.

Since we're downtown, the vast majority of the stores that are open (as opposed to being boarded up) are way out of my price range, and not too close to his ability to pay without causing critical damage to his finances, either. We are not here to do any real shopping. Mostly we're just looking at Christmas displays: elaborate train sets, giant Christmas trees, light displays, fake snow in fake wooded winter wonderlands. Bears dressed up as Victorian-era carolers. Our gloved hands reach for each other and embrace, creating a mingling of leather and acrylic yarn. A stray snow flurry lands on my cheek.

Something sparkling catches my eye, and we pause to look in the window. We're in front of a jewelry store.

"Oh, those are beautiful," I sigh, gazing in rapture at a pair of small, teardrop-shaped garnet and opal earrings set in white gold. They're my two favorite stones. The price of the earrings is surprisingly not obscenely high. No, neither garnets nor opals are considered precious, but the jewelry store whose window we're looking into has a reputation for charging its clientele a fortune.

"Would you like them?" he asks. "I'm still thinking about Yuletide presents."

"There wouldn't be much point. Those are studs. I don't have pierced ears. I'm surprised you hadn't noticed."

The snow starts to fall in earnest, in large, wet flakes. He has snow in his hair. As he leans in to kiss me, taking my face in one of his leather-clad hands, I reach up to brush the snow away.

WE SIT SIDE BY side on the couch, near the tiny tree he has set up on top of one of his shorter bookcases. The little white fairy lights shine through prisms we've hung from the artificial boughs, making rainbows scatter along the walls of the living room.

"You first," I say. I hope I'm cute when I wheedle. "Go on. Please?"

He smiles, kisses me lightly, and reaches for the larger of his two presents. I wrapped them in notebook paper because I couldn't afford wrapping paper after I bought his presents, but I decorated the paper with drawings of trees, to make it at least a little more festive.

"Baudelaire! In the original French, too, no less! Thank you. That was perfect. I'll have to read some of them aloud to you tonight. Have you ever read *Les Fleurs du Mal*?"

"Some of it. In translation. It's been a long time. I didn't quite get his poetry when I was a teenager. No doubt I was missing something. I did think it was beautiful, though, even though it mostly went over my head."

His "Litanies to Satan" gave me the creeps when I was sixteen, because I was still Christian at the time, but the stanzas were so gorgeous that they swept me away anyway. I'm sure there's more to Baudelaire than Satanism, though. He has a reputation. Which is why I grabbed the paperback copy of *Les Fleurs du Mal* to get *Magister* as a present when I saw it on display.

"Very beautiful. Also very strange, rather like us." He opens his other present. "A replacement silk! My tarot deck will thank you for it." He kisses me again, this time running the silk lightly across my cheek. "Although I might put it to other uses first. Your turn, *eromene*."

There are three packages, one large and long, one medium-sized, and one quite small, all of them wrapped in brocaded midnight blue and silver cloth, tied with braided silver fabric trimming. The fabric and trimming alone could be gifts; I could sew them into a pouch or a pillow, or maybe an altar cloth. Where on earth did he find them? The local fabric store wouldn't have something this precious, surely. Then again, if it carried silk gauze for my ritual robe, it probably has a wide selection of luxury fabrics. Sewing has never really been my thing, so I didn't really explore the store too thoroughly when I visited it.

I decide to go for the package that looks and feels like books.

They're books.

"The collected letters and writings of Abelard and Heloise?"

"Are you familiar with them?"

"No."

"In that case, I have some ideas for your next reading assignment." He smiles and strokes my jaw, until his palm rests against my cheek; I tremble and melt into his touch. "Go on. I want to see your face when you open the other two."

The small box looks suspiciously like a jewelry box, which sets off paranoid and no doubt silly worries about his having spent a king's ransom on me, so I pick up the larger box, which is about three feet long, and rather slender and flat. It looks like it ought to contain a bouquet of long-stemmed roses, and when I pull off the fabric wrapping, there is indeed a florist's logo on the box, but it's very heavy, much too heavy for flowers. How curious.

Inside, wrapped in multiple layers of tissue paper as if it were a floral bouquet, is a braided cat-o-nine-tails made of what appear to be many fine strands of black leather, interspersed with strands of rubber, both types of strands about three feet long, and with both the knotted braid ends and the rubber lash ends capped with tiny lead weights and smooth, sharply pointed tips of polished steel. The foot-long handle of the flogger is sterling silver. It's repoussé all over with patterns of climbing roses, some open, some merely budding, vines covered with leaves and thorns. The end of the handle is shaped, with loving anatomical detail, like the head of a phallus.

It looks like it belongs in the hands of a Dionysian priest, or maybe a crazed maenad. If Louis Comfort Tiffany had been into erotic pain, he probably would have designed something like this.

How could *Magister* possibly have afforded it? Even I, with my relative lack of experience in purchasing such items, can tell he spent a small fortune on it. No wonder we never bought Halloween candy this year, and hardly ever go out on dates. Dates cost money.

It's so beautiful that it brings tears to my eyes.

"It does come with a catch," *Magister* says quietly. "You must earn it. That whip came dearly, although once I saw it, I couldn't *not* get it for you – it was so beautiful that I decided it had to be yours; the roses, in particular, reminded me very much of you. Probably a bit rash on my part, but the handle and the lash ends were custom work. They, and the leatherwork for that matter, were done by a friend of mine who is a silversmith who makes a living selling jewelry and occult items at pagan festivals. He gave me the first chance to purchase it before he put it in his inventory of booth goods, I think because I'd told him I was in a relationship again for the first time in years, and I told him a bit about you. I couldn't bear the thought of anyone else buying it, so I bought it, despite the extravagant price. It seemed so very *you*, somehow. And really, who or what else would I spend my money on? I have everything I need, in terms of basic creature comforts, and a little bit saved against a rainy day, and beyond that, I see little point in hoarding money for its own sake. Well. The whip is yours now. It would be good to see it put to some use while we are partnered together as teacher and student, and there is only one of us here who makes an appropriate target for its blows."

Yes, once I laid eyes on the whip, I'd rather suspected there would be conditions of this kind.

Although I already know what the answer to my question will be, because I can see it with my own two eyes, I ask anyway. "This one you just gave me is nastier than the floggers you've used on me so far, isn't it?"

"Much."

My hand trembles when I caress the handle and the silver-tipped cords. He has several cat-o-nine-tailed whips; one of them is large and heavy and has a plethora of wide strands made of soft black suede, and looks intimidating, but it isn't all that bad. It's more for deep tissue massage than anything else. A "thud toy," he calls it. The others, however, aren't so innocuous. The one that gets the most frequent use is the one with thin leather braids that he used to work me over during my initiation ritual, and just thinking about it makes me want to squirm. This one is "much worse?" How much?

Well, I might as well brave the last package. I pick up the small parcel and untie the silver trimming that keeps the cloth wrapping shut. As I suspected, it's a jewelry box.

Inside it are the earrings that I was sighing over when we were looking in the window of the jewelry shop.

"How am I going to wear them?" I ask, knowing that I'm missing something obvious.

"I thought I'd pierce your ears for you."

A PAIR OF PLAIN, thin, black hoops made of some inert metal – I think he called it niobium – sits on the table in front of me, next to a box of rubbing alcohol pads and a type of slightly curved needle I've never seen before, although given how I avoid needles for anything but the usual basic sewing and mending, it's not surprising that I've never seen anything like them before. Maybe they're extremely common and I just don't know it. The needle glints in the afternoon sunlight. I assume it's a piercing needle. I suppose I shouldn't be surprised that there might be special needles manufactured for that specific purpose. I fidget in the kitchen chair as he washes his hands. When he comes up to wipe my left earlobe with an alcohol pad, I shiver.

"Nervous?"

"There's a reason why I never got my ears pierced when I was growing up."

"It shouldn't hurt too much; earlobes have almost no nerve endings. I'll be quick about it." He picks up a fine pointed felt tip marker and marks a dot on each earlobe. "There. That looks even. You'll need to hold still. Jerking could have unfortunate consequences."

I nod miserably and try to think about pretty jewelry made with opals and garnets, rather than about unfortunate consequences.

He stands beside me for a minute; then he changes his mind and pulls up another kitchen chair and sits across from me, so that his face is more or less level with mine. I feel the blood drain from my face as he tugs gently on my earlobe with one hand and picks the needle up with the other.

"My *eromene*, I had no idea this would be such an ordeal for you. Would you rather I not do this?"

I think of the earrings he gave me for a Yuletide present. Every time I wear them, I will be reminded of him.

"No. Keep going."

"If I could hold your hand, I would, but I don't have enough extra hands for that." He thinks for a moment, and then slides one of his legs over my left thigh, pinning me down. His warmth, and the weight of his leg, are like a heavy blanket. "Does that help?" he asks. "It's the best I can manage, under the circumstances."

I nod.

"All right. This will probably feel like a pinch or a slight sting, depending on the angle of entry, but that's all. Here comes the first one."

I whimper when the needle goes through my earlobe, but it's through me quickly enough, and he's right – this didn't hurt nearly as much as I'd feared. I try to not think about the needle that's still resting in my earlobe.

"There you go," he murmurs, and strokes my head. "That wasn't so bad, was it?" Then he pauses, and his face gets a stricken look for a fleeting moment before he quickly composes himself again. "Now, I think the easiest way to go about finishing off *this* ear would be to press the hole down just a little to allow me to thread the hoop through, then remove the needle. I'll use the piercing needle the proper way on your other ear and thread the hoop onto it first. I'm so sorry."

"*Wait. You've never done this before?*"

"This is the first time I've ever installed permanent jewelry. I've seen rings and studs placed before, at play parties, and of course I know my way around using needles on people, or I wouldn't have offered to pierce your ears for you, but this is the first time I've ever placed hoops, myself."

Now he tells me.

"Nervous?" I snap, before I think better of it.

"A little. I do want the end result to look good, since it's going to be permanent. There, that's one ear done." He gets up, has me stand, switches chairs with me, and drapes his leg over my other thigh, and then reaches for another alcohol pad to use on my right earlobe. And sighs and marks it carefully with the pen again.

"What's a play party?"

"Pretty much what it sounds like: a bunch of perverts getting together and doing creative things to each other. Not really my cup of tea – I've found that I'm too much of a private person to enjoy myself in group settings as much as I otherwise might – but when I was young, I was curious, and they were a part of the scene – still are – so I went to a few. Maybe more than a few. It seemed," he says with a grin, "a reasonably good way to learn the ropes. Now. I'm going to put the needle through your other ear; here it comes." His mouth curves into a wry half-smile. "And yes. This time I remembered to thread the hoop onto the needle it was designed for. I can't *believe* I ditzed like that."

I grit my teeth, close my eyes, and focus my attention elsewhere. I think about his leg draped over mine, and how it stands in for his arms now that his arms and hands are otherwise occupied. He busies himself with the other hoop for a couple of seconds, and then it's done and he's holding my face between his hands, inspecting his work.

"Oh, good. It's perfectly even. You'll need to clean the holes and rotate the hoops twice a day for a few weeks until the skin heals," he says. "I don't know how soon you can take the hoops out and wear your Christmas present. If those were studs in your ears, I'd say give it a couple of months, maybe, but the wire hoops are a little finer, and I'm told that makes a difference. I'd give your ears a good four months before you try out other earrings. April, maybe May." He kisses me lightly on the lips, then on my cheek, and on my forehead, and on my lips again, this time lingering a little bit longer. "You did very well. I presume you aren't about to kill me for that first ear?"

I smile. "No. Not immediately, anyway. I'm glad it was you, and not some stranger in a mall kiosk holding a piercing gun." Not that I'd ever have gone to a piercing kiosk in a mall of my own volition, anyway. "Much less scary. Certainly, more romantic. I like you better than a store clerk I'd be paying to punch holes in my earlobes."

"Happy?"

"Yes. Very happy."

"Good. I'll put the rest of the sharps away, then. I won't be using them on you, after all; you turned out to be much more frightened of needles than I had expected."

"The rest of the sharps? I take it you mean needles. You mean there's *more*?"

"Yes, of course, there's more. I have a bit of a collection. Needles, a few other useful things. You can take a look if you're curious." His eyes flick over my shoulder to the rolling kitchen island he sometimes uses for food preparation.

Holy Mother of God.

There's a tray on the island; somehow it had escaped my notice. Having needles pushed through my earlobes might possibly have been something of a distraction. "What is *that*?" I rasp. "A supply kit for a correspondence school's brain surgery course?"

"There would be a cranial saw included if that was the case," he replies. "It's just various kinds of needles, plus a few other basics. A box of disposable lancets. A box of safety razors. Scalpels. Knives. Several types of tourniquets. My first aid kit, which of course you've already seen."

A squeak escapes from behind my mouth.

"Far less painful to make shallow cuts or jabs with something extremely sharp, that's been designed for the purpose of cutting skin, than with something dull, such as an Exacto blade or a kitchen knife."

I had to ask. I just had to ask, didn't I? Ask, and you shall receive. Imagine, and you shall regret. "Um. You just said this was the first time you. Um. My ears." I want to get my voice to stop cracking, but it won't obey me. Stupid voice. It keeps making noises. High-pitched, incoherent noises.

"It wasn't just a case of nerves when I was doing your ears, was it? You have a phobia."

I nod.

"I didn't say I'd never used piercing needles," he says softly, "merely that I'd never installed jewelry. Also, when I brought in my supplies, I had no idea you were *that* scared of needles. Most people get a little nervous, some people get very frightened indeed, and I'd had a tentative idea for playing with fear, and seeing what came of it, but I wasn't expecting you to have a full-blown phobia – especially since you consented to let me pierce your ears. It's a common enough phobia, as far as phobias go, though, and I should have asked first. I'm sorry."

My teeth are chattering.

"I'll put my sharps away and make a mental note that this is one of the activities I need to add to your list of things you absolutely do not want me to do to you."

"No," I say in a strangled voice. "Go on with it."

He stares at me incredulously.

"How could I possibly do this to someone else, later in life, when my education is complete, without ever having endured it? As far as I am capable of submitting, I must. If I am to be a guide in the darkness, I need to go into the shadows myself. I have to. *It's who I am.* Besides, I don't want fear to be my master. I want you to be my master."

It's out. I can't un-say it. Today is quite the day for sharp things.

After a claustrophobic silence that seems to stretch into eternity, he sighs. "Oh, my *eromene*. You never cease to amaze me... Promise me you *will* stop me before I exceed your limits. As your teacher, it is, of course, my duty to push you as hard as you can endure, and then some, but we have somehow become much more than *Magister* and *ancilla*, have we not? And as your lover, I want you to delight in me, not suffer me."

I nod. I don't trust my voice.

"Do you really want me to be your master, now? Outside of the bedroom and the circle of light? Or were you just saying that in the heat of the moment?"

"I don't know. I didn't know I was going to say it until it escaped my mouth."

"We're going to need to talk later... although for now, I think it best to not assume you meant it literally. Fear sometimes makes people say things they do not intend, and in translation, the meaning is usually about needing security."

My gaze keeps getting drawn to the tray of needles and sharp things behind me, and every time I force myself to look forward to *Magister* again, the effort required drains me. A part of me – a large part of me – would rather be running naked down a crowded street right now, pursued by hornets and rabid dogs, *en route* to jumping off a high cliff into the wild blue yonder, to fall endlessly through thunderclouds full of lightning, until landing at last in a sea full of hungry sharks. Anything but this.

The other part is insane.

"Could you hold me when you do it?" I whisper.

He takes me by the shoulders and kisses me, long and gently. "Yes. Whenever that is possible." His mouth moves to my eyes, my cheeks; I realize that he is kissing me and drinking in my tears. At some point, I must have started crying. I hadn't even noticed. How can anyone not notice when they start crying? Impossible. "It takes incredible strength and courage to face down a phobia, you know. I am honored to have you as a pupil. Sometimes, however, I think you push yourself farther than even I do, my *eromene*, and I shudder to think to what lengths you will be capable of taking your future lovers if you expect them to follow you into the darkness."

I lean into him.

"I need to make sure before we go any further. Were you *really* asking me to help you face down your fears by playing with them? If this is what you want, I am willing to go on with the original activities I had tentatively planned. But it will be harsh. I think you will find it an ordeal."

"Yes."

"Very well, then. Take off your clothes."

My hands are shaking too hard to work the buttons on my shirt. He has to help me undress.

"I will do my best to explain technique when I push the needles through your skin, although given your state of mind, your retention will probably not be very good. If you do retain any of this, and it comes in handy later, I am glad to have served you well. The important thing to remember about piercing flesh is that needles slide through loose skin. The safest places to target are those that you can manipulate easily when you pull on them. If you can clamp a part of the body safely, you can most likely pierce it safely as well. Avoid arteries and veins. Avoid tendons. Avoid areas near major organs. Avoid tight skin, to minimize risking damage to muscles and nerves. Some piercings are inherently more painful than others. The more tissue the needle must pass through, generally, the more the piercing will hurt. It will also require more physical effort on your part if you are doing the piercing. You might want to practice ahead of time on something thick and meaty, like a raw steak, or maybe soft leather. And remember, unless you are doing the piercing to install jewelry, the piercing is temporary. The needles must all come out. That, too, can be a painful experience. Jewelry can be put in temporarily as well, if it is removed immediately after play to allow the hole to close back over. So can sutures. Hopefully, you will never need to give a play partner stitches, though. Does all this make sense so far?"

I nod mutely.

"Remember, *eromene*, that you can use your safeword at any time if this gets to be too much. Would you rather I start with the least painful areas, or would you rather I get the nastier piercings out of the way first?"

"Least painful," I mumble.

"All right. In that case, and I suspect this is going to be more than a little hard to believe due to your not having had personal experience, I need you to open your legs wider to give me some room to work. I'm going to start with the hood of your clitoris."

My legs slam shut.

"I rather figured that would be your initial reaction. It's actually one of the easiest parts of the body to get pierced. The skin is very thin and loose there. It's not the clitoral glans itself that gets pierced – that would be horrifically painful – just the hood. Do you trust me?"

I nod. There is a lump in my throat that won't go away.

"Open your legs."

I force myself to do so. I hope my trembling doesn't cause problems. I try to not think about what will happen if his hand slips due to my shaking.

"Please, don't make me look..."

"No. I won't. You can close your eyes."

I feel the dry, cold, stretched sensation of alcohol on my skin. Then stinging.

"It's in."

That was it? I open my eyes again and look at him with astonishment.

"There. That was a pleasant surprise, wasn't it? This is one of the more common areas to get pierced, at least, in the scene. Some women wear a hoop ring with a ball at the end that rubs against the clitoris. As I understand it, it can enhance certain sexual acts. I'm going to assume, however, that you aren't interested, given your overall reactions so far."

"No," I manage to squeak, "no jewelry."

He nods. "I thought so... Hmm." He brushes his hand up my thigh until his fingers find a needy, drenched spot between my legs, making me gasp. "Your brain might not be enjoying this very much, but it would appear your body has other ideas. I'll have to be careful to avoid the section I just pierced, of course, but that shouldn't present too much of a problem." He kneels in front of me, places his cupped hands under my buttocks, lifts me, and bends down. Then he begins to do impossibly tender things with his mouth. "Go on?"

"Yes," I gasp.

Time stops in place, shaking.

I cry out. "I wasn't expecting..."

"Are you sure you're done?"

And just like that, I am aware of not being finished after all. "More," I say in reply. "More. Please."

He presses his face into me again and resumes working at driving me into yet more ecstasy with his tongue. Every now and then, he pauses lapping near my clitoris to drive his tongue inside me. I am not so far gone that I am past noticing that he always seems to do this when my second orgasm is near.

He doesn't tease forever.

"YOU'RE NOT GOING TO like hearing this. The next easiest spot, due to the looseness and shape of your skin in that area and the relative ease I have in manipulating it, is going to be along the edge of your labia. If I really wanted to cause pain, I'd target a point a little further in, where the tissue is thicker; as it is, the outer edge will definitely hurt, but not as much, and not as much as other parts of the body. I think I'll target just two points, on either side. I promise to not turn you into a pincushion."

He's right. I don't like the sound of this. I feel my stomach start to tie itself in knots.

"And again, I am very sorry, but this *will* hurt. I think it would be best from now on if you had something to bite down on." He casts his gaze about, then starts rooting in one of the counter drawers. "Here. Wooden stirring spoon. It's smooth enough that it shouldn't give you splinters."

He puts the handle against my mouth; I bite down.

"Move forward a little, so that you are just a little closer to the edge of the chair, please."

I comply.

"There. Stop. That's a good place. All right," he says with a sigh, "brace yourself. You don't need to watch if you can't force yourself to do it, although I do recommend you watch me work if you are able. You might want to count each needle as it goes in, to remind yourself that this won't go on forever. There will be four."

Counting would involve acknowledging the needles as they enter me. No, please no.

He was right. This hurts. I bite down and whimper, but I somehow manage to avoid flinching. Eventually, tears start flowing out of me in a soft, steady torrent.

He rests his hand gently on the top of my thigh. "You aren't moving from this position until the needles come out. Open your eyes and look down."

I look, and instantly regret it.

He's pinned me to the chair by my labia.

"I hope you are as comfortable as possible under the circumstances. None of what I do next will be painless, and I apologize, because I know this isn't the sort of pain you usually welcome." He reaches up and strokes my cheek. "If it's any consolation, from here on I can hold you or lean you against me for support for most of what I do, even when I'm putting needles into you."

"Yes, please," I sob. The spoon falls out of my mouth, clattering to the floor.

"There, now. I have you. I won't let you go. It's all right." He drinks in more of my tears with kisses. "You're dealing with this very well, you know."

"I am?" I manage a half-laugh. "I think I'm a wreck."

"You're doing better than you think you are. I've seen people break down much more dramatically from playing with sharps, and none of them had your extreme fear of needles. Phobias are serious things. Working with them requires bravery, especially if you face your phobia head-on without any prior desensitization. I might also point out that up until now, you've been holding yourself in place of your own volition. That takes an incredible amount of willpower, especially when you are terrified. Most of the other people I've subjected to this, or seen subjected to it, were well restrained; and that was simply to immobilize them while they were enduring something painful. None of them had phobias of needles, or of any other sharp things – although most of them were a little nervous, which was to be expected." His hand strokes my hair as he continues kissing me, and eventually, my need to weep subsides. I sag into his arms, exhausted.

And that hurts.

"*Magister.* Could you please add more restraints? Please? I'm afraid of slipping down the chair."

"Yes, of course. Let me get the clothesline." He goes back to the counter, opens another drawer, and pulls out some cotton rope.

There is just enough to wrap around my midriff a few times, under the armpits, so that I am propped up on the chair. He also rolls a towel and places it behind the small of my back. While I still need to use my feet to push my weight back to avoid putting any kind of pressure on the pins affixing my painfully throbbing genitals to the chair, at least now I have a safety line. I pretend that the rope is a part of him. That way he is always holding me, never letting me go.

"Perhaps you will like what I'm about to do next," he muses, "since it doesn't involve needles."

This ought to be a relief to me, but somehow, it's not.

"You will have noticed that I left your arms free. Do you remember my lessons on nerve endings and meridians? So far, I have limited myself to stimulating them by stroking, or, if the sensation I want to produce is pain, pressing down on pressure points. Now, I think it's time to use some sharper tools. I'll start with a scalpel." He pulls one of the foil-wrapped packages off the baking sheet and opens it. "As you can see, this scalpel has a single-bladed edge, and a sharp point. The edge and point can both be used on nerve paths. The point can also be pressed into meridians, either with or without drawing blood."

He lifts my right arm, holds it against him, and starts stroking me gently with the blade. Down my shoulder, along the inside of my arm, down to just past my wrists. He repeats the process on the other arm.

At first, it tickles, because the touch is so light and delicate, but after a while, the tickling starts to feel like burning. I don't feel anything trickling down, so I don't think I'm bleeding, but it's hard to say whether I'm being stroked or being cut. I glance at my arm to make sure. No blood. He's not cutting.

"I'm pressing very lightly, and holding the blade at such an angle that it won't cut your skin, so you aren't bleeding. The burning sensation is just your *ch'i* awakening," he says. "I'm bringing it to the surface. As was the case after your initiation ceremony, there will be lines. They won't be permanent, though."

If he pushes the blade harder, there *will* be cuts. He doesn't need to say that part out loud. Try not to shudder. Try...

But he stops, then flips the blade over, so that it is upside down, and places the point on my arm.

"I use the point to stroke if all I intend to do is produce strong sensation. Even though disposable dental scalpels like the one I've been using aren't the sharpest tools available, it's a bad idea to push down hard using the blade itself, especially if you're near veins, arteries, or nerve endings. It's also a bad idea to use the point directly on top of veins, arteries, tendons, or the like. That could cause serious damage. It's best to stick to what only shows as flesh. Your unhealthy thinness is very fortunate, here, because it lets me see what areas I need to avoid."

The tip engraves itself into my skin, just hard enough to mark, just light enough to not cut. Lines swirling up and down my arms, lines curling across my chest. I bite down on my spoon.

"Now, this is interesting. Notice what happens when I use the sharp tip of the scalpel to stroke the kidney meridians along your legs. They run from your foot to your chest. I won't be applying the sharp tip to your feet, though – I don't want to risk tickling you, given the method I've used to pin you down." Holding one of my legs gently, he crouches down on his haunches so that he can reach my ankle better.

The tip scrapes up my left leg.

Pain.

Fire.

Need. A terrible, consuming, desperate need that makes my genitals throb – quite separate from the painful throbbing there that's never gone away. The wood

I am pinned to feels slick; it would be a pleasant surface to rub myself against. But I can't twitch my hips or grind in place without ripping myself free of the needles that pin me down. I groan.

"And that is another use of the blade," he says. "And to think I haven't even cut you with it. Yet."

AFTER WHAT FEELS LIKE an eternity of lines being engraved into me, none of which bleed, and most of which put me just this side of another orgasm, for all that they hurt, he puts the scalpel down at last. "If I use this much longer, I'll make it dull, and that won't do," he says. "Not for this." And then he pulls another blade off the tray and shows it to me. This one is not disposable. It looks like it has a sharper edge, too. "This is a Liston knife. In medicine, it's usually used for sawing through bone. I don't use it for that. I use it for bloodletting. I find it a little more sensitive and precise than my fleam, although it's not appropriate for finer work, such as cutting sigils, brands, and designs into flesh. That requires a very sharp surgical scalpel." He puts it against the left side of my neck, directly on the pulsing vein. Or is that my carotid artery?

I draw in my breath sharply.

"This would be a remarkably inappropriate place to cut. Which is why I won't cut you here." The blade slides down, slowly and gently, to the center of my chest, just between my breasts.

And he presses down, parting my skin as he cuts. A sudden pain burns coldly where he has slashed my chest.

"There. That's what I was looking for," he murmurs; then he lays down the blade, puts his mouth to the surface wound he made over my heart, and drinks me in.

As he drinks, my chest grows cold, in contrast to the soft warmth of his mouth and tongue. Then the rest of me grows cold. The room spins around me. It feels almost pleasant. *Don't faint. Don't faint. If you faint, you might slip, and then you'll tear yourself off the chair. Don't faint...*

My outer labia are on fire. I wish the sensation would stop.

He has set aside the scalpels and knife and gone back to the needles.

"Ordinarily I'd insert many more needles into the safer areas to target, but for your sake, I'm keeping my needlework to a minimum. One can confront phobias without going overboard. I think next, I'll target the side of your nose, the corner of one of your armpits, and the cartilage of one of your ears. That last one will be extremely unpleasant. Ear cartilage is considerably harder to pierce than a flap of skin. It's one of the more common areas to pierce, but it presents certain problems, especially if the person being pierced is going to be wearing permanent jewelry there. Earrings in that area pose something of an infection risk."

I blink. "My *armpit*?"

He pinches a flap of skin between his fingers. "You have very loose skin there."

"Oh."

"But with an abundance of nerve endings, and in an awkward and frequently stretched location, which is why this is seldom done except as a temporary piercing, with a subject who can reasonably be expected to not move out of a restrained or held position, and who for whatever reason does not mind getting hurt. Just so you know, it's also quite common to pierce lips and tongues and navels for reasons of adornment as well as for play piercings, not just in the BDSM scene but also in the vanilla mainstream, especially among members of certain fashion and music subcultures, but I'll avoid doing that to you. Hmm." He brushes the top of my inflamed, cut chest with a tentative finger. I wince. "The chest is a fairly common site, for temporary piercings anyway, as is the back, but you don't have much skin there. Or much of anything else, other than bone." He reaches to the side for another alcohol pad. "We need to fatten you up some more, *eromene*."

He puts the spoon back between my teeth.

I start crying again when he resumes his work. If it wasn't for his arm around me, and the warmth of him at my back, I don't think I could bear it. I'm not sure I can bear it now, but I bite down on the spoon harder and keep telling myself that this can't go on for too much longer. Surely.

When the needle selected for my armpit goes through, I scream into the spoon. Agony remains after *Magister* is done pushing and I am done screaming.

Blood trickles down my side.

Magister kneels down and licks it from my skin.

WHEN HE'S DONE, HE releases me and tilts my chin so that I am looking him in the eye. He is at once grim and distant.

We stare at each other wordlessly for a long moment. He doesn't blink; nor do I. We hold each other's eyes without speaking, even as he moves a hand toward the tray of needles and blades. A part of me is astonished that he can reach for things like alcohol pads and sharps without even looking at them, and not get cut or stabbed in the process. The other part of me is noticing that he is using his other hand to tease one of my nipples. Around and around, then gently back and forth. I shudder and keen with pleasure. Then it dawns on me what he's doing.

I let out a strangled scream as I push my feet against the floor with all my might, as if I could fly if only I pushed hard enough. My back arches in an attempt to get me away. Anywhere away, so long as it's away.

He picks up the spoon I just spat out off the floor and places it in my mouth again. The cold evaporation stiffens me more, whether I am ready for it or not; of course, I am not. His hands are busy. My body is shaking in quiet convulsions. I have become a sine wave.

When the needle enters me, it is agony. I scream again. The spoon drops to the floor, clattering.

He stops and looks at me speculatively. "You do have a safeword, you know," he says.

I can't stop sobbing and shaking.

"Have you – have you forgotten it?"

I think I nod. I'm not sure. I've finally gone over the edge.

"I'll assume that's a yes. I'm stopping now. I was beginning to wonder what would make you safeword. Or try to, anyway."

"Stop, please," I hear myself croaking. "Please make it stop..."

He stops.

After he gets all the needles out of me – which is a whole new exercise in misery – he holds me close until my sobs subside.

"Oh, *eromene*. You do know that safewords aren't a form of 'giving in,' right? You need to feel secure about it being acceptable to say no to something, even when you're in the middle of it, or to ask for a break. Even I might need a break, although admittedly, almost nothing we have done together has been too intense for me, which I'm not sure I should find worrisome or not. You haven't been enduring things you didn't like all for the sake of avoiding using your safeword, have you?"

"No."

"Do you remember what it is now?"

"*Mate*."

"Good. Wait. You've never even simply said 'no' in the heat of passion to anything I've done to you, have you? You've never said 'no,' you've never asked me to stop, no matter how intense things got between us; you certainly don't seem to be one of those people who needs to go through the motions of resistance or denial to find release, and thus needs to use a safeword to stop play rather than use literal words like 'no' and 'stop' – which is just as well, because I prefer to not tap into that, consensual nonconsent makes me nervous. For that matter, the closest you've come to so much as asking me to *pause* has been when you touched or squeezed my hand to ask me if you could scream into my mouth when your climax was near. I think we should avoid playing chicken like this again, in the future; the result would be traumatic."

I nod and collapse against him, smearing him with my blood and sweat and tears.

CHESED

"ARE YOU SURE YOU don't want me to order you some bacon and eggs, or something? You look like you're starving."

"No thanks."

We were lovers, once. Now we are former lovers, trying to be "just friends." It's easy enough to manage when one was not much more than a friend in the first place. Trying to bury the memory of passion and pretend that it doesn't matter that there was once romance and now there is no more, is another matter. At least for us, it is.

We're still trying anyway, because as awkward as being "just friends" has proven to be, the thought of being enemies or, worse, ghosts of memories to each other is more painful.

"I don't think you get to be angry at me for having dumped you for a man, after this." My ex-girlfriend stabs at a pancake with her fork. I must still love her, at least a little. Ordinarily I wouldn't even consider meeting a person for breakfast before a civilized hour – say, eleven o'clock. The only way I can even think of being awake at dawn involves an unhealthy amount of caffeine. It's a good thing the diner has bottomless cups of coffee.

Those pancakes she's eating look delicious. Oh, well.

"That was different. I was dating you at the time. We moved in together. I thought we were in love with each other. I thought you *loved* me."

"I did love you. I still kind of do. Just not..."

"Not enough?" I grimace. "You left me hanging for rent."

"Get a roommate."

"Easier said than done. This is me, remember? I have to keep the roommate after I get the roommate, assuming I actually do manage to get the roommate." It's been months, and not one person has followed up on my campus posters yet, so the point is moot. I suppose I'd have better luck if I paid for a classified ad in the newspaper, but I can't afford to do that. Working for the local newspaper as a telemarketer gives me a steady supply of free newspapers. It doesn't give me free classified advertisements.

"You yelled at me because you said I treated my relationship with my boyfriend as more real than the relationship I had with you. You used to tell me that back when you actually *had friends*, your friends would leave you hanging when they got into romantic relationships, only to get friendly again when things didn't work out with their boyfriends, and they were single again. The last time you contacted me to hang out was *last March*."

I hang my head. She's right. As it turned out, we were more compatible as friends than we were as girlfriends, anyway, for all that we had managed at some point to convince each other that we loved each other; and nursing resentment isn't exactly the best way to keep a friendship alive, any more than ignoring your friend is. But I've done one of the things I used to rail against: I've ignored people I call friends entirely and let myself get drunk on being in love.

It's a great way to lose friends.

And it's not like *Magister* wants me to do it. Every now and then, he asks me if maybe I'm neglecting the other people in my life, since he never hears me talking about them or sees me with them. I blow him off every time he asks because I never really know quite how I should respond, but it's a reasonable question.

"I'm sorry," I say, looking up from the cup of coffee I've been toying with. I think it's my fourth, but it might be my fifth. She wanted to buy me breakfast, too, but coffee is about as much charity as I'm willing to accept from most people.

"So, who is he?" she asks, amusement tingeing her voice. At least I think it's amusement; I'm not sure. I hope it is. "He must be pretty special if he's the reason you haven't even called me for the past ten months."

"He's a librarian. He works at the downtown public library."

"Well, that makes sense. Anyone you fall for would need to be all about the books."

"We did meet in a bookstore."

"Mmm-hmm. Is he cute?"

"Um. I don't know. I guess. I mean, isn't that kind of subjective anyway, based on the things any given person finds cute? I think sometimes he's cute. He's good-looking. He has beautiful eyes and cheekbones. And his hair is incredible, all thick and wavy, black and silver. I love touching it."

"Black and silver? How old *is* he?"

I tell her.

After spitting out her coffee, she says, "He's twice your age? Wow. Congratulations." She grins lasciviously. "He must be good in bed. You know what they say."

"Oh, good grief. You actually expect me to answer that? That's an awfully personal question." Know what who says? About what? "Yes."

"Mmm. I bet. You're glowing." Her eyes flick down to her wrist. "I'm going to be late for my shift if we stay here much longer. Can we get together sooner than another ten months from now, do you think?"

"I'm going to be running a game this Sunday. Not a long campaign, just a one-off. Are you free?"

Magister and I decided to try setting up a gaming group for me to help me make more friends and get a life outside of him. It's worth a shot. And I do miss gaming.

"Does joining the party mean I get to meet your significant other?"

"It does."

"I'll be there. I'll steal my boyfriend's dice since he has to work that day." She shrugs. "Well, I'd be there, regardless, but this gives me an extra incentive. So, what are we playing?"

"I thought I'd have you do a little computer troubleshooting."

IT'S A SMALL PARTY sitting around the card table we set up in the living room – the only other two players besides *Magister* and my ex-girlfriend are a couple of *Magister's* co-workers from the library, who I think I've bumped into a few times, because they look familiar – and that's fine by me, because it's easier to roll up canned characters for a one-day campaign when you don't have to create very many characters. Also, the living room can only hold so many people. I suppose we could squeeze in a few more players if they were willing to be very friendly with each other. We do have the couch. For now, though, it's just the five of us.

"It looks like there's nobody else joining the four of you in the empty classroom. Suddenly, you hear a tinny voice coming out of the public address system: 'WELCOME, RED TROUBLESHOOTING TEAM ALPHA ONE ONE EIGHT POINT SEVEN. THE COMPUTER HAS A VERY IMPORTANT MISSION FOR YOU TO COMPLETE. IT IS IMPORTANT THAT YOU PERFORM THIS MISSION TO COMPLETION AND COMPLETE IT TO ITS COMPLETEST MAXIMUM PARAMETERS. THE COMPUTER IS YOUR FRIEND.'"

"Is the computer always this redundant?"

Magister has never played this game before. He's more of a fantasy and horror role-player.

I smile sweetly at him. "A ceiling panel slides open directly above you. Suddenly, a beam of red light falls on you; you are vaporized within seconds."

"*What?*"

"Don't worry," one of the co-worker players says soothingly, "you have five more clones. This is normal in the game."

"It is?"

"The ceiling panel remains open," I say. "From the ceiling, your clone replacement drops to the floor, and proceeds to bounce around the room, ricocheting off the walls and floor like a rubber ball."

"It does what?"

"Mutant!" cries my ex-girlfriend. "Destroy the mutant! Down with mutants!" She looks at me and says, "I aim my laser side-arm at the bouncing mutant and shoot it in the chest."

"Roll for – uh – roll for accuracy."

She rolls.

"Success. The mutant dies, shot through the heart, and continues to bounce around the room like a rubber ball, splatter-painting the walls, furniture, and floor as it does so. Meanwhile, a metal robot the size and shape of a bread box emerges from a wall panel at the other end of the room and proceeds to vacuum up the small pile of ashes that used to be a traitor. From the ceiling, a second clone replacement drops to the floor."

"What?"

"Is *this* clone bouncing?" asks another party member.

"No."

"I think we can assume this one's not a traitorous mutant commie," she tells my ex. "All clear." She turns to *Magister* and whispers, "You only have four clone replacements left. One of them is the one you're about to use right now. Let us do the talking for a while if you want to live."

"Maybe that's for the best," he agrees.

He learns fast.

"A FOOD TERMINAL IN GREEN MAUSOLEUM SEVEN TWO NINE B IS MALFUNCTIONING. YOUR MISSION IS TO REPAIR THE MAL-FUNCTIONING FOOD TERMINAL. IT IS A VERY IMPORTANT MIS-SION. FAILURE TO PERFORM THIS IMPORTANT MISSION IS TREA-SON AND WILL BE PUNISHED BY DEATH. THIS MESSAGE WILL SELF-DESTRUCT IN THREE SECONDS."

"There's a food terminal in a mausoleum? *What*?"

"As Chief Happiness Officer, I think our new team member needs a Happy Pill to improve his morale. That, and I need to test them out on somebody."

"Yes! Absolutely! Give him an experimental Happy Pill!"

"*What?*"

"Looks like you're being given an experimental Happy Pill. Don't worry, they're – " I roll – "orally delivered, as opposed to the last experimental Happy Pills, which were rectal suppositories. And within seconds, you are radiantly happy, and the pill failed to blow up on contact, which is great news for pharmaceutical research," I chirp. "The suppositories were a bit more explosive."

"The last time I was in a role-playing game, I played a half-elven Druid," *Magister* mutters. "This is a little different, isn't it?"

"Just a bit. Okay, you two," I say, gesturing to my ex-girlfriend and the co-worker of *Magister's* who hasn't said much yet, "if you could follow me into the other room, the Computer has an additional top-secret assignment *just for you.*"

These two players are members of a secret society, and they have orders from their society to carry out. Actually, all the players are members of secret societies – for instance, *Magister's* character is a member of Save the Redwoods, which is a seditionist cabal in the dystopian future of this game – but my ex and the other person are in the same society, a different one from the one *Magister* is in and the one his other co-worker is in – so it makes sense to debrief them together. Besides, I've found that talking to players in another room where their gaming partners have no idea what is going on is a great way to raise levels of paranoia and general unease.

As I lead them into the kitchen, a doorway materializes unexpectedly where it wasn't supposed to be – alternatively, my perception of the doorway is lacking, which is probably the more likely explanation – and I encounter the doorway with my hip, stumble, and land hard against the corner of the kitchen table on the top of my thigh.

Unfortunately, the part of that thigh that crashes into the table is still recovering from last night. Other parts of me are still recovering from being pierced, engraved, and sliced, but they don't come into contact with the table. Small mercies.

I let out a yelp, and add a few choice swear words for good measure.

"Are you all right?" *Magister* calls out.

"Yes. I'm fine. I just crashed into the table and landed on my welts, that's all." I walk back into the living room, because of course, I remember that my campaign notes are still in there, behind my GM screen. That's not a good practice to get into, even when one's players are trustworthy. Oops.

A sudden silence fills the room.

"You landed on *what?*" asks my ex-girlfriend, from the kitchen. "How on earth did you get welts?"

"How does one usually get welts?"

She gapes at me.

The rest of the gaming party stares at me, then at him, then at me again. From the appalled looks on the faces of just about everybody in the room, it looks like there is concern for my well-being.

Then my ex turns her head to stare at *Magister*, who also has an appalled look on his face, though for an entirely different reason.

She gives me an astonished look again. "I didn't know you were into that. Wait. You aren't the dominant?"

I have no idea what put that idea into her head. Then again, we did date one another for a while. Perhaps I was more of a character in bed than I thought I was. "I probably would be, if it was anybody else. It's a bit complicated to explain."

I can almost hear *Magister* blushing, he's blushing so hard. On the other hand, at least now his co-workers no longer think he's abusing me.

"You owe me lunch. And a copy of *The Claiming of Sleeping Beauty*," says one of his co-workers to the other.

"What?"

"Oh. We had a bet going," she says, turning to *Magister*.

Magister groans and covers his face. It doesn't help. He's blushing all the way down to his collarbone. "Can we get back to the game?" he mutters. "I think I'd rather be shot with lasers and fed mood-altering drugs for right now, if you don't mind."

"No, I don't mind," I reply.

I STAND IN FRONT of the couch expectantly. He's been parked there since early this morning, going through a pile of books. I don't think he even noticed when I excused myself, walked to the local thrift store, and came back with a large bag. When he starts reading, he gets totally absorbed in it.

"Happy birthday!"

He looks up from the book he's currently working on – the collected writings of Marcus Aurelius, in the original Latin – and gets a bemused look on his face. "It is my birthday, isn't it?"

Since he has his earplugs in, I assume he is having one of his more hypersensitive days. Sometimes noise bothers him, and if he doesn't protect himself from it, he gets wicked headaches. Bright light sometimes does it to him, too. He says some days are worse than others for him. I make a note to do my best to keep my voice down. He'll still be able to hear me through the earplugs even when I'm using a quiet voice – from what he says, the earplugs don't so much muffle all noise as drown out chaotic background noises and make it easier for him to focus on what one person is saying without getting overwhelmed, and they keep the "projection" level of the person he's focusing on down to a dull roar so his ears and head don't hurt. When I asked him what the difference was between noise level and projection, he gave me an odd look and asked if other people's noise didn't push at me or feel like it was jabbing me.

I don't perceive sound the same way he does. I also don't seem to perceive light the same way he does. Then again, he doesn't perceive other people's *ch'i* through the layers of his skin all the way into his nerves quite the same way I've been doing since November. I guess we both have hypersensitivities, just different ones. His hypersensitivities seem more awkward and annoying than mine are. I deal with mine easily enough by not letting most people get anywhere near me, which is natural enough because I've never really liked being close to other people anyway. On his more sensitive days, he doesn't seem to have any way to escape the unpleasant stimuli at all – the best he can do is stay in the shadows and muffle the noises that bother him.

"You just turned forty-two. That makes you the meaning of *life, the universe, and everything*. Come on. We have to celebrate it. It's mandatory."

"Hmm. It sounds like you have something in mind."

"Absolutely," I say with a grin. "I have a present for you. Sorry I couldn't wrap it properly, but I did find a nice bow. Here's the bag." I hand it to him.

He puts down the book and holds out his hands for the bag. When he opens it, he pulls out my present and turns it over a few times, looking at it from different angles.

"A baby harp seal plush? Er. Hmm. *Eromene*, why a harp seal plush?"

"I was originally scouring the thrift store for books, but it was cute, it was there, it was cheap, and I couldn't resist buying it for you. Isn't it adorable?"

"Looks cuddly," he agrees.

"There's only one catch," I say, trying valiantly to keep my face deadpan as I do so. "You have to earn it."

"Earn the harp seal."

I grab the stuffed seal by the tail and chamber it into position on my shoulder. "Turnabout is fair play!" I declare emphatically, and then I swing the harp seal at his head. It lands just hard enough to make a muffled noise.

The look of sheer astonishment on his face needs to be captured for posterity. If only I had a camera.

"Forty-one more to go. Hold still, this is supposed to be character-building, you know."

Stuffed harp seals make great pillow weapons.

After whacking at his head and various other body parts – both he and the harp seal survive – I hand him his seal back. "There. It's yours."

"Thank you. That was probably the most surreal birthday present I think I've ever received." He smiles. "Although I'm pretty sure I didn't need the character-building. I'm enough of a character already."

"I'll go start baking the cake," I say. "It's from a mix. I hope you don't mind."

"I'm flattered that you even thought to bake me a cake," he replies. "And cake mixes are a very good way to practice baking cakes. After you get confident at it, you start playing around with the instructions by adding or substituting things, and from there, it's a short step to cooking from scratch. That's actually how I first started using an oven..."

I kiss him on the lips in mid-sentence before he has a chance to expound anymore. "Hush. It's okay to just *enjoy the chocolate cake*. Really."

He glances down at the seal. "I think I'll name him Approval."

He gets a really cute look on his face when he's confused. I should find a way to get him to make that look more often.

Later, as we drink mulled wine to chase away the cold January night, and cuddle together on the living room couch to watch Stealing Heaven (which seems fairly faithful to the written records Heloise and Abelard left of their affair, at least for the duration of their brief physical involvement) he whispers in my ear, "Of course, what I really want for my birthday is you."

"You already have me."

"Really? I had some rather specific ideas in mind."

"You always have specific ideas in mind."

"True," he agrees.

"And you *definitely* have me. You had me before we even formalized our relationship."

"I did?"

"Good grief, couldn't you tell? Yes. You did."

"And I have you now, do I?" He turns so that he is leaning on me, pinning me to the couch. I feel his hands close about my wrists.

No matter how many times he does that, it never ceases to transform me into a puddle of molten want.

"Oh, yes. Always. Even when you use cheesy, horrible lines like that." My mouth seeks his and finds it. "You have my heart always. So, what does this specific idea of yours entail?"

"Unwrapping and enjoying you, of course," as he presses his weight against me, grinding me into the cushions. I moan in expectation. "Slowly." He thrusts. "And thoroughly. And very deeply." Another thrust, this one hard. I moan again. The things he then proceeds to do to my ear while he has me pinned under his hips, using his tongue and the tips of his teeth, make me writhe and thrash, crying out in need. I strain against his hands; they tighten, clamping me down, until I feel my own wrists and hands start to tingle.

"Don't stop," I gasp, "please, please, whatever you're doing, don't stop, I'm so close..."

"Oh?" He rolls his pelvis against mine, wringing yet another moan of desperation out of me, and I feel myself shaking. "Well. This seems like the perfect time to try something."

"What?"

"*Come,*" he says softly into my ear.

Body arching. Shaking. Convulsing. Burning in a fire of pleasure. White heat. I need to scream.

Gasping for breath. Weak at the knees.

He stares at me, flabbergasted. "I hadn't expected *that* to work," he says. "It's a BDSM porn cliché. It almost never works in real life. And when it does work, usually there is some suggestion and behavioral pre-conditioning first. I hadn't got around to that yet, with you." Then he smiles. "I hope you don't mind, but I have decided to make this a very long evening."

"No," I manage to whisper, "I don't mind at all."

I HAVE BOOKS PILED around me on the living room floor in my usual cross-referencing mess. The compilations of love letters between Peter Abelard and Heloise; the Hilaire Beloc translation of the Bedier *Tristan and Iseult; The Romance of the Rose; The Art of Courtly Loving* by Andreas Capellanus, which I'm pretty sure was thrown in with the other books as my weekly red herring, because it's obviously written as a satire of Ovid, and Ovid's original was not exactly written as serious advice to lovers, either.

I'm looking for the chivalrous roots of the BDSM subculture in the cult of courtly love, which puts a whole new spin on the more romantic aspects of Arthurian legend. Guinevere and Iseult, for instance, can be seen as dominants. The concept is amusing, and not entirely out of the realm of the possible, although plausibility is another matter – I have a very hard time seeing a Western tradition of BDSM customs that stretches back all the way to the Middle Ages. It works better as a thought experiment than as history.

I scribble:

> I think this modern revival of courtly love, under a new name, so to speak, is rather more romantic and genuine in its own way than the actual medieval cult of courtly love ever was. At least it seems that way, going by the disgruntled poems of Beatritz, Countess of Die and the other *trobaritz* women, who wrote in response to the obviously insincere professions of love and adoration made by their more well-known male counterparts; and of course, there are the tongue-in-cheek opinions of Capellanus. Even the later part of *The Romance of the Rose*, consisting of those chapters completed by Jean de Meun rather than the ones written by Guillaume de Lorris, the book's earlier author, is rather cynical about the whole courtly thing. Courtly love, in the literature of the high Middle Ages, seems to only exalt the impossible and fantastic. Bringing fantasies down to the level of enactment does not appear to have often been done. There were simply too many impossibilities.

> In the Arthurian romances, the most romantic lovers were those who transgressed the rules of courtly love to succumb to something a little more earthy, but it usually meant certain death, by

execution or trial by ordeal or getting sent on a quest that was a
suicide mission. Even if the result of carnal pleasure was not death,
the consequences of getting caught were dire. If a lover was very
lucky, like Lancelot and Guinevere were, he or she might survive
trials by ordeal and combat, suicide missions, banishments, accu-
sations, and so on only to spend the rest of his or her life locked up
in an abbey or a convent.

The legends were created during the Age of Faith, and they reflected their times; it was not uncommon for widows, second sons, et
cetera to take religious vows due to having no other recourse, but
religious devotion notwithstanding, taking vows for purely prag-
matic reasons was probably a let-down. The Church told people
that sexual desire of any kind was sinful and should only be used
for the purposes of procreation, not pleasure. Living vicariously
through transgressive characters in songs and stories could have
helped relieve some of the tension of pent-up desires for those
people who could not defy convention.

It thus seems unfair that Lancelot and Guinevere and similar
chivalric characters should go through decades of sneaking around
with each other, surviving accusation after accusation, trial after
trial, only to end their days separated by religious vows. But there
it was, and in real life, their story probably would have ended in
death; retiring to the convent or abbey to spend the rest of one's life
in a sort of second chastity was, relatively speaking, a "happily ever
after." It hinted at some kind of heavenly reward when a garden of
earthly delights had nevertheless been sinfully enjoyed.

Lancelot and Guinevere and Tristan and Iseult were legends. More than that, they were fantasies. Ordinary people would not have subjected themselves to the torments those legendary figures willingly endured; if they had, they would not have survived. Then would come an eternity of Hell.

In poetry and song, meanwhile, the convention of "passionate poet writing love poems to a noble lady patron, whom he loved from afar" seems, in practice anyway, to have been given little credence, except as a form of ritualized flattery aimed at getting money and other forms of material support from the patron. Hardly surprising, given that seducing the lady of the manor would have been a punishable transgression. There was one troubadour who wrote love lyrics not to his patron, but to his wife, and according to his *vida*, he was ridiculed for it, even though his confessions of abject love were probably quite sincere. Uxoriousness was not considered a courtly sin. Dressing up like a wolf and howling outside the window of your patron, making yourself the quarry in a wolf hunt, the way Pierre Vidal did, all because the married noblewoman you write poetry to has a name that translates as "she-wolf?" Courtly.

If indeed it ever happened, which is hard to believe.

The only two genuine courtly lovers who left behind reasonable proof of their romance were Abelard and Heloise, and it wouldn't have been a relationship based on courtly love had he not been

castrated almost immediately after marrying his young lover. Their
relationship (which was technically inverted, because the conven-
tions of courtly love required a submissive male suitor and a dominant female of higher standing, not a dominant male tutor and a
submissive female student who wound up being submissive *wife*
for a short while, then a submissive *nun in an abbey*) also seems to
have been subject to a certain amount of degrading due to religious
fervor. Poor Heloise. Poor Abelard. Well. Maybe not so much poor
Abelard, since it was his religious fervor that caused his relationship
with his abbess-wife to deteriorate – when he was castrated, he
lost his testicles, but the rest of him was untouched. At worst that
might have caused impotence. Surely, in that case, he could have
found other ways to make love with Heloise, inventive man that
he was? Poor Heloise.

Oh, well. It's still a fun assignment. Valentine's Day is coming up, and this
provides inspiration, as I am sure *Magister* intended.

"The first letter, written by Heloise to Abelard, begins: "*Domino suo, immo
patri; coniugi suo, immo fratri; ancilla sua, immo filia; ipsius uxor, immo soror,
Abaelardo Heloysa.*" The parts about being brother and sister probably just reflect
the fact that both of them have taken vows, at the time of writing, but she refers
to him as her husband and her father, among other things. I really don't think
that when she calls him her father, she's thinking of him as her abbot, especially
since she also calls herself his servant. You did tell me that some power exchange
relationships play on familial dynamics. Just because we don't have that in our
relationship doesn't mean they didn't have it in theirs.

"Then there's this: "*Qui tanta hostibus largiris, quid filiabus debeas meditare;
atque, ut ceteras omittam, quanto erga me te obligaveris debito pensa, ut quod
devotis communiter debes feminis, unice tue devotius solvas.*" Heloise speaks of
Abelard's "debt" to her, and it's very clear that this is not a monetary debt – it's
a debt of obligation, of responsibility. I think she is speaking of a debt owed by a

master to his servant, especially since she concludes this paragraph of her letter by calling herself Abelard's alone. She makes it clear that she *belongs* to him.

"And of course, there's that notorious paragraph in which she calls herself Abelard's whore, his strumpet. His concubine. "*Non matrimonii federa, non dotes aliquas expectavi, non denique meas voluptates aut voluntates, sed tuas, sicut ipse nosti, adimplere studui... Deum testem invoco, si me Augustus universo presidens mundo matrimonii honore dignaretur, totumque mihi orbem confirmaret in perpetuo possidendum, karius mihi et dignius videretur tua dici meretrix quam illius imperatrix."* Yes, she was originally hesitant to marry him because marriage would have been the death of his ambitions and his academic career. At that time, the only route to scholarship was through the church, which meant taking orders, which meant taking vows of celibacy. That was why they tried to keep their marriage a secret. Marriage was not allowed for monks and priests. It was common enough for clerics to have lovers, but Abelard wanted to pacify Heloise's uncle by making her an honest woman, as the saying goes, fat lot of good that it did him. However, by the time Heloise wrote her letter, all this was in the past. She had no reason to think of herself as Abelard's concubine. They were already married. The only reason she could possibly want to be his concubine, his whore, was to tickle her own fancy.

"So. How much of her subordination to Abelard was purely conventional, the result of wives being required in those days to submit to their husbands, abbesses to their abbots, and how much of it was sincere? Was she only playing on words, or was she using her words to subject herself to Abelard? And would it have meant the same thing, in context, for those two as it would have meant for us?"

"That," he says, "is an interesting question. I would like to doubt that any of it was purely metaphorical. Heloise in particular seemed to be the sort of writer who said what she meant and meant what she said, and if a metaphor was involved, she'd preface it by informing Abelard of the metaphor. The two of them did have some rather extreme and unusual obstacles to their love that they could never manage to overcome, which would necessitate some equally unusual coping strategies. Would they have had a relationship based on power exchange, as we define it today, before and after the violent annulment of their affair? That's an interesting conundrum. I'm inclined to think so. Here."

He pulls Abelard's *Historia Calamitatum* from out of the pile.

"*Quid plura? Primum domo una coniungimur, postmodum animo. Sub occasione itaque discipline, amori penitus vaccabamus, et secretos recessus, quos amor optabat, studium lectionis offerebat. Apertis itaque libris, plura de amore quam de lectione verba se ingerebant, plura erant oscula quam sententie; sepius ad sinus quam ad libros reducebantur manus, crebrius oculos amor in se reflectebat quam lectio in scripturam dirigebat. Quoque minus suspicionis haberemus, verbera quandoque dabat amor, non furor, gratia, non ira, que omnium ungentorum suavitatem transcenderent. Quid denique? Nullus a cupidis intermissus est gradus amoris, et si quid insolitum amor excogitare potuit, est additum; et quo minus ista fueramus experti gaudia, ardentius illis insistebamus, et minus in fastidium vertebantur.*

"Or, loosely translated: *Our hands sought our books less than they sought each other's bodies; love drew our eyes together far more than the lesson drew them to the pages of our texts. In order that there might be no suspicion, I did sometimes beat her, but it was in love, not anger; the marks I left were the marks, not of wrath, but of a tenderness greater than the sweetest perfume. What followed? Everything we could imagine doing to each other.*

"In order that there be no suspicion? Really? When the blows were hard enough to leave marks? I *highly* doubt deflecting suspicion was the motivation, especially given that he confesses to trying every single possible sexual practice imaginable with Heloise, in the sentence immediately following." He smiles. "I wouldn't rule it out. I think it would be silly to say bizarre love games did not exist until some arbitrary point in modern history – that would be like saying the human race didn't invent sex until the twentieth century, and as long as sex has been around, I'm reasonably sure variations on it have likewise been around. And the two of them were, after all, the foremost academics and intellectuals of their day. The BDSM subculture seems to have always had a higher-than-average percentage of intellectuals in it than the general population as a whole. Awkward intellectuals. Perhaps we gravitate to the imposed structure as much as we do to the intellectual stimulation of twisting and bending sex to the dictates of our own imaginations. We thrive when we have fetters to wear, outlines to follow, roles to play. We're graceless, otherwise. Like stilt walkers on a field of eggs and land mines."

"Geeks and nerds have a tropism for kink? Yes, that would certainly explain us. Maybe not every pervert in the world, but that's us." I go back to my outlining and quote hunting.

The living room is silent except for the clanks and hisses of the ancient steam heater coming to life, and of my pen scratching paper.

It's so delightfully warm in here. I don't even need to wear four layers of clothing or a coat when I visit, despite the recent cold snap. So different from my own apartment.

"You should be back in college," he says softly. "I love coming up with essay assignments for you to entertain you, but ultimately, your mind needs more challenging than can come from one tutor who doesn't even have any formal ties to academia beyond a master's degree in library science. You need to use your academic inclinations. Did you envision a lifetime of telemarketing when you were a girl, dreaming of what you would be when you grew up?"

"College professor," I reply shortly. This isn't a subject I like to talk about much.

"You won't get that without a degree – preferably a doctoral degree, for most colleges and universities. You need to get back into college."

"Can't do that without money. Can't get money without financial aid. According to Uncle Sam, I can't get financial aid until I'm classified as financially independent, which can't happen until I'm a grad student, a veteran, a head of household, married, or twenty-four years old. That's what my college's financial aid office told me when I begged for emergency assistance after my parents disowned me, anyway." Not that I'd expected much success – the few students I know who received any kind of financial aid told me horror stories about how hard it was to get either need-based scholarships or help applying for federal assistance at our college – but I'd had to try anyway. And at least it had bought me a couple of weeks more time. That was time enough for my sisters in the sorority to brainstorm ways to find me new accommodations since only students could live in the dorms. "I won't be twenty-four for another two years. I can't skip straight past an undergraduate degree to apply to a grad school. The other options are not options."

"Two years is not that much time; we've been together for nearly a year, and it doesn't feel like much time at all, does it?" he asks in a quiet voice. "In the meantime, you might want to try attending the local university. The spring semester has already started, so it's a little too late for now, but you could apply to enroll in summer classes, or to start in the fall. One course would cost approximately three hundred dollars in tuition. That's not so bad. You haven't told me how much your monthly rent is, but it probably costs more than that per month. Taking a course or two every semester would help you build up your transcript and maybe get a few academic references, and you could use those to get a scholarship somewhere, or at least a place in the honors program of one of the better state universities here."

"I can't even afford groceries most of the time," I snap. "How can I possibly afford college tuition?"

He takes a deep breath. "You could move in with me."

My jaw drops.

"You're not serious."

"I'm very serious. It's something I've been stewing over for some time, now. I definitely have my reservations, but the arrangement makes sense from a purely financial perspective. Take whatever money you spend on your apartment rent now, and you can use it to pay for college. Factor in what you'd save on your other monthly expenses, and you could probably even manage to come up with enough tuition money to attend college full-time, if you opt for a monthly tuition payment plan – although between the demands of your job and the readings and occult study I plan to keep giving you, I'd recommend taking no more than two courses at a time, to make sure you will still have time for some sleep at night.

There are other practical benefits as well. Food, for instance. It worries me that I can still count your ribs just by looking at them. I give you food for your cupboard, but do you eat any of it? Then there's the neighborhood you live in. I imagine you would prefer to live on a street that did not have gunfire waking you up on random nights. I know *I'd* prefer you to live on a street that lacked gunfire. For some strange reason, I like the idea of you not getting shot."

"My street is safer than that," I protest. "You have to go a few blocks south or west before you really have to worry about gangs. Where I live, most of the loud noise at night just comes from drunks getting into fights."

If I move in with him, I sacrifice my independence.

I have been living on my own since my parents locked the door behind me. For a brief while after the furnished studio my sorority sisters found for me got sold to a new owner, who jacked up its monthly rent by two hundred dollars, which meant I had to move out, independence meant living on the streets, looking for space in shelters, bouncing from the living room floor or dorm room floor of one friend to another until I finally found a cheap efficiency in a rundown section of town, near the railroad tracks. I gave up everything for my freedom. I don't want to lose it. What *Magister* and I do together might involve a temporary kind of giving up of freedom, but ultimately, I belong to myself – the arrangement was at my instigation, and he doesn't own me. He might have me under his domination during lessons, and often as a part of lovemaking, but I am still my own person, and I have always been free to negotiate my own terms or to end the relationship altogether.

Moving in with him threatens this. If things sour between us, where would I go?

And how do I maintain my own space when I am permanently a part of his?

No.

"Believe me, I have mixed feelings as well," he says. "However, from a practical and financial perspective, this seems to be the most sensible approach to take. I think we can work it out if we keep in mind that the purpose of this is specifically to get you back into college, rather than to make you a kept woman. Something tells me you'd like it even less if I offered to pay your tuition directly, although I suppose if you'd rather I charge you rent for moving in here, I could. I can't afford to cover both your housing and your university classes, though."

He's right about my not wanting him to pay for my tuition. The thought of moving in with him for free feels uncomfortably like mooching; letting him pay for my tuition would make me his sugar baby.

Damn it.

"Why are you pushing for this?"

"It's the only way I can think of to help you get your dreams back." He shakes his head. "I can't become a new dream for you. I can't replace your ambitions. I don't *want* to replace them. You need more than I can give you, not that anyone should make another human being into the embodiment of their ambitions, anyway. Can you think of another way to get back into academia, short of waiting for your twenty-fourth birthday, which is what you have apparently been doing so far? You have told me of a calling to teach, to guide. How do you see yourself following this path, if you try to do so through me? You can't be my student forever... I'm sorry. I don't mean to be pushy. Well. Perhaps I do, but I don't mean to make you feel like you have no choice in the matter. I've wrestled with this problem for a while. I simply don't see any other way to help you get what you want."

I try to answer that. Of course, I can't. There are no good answers.

"Aren't you worried that we might try to kill each other if we try to live together in close quarters?" I ask him.

He shakes his head. "We're together on the weekends, and we haven't killed each other yet. I think we can find a way to give you enough personal space that you can escape to it when you need to, while preserving enough space for me to escape to when I need to recharge. I'm more worried about Stockholm syndrome. You seem to lead a very isolated existence. We've talked about that. Getting people together for a gaming session was the first time I saw any sign of your having a social life that might not include me, and even so, two of my co-workers and I were part of the session, so I'm not sure it should count. If I'm the only person you see, other than superficial interactions with co-workers, you're mostly dependent on me for your friendships and social transactions, and the fact that we have a relationship based in part on power exchange makes the dynamic between us extremely intense. The spiritual bond we've formed as a result of our magickal work only adds to that intensity. I worry that if we live together, the intensity will overwhelm you entirely. It's the reason I hadn't invited you to move in with me before, when you had to vacate your old attic apartment."

"Isn't Stockholm syndrome something that happens under conditions of captivity and hostage-taking, though?"

"Yes. It also happens in situations of domestic abuse, because the abusive partner manages to cut the victim off from friends and family and creates a situation of social and financial dependence through isolation. Obviously, I'm not abusing you in this relationship, but the intensity of our personal dynamic combined with your being more or less a recluse could make for a bad situation. I'm worried about accidentally swallowing you up."

Oh, God.

I FLICK ON THE lights and open the door. We are using the back entrance, having taken the narrow back stairs that were the only entrance to the illegal attic apartment on the third floor, back when it *was* an apartment, but we stop at the second floor rather than climbing up to the attic. That unfortunately gives him a perfect view of my kitchen as we walk in (there are only two roaches on the wall by the stove, surprising me – they usually start to get frisky in the late afternoon).

Expressionlessly, *Magister* fiddles with the knobs on the nonfunctional gas stove, and the hot water handle on the sink that only produces cold water. I've been letting a small but steady trickle of frigid water drool out of the faucet for several days now; I don't want the pipes to freeze and burst. I have no idea when my landlord would get around to calling a plumber to fix the problem were that to happen, and I'd probably be charged for it, anyway.

We walk through the bare living room to get to my bedroom. There might have been some roaches in the living room. I've never paid attention, having had nothing to put in it. The same goes for the second bedroom.

He takes in my bedroom as I gather up my worldly possessions, such as they are. At least, thanks to the little ceramic heater I splurged on last month, the air in here does not make his breath fog, the way it does in the rest of the apartment (he would be seeing my apartment during the week we had a severe cold front sweep in, cold enough to make breath fog in the unheated rooms – usually, now, it's cold, but it's not *this* cold). The heater isn't powerful and doesn't warm the room well, but it's better than nothing at all. I do my best to give it some help by keeping my room well sealed with a rolled towel shoved up against the door. Drafts don't get in from there. I also have newspaper taped over two of the three windows for extra insulation, and I've put plastic sheeting on the third. If I stay in bed with the electric blanket on, I can take off my coat, and sometimes even my sweater.

I'm not supposed to leave the heater on when I'm not in the room. Abandoning an electric heater is a fire hazard. However, if I turn it off when I'm gone, my room never gets warmed. It's UL-listed, so that makes it kind of safe to walk away from if I absolutely have to, surely. And it's a ceramic heater. And it's new. It's not the kind of heater that's likely to make sparks.

"This... this is where you have lived since November?"

"Yes."

"How much have you been paying for it?"

"Three-fifty. Not bad for a two-bedroom apartment. I would have preferred staying in the attic; it was only a hundred and eighty-five per month, and it cost less to keep the utilities on, but the health department made my landlord evict me from it because it wasn't zoned for rental."

"You're paying for all your utilities?"

"Everything but water and sewer."

"I presume that's why you have no heat. I wish you had said something earlier. I could have told you how to apply for heating assistance if you didn't want to accept help from me." He looks out the window at the setting sun, and at the street, with its sidewalks covered with broken bottles and used diapers. Then at my bedroom again. "This must have been hard to adjust to, after the wealth you grew up taking for granted. Oh, my *eromene*, why did you not say anything? This? *This* is where you have been living this past year?"

"Well, you know what they say. Freedom isn't free."

"No. I suppose it's not." His voice is shaking. "Well. Let's get everything packed up. I'm going to go to the kitchen to see if there is any food we need to take back with us, since I have had reason to suspect you might not have been eating the grocery items I gave you to keep you from starvation."

"Just a box of granola bars."

"I'll get them. *I am not going to let this happen again.* Your living conditions are endangering your health and your well-being. You should have told me. I do not like that you have done everything in your power to conceal the misery of your situation from me, and we *are* going to have a discussion about that when we get home. Concealing an unpleasant truth is a form of lying by omission. Lying to me is unacceptable, no matter what the reason was for lying. You knew that. The foundation of our relationship, you will recall, is perfect love and perfect trust. I made that clear from the very beginning. We do not lie to each other. We do not keep secrets from each other. People who trust each other do not conceal things from each other. I thought you trusted me." He sighs. "Suddenly, I feel better about asking you to move in with me. It may not be comfortable for you, but at least it will keep you safe and well-fed."

He leaves the room. I hear him opening and closing cupboard doors. He's looking for food.

I didn't lie to him about that. There really is only a box of granola bars left.

I sink down onto the floor, sitting hard, and crush my head against my knees. It doesn't make the room disappear, or make me disappear from the room, but I can at least wish.

Oh, that this too, too solid flesh would melt.

As if things weren't bad enough, when he comes back, granola box in hand, I start to cry. "I'm sorry. I know I should have said something about my utilities being cut off, and my not being able to afford anything. I just didn't want you to worry about me. Or – or feel sorry for me –"

The wooden floor is an interesting study of discoloration. I'm not sure what needed to be ripped up from it after some earlier tenant moved out. Soiled carpet? Shredded linoleum?

He kneels in front of me and tips my chin up with his finger so that I am forced to look him in the eyes. "I know you are proud," he says softly, "but there is such a thing as going too far. I trusted you to be honest and share the important details of your life with me. As your *Magister*, I need to know these things, because they may affect the lessons I give you; as your lover, I am very hurt that you would not tell me about your sufferings. I think I've mentioned that it hurts me when you hurt. How could it not? You have crossed a line. *You will not do this again.* Do you understand me? We will talk about the consequences when we get back home."

"Yes, *Magister*," I sob.

"You are forgiven. Well. Let's get your things and help you escape your slumlord. Your new dwellings will not be a mansion like the one you grew up in, but I think we can agree that they will be a vast improvement over this."

My belongings, aside from about twenty plastic milk crates filled with books, fit in two old, battered suitcases, both of which are now sitting in his living room. My landlord can worry about my old mattress. I wasn't that attached to it; used mattresses are easy enough to come by. If you don't want to spend fifty dollars at a thrift store, you can just go curb crawling, which is how I acquired mine.

My landlord can also have the toaster oven my ex-girlfriend left behind when she left me.

My lease is officially broken. It's going to hurt my credit rating, but I'm not planning on applying for any credit cards, given my likely inability to afford making monthly payments on anything I borrow. I don't like the idea of breaking my formal agreement to lease the apartment for a set period, though. An agreement is an agreement. This just doesn't feel right.

It does, however, get me back into college in the summer.

Going through the recent course catalog *Magister* picked up for me is like being let loose in a candy store. It's been so long, so very long, since I sat in on a real lecture, or took a seminar. I want to sign up for everything, even the math classes and the paralegal studies classes that I know I have no aptitude for and won't ever actually use.

He watches me as I sit on the couch circling classes, my unpacked bags completely forgotten; when I emerge from my daydreams of lectures and seminars to look back at him, his eyes are wistful.

THERE ARE, OF COURSE, some nice things about moving in with him. Aside from my not having to constantly worry about how to make too-short ends meet, there is *Magister* himself. Every day, he cooks for us (unless I'm taking a turn in the kitchen, which he has me do every few days or so – he wants to get me comfortable working from a cookbook and making meals that don't rely on pouches or boxes of something cheap and preprocessed, for some reason). Every day, we do our *tai ch'i* together in the living room. Every day, we read to each other. He reads me poetry or short stories (not all of which are erotic in nature) or essays he thinks I might find interesting; I usually read him poetry when I do the reading.

His work schedule generally involves afternoons and evenings, so it's compatible with my own evening shift at the newspaper call center (I've cut my hours at his request – he thought the dark circles under my eyes indicated a lack not just of nutrients, but also rest, and it was his opinion that I ought to get caught up on the rest I've been denying myself, especially if I'm recovering from food insecurity and cold exposure. He was correct in his assessment. Damn him). So, every night, I have him.

Every night, I have him. And every night, when he is done with me, I tie our wrists together before we sleep, our hands entwined, our flesh united by a length of securely fastened black silk.

THE LIVING ROOM STEREO plays Rimsky-Korsakov's *Scheherazade.* We're eating truffles and celebrating Valentine's Day, although it's a week after the official date. The main reason for this is that we like chocolate, but we also like buying said chocolate on clearance. It makes no sense to pay extra money just to celebrate a holiday on time, especially not when the holiday is a commercially hyped celebration of a romantic love that we two celebrate every day that we're together anyway. Chocolate gets celebrated here on a fairly regular basis as well, come to think of it.

"Roses," he murmurs into my ear, as he slides a chocolate cherry truffle into my mouth. "It wouldn't be Valentine's Day without roses."

"It's a bit late to run out to the florist." I lick chocolate from his finger.

"We already have the roses."

"We do?" I start unbuttoning his shirt, to run my fingertips lightly along the nerve endings he showed me. When I start flicking my tongue along one of his nipples, his breath quickens. I like the way it sounds. "Maybe I could get you to turn a nice shade of rose. The color would rather suit you." I start unfastening his belt, then his trousers, and use my lips to coax his member out through the flap in his boxers. It's a shame there's no chocolate syrup nearby. He's pleasant enough without chocolate syrup, but the holiday we're celebrating makes chocolate syrup seem appropriate.

He reaches for my head. "Not that I object to your ideas for the course of the evening, but let's save them for later. No, I was thinking of different roses."

He runs his fingers through my hair caressingly before grabbing a handful and holding me firmly in place, making me inhale sharply. "I was thinking of the roses I gave you for Yule."

Oh.

Those roses.

I gulp. "That does seem fair," I say, my voice carefully steady. "It has been almost two months since you gave me my Yule present, hasn't it?"

"Yes," he agrees, and somehow manages to rise off the couch while still holding me by the hair. He lets go of me just long enough to pull up and refasten his trousers, then takes me by the hair again. I have no choice but to follow him when he pulls me along to the center of the room. "Strip," he says, in that incongruously soft, velvet voice of his. It's amazing how many different ways that voice can send chills up my spine, some of them more comfortable than others. The chill I feel now is not one of the comfortable ones.

As I go about removing my clothes, he disappears into the bedroom and returns with the silver-handled flogger, two sets of manacles, and rope. "If I was feeling particularly evil, I'd make you use your own effort to stay in place," he says, "but I'm not feeling that evil. Besides, I think that would involve unrealistic expectations on my part. I doubt even you could hold still for what I'm about to do."

Oh. Thank you. You're so very kind.

He arranges me over the wooden chest and ties the rope between the manacles and around the chest and the bottoms of my thighs, just near my knees, so that I can't move anything other than my head. I'm not sure how he's fastened the manacles at my ankles, to keep me from lifting my lower legs, but he's managed to fasten them to something. "You're still far too thin in your upper body," he muses. "I can only safely target the area between your hips and your knees right now. Given the way your voice carries when you are not under silence, I think we'll also have to address that. It wouldn't be fair to not allow you the release of screaming tonight. Would you prefer a gag, or something to bite down on?"

"Biting," I reply faintly. I imagine the repoussé silver of the whip handle, roses shining in candlelight. I will suffer for this beauty tonight. I doubt it will be the last time that I do so. At some point, I should probably reflect on this.

He disappears for a moment to go into the bedroom and returns with his riding crop, which he puts between my teeth. It is covered with bite marks that hadn't been there a year ago. It's been put to this use many times.

I whimper. Some Stoic I make. It occurs to me that I've shed more tears in the months we've been together than I had in all the years of my life combined before I met *Magister*. I'm not quite sure what to make of that. For the most part, they haven't been tears of sadness, exactly, and I'm not sure what to make of that, either. It is just an odd fact: until I met *Magister* and gave myself to him for apprenticeship, I seldom cried. I could go for years without shedding a single tear.

"I think ten blows would be appropriate," he says. "It would certainly be at the upper limit of your endurance, but I'm reasonably sure you can handle it. I'll count them out loud to help you know that they won't go on forever. Later in life, should you inflict this on one of your partners, please remember that the business end was designed for causing two things: pain, and lacerations. Go light. Do not lay into a person with all your might when you wield it, do not allow the whip's weight and momentum to escape your control. You can flay a person to ribbons that way, and I'm not being metaphorical when I say that. Make no mistake about it: the handle may have its own recreational uses, but as a whip, this is not meant to be a toy. It was designed as a weapon. Be very careful. Use minimal force only, or if you want to play with momentum, step far enough back from your partner so that only the steel tips make contact with their flesh. And then beware of wraparound so that you don't accidentally tear your skin apart. Speaking of which, I recommend testing it out on your own skin, by yourself, to get an idea of how much force to use. It will be a distinctly unpleasant experience for you, but it would be the responsible thing to do. Your whip is as dangerous as it is pretty."

Lacerations?

"Brace yourself, *eromene,*" he murmurs. "One."

When the steel tips bite into my flesh, I scream behind the stick and bite down hard enough to make my jaw ache.

I don't think my brain could even have encompassed this.

"Two."

After the fifth stroke, I am sobbing hysterically.

I STAGGER, MY ARM draped over his shoulders. My knees are so wobbly that I can barely walk. My vision is blurred from the tears I am still shedding. He has to help me to lie down before he can start performing basic first aid on my wounded backside: warm soapy water, followed by a medicated antiseptic ointment that, blessedly, has a topical anesthetic in it. I don't know how I will be able to fall asleep tonight. I've rested on top of injuries he's left before, but they were never quite this extensive.

When his fingers enter me, I moan.

"I thought you might need some consolation," he says softly. "Is this a good consolation?"

"Oh, yes," I cry out, as I rock my hips to get him deeper into me. "Console me more." My sobs become slightly crazed laughter; my laughter becomes sighs and gasps; my sighs and gasps become ecstasy.

Our days pass in poetry and philosophy and meditation, our nights in love and pain. We move together in a golden glow, bathed in sweetness.

BINAH

I write the check and sign my life over to the clerk at the counter. Unlike full-time students, who pay a flat rate tuition, my credit hours are multiplied by a dollar value and added to my matriculation fee and student activity fees. At least I'm able to pay for my eight credits of fall semester study on a monthly plan. I had to pay for the single composition course I took this summer up front.

Tuition indeed costs less than the rent for my old two-bedroom apartment. It would still be more than I could afford if I wasn't accepting *Magister's* help.

I do need to pay for my books and materials, but one nice thing about sticking to humanities courses is that the reading material is generally cheaper than science textbooks and career-oriented textbooks are. English literature, philosophy, and religion classes have particularly cheap reading material, at least, when it's the original classics rather than something put into a Norton anthology. Anthologies cost a little more.

Out of the air-conditioned climate of the Office of the Registrar, into the August heat. The campus bookstore awaits.

Classified as I am as a part-time, nontraditional student, I am not eligible for admittance into the honors college, which limits my choice selection somewhat, but I was still able to find an art history survey course yesterday when I picked out my courses for the upcoming semester at the registrar's office. It's a repeat of the course I took as a freshman at my last college, but the hours for the Introduction to Art History course were convenient. It should be an easy A. I already pretty much know the material. There had still been some space left in an upper-level course on existentialist philosophy, too, which I'll need to study formally sometime if I stay in my major, so I'd grabbed that before it was gone.

As it turns out, the Existentialism course uses cheap paperback reprints of the original writings of various philosophers, just like I'd expected it would. It doesn't even look like the books have been marked up any from the price I'd pay if I was buying them in a regular bookstore in one of our local malls.

The art history course has an expensive textbook, though. It's a different one from the one I had the last time I took an introductory survey course in art history, so I don't have the option of just using my old textbook like I'd hoped I could when I signed up for the class in the first place.

Maybe I can study in the bookstore for the first week or two until I can afford to purchase it. If that proves too difficult, I will ask *Magister* to pay for the book, then reimburse him – it still makes me feel awkward asking him for money, but I did agree months ago, after a long and emotionally painful discussion, that trying to do everything on my own is only acceptable when it does not hurt me. If my grades suffer, that constitutes harm, as harmful to me as starvation, freezing, and overwork.

And harming myself that way, it has been pointed out, makes it hard for him to trust me, especially when the harm would be prevented by my asking him for support that he can easily provide, and my trusting him to not look down on me for asking.

Harming myself is its own punishment, but its consequence is that I must earn back his trust.

"I can't *believe* I've found another girl gamer," the woman who sits next to me in my existentialism class gushes. "Are there any openings in your party?"

I can't believe my good luck.

My ex, promising to stay in touch with me via regular letters and phone calls that I'm fairly sure she will never make, moved to another state with her boyfriend because he wanted to be closer to his family, and she wanted to be closer to him.

That left the group deprived of two players. I'd been wondering how to drag in more people.

"I have a couple of openings. It's funny you mentioned being astonished to find another woman who plays role-playing games – there are two other women in my gaming group. In fact, the only man in the group now is my, um, boyfriend. It makes for some interesting dynamics."

There are no sexist jerks in the group, no players who see gaming as a pastime for male geeks only with no female players allowed in the troglodyte cave. My players have told me that it's refreshing to be in a group where they are allowed to play something other than healers or sexy rogue courtesans, and to actually speak up and contribute to the game as it plays, rather than lurking quietly and meekly until needed. I find it even more refreshing to get to be the game master. I've had so many ideas for games, and no opportunity to use them until now. "Are you free on Sunday afternoons?"

"I am. So is my boyfriend. Can I drag him along? He plays, too. And he's done eldritch horror campaigns before."

"Since you'll be replacing two exiting players, that works. Perfect timing."

She has a boyfriend. I don't know why that's disappointing. True, she is not only a really cool person who's another philosophy major and into gaming, she's also a *cute blonde goth chick* who's a philosophy major and into gaming – but I'm taken. And really, I don't have room in my heart, or free time, for anyone else right now. I'm just noticing that she's cute. So why am I disappointed? Shame on me.

"Awesome! We'll be there!" she says.

I can't wait.

I STRUGGLE AGAINST THE manacles. Every time the sharpened quill presses down into my skin, the sharp scratching sensation makes my body jerk. I can't believe he isn't drawing blood. Who would have thought the sharpened end of an ostrich feather – a *feather*, for crying out loud – could be so nasty? All the nerves along my arms and torso are on fire.

He presses the tip against the pressure point under my collarbone again and drags it along the nerve endings and skin he's scratched to angry, weeping redness. I hiss.

"Maybe it's time to give you a bit of a break," he muses.

Yes. Let's do that. That's an excellent idea.

He starts tickling the raw welts with the feather end. Better – even though I hate being tickled, it's still better. Much, much better.

"Can I ask a question?" We're not doing this as part of my magickal training, so I have my voice. Over the past few months or so of living together, the lines between formal training and informal lovemaking have blurred considerably, but there are still some boundaries we've kept intact, one of them being that if a circle is cast, energy work of any kind is performed, or actual lessons have commenced, I remain silent and attentive. He thinks the formalities help keep me from losing myself and my identity in a romantic haze of submissive ecstasy because the formalities separate what is fundamentally me from what is a position I happen to be in, something of critical importance now that I am part of his household rather than living independently, and I'm inclined to agree with him.

He smiles. I'm sure I'm only imagining that his smile looks like something the wolf would have flashed at Little Red Riding Hood. "You can certainly ask."

"Why is it that when you tie me down or otherwise restrain me, you so often spread-eagle me?"

"Several reasons, although that was a nice reminder to employ a bit more variety in the future. The first, and simplest, is that I happen to think you look quite fetching that way. I enjoy feasting on you with my eyes. Second is that it's a very convenient position, in that it creates all sorts of vulnerabilities. Your skin, for instance, is stretched taut, making it easier to mark and making that marking, regardless of what form it takes, more physically intense."

"You mean it hurts more."

"Of course."

He smiles again, although it would be more accurate to describe it as a cheerful baring of teeth. Definitely wolfish. I was absolutely not imagining it. I wonder how many years it took him to perfect that "smile." I hope he's never accidentally broken into that smile in front of any young children, or any overly imaginative or nervous adults, for that matter.

"Also, it's easier to fit you onto the futon while still supporting your extremities if I spread-eagle you. In some stretched positions, your feet dangle over the edge, and that's a form of discomfort I would rather spare you, as it can be distracting, not to mention bad for your circulation. I need to accommodate your height properly. Then, of course, there's the way arranging you like this leaves all sorts of body parts exposed. Your imagination can probably supply enough details, there."

I sigh melodramatically.

"Well. Maybe I can provide a bit of a demonstration." His weight presses into me as he covers me with his body; our lips meet, then our tongues, and I moan into him when his hand reaches down between my legs and illustrates, over and over, just how vulnerable I am.

"And finally," he says, unfastening and shedding his trousers, "the spread-eagle position has a certain amount of esoteric significance, or at least, it can. Our souls are stars, each of us burning brightly in this universe with the spark of the divine; we are all, every one of us, stars. It is our task to remember this. We must learn to hear the music of the spheres and our place in the sacred harmony. When you are restrained in this position, you bear a rough resemblance to a five-pointed star. It's a visual and kinesthetic reminder of your divine fire." As he enters me, he asks, "Did you know your aura glows when you climax?"

"It does?"

"It does," he says, and proceeds to set about demonstrating it to me.

"HAVE YOU STARTED YOUR college hunt yet?" he asks me out of the blue.

I blink at him. "What? But I'm already back in college."

"You'll be twenty-four in just a little over a year from now. That means you'll qualify as financially independent, and you'll be able to apply for financial aid without a parental co-signer. I looked into the details after you told me how that worked, because things have changed a little since I was in college. I do remember it took me the better part of a year to look for graduate schools, though, and longer than that when I was searching for places where I could get my bachelor's degree. I know you've only been attending classes at the university here for a few months, now, but have you thought about where you want to apply the credits you're earning here?"

"No. I haven't thought that far. I could just stay here, couldn't I? That might be easiest."

"You could. You could go full-time and then apply to be part of the honors college; if you are a part of it, it would look good on your record when you send off your grad school applications. You would have more opportunities at a different university, though. A wider selection of classes in the humanities, since the university here is geared more toward practical degrees than degrees in the liberal arts, which I'm sure you've noticed; you'd have better professors in a private college, also better name recognition, both of which improve your chances of being accepted into a good graduate school. I don't think you'd need to worry about cost – there are scholarships everywhere, as well as grants for people who show obvious financial need. And it wasn't so long ago that you were telling me how much you were looking forward to searching for a new college where you could get a fresh start."

"But why can't I just stay here with *you?*"

"You like the idea of living with me indefinitely, now?" He smiles. "I would have thought I'd be impossible to live with."

"This comes as a surprise? I love you. I am yours. Yes."

"Oh, *eromene*! That you want to be a part of my future, and not just my present, is a delight. We should talk about this, though, because I am not sure that what you envision for a future with me meets my vision of a future that contains you. Were you... were you asking about making things more formal, more permanent?"

His face is either glowing or blushing. I'm not sure which. Meanwhile, I'm not sure whether seeing his hopes bloom delights me or makes me uncomfortable.

"Maybe. I don't know. I hadn't thought about it. I just know I want to be with you."

"Ah. Of course."

Great. Now we're both confused. Also, I might have just broken his heart. And maybe broken my heart, but I'll determine that latter bit when I'm not confused.

"I don't want to go away. My first girlfriend and I didn't work out because it was long distance and it hurt too much to never be able to see each other."

He sighs. "Did it occur to you that, unlike your first girlfriend, I have a car, and I can visit you on weekends if you're only an hour or two away?"

"Uh." That actually hadn't occurred to me.

"If you want to stay near me, an Ivy League university is out of the question. However, I can think of at least ten colleges and universities that are only about an hour away, at most," he says, "some of them quite prestigious. It wouldn't hurt to start ordering admissions brochures and looking through them now, to get a better idea of what might be a good fit for you. Also, perhaps now would be a good time to think about whether you want to live off-campus if you go off to college somewhere a little way away from here, or if you want to live in a dorm. If you don't mind my visiting your dorm, I won't mind. Although I think it would be better to bring you back here for our dates, all things considered... At any rate, it's in the future. There's plenty of time. But it doesn't hurt to do a little research in advance."

THERE IS NOW A box of college brochures taking up space near the futon in our bedroom. It's packed to the gills with course catalogs and prospecti. Once I've narrowed down my choices to fewer than ten institutions, I'll put the literature from each place in a folder and keep my folders in alphabetical order, but for now, it's a jumbled mess.

I have tentatively put my former college plus seven other colleges and universities aside as top choices. Most are about an hour away if you drive on the highways or take a Greyhound bus.

I'm hoping all the options I'm looking at, whether public or private, have good departments of financial aid. My former alma mater probably still doesn't, but it won't hurt to apply for a full scholarship after submitting my financial aid paperwork. At worst, my request will be turned down, and I'll have to go somewhere else. Mostly I'm considering it as an option because I had a high grade point average when I was there, so simply getting accepted back into the college and into the honors program should be fairly easy.

Limiting myself to a relatively small geographical area that I can access on my own using the local interlinked public transit networks, or failing that, a Greyhound coach, means I won't be able to consider several small but excellent rural colleges, due to their lack of access; and I almost wish I had a car of my own, until I remember that for me, my financial priorities place having a roof over my head higher than having transportation, if a choice must be made, which, so far, it invariably has. I probably shouldn't even be considering rural colleges at all, but the two I have set aside for future consideration, my former alma mater included, both have music conservatories, and are at least both on Greyhound routes. I miss singing. I miss studying music. It would be so nice to belong to a campus that has its own conservatory of music. And again, my former college is likely to accept me again if I apply for re-entry, so there's that.

Further narrowing the field is my need for room and board. I won't be able to afford to rent an apartment and commute, especially if I'm living in a city. Cities are more expensive than small towns. I could probably afford a furnished room or a small apartment in a small town, but all problems with the financial aid departments of the rural colleges I short-listed aside, the thought of living in a small town again makes me nervous. I'd feel safer living on campus if I'm in a small town, even if I can afford to rent off-campus housing. Visions of next-door neighbors with shotguns, and of pick-up truck drivers who yell "fag" at me as they drive past me, dance in my head.

(I have no idea why the locals did that, when I was living in town near my former college. I don't think I look like a man. I'm tall enough, okay, and I don't have much of a figure, so from behind I might look like a scrawny fifteen-year-old-boy, maybe, but I'd be a fifteen-year-old boy with almost hip-length hair, which I have a hard time imagining being an expected sight in a small, conservative town in the Midwest, especially one where the locals all seem to know or at least recognize each other. Once, when I got yelled at this way, I even felt compelled to call back, "I'm not a *fag*, I'm a *dyke* – get it right!" Lesbians would take exception to that self-description on my part since I'm bi, but correct grammar does require correct gender. Fortunately for me, correcting my harassers did not inspire them to stop their vehicle, get out of it, and beat me to a pulp on the sidewalk. I really ought to watch my mouth).

Although I have no idea which one it will be yet when the time comes, I think I want to apply to a single college via early acceptance, rather than simultaneously to several colleges and universities later in the academic year. I'm more likely to get approved if I show my keen interest in the institution, and it would give me a chance to get a jump on setting up financial aid. Besides, if I only initially apply to one college or university, and that place accepts me, I will only need to pay for one copy of my standardized test scores and transcripts from every institution I've attended, rather than for several copies, and I'll only have to pay one application fee. If the college or university of my choice turns me down, I'll worry about coming up with several hundred dollars for necessary multiple copies of documents, but hopefully, it won't come to that.

The local university here will be a perfectly good fallback if none of my top choices both admits me and gives me adequate tuition assistance. *Magister* thinks I'm selling myself short, especially since there aren't many course selections in philosophy, and attending college here full-time will require me to consider changing my major, but it never hurts to have a safety school as an option. For that matter, I'm not as deeply and profoundly attached to my declared philosophy major as I could be. English, Classics, art history, and music history are just as interesting. The former can be studied cheaply pretty much anywhere. Most colleges and universities offer English courses.

WE'RE CLUSTERED AROUND THE card table again. There are only five of us now – me, *Magister*, the other two librarians, and my classmate. When she and her boyfriend broke it off in an acrimonious sort of way back in October, she got custody of Sunday gaming nights. Some of that custody arrangement might have been due to his character's having lost so much sanity after summoning an Elder God that the character wound up permanently institutionalized as a drooling, gibbering wreck, an encounter only even survivable by his making an astronomically good save roll; but had also recently picked up a new part-time job that was going to get in the way of his gaming, so he didn't really have a good reason to fight for his spot at the gaming table.

Interestingly, this means *Magister* is now the only male in an otherwise all-female group of role players. That doesn't happen very often. If I'd been in his position, I think I would have made one obligatory teasing comment about having a harem, just to see what kind of reaction I'd get, but so far, he's refrained.

"Make a perception check," I tell my classmate, who is playing an archaeologist. It's a fairly easy challenge – the party needs to find out somehow that there's something a little off about the hieroglyphics on the wall of the pyramid. If all else fails, another character can spot the alien drawings. In the meantime, though, my classmate needs to roll, and she needs to borrow my dice, because while she got custody of Sunday game attendance, her ex-boyfriend got custody of all the dice. She still hasn't replaced her dice.

It was an extremely messy break-up.

When I pass her my twenty-sided die, our hands brush up against each other.

"Sorry," we both say, more or less at the same time. Of course, this makes us apologize again, with similar timing.

I feel blood rush to my cheeks. No doubt I'm blushing as hard as she is. Her roll is successful.

THE GRAPE AND YOGURT salad chills on a shelf in the refrigerator. That was the easiest dish to prepare. Everything else we're advance-prepping for our Yule feast – tiropitas, spanakopitas, and baklava – requires actual work.

If I roll any more phyllo dough, I think my arms will fall off. I have rolled so much phyllo dough that I know I will be dreaming of rolling pins and dough when I fall asleep tonight. I think I've rolled about eight feet of dough so far. If it hasn't been that much, that's only because after a couple of hours I lost track of how much dough I rolled. Maybe I've rolled more than eight feet. I can't tell.

Large plastic containers filled with ingredients sit on a section of the kitchen counter – feta cheese, parmesan cheese, ricotta cheese, and a thawed bag of spinach leaves. Next to them are cartons of eggs, freshly ground cinnamon sticks, the grater I used to grind the cinnamon, a massive jar of raw local honey, and, mixed in with sugar and cinnamon, several pounds of pistachios and walnuts that were a royal pain to chop fine, even using a blender. A saucepan containing several packages of butter I'd clarified earlier this morning sits on a warm stove burner to prevent the butter from firming up when we want to be able to drizzle it over pastry. It sits next to a smaller saucepan of homemade simple syrup that he had me cook up from rose water and sugar before I clarified the butter.

We're making everything from scratch this time. That is if my arms don't cramp up and freeze in mid-roll.

Magister is bent over a funnel, sprinkling herbs he ground in a mortar into a bottle of ouzo. Contrary to popular belief, real ouzo is not illegal to import into the United States, and it does not contain extract of opium poppies. Real ouzo is just absinthe without the wormwood, but with a lot more sugar added; it's an alcoholic jellybean. There are no controlled substances in ouzo.

That's why he's adding them himself.

"Exactly where does one find poppies and wormwood?" I ask. "Aren't they kind of illegal?"

"The dried poppies came from a craft store, where they're sold as flower-arranging supplies. The wormwood leaves and roots came from an occult supply catalog, which is also where I got the mugwort, which is a cousin of wormwood that is traditionally used to induce vivid dreams and prophetic visions. There's no 'kind of' about it. Both the opium poppies and the wormwood are illegal." He frowns. "Quite silly that wormwood is illegal. Wormwood and other plants that have thujone in them, and those would include oregano and sage, aren't even psychotropic – the notion that absinthe causes delusions and seizures is based on pure propaganda, and maybe on patent medicines labeled as absinthe that were tainted with wood-grain alcohol. Some of the things medicine show salesmen peddled were astonishingly unmedicinal... The closest thing to a consciousness-altering side effect from thujone is that some people who ingest it experience temporary mental clarity, like what you'd get from caffeine, only without the jitters, as thujone is not a stimulant. I suppose it would be possible to experience weird side effects or to poison yourself if you consumed an essential oil made from wormwood, because that would contain a much higher concentration of thujone, but only an idiot would want to do something like that."

He's cute when he harumphs.

"And the pieces of dried poppy I'm steeping in the bottle – if you made a tea from the entire poppy, it would probably be no stronger than a dose of codeine cough syrup, and drinking one shot of infused ouzo won't even give that high a dose. Really. The overall effect of this should be to create intense and lucid dreams if taken before bedtime, or clarity of thought and openness to visions if used before meditation, no more." He removes the funnel and recaps the bottle. "There. It should be ready to strain in about two weeks. It won't taste like ouzo anymore, of course, because the herbs I added are very bitter, but the taste will probably be the closest thing to real absinthe one might get, outside of Portugal. Let's see how you're coming along with the dough. Gracious. That's a lot of dough. After we're done making Greek pastries, there might be enough phyllo dough left over for me to make a strudel and use up the rest of the apples we have in the fridge. Ready to start?"

He pulls out baking pans and paintbrushes and brings the various ingredients to the table, and after oiling the pans, we get to work on pastry-making. He puts the kettle on for tea; when it starts to whistle, we each pour water into mugs so that we can drink herbal tea while preparing pastry. Almond Sunset. I bought it mostly for the romantic picture on the box, which made me think of Christopher Reeve and Jane Seymour in *Somewhere in Time*, but I found I like the taste, especially after I've added a little milk and sugar. It's one of the sweetest herbal teas I've ever had.

"There was a Greek restaurant a few streets down from my old college," I say as I brush honey on layers of phyllo, before sprinkling candied nuts on top of the honey and drizzling everything with melted butter, repeating as necessary. Usually, the honey does not come until the very end, when one pours simple syrup over the freshly sliced pastry, but *Magister* has always liked his baklava extra sticky and sweet, hence the extra step. If I'm careful applying the honey and the butter and don't go overboard the way I did the first time I helped him make baklava, the baklava should be crisp, rather than soggy. "The food was delicious – the proprietor came from the old country. I loved the tiropitas he made. They were huge, not like these little ones we're making. They were the size of large burritos, and came in ceramic dishes, piping hot, straight from the oven. Tiropitas the size of your head. One of those would fill you up for the rest of the evening. They were incredible. The two of you should have a cook-off someday. I don't know who would win."

"He's a Greek chef? And a first-generation immigrant, at that? Ah. Well. He'd probably win. Cooking is a hobby for me, one that I happen to love very much, especially when it's Mediterranean food, but it's still only a hobby. And Greek cuisine is not in my blood."

We continue to sprinkle cheese and spinach, layer dough, and paint honey. Eventually, we have several pans of tiropita and spanakopita that go into the oven, and two pans of carefully sliced baklava that he pours simple syrup over before cramming them into the large convection toaster oven that sits on a corner table. (The convection oven is his latest kitchen toy. I suspect he planned our Yule feast intending to test out the toy). The oven timer gets set for twenty minutes. The leftover ingredients go into the refrigerator, as will the pastries themselves, once they're done. Much of our handiwork will be stored in the freezer for later reheating. Meanwhile, we've run out of baking pans. Darn. I was hoping for more baklava. I've developed a taste for extra-sweet, extra-sticky baklava, myself.

"Much better than frozen burritos or breakfast pockets," he says. "And less expensive, in the long run. Food is generally cheaper and more nutritious when you are willing to do everything from scratch."

I sigh. "Yes, Mr. Miyagi."

"Just wait until you taste the pastitsio I'll make for you. I'm doing all the work on that one."

He reaches over the corner of the table to stroke my cheek. I close my eyes and lean into his caress. One of his fingers brushes against my mouth; it tastes of honey. I take his hand in mine and suck the honey from his finger.

"Mmm. More."

"More what?" he asks, amusement in his voice. "More honey, or more of me?"

"I'm not sure. I like both. You do go very well with honey."

"I do?"

"Mmm-hmm. You do." I feel a wicked smile start to play at the corners of my mouth. "The jar is just a bit out of reach. Could you help me get it?"

I start unbuckling him when he reaches across me for the honey jar, which causes him to chuckle. "I think I have an idea of what you have in mind."

"I'd be worried if you didn't." I dip into the jar with the tip of my finger, draw out some honey, and dip it onto the obvious target.

He goes very well with honey.

The oven timer goes off. Stupid timer.

"Time to check the tiropitas," he mutters. "Well. We can come back to this in a few seconds. The honey will still be here, as will I, I think."

He refastens his trousers and gets up to open the oven door; upon inspecting the pastries, he decides that it is indeed time for them to come out. The next set of tiropitas and spanakopitas go in. He closes the oven door, sets the timer a second time, and comes back around the table to where I am. When he puts his arms around me, they burn with warmth, despite the cotton barrier of his shirt. He kisses me deeply on my mouth, then my neck, making me moan with expectation. I feel his hands quickly and deftly unfastening the buttons on my own clothing, and I reach down to help him, but by the time I get there, I'm already completely unbuttoned and unzipped. I lift myself off my chair to help him pull off my jeans. Stupid things are in the way. Can't have that.

"You gave me an interesting idea a few minutes ago," he murmurs into my ear. "Onto the table, please."

"I hope I give you lots of ideas." I hoist myself up onto the kitchen table.

He smiles. "Always. I find you a wonderful source of inspiration." This time, when he kisses me, he pushes me gently but firmly onto my back. "I'll need you to hold yourself still for this. If you wiggle too much, you might make a mess of my work." The mugs of tea are still on the table, as is the jar of honey; he moves the still-steaming mugs to the counter and covers them with saucers to keep the tea inside them warm before returning to me, this time with a paintbrush in hand. He dips the brush in the honey jar, lets a single drop fall back into the jar, and then brushes the honeyed bristles across my lips. He's painting my lips with honey. It tickles. I find myself giggling. Then he bends down to lick the honey off my mouth, and I gasp, because I like what he's doing with his tongue a lot more than I like being tickled. When he bites down on my lower lip with careful, methodical slowness, the sensation makes me writhe.

"Hold *still*," he whispers, and picks up the brush again.

I am covered with honey and cinnamon. The table is getting messy, too; we're going to have to really scrub to clean it off. I'm not sure what holding still is accomplishing, given the incredible amount of inevitable splattering, but I continue to do so. It's *for art*. Besides, he asked me to.

Holding still is getting difficult, though, because he's started painting my nether regions. Every stroke of the paintbrush makes me want to roll my hips in ecstasy.

"It's amazing how many euphemisms and slang terms for the female genitalia reference honey or sugar," he says, and does something particularly interesting with a corner of the brush. "Jelly hole. Jelly roll. Honey pot. Honey hive. Honey trap. Sticky bun. Sugar basin. Donut. It makes the female genitalia into a dessert. Linguistically speaking."

"Oh," I reply.

I can't tell if I'm automatically commenting on his words or on what he's doing with the paintbrush. It probably doesn't matter too much, really.

"Rather makes one wonder if terms of endearment like 'my sweetness' were used innocently."

He pauses his monologue.

That's not a paintbrush. I cry out. I don't want him to stop what he's doing...

...and he stops. And he gets up to go to the refrigerator. And he starts rummaging. I groan. This isn't fair. Just now, the oven timer also chooses to go off, so he takes spanakopitas and tiropitas out of the oven and baklava out of the toaster oven, and then turns off the heat to the ovens and sets the baking dishes on the counters to cool. We're running out of counter space. I'm running out of patience, but that's my problem.

When he returns, he has the bowl of grape and yogurt salad in the crook of his arm. "You didn't really think I'd forgotten about you?" he asks. "Tsk. You know better than that." Then he starts inserting the grapes.

"They're... they're cold," I gasp, displaying fine mastery of the obvious. Not that coldness is a bad thing. Actually, it feels quite interesting. Interesting, that's a good word for it. I think he could hold my attention this way for quite some time.

"Don't worry; I'll warm you up. Stop wriggling, please. You'll undo my work."

How many grapes is he going to try to fit in there? I feel frozen and stuffed. The filling sensation is not at all unpleasant; I've accommodated his hand on numerous occasions, and the grapes aren't much different in that regard, except for the fact that I can't move around the grapes to get myself off, the way I can move around his hand. The chill, however – I'm not sure whether it feels uncomfortable in a bad way, or uncomfortable in a good way. I do know it's starting to feel uncomfortable. I'm shivering from the cold.

And then he gets up, lifts the saucer to drink tea out of the mug, sits back down again, and puts his mouth against me. Warm tea spills against my flesh. After the cold of the grapes and the yogurt, it feels like sunlight. I moan.

"Fire and ice," he murmurs. "This is usually done with round ice cubes, not refrigerated grapes, but I thought you'd go well with grapes."

"Could you... could you do that thing with the tea again? I... I liked that..."

"I think I can manage that."

Tea. I never before thought of tea as a sex toy.

Tea.

Oh, God.

He does that for a while, perhaps because he likes the way I sound when I beg.

"Hmm. Something's missing. I think a little more honey would be appropriate... Yes. Let's try that." He picks up the paintbrush again.

My breath has become gasping and hoarse.

"I think, maybe, just a touch of cinnamon. There. That should do it. You make a lovely canvas for art. Alas, everything that is done must be undone. It wouldn't be practical to have you walking around the house dripping honey, yogurt, and grapes, after all." He bends down, murmuring, "Then make my joys at full. And drop down nectar from thy honey lips..."

Eventually, the grapes are all out.

My knees are shaking. The kitchen reverberates with the sound of my cries.

When he surfaces, he tastes of honey, grapes, cinnamon, almonds, and me.

"Oh, you," I sigh, when we are done with each other's mouths. "I never did finish what I started. Those clothes are going to have to come off. Now, where's the honey?"

THERE IS A LULL between my Formal Logic class and my Victorian Literature class; my gaming buddy from last term's course on existentialist philosophy is in both classes with me (apparently, she shares my intellectual tastes) so we generally spend the hour between the two classes hanging out together in the student union lounge. It gets a little crowded and noisy for me, to the point where sometimes my skin feels like it wants to crawl, but it's easier to hang out here than it is to wander around looking for an empty classroom to occupy. Warmer weather will be here in a month or two, though, and then we'll be able to sit outside on nice days.

"Why do you always wear that black scarf wrapped around your wrist?" she asks. "I've never seen you without it."

I suppose someone was bound to ask sometime.

I could just give a simple answer. *My boyfriend gave it to me.* However, some impulse in me makes me blurt out the truth in greater detail. "I wear it as an outward sign of my submission to my *Magister*."

"You what for your what?" She blinks at me.

"My boyfriend. He also happens to be my magickal teacher, my tutor, and my mentor in the erotic arts." If I'm going to come out with it, I might as well go the whole nine yards. I couldn't just keep it quiet, could I? Oh, well. The only reason I've been discreet so far has been because *Magister* is easily embarrassed, but my friend from class is unlikely to tease him. And it's not like the rest of the gaming group doesn't know, although it's not the sort of thing we talk about while sitting around the table.

"Oh. Oh, wow."

It seems like whenever there is an awkward pause in the conversation, it's not just you and the person you're talking to who are hushed – the entire room suddenly stills, and everyone seems to be listening to you, waiting to hear what you have to say. No doubt that's completely illusory.

"So," she asks at last, "that means you're into bondage and stuff?"

"Among other things."

"What kind of magic is he teaching you?"

Where should I even begin? "Are you familiar with the Neoplatonists of the Renaissance? The Hermetic scholars? The occult philosophers of late nineteenth-century Europe? That's a part of what he's teaching me, for the philosophy part of my studies. He's also been devising practical lessons in magick based on what I'm studying. A lot of it is Thelemic sex magick, with an eye to gnosis through ecstasy and self-perfection, but a good part of the practicum comes from Siberian and Finnish shamanism because we found my personal energy works better with primal stuff and chaos than it does with ritualistic ceremony."

"Sex – oh, wow." She stares at me. "That's amazing. I didn't know there was such a thing. Does it work?"

"Sex magick?"

"Yes."

"It depends on what you want it to do," I reply quietly. "Mostly we use it to search for our higher Selves, and to share our souls with each other." *We drink from each other as if we were wine.*

"How long have you been together?"

"About two years, now."

"It sounds beautiful. Weird, but beautiful. You must love each other very much. You're glowing. Your whole face just lit up."

"Yes," I sigh.

"Oh, it's beautiful down here! And you say there are *swans* on the lake when the weather is warmer?"

"Yeah, we have swans. If I'm still living here in the spring, maybe we could have a picnic, and I could show you the swans. The trees around the lake are all in bloom. It's like being in a postcard."

"What do you mean, if? Why on earth would you want to move?"

"It would be nice to be closer to campus. Also, my rent is four hundred fifty dollars, even though it's only a one-bedroom apartment, and I don't even have any air conditioning. My mom would rather I just stay here because it's safe and quiet, but it's so far away from everything." She grimaces. "Then there's the type of people who live here. It's not like Portland, where my dad lives. You'd think people out here never even heard of goths before. If I hear one more person ask me if I'm Amish, I'm going to scream. Just because a person dresses in black does not mean that person is Amish."

"*But you have swans!*"

She laughs. "And a long bus ride. I'm going to need a car if I keep living down here."

I don't quite see eye-to-eye with her on this one. I've never had my own car, and I've endured longer bus rides to get to work, from neighborhoods that were considerably less scenic. Swans were never part of any neighborhood I ever lived in, for that matter, not even when I was a child living with my parents, in a historic gaslit district, in a large Tudor revival house. Swans would certainly have gone well with the place, but we didn't have any.

"If I come down to visit you in the spring, and we have a picnic by the lake, can I kidnap one of your swans?"

"You don't know much about swans, do you?"

"Uh…"

"A swan probably has way more hit points than you do. If you don't get bit all over, you might get a broken bone or two from the swan's wings."

"Birds have hollow wings. That can't be right."

"They still bite. They're nasty. Please don't try to run off with one of our swans. I like you. Besides, can you imagine what kind of havoc the swan would wreak on the bus, assuming you could fit the swan through the door? I presume you'd be taking the bus home."

"Well, yes."

She pulls out her keys. It was a short walk from the bus stop because her ground-floor apartment is in the "downtown" of her suburb. Her apartment building, a Victorian house that's been subdivided into four units, is quaint. The view from her building's front porch is quaint. Everything here is quaint. She lives in a sugar confection of a town that belongs on a Holly Hobbie print, or maybe in a dentist's office as an advertisement for what to avoid if you don't want cavities.

We don't have class today, I don't have work today, although *Magister* does, and it's not gaming day, so when she asked if I'd like to come over and watch movies and pop some popcorn, I said yes.

"Would you mind if I hung out with my friend from campus this afternoon while you're at work? I might get home a little bit after dinnertime. I have to transfer buses downtown."

"Mind?" *Magister* asked. "*Eromene*, how long have I been urging you to try to make more friends? You need a life outside of me. Go. Spend some time with somebody other than me, outside of work and classes. Enjoy."

Her living room window has stained glass in it. The stained glass is mostly in shades of pink and purple, with a little white and green here and there. Flowery quaintness. Of course, it's quaint.

We settle onto her couch (which, surprisingly, is not quaint; it's an orange burlap monstrosity that looks like it was rescued from a basement somewhere) and watch *Labyrinth* as her air popper pops the popcorn. Sitting right next to her, I notice that the two of us are a study in contrast. Where my hair is blazing auburn, hers is a pale blonde that is almost snowy white. Where I am freakishly tall, she is short. Where I am angles, she is all fascinating plumpness and curves. I probably should stop looking at her. If she notices me looking, it could make for awkward conversation, not to mention, there's a chance that she might be one of those people who is uncomfortable when being watched.

People seem to think that all goths are built like skeletons and that there are no plus-sized goths, but then, people also seem to have the idea that all goths have their hair dyed black. I suppose we could talk about that if she asks. It would be better than my simply saying I have no idea why the differences in appearance between the two of us fascinate me so.

"Do you have any owls that I could take home with me if I can't have a swan?"

"You mean like the one that turns into the Goblin King? No. No owls. Sorry. Anyway, what would you do with the Goblin King if you took him home? Don't you already have one... um..."

"*Magister.* Yes."

"Also, I have dibs on David Bowie."

That reminds me you're a babe.

"What's he planning on doing with that thing, anyway?"

I note the direction of her bugging eyes. "What 'thing?' His riding crop, or his codpiece?"

"Yes!"

I shrug. "Probably whatever he likes, I would imagine. He's the Goblin King, isn't he?"

"Well. I wish he'd come do it over here."

"You wish?"

"Yes. I wish he'd come do it over here. *Right now!*" She closes her eyes and waits, then reopens them. "Darn. It didn't work. Oh, well, a girl can dream. Popcorn?"

MY VICTORIAN LIT CLASS is over, and I have some time before I have to clock in for my shift at the call center, so I'm at the library. *Magister* is filling in at the circulation desk this week. Usually, there are one or two other librarians there with him, but since he is alone, my guess is that someone made herself scarce after sighting a problem patron, and since the person *Magister* is helping is male, and is wearing a disappointed look on his face, my guess is probably a sound one.

No, he's not burly, nor does he look particularly intimidating, despite his height, but *Magister* is male, which means his female coworkers sometimes call on him to obstruct sexual harassment. He stays at the desk to "provide help." Meanwhile, the co-worker makes herself scarce. Exit, hopefully not pursued by the bear.

I wait until the patron is gone, partly because I don't want to interrupt, partly because I don't want to be a possible new target, and then walk up to the desk.

"Another Harold Hill?"

"Yes." He sighs. "At least this one didn't decide to wait around."

Sometimes they do that. Breaks only last so long. Sometimes *Magister* being the only librarian around to help a patron effectively discourages that patron from hitting on the woman he's looking for at the help desk. Sometimes the patron decides to wait for the librarian he had hoped to interact with, and *Magister's* presence only delays the inevitable. Unfortunately, if the patron in question isn't mauling his target, and his attentions stay within the boundaries of plausible deniability, the only way for the harasser's target to deal with the situation is to politely endure it and to try to avoid showing any kind of reaction.

I do my best to not flirt with *Magister* when I visit him because I don't want to set a bad example. When I first heard about the problems his co-workers had with patrons making lewd comments, asking them out on dates, getting overly friendly, and otherwise verbally harassing them, and the library's administration refusing to get involved on the grounds that the library should always be a "welcoming place for patrons," I was horrified.

A familiar voice beside me says, "I'd like to check this out," and Gaston LeRoux's *The Phantom of the Opera* appears on the checkout desk.

My classmate is in black from head to toe, as usual. She went to a few extra pains with her outfit this time, though. I have no idea where she found that corset dress, although the pointed witch's hat looks like it was part of a Halloween costume. Possibly the dress was part of the same costume. It is now February, but I think a good argument could be made for celebrating Halloween outside of October. Take now, for instance. Thanks to my classmate, I have realized that both Halloween and Valentine's Day feature the devouring of copious amounts of candy, and it would only be a small tweak to change Valentine's Day to Winter Halloween.

"Wow!"

"Do you like it? It looks like something out of *Beetlejuice*." She twirls in front of me. "Strange and unusual!"

"Yes, Lydia." I grin. "Where on earth did you find that dress? I love it."

"Used clothing store. I got lucky."

She makes a little bit more small talk, then flits off with her book, black lace trailing under her velvet coat. I should have asked her where she got the coat, too, not that I could afford anything like it.

Magister gives me an odd look.

"*Eromene*? Your classmate seems to have a bit of a crush on you."

"What? No, that's impossible. She knows I'm with you."

He frowns and shakes his head. "I doubt an object of desire being attached to another person has ever stopped sexual attraction from happening."

"I don't see it. Really."

"I hope you're not leading her on. That wouldn't be fair to her. Be a little more careful."

I shake my head. "I don't even think she's *interested* in me, but I can assure you, I'm not flirting with her."

When it's time for me to go to work, I pull a piece of paper out of my purse and leave it on the desk. I like to give *Magister* little presents when I visit – love notes, quotes, poems. In warmer weather, I sometimes leave flowers. Today it's a Catullus quote. *Da mi basia mille, diende centum, diende usque altera mille.* Give to me a thousand kisses, then a hundred, then another thousand.

A COUPLE OF WEEKS ago, it was bitterly cold out, but now it's warm enough that I'm tempted to not only skip wearing a winter coat but also go around in my short sleeves. I resist the temptation. It's March. The temperature can drop forty degrees in the space of minutes this time of year. It has in the past.

Since Lydia and I are planning to do a photo session in the cemetery, I'd rather not be caught outdoors without a coat if temperatures suddenly drop. Yes, it's a short walk from the northern part of the cemetery to the apartment, but it would be a short walk in freezing cold, which I'd rather not have to deal with if all I'm wearing is a short-sleeved tee shirt and leggings.

I could, of course, summon Fire. Summoning enough Fire to keep myself warm for the duration of the walk, though, requires a certain amount of energy, and right now, there are other things I'd like to save my energy for, such as cooking dinner. It's my turn to cook something tonight. We have some tilapia to use up, and I was thinking of steaming it and serving it on top of a lentil and rice pilaf. It's not a very labor-intensive meal to prepare, which is one reason it appeals to me, because I still have my weekly essay to write.

And then *Magister* has some plans for the evening tonight that he doesn't want to share all the details of, but apparently what he has planned will keep us both busy until well past midnight, so using my energy and willpower to summon Fire to keep myself warm for a brief walk through the cold, resulting in me crashing halfway through the evening and nodding off at the table before the night's festivities have even begun, would not be useful.

Easier to just wear my coat.

"You're so lucky to live across the street from a cemetery," Lydia says. "I wish I did."

"You can look out your living room window and see a lake. With *swans* swimming on it. That's better. Has the town brought the swans back from their winter home yet?"

"Not yet, but it shouldn't be too much longer. The ice on top of the lake has melted."

We continue to walk south, downhill. The northern part of the cemetery doesn't have much to look at that's interesting, nor does the middle part, unless you want to visit the gravesite of a famous preacher and sobriety advocate, in which case you can look for a plain, modern tombstone that looks like all the other plain, modern tombstones near it. (In June, you can also look for motorcycles and a crowd). There are better photo opportunities in the older section of the cemetery. The monument art there is spectacular.

"Lydia, why did you want to take pictures of me in a cemetery?"

Magister was wondering the same thing just a short while ago when Lydia knocked on our door to come pick me up. Which, in turn, got me wondering. It's not so much the cemetery I'm wondering about – this is Lydia, after all – but why include me in the pictures?

"I thought you'd look really cool standing by the graves and stuff."

Oh. Well, then.

Lydia pulls out her camera – a fancy single-lens reflect camera, the kind that requires the film to be threaded on, and lenses to be manually adjusted – when we are near the bottom of the hill. She takes some pictures of old tombstones that she says are beautiful and deserve to be captured for posterity, then sees the old mausoleum and squeals with delight.

"I have to get your picture here! Oh, my God, it's *huge!* And look at all this ivy! It's like something out of Edgar Allen Poe. Whose tomb is this?"

"Nobody's. The cemetery built it, but it never got used."

"I wonder why? There. Stand there, in the shady part. That's good." She fidgets with the lens, snaps a couple of pictures, then says, "Take your coat off. I want to get a picture of you that doesn't make it look like you're trying to protect yourself against the cold. Something that makes you look like you belong here."

"Oh, gee, thanks." Anybody other than Lydia would have been wishing me dead with that statement. Fortunately, this is Lydia, so I don't have to worry.

"That's it. Now melt into the ivy."

"Melt into the ivy?"

"Yeah. Bury yourself in it, kind of."

I check to make sure there's no sign of poison ivy growing in or around the English ivy that covers the mausoleum, then do my best to comply. All I have on besides my shoes and socks are my black tee shirt and leggings, now. On the sunny side of the mausoleum, this would be enough, but here in the shade, it's actually chilly. My hands are cold where they encounter the stone of the tomb under the ivy. Underneath my tee shirt, I feel my nipples start to stiffen.

She gets a few pictures of me from various angles, including two close-ups of my face, one with my eyes closed, the other with my eyes open, and then she puts her camera down and stares at me.

"Um. Lydia? Is something wrong? Why are you looking at me like that?"

"No, no, nothing's wrong. It's just. You're so beautiful there."

"I'm beautiful with my backside crushed up against a tomb?"

"Yes. You *are*."

AFTER WE GET DONE exploring the cemetery, we trudge back up the hill to hang out at the apartment for a bit, while we catch our breath. *Magister* is sprawled on the couch reading an Ursula LeGuin novel. He looks up when we walk in the door.

"Get some good pictures?"

"I did. I think I'll get doubles when I get the film processed; that way you can have copies."

The apartment smells like warm cookie dough. He must have been baking while we were gone.

It occurs to me that I still don't have a single picture of *Magister*, nor does he have one of me. It's been nearly two years, and we still don't have pictures of each other. I'm not sure why not. Neither of us is exactly camera-shy, although neither of us seeks out opportunities to be photographed, either. It's just something we never got around to doing. We had too many other things to do, maybe.

"Lydia? Could you get a picture of the two of us?"

"I'd love to! There, on the couch – is that good? Maybe you could lower the blinds? I don't want you backlit."

I lower the blinds, and then *Magister* and I sit close together, his arm around me.

His arm seems a little tighter than it ordinarily might be. He must be more uncomfortable having his picture taken than I thought he was. I should have asked his permission first.

Lydia takes several pictures of us before leaving, including one of us kissing.

THERE AREN'T MANY POSH places downtown – this city is one of the rustier parts of the Rust Belt – but there are a few. I found this one when I first moved here and went through the rounds of signing up with several temp agencies, one of which was in this office building. The building has an atrium on the bottom floor, and the atrium has an orangerie in it. There are little bistro tables placed among the potted orange and fig trees. Sometimes I come here to sit and read in between classes and my job, rather than the library.

Lydia and I are sitting at one of the tables, looking through cemetery photos. I've already pulled aside a few copies to take home with me. In the little pile of photographs to take home are also all the pictures of me and *Magister* sitting together on the couch. There's one I want to frame and put on a bookshelf in the living room; maybe I could put it on the shelf where *Magister* keeps the books of poetry.

"I'm probably going to need to take out a student loan," Lydia says. "My dad stopped paying my mom child support again, and Mom doesn't want me to get a job to pay for my apartment rent. She says I need to keep my grades up. Dad wants me to move out to where he is and transfer to one of the colleges there. It would be more expensive, though. And I love my dad, but I don't want to leave Mom. I visit Dad during the summers and on holidays. It's not like he never sees me. I think he's just trying to make Mom upset." She sighs. "It's not too late to apply for a student loan, is it? I've never done it before."

"I think if you haven't already submitted a loan application for this year, you should be fine."

"Yeah. I guess. I wish Dad would stop trying to force me to transfer. Portland is a lot nicer in a lot of ways – it's really pretty there, for one thing. There are mountains, and the ocean is nearby, and there are roses. Everywhere. And they're used to people being a little weird. People don't stare at me for wearing black clothes and lipstick. And the city is queer-friendly. Not like this place. Nobody bats an eye there if I say I'm bi. But it's so far away. I don't want to move out there. Not when my friends are here."

Nobody bats an eye there if I say I'm bi.

"Is Portland really that open-minded?"

"Yes. You'd love it. I'd love it if it wasn't so far away. It would be nice to be able to go back and forth between my parents more easily. What about your parents? Do they live here? You don't talk about them much. What are they like? Do they get along better than mine do?"

I take a deep breath. "I don't have any parents anymore."

"You're an orphan? Oh, my God. I'm so sorry..."

"I'm not an orphan. I just don't have parents anymore. Look, let's talk about something else, okay?"

After a few moments of awkward silence, we do.

HAVING YOUR PARTY FACE down a group of cultists is thirsty work. My glass is empty, so I get up from the table to go to the kitchen for more iced blackberry tea.

Lydia follows me into the kitchen.

"Did you want a refill on your tea, too?" I ask her.

"Actually, I wanted to talk to you for a couple of minutes. Alone. I didn't have the nerve to say this at school. Um. I've never. Um. You and your um. You don't have an open relationship, do you?"

Um.

"That's never come up in conversation," I reply, truthfully. Now that she mentions it, I think it's strange that *Magister* and I have never actually talked about whether our relationship is an open one or a closed one. Then again, neither of us has been interested in anyone else since we first started seeing each other. "I don't think we do."

"Oh." She looks away. "Do you like me?"

Somehow, I don't think she's asking that in the casual sense of the word "like."

"Yes," I hear myself saying, also truthfully, wishing instantly that I hadn't admitted it out loud. Nothing good is going to come of this, I'm pretty sure.

"May I kiss you?"

Um.

"Yes?" I whisper.

And then her arms are around me, and she's standing on the tips of her toes to reach my mouth with hers, and she tastes sweet, sweet like blackberries and sugar, and before I can stop myself I have her gathered up in my arms, her soft pale hair wound tight in my fist, her pelvis crushed against mine; and she's moaning as I push her up against the kitchen wall, devouring her lips with my teeth and tongue. She clutches me tighter; I force her arms down and out, pinning them against the wall as I grind into her. "Yes," she gasps, "oh God I like that, that's what I want, I never, oh God don't let go," and she throws her head to the side, baring her neck, and I lean down to kiss it and graze it with my teeth before sinking them into her flesh, worrying at her until she cries out. Such soft skin, such need. I think I'm getting drunk on her.

Magister coughs.

Oh. Oh, dear.

SOMEHOW, WE ALL MANAGED to make it through to the end without anyone mentioning or even acknowledging that something awkward had happened in the kitchen; but the guests are gone and it's just the two of us in the apartment, now.

He sits hunched over on the couch. I've never seen him look so small.

"I know I can't meet all of your needs," he says, his voice trembling, "and some of those needs are important enough that they can't be ignored for your whole life. I know you were disowned for loving a woman, and that you like women. I also know that you have always had a strong need to be dominant, and what the two of us have is probably unusual for you. I can't be a woman for you. I might possibly be able to play the submissive for you, sometimes – for one thing, you are supposed to be learning domination from me, and it would give you a chance to practice and to find your own style – although I suspect it would not go as far as you would like. There are certain lines I cannot cross. But *eromene*, did you have to remind me *now*?"

"I'm sorry. I wasn't thinking. She kind of threw herself at me, and I kind of caught her."

"You caught her and pinned her against the wall of our kitchen?"

"You never told me not to."

He sighs. "It would have been polite to at least ask my permission."

I feel a lump form in my throat. "I'm sorry. It just happened before I could stop. I didn't mean to do it. Really, I didn't."

"Didn't you?" He finally meets my eyes again. I almost wish he hadn't. "That kiss seemed full of intention, from where I was standing."

"I don't want her. Well. I do want her, in the sense that I think I lust after her, but I don't want to date her. I don't think. I only kissed her. I want you." Then the tears start, and this time, I'm crying not from passion, but from sheer misery.

"I love you, *Magister*. My *erastes*. I want you. I'll never stop loving you. I'm yours forever if you want. I didn't mean for that to happen…"

"No. You're not."

"What?"

"You are not *mine*. Much as I often wish you were. I love you, too, *eromene*," he murmurs, so quietly that I can barely make out the word *love*, as I realize it's the first time he's ever spoken it aloud in a language that isn't dead; and he reaches for me. "It was partly my fault for not ever having thought to discuss the possibility that you might find an outside partner. Monogamy is a cultural default, but it's not something I should just take for granted. And arrangements of convenience between couples that allow one or both members of that couple to seek play partners outside the relationship are extremely common in the BDSM scene, especially when one primary partner is dominant and the other primary partner is not submissive, or when one primary partner is submissive and the other is not dominant. It happens all the time. Just because two sexually kinked people make a perfect couple in most of the more conventional ways – values, common interests, that sort of thing – does not mean they are going to be perfectly compatible in their specific kinks. We are no exception to this. Nevertheless, I don't want to share you. Is that all right?"

"Yes. Yes, *Magister*."

"I know it's one of the oldest and most stereotypical male fantasies in existence – having two girls at once, having a girlfriend who is attracted to other women and is willing to do things to another woman in front of you and possibly even let you join in – but that's never appealed to me. It hurt me to see you with someone else. It reminded me of everything I am not, and can never be; and it showed me in no uncertain terms that you can't and shouldn't be truly *mine*, regardless of how badly I might want you to be *mine*." His voice has been a near-whisper, and I realize it's because he's trying not to cry.

Meanwhile, I'm crying hard enough for both of us. One way or another, I guess, the tears will all get shed.

"I'm sorry. Forgive me? Please?"

"*Se philo*. Of course, you are forgiven, *eromene*." He sighs again. "This was my fault. We should have had this discussion years ago. I can't blame you for doing something you didn't know would cross my limits if I never even told you that I needed monogamy in the first place."

He buries his face in my hair, and we stop trying to patch our wounds with words. Holding each other seems to work somewhat better for mending ourselves, although it, too, only goes so far.

"But now I know I can never be enough for you," he says in a choked voice.

Then his tears start, landing harder on me than blows.

"I'm sorry about the kiss. It was amazing. You are beautiful and taste like heaven. But nothing can come of it; it would hurt *Magister* too much if I date other people outside our relationship. I'm not sure I have enough time or energy for another relationship right now, anyway. I barely have enough time to sleep."

Thank goodness this is one of those days when the student union is mostly deserted, so we can talk in the temptation-free zone of a public place and yet not be overheard, keeping the conversation itself private.

"Oh. I was afraid of that." She looks up. "He wasn't, you know, mad at you?"

"Of course, he was angry. He was jealous, and it was my fault."

"No, I mean – he didn't hit you or anything?"

"He doesn't do that. Well, not when he's angry. He hits me when we're making love, sometimes, but only because then, it's part of lovemaking. Think of us as being part Klingon."

"You didn't get punished?"

"That's not how our relationship works, except when formal lessons are going on."

I had to hold him while he cried. I suppose that counts as a sort of punishment.

"Oh." She looks down again. "I'm sorry I threw myself at you. I'd say I was drunk, but you can't get drunk on iced tea, can you?"

"I don't think so, no."

"Can we pretend it never happened?"

I sigh. "Yes. Let's do that."

Well. We can *try*.

MY TWENTY-THIRD BIRTHDAY – our official second anniversary – is coming up in a few days. A nearby symphony is performing *Tristan und Isolde* in its entirety as an orchestral piece with chorale and vocal soloists on that weekend, so this year, we're celebrating by traveling up north to hear it from the good seats in the front of the lower balcony in the concert hall. Since neither of us likes to go through money as if it's water, we're hearing it as a matinee.

That will also leave us plenty of time later that evening to find other, more private ways to celebrate the occasion.

I don't have anything particularly nice to wear to the symphony, having by now outgrown the vintage granny gown I wore to my sorority formal years ago, and decided, after adding an extra tier of lace to the bottom of the gown so that it would cover my ankles again, that the result just looked weird. This is why I'm browsing the racks at the thrift store that's within walking distance of our apartment, searching for any kind of clothing that might be useful for occasions requiring fancy dress. (The thrift store, fortunately, is not a Salvation Army store; after the Salvation Army turned me away from a shelter on one of the coldest nights of the year for being "sinful" and "unnatural," I have no desire to give them any of my money. Yes, it was years ago, and it was probably my fault for answering truthfully when the captain who ran the shelter asked me why I had nowhere to sleep that night, but there are some things I just can't let go of).

One of the nice things about not seeing my bank account in a constant state of hemorrhage due to household bills is that I actually have some money left over from my job after paying tuition for my college courses and contributing some-what to my upkeep. *Magister* objected to my helping with non-rent household expenses at first, on the grounds that I should be saving for any present and future college-related expenses, but my argument for a while has been that as long as I can afford to help out a little, I will; I refuse to be a burden or, worse yet, something of a cross between a dependent and a household pet. This month I have enough disposable income that I can splurge some of it.

Usually going shopping would involve browsing for books, but today I'm looking for clothing. It doesn't take long for me to remember that I find shopping for clothing to be a purgatorial experience.

Almost nothing ever fits me well. I like to borrow *Magister's* shirts, because they cover my arms down to the wrists rather than halfway past my elbows, which means I can make up my own mind about whether I want to roll them up or down; they don't seem fancy enough on their own for a symphony outing, though, which means I'm looking through racks of women's apparel for something that's pretty, but that also has sleeves long enough to cover a gorilla's arms, and preferably is long enough in the trunk that I don't wind up displaying my navel when I wear it.

Eventually, an unusual black velvet blouse appears, peeking out from a hidden spot on the plus-size shirt rack. It's long enough that I guess it must have been a tunic or a short minidress on anyone of a more normal height than mine, and the lace accents and black faceted buttons (surely, they aren't made of *real* jet) make it look vaguely Victorian. The velvet is soft and reminds me of nights spent between the sheets and of the things *Magister* and I do between those sheets. It wants to be touched.

I grab it before someone else can find it and look for a coordinating skirt. All I own for bottoms are leggings, sweatpants, some jeans and slacks sized for adolescent boys, and a hand-sewn drawstring skirt I made from a massive tube of calico fabric on one of my more creative days. None of these are appropriate formalwear.

It takes some poking around, but I find something suitable, a filmy number made of silky black gauze that flares in a full circle when I twirl in it, and manages to at least go down to my calves, which is more than I was expecting from a maxi skirt that was designed for a normal person, rather than someone built along the lines of a flagpole the way I am. It has a built-in slip for modesty, too, thank goodness. I don't think I'd have much luck finding a long slip here. I'm not sure where I'd find a long slip anywhere. A bridal shop, maybe.

I head for the cash register with my findings. The counter near the cash register has a bin of used records and cassettes sitting on it, unsorted; on a whim, I grab the Jefferson Starship cassette that sits at the top of the pile and offer the person tending the cash register fifty cents for it. She adds it to my pile of clothing, and I walk out into the light of day, squinting at the afternoon glare. April here is chilly, but as bright as summer.

A BUS PULLS UP to the stop just as I'm walking past the stop, and I have change in my pocket left over from my thrift store expedition, so I decide to ride downtown for one more shopping trip. There's a mall near the university that used to be a cereal factory before it got converted into retail stores and office space as part of a halfhearted attempt on the part of the city council to revitalize the downtown area. In it is a little perfumery that sells essential oils and perfume oils, and toiletries that a customer can add personalized scents to. It's where *Magister* gets his sandalwood products. I sometimes browse here on less busy days just because everything smells so good.

After going inside and spending time sniffing various tester vials, including one with the white musk the shop is locally legendary for, I purchase a couple of bottles of essential oils: frankincense and spikenard. I like the way they smell on me, and the frankincense in particular reminds me of when *Magister* and I cast circle. I also have the oils added to shampoo and conditioner. I like the idea of my hair smelling like magickal work.

I decide to go home before I spend any more. I don't mind being decadent, but I don't want to cross the line into profligacy. It isn't a good habit to get into.

"WHAT IS THAT YOU'RE wearing? There's definitely some frankincense in there, but there's something else blended in that I can't identify. It's not myrrh. Is it vetiver, maybe?"

"Spikenard."

He pauses for a few minutes. "It smells like consecrated savagery... It's very you," he says at last. "I like it."

"Want to see what else I picked up to wear to the concert? It's really snazzy."

"I've never seen you in formal clothing before. This should be interesting. Yes, please."

I make a hasty exit to the bedroom, where I shed my street clothes and don my new apparel. It occurs to me as I do so that I don't have any shoes that would go with it – all I have are a pair of sneakers and a pair of penny loafers, neither of which are appropriate for coordinating with formal wear – and I will have to go out again sometime in the next few days to purchase a cheap pair of black ballet flats or sandals or something, and coordinating hose, if I can find pantyhose that fit me. Terrific. More shopping. The last time I wore pantyhose was when I was a freshman in college and was only about five-eleven. Do they even make pantyhose in my size?

"You can look now," I say at last, once I have on the velvet blouse and the skirt. It took a long time to button up the blouse; there were a lot of buttons to push through loops.

The expression that appears on his face is extremely gratifying.

"Well, well," he breathes. "Very striking indeed. Black is certainly a good color for you. I'm surprised you don't wear it more often. It makes your red hair stand out." A corner of his mouth begins to twitch into a smile. "The effect is rather intimidating. You might want to make note of that; it could come in handy later. That blouse, in particular. I'm not sure what I want to do more, run my

hands over it, or congratulate you on your instinctual good taste in domina-
trix couture..."

"Run your hands all over it, of course, and then devour me. That's my
suggestion," I offer helpfully.

He grins. "Certainly. Your wish is my command."

"Oh, stop," I reply, giggling, and fall into his arms.

"HAPPY BIRTHDAY," HE SAYS, and hands out a small box.

Oh, dear.

Inside is an opal pendant set in white gold, on a matching chain.

"It looked like it would go well with your earrings. Don't worry, it didn't
set me back too much."

I love opals, especially fire opals like this one. "It's beautiful," I sigh. I
shouldn't fret so much; he's right, if the necklace only cost as much as my
Christmas earrings, which seems a reasonable assumption, the symphony
tickets cost more than the earrings and necklace combined. Semiprecious
stones are not generally very expensive. "Would you like to put it on me?"

"That's a very loaded question. And yes. I would."

When he fastens the clasp, tightening the short chain, the pendant barely
brushes the hollow in my collarbone.

The longing look he has on his face pierces me to the core.

WE SIT SIDE BY side, hands clasped, under a ceiling of gold, watching a lit
screen above the orchestra and singers display an English translation of Wagner's
German lyrics as we listen to the performance. The lovers have just drunk wine
that has been adulterated with a love potion – a potion that was supposed to have

brought instant death, except that Isolde's maidservant, Brangaene, substituted a love potion for the poison at the last minute.

Isolde! Tristan!
Escaped from the world,
I have claimed you!
Supreme joy of love,
Now I am yours, I only know you!

Our hands squeeze. Yes, this is something we know very, very well.

The chorus of sailors chants in rhythm as they unfurl the sail and bring out the oars; the steady pulse of song that is the beating of oars against water is the rhythm of our hearts beating as one.

When the second act begins, and the soprano soloist sings,

However the Goddess of Love turns it,
however she ends it,
whatever she reserves for me,
wherever she leads me,
I have become her very own:
Now let me show my obedience!

I shiver and grasp *Magister's* hand more tightly. This, too, is something we know very well.

I glance sideways; I find that he is looking at me with both sadness and hunger. It cuts me to the bone. Oh, the fibers that we have braided into this rope we wind about ourselves. I bring his hand to my lips, quickly, furtively. I would do more, but this is a crowded concert hall, and there are certain things one just doesn't do in public.

We do manage a quick kiss on the lips during the intermission. Our hands remain clasped; in my mind, I pretend that our fingers are our limbs, our bare hands our naked bodies, fused in love, and I imagine that he is having the same longings.

In the surging swell,
in the ringing sound,
in the vast wave
of the world's breath –
to drown,
to sink,
unconscious –
supreme bliss!

Liebestod. And with it, the end of the concert. I wipe tears from my eyes. I look to my side; *Magister* is not crying the way I am, but his face is tensed, and his eyes are bright.

"The ending always makes me cry," I sniff. "Silly."

"Personally, I find it strange that more people do not cry at the ending." He flashes a melancholy half-smile at me, and we sit together while other patrons rise up around us and head for the exits. Eventually, my legs are strong enough to bear my weight again, and after making a brief detour to pay our respects to the case where Wagner's jeweled baton stands on display, we leave the gilded hall behind us.

Late afternoon sunlight pours down on us as we emerge, and we blink until we have adapted to the unaccustomed brightness.

Across the street from the concert hall is an art museum, which appears to be part of a well-manicured urban park. We recline side by side on a grassy slope, gazing at the waters of the shallow artificial lagoon that sits on the grounds, and at a statue of mermaids that watch over it.

"I wish this day could last forever," I say. "I wish we could last forever. Like this." This sunlight, which seems to fall on us almost brightly enough to blind, so that I have to close my eyes and turn my head away from its angle. These first violets of April. These shining waters. These arms, wrapped around me.

"Yes."

We fall silent in the face of the enormity of our longings.

I let my forehead fall against his. Our third eyes meet. I feel a warm, tingling sense of dissolving.

"*Magister* - my *erastes* – what would happen if we could make it last forever?"

"The day? Our love? Our relationship?"

"Our love already is forever, I think." I run my hand through his hair, reveling in the way it ripples under my palm's flesh. "While no day lasts forever. I meant *us*. What would happen if we made it permanent?" My lips seek his. He is so warm. I want him, now; I want him so much that it hurts me. I wish I hadn't said anything out loud. Desire makes me tremble – desire, mixed with fear. "Could we?"

It would be so sweet, to never have to let go, or be let go.

His eyes open wide. "*Eromene*, was that a proposal?"

Yes. No. Maybe. "I don't know."

As usual, I can't commit myself, and I hate myself for it.

His mouth quirks. "Well. Shame on me for getting my hopes up when tempted. However, you want an answer, and I suppose I had better provide it, because I too need to be reminded of what is advisable and what is not. So. What would happen? Permanence. Commitment. I would need an absolute commitment from you if I were to commit myself to you forever. It wouldn't be fair otherwise. This is not the first deep romantic relationship I have been in, and you are certainly not the first woman who has been in a submissive position with me, and on a couple of occasions the two states have, in fact, coincided; but I do not give my heart easily, nor do I give it lightly, and neither do I give the rest of myself lightly. I wouldn't need marriage if you didn't want it – I see a marriage license as a legal convenience, since vows of commitment can be made in private without any signing of formal paperwork, although later in life, legal marriage comes in handy because it provides such civil niceties as power of attorney, inheritance rights, tax benefits, and so on, and those can become important. However, although I see marriage itself as optional, commitment is not. I would demand monogamy, for one thing, since I myself am monogamous. What happens when you realize you need to find a slave of your own? I can't be that for you. Nor can I be a woman for you, and you would not have kissed your friend with such abandon had you not needed her to be in your arms to be kissed. You are still young, and you have a life that wants to be discovered and lived. I think you would eventually find the situation frustrating."

I sigh.

"Then there's the other aspect of commitment: ownership. What we have right now is an unusual and unique situation. I could be your lover and your partner forever, although not your teacher, since students do eventually move on. At some point, I would run out of things to teach you, anyway. What would be left, then, would be our romantic relationship. Well. If you have me forever, then you have *all* of me forever, as I don't think I would be happy spending an entire lifetime with my beloved without giving myself utterly, weaknesses as well as strengths; and I would want to have all of you forever as well. I would insist on possessing you, because I do happen to have quite a possessive streak that I've been trying to keep in check out of consideration for you. At the very least you could expect yourself to wear a collar. For the sake of discretion, I could make sure it looked like a necklace or a choker of some sort, but we would both still know full well what it meant." He traces his fingers along the skin of my neck, where it touches the white gold chain of my recent birthday present, and I tremble. It feels terrifying. It feels exhilarating. "Permanent marks made not just as a result of heavy play, but specifically and deliberately to display my ownership of you, would no longer be out of the question, either; we'd need to discuss that.

"And perhaps your hesitation to commit to anything permanent is wise. Perhaps commitment would destroy us both. What we have now may very well be beautiful and priceless because it is not compelled. You are your own person, for all that you surrender to me in the magickal circle we cast, and in the bedroom. You control the terms of your own bondage. You control your own destiny. What would happen if you were completely and utterly mine? Would you still be so keen to return to academia?"

I ponder this. No, maybe I wouldn't. It doesn't make sense to me that my longings would change, but they could. I might not want to go back to college full-time and get my degrees. Instead, I'd want to get lost in his arms all the time. The delirium he induces in me is heaven and hell combined; what need would I have for my dreams? I'm only back in college because he nudged me in that direction. He was the one who insisted I take courses to build up my transcript, even if I had to move in with him to afford them. He pushed me into starting my college hunt afresh. I doubt I would have ever returned of my own volition. Going back to college felt too much like trying to go back to the Garden of Eden, with its gateway guarded by an angel with a fiery sword. I had no strength to face that. I am doing something for myself to bring myself back to a life I had always wanted, and needed, only because I was initially doing it for him. If I made my life with him, for him, what need would I have for my own life?

Even if I did go back to being a full-time student – and I grudgingly admit to myself that he would have to request it – it might be nothing more than a passing of time to me, and all because I wouldn't be following my inner voice. That voice has prompted me throughout my life, telling me to teach, and not just in a classroom. It's in my blood. It's always been who I am. I apprenticed myself to *Magister* not because I wanted to submit forever, but because I wanted to learn the physical and spiritual arts of domination, to which my desire to teach and guide seems to be related, a sort of weird vocational cousin if not an actual twin sibling. I could forget all that if I fully enslave myself to him, however, because the part of me that defines me would never see much, if any, use. I would then cease to be myself. It wouldn't happen overnight if it even happened at all – we'd probably have years of happiness – but eventually, it could happen.

He nods. "You begin to see. And with the loss of your ambitions would come resentment. To this day, astonishingly, although we have had a painful discussion or two, we have never quarreled outright. I think that would change. You have a calling – as do we all – and *calls* are not meant to be ignored or denied. Abandoning your calling, which is part of your Will, would make you bitter and shrewish, and with time, that would poison us. Your love would turn to resentment, and then to hate, and – oh, God! I could not bear it if you hated me. My *eromene*, permanence between us might be a disaster. What we have now is incomplete, but it is happy. If that does not change, at some point we may part, but we would be left with mostly happy memories of each other. I shouldn't let myself get too attached to you. It would not be fair to you. That you bring me such joy, that I want you forever, is irrelevant. I can't own you." He trails his finger along the chain on my neck again.

Oh, my love. So much pain. All my fault.

I tighten my embrace and cover his mouth with mine.

The afternoon sun beats down on us like fire.

We burn like moths.

As usual, he went all out. Dinner was an assortment of shellfish in garlic butter sauce, served over linguini; a tossed salad of mixed spring greens, violets, and pansies with a light dressing of oil; steamed asparagus drizzled with orange butter; and, for my birthday cake, an impossibly rich New York style cheesecake he made with added sour cream and dark chocolate and allowed to age for several days in the refrigerator. White zinfandel accompanied the food.

A balmy spring breeze pushes at the kitchen curtains.

His head rests on his arms. He's been lying there slumped at the table for a while now. It doesn't look like a very comfortable position to fall asleep in.

"Come to bed," I say. "You look like you could use a rest."

He nods, and we head off.

When we sit on the futon, I start working his suit and other clothes off. He doesn't object. The tie presents an interesting challenge, but ultimately, it's much easier to undo a Windsor knot than it is to tie one. The tie is silk. "I love the way this feels against my skin," I murmur, rubbing the tie against my cheek as I take it off. "You should wear these more often, to give me an excuse to take them off. Or give yourself an excuse to do something with the tie once it's off."

He doesn't bat an eye.

"My word. You must be tired, to ignore an opening like that." I run my hands along his shoulders as I unfasten his shirt. "Knots. You're in knots... Let me help. Please." When I dig in my fingers, the tension in his muscles feels like stone. He is a study in alabaster.

I bite a shoulder gently, then dig in, wrapping my teeth around the knot to loosen it, and he groans.

"My love, how much are you holding in there?"

His only response is a sad smile.

"Like Atlas, with the weight of an entire world on your shoulders. No wonder your shoulders are all tied up."

"Only when I let myself brood."

"Then don't brood," I reply. "Silly. There. Problem solved." I kiss his mouth, long and hard, taking his face between my hands, and in a few moments am gratified to hear him let out an odd little gasp, almost a sigh. It's a lovely gasp. I could get used to hearing it.

"Thinking about what I mustn't have does tend to make me brood somewhat, eromene," he says, and leans forward to kiss my neck where the chain of my birthday necklace brushes my flesh. His lips are light, no more forceful than thought. They feel like a soft wind.

"No. I did just tell you not to brood, didn't I? Stop brooding. Stop even thinking." I lean into him, unbalancing him and knocking his naked body back down onto the pillows, where I pin him between my forearms as I bend over him.

"Do you know what I want most for my birthday present? Your happiness."
His lips need kissing. I kiss them. "I want you to be blissfully, radiantly happy.
I want you to be positively drunk on happiness." He has such beautiful eyes.
The lids tremble when I put my lips to them. "I want you to be so happy that
you forget how to be sad. I want you to be so happy that you can't think. I
want your ecstasy. Let me give it to you. Let go. Just this once." I reach down
and rub my hand up against the hardness between his legs. "Let go."

He moans. It sounds like music.

"I think you finally want the rest of me," I whisper into his ear.

"Yes." More gasps. I love his gasping.

It's made me hungry, although I don't seem to be hungry for food, exactly.

"Oh, yes. Yes, you do." He seems almost like a delicacy now, one that I
ought to sample; I lick and nibble along his neck, until I feel his pelvis twitch
and roll under my hand. His cock is so hard. "Don't worry, my love. My
Erastes. My beautiful one. I'll be gentle deflowering you."

I can't tell if that's a laugh or a choking cough. Maybe it's a little of both.

I think fast about what the most convenient way would be to place him
if I want him to be able to move his hips when I have sex with him and
decide a straight horizontal line would probably be the most practical for my
purposes. "So," I murmur casually as I fasten his cuffed wrists to the middle
eyebolt at the head of the futon, "*is* this your first time on the bottom?"

"No."

Well. I wasn't expecting that. How interesting. I raise an eyebrow.

"I was curious."

"How did it turn out?"

"Not very well. Curiosity by itself doesn't seem to make for very good love
play, at least not for me; and since I don't usually incline that way, anyway...
well. It was a valuable experience for the both of us, in its own way."

"Oh, my love. That's not right. You deserve happier memories. I'll do my
best to make it up to you."

There, that's the ankles taken care of. I rise and begin to run my fingertips lightly down his chest, massaging meridians and pressure points with my fingers when I find them. With any luck, this will also help unknot some of his muscles. His breath catches when I take a nipple between my teeth and start flicking at it and around it with my tongue. So sensitive. It's a sweet, lovely sound when he gasps and sighs like that, so I keep doing it in the hopes of hearing it again.

He strains underneath me; I roll onto him and let him ride up against my crotch. My pantyhose is soaking wet now, and very much in the way, but I want to drag this out a little longer. I'm not ready to let him go yet.

When I brush against his face, on the way to giving him my breast to pleasure, he rubs his cheek against my blouse.

"Heavens. You do like that velvet blouse, don't you?"

"It's... very nice velvet. And you do look very good in it..."

A throaty laugh bubbles from somewhere out of me. I make sure he has plenty of contact with the velvet of my blouse as I suggest other places for him to kiss, and I crush myself against his chest when I swoop down once more to steal his tongue from his mouth and tease it with mine. His face, when I wring more and yet more pleasure out of him, fills me with awe. He looks for all the world like a chained god. Prometheus, on the mountaintop, must have looked something like this.

I lower my head to strike my hair against his chest.

He groans.

"Oh, you liked that? Let's do it again, shall we?" I toss my head down again and trail it in swirls after it falls on him. "Unfortunately, I can't keep it up for very long without getting dizzy, but I think I can manage a few more times."

I make sure to writhe against him, grinding my genitals upon his, every time I lash him with my hair.

I'm tired of waiting.

The skirt can stay – I like the way the chiffon layers and satin liner feel when they rub up against my skin – but the hose has to go. The very act of removing pantyhose involves a certain amount of friction, and I nearly come just from that, but something tells me he'd find it more arousing to have me climax around him, so I manage to hold myself off until I mount him.

His erection is like marble.

Pleasuring my clitoris with my hand, I ride his cock until I scream, which doesn't take long. I had no idea I would find my own need to be so urgent. How does he manage to keep his passion contained for so long when he plays me? He must have inhuman patience. Practice makes perfect, perhaps. I hope I get more practice in the near future. He did mention wanting to let me rehearse things with him.

This is something I'm going to discuss with him at greater length, later.

I lean down and gently, firmly, grasp his face in my hand. His mouth wants more kissing.

When I lean back to gently hold and stroke his testicles with one of my hands, he moans and bucks up hard against me. That's a nice reaction. I decide to prolong it for a while before going back to scratching his body's nerve endings with my fingernails.

He arches, crying out my name as he tosses his head. "*S'ero,*" he rasps, "*s'ero...*"

I lean back down to ravage his mouth with mine. He's still straining underneath me. Oh, such sweetness. "Is this an improvement over the last time, my love?"

He lets out a faint laugh. "Yes."

"Good." His lips are so very warm and alive. I want to draw all that warmth and life into me and let it fill me. Dear God. "Before you come, I have a request."

"Yes?"

"Tell me you love me. In English. I want to hear you say it in English. Audibly. And look at me, now. Look at me when you say it."

His eyes fly open. We gaze into each other, falling, drowning.

"I love you," he whispers, his breath trembling.

"Again. Louder."

"I love you. I love you, *eromene*. I love you..." And then he is crying it out, over and over, and his body shakes and he spends himself, calling my name, calling out his need.

I remember to unhook and unbuckle him before we collapse against each other.

"I love you, too," I murmur, and kiss sweat from his body. "My God, how I love you."

Just before we both succumb to sleep, I feel him smile against my shoulder, and hear him murmur, "My beautiful rose, you have grown some interesting thorns."

"Roses generally do. Do you like my thorns?"

"They seem to suit you."

CHOKMAH

"You can't seduce the Orc. The Orc does not care that you have a comeliness score of eighteen. The Orc only sees that you are a High Elf. From an Orcish standpoint, you're rather ugly."

"*Ugly?*"

"You're short, thin, pale, and have weird purple eyes. You can't be very sturdy, because you have no muscles to speak of, and your bones are as thin as a bird's. What self-respecting Orc would find that attractive?"

"I have big tits!"

"Which means most Elves would probably find you unattractive as well," *Magister* mutters, *sotto voce*. Fortunately, the High Elf mage in question is too distracted by his frantic rule-searching to notice.

I suppose I shouldn't be too surprised that the new guy would want to play a character of the opposite gender from his own solely as an excuse to get his character laid and would want the character to be a stereotypical porn star, only with purple eyes, pointy ears, and enough magical ability to take down a balrog when she is not coupling with other characters in the adventure. So far, "Perditiel" has seduced nearly every non-player capable of consent, regardless of race or sex, or killed them, regardless of whether the NPC was even an adversary. At least the other player characters have so far been deemed off-limits. Small mercies.

"Why do you want to seduce an Orc?" I sigh. "You're an Elf. Your race doesn't like Orcs any more than Orcs like yours."

"I need to interrogate her. Where there's one Orc, there's a war party."

This is one of the few things Lydia's cousin has said all afternoon that even makes a modicum of sense, although seduction is not the usual method an Elf would probably choose to pry out an Orc's secrets. Unfortunately, in this case, the Orc in question is not part of a war party; she's the rogue employer who is about to hire a band of adventurers to break into a powerful wizard's house and steal a valuable enchanted artifact. We already exhausted what was going to be a two-weekend dungeon crawl in a home-brewed campaign, courtesy of Lydia's cousin finding a loophole in the game rules that allowed him to charge up a jeweled golden falcon the party found in a treasure hoard, turn it into the equivalent of a heat-seeking nuclear missile, and slay the red dragon that was guarding the dungeon. Now I'm on my second adventure. I'm not sure I want to know how the cousin will make himself temporarily as powerful as a demigod and kill the rival wizard. It probably won't involve something as boring as cooperation with other players, though.

I sigh again. "Fine, Perditiel. Have it your way. Make a charisma check."

He rolls.

"Terrific. It's a success. You seduce the Orc. You don't expect me to describe what happens in detail, do you?"

"I want to know all the Orc's secrets. Where is she from? Who is she working for? What does she want? Where are the other Orcs?"

This may be the only opportunity I get to get the game back to its plot, so I quickly launch into debriefing my characters on their mission.

And then I realize that it's time for a summit meeting. Things have gone far enough.

We confer in front of the refrigerator. Ostensibly, Lydia and I are in the kitchen for more soda and chips to take back to the living room, but of course, that's only an excuse to be here. Our real reason is a little more serious.

No, this isn't awkward. Not at all. It doesn't matter one iota to either of us that at one point about a year ago, we were in a passionate clinch a couple of feet from where we're now standing. We're not even thinking about that. And if we are thinking about it, we're not going to discuss it.

"How do I put this?" I try to think of a way to bring up the immediate problem with the gaming dynamics tactfully, but there isn't one. "Your cousin's gaming style leaves a bit to be desired. He's making it hard for me to run campaigns for everybody else."

"If he was any more of a munchkin, he'd be handing out lollipops on behalf of the guild," Lydia says flatly. "Sorry. I had no idea he'd be this much of a problem. He flies back home tonight, so this is the last time we'll have to deal with him in the game."

"Mind if I kill him off early and remove him from play?"

"You sound like you already have a plan."

I smile nastily. "You could say that."

"THE WIZARD'S GARDEN IS bathed in spring sunshine. You hear bees buzzing as they go about their work, and birds singing, and the gurgle of a nearby stream as it flows along on its way to the ornamental pond that you can see at the end of the garden. All around you are roses and irises, and lavender at the start of its bloom. In front of you, sitting in the middle of the neatly manicured lawn, on a small hill, is a gazebo."

"How big is it?" the cousin asks suspiciously.

"It's – gazebo sized. I don't know. Fifteen feet around, ten or fifteen feet high, maybe?"

"Built like a brick house. It must be an ogre of some kind."

Astonishing. The cousin has never heard of gazebos, let alone the gazebo joke? Good grief, the gazebo joke is several years old. Doesn't everybody read *Dragon* magazine? Is he setting me up? I had originally been preparing some killer clematis and ranunculus. This is too easy. I do some quick mental calculations.

"No, it's not an ogre. It's a gazebo."

"It's toast. I'm going to roast it with fireballs!"

Not a set-up? Surely this opportunity has a set-up attached to it. Then again, to have a set-up attached, Munchkin would need to know my plans.

Well, if anything would "kill" a wooden gazebo, it would be fireballs. "Okay. Roll against intelligence, with a difficulty of two." He'd better not get a critical success.

He rolls.

I chortle maniacally.

Silence falls.

"You rolled a *one*? Oh, dear. You couldn't have picked a worse moment. The gazebo, which had been slumbering on the grassy knoll, wakes up to the sound of your botched incantations and finds your off-key voice offensive. Roll for initiative."

I decided two minutes and thirty seconds ago that a gazebo, if awakened, should be as powerful as a greater deity. No matter how high Lydia's cousin rolls, he won't be able to beat the gazebo's power.

Within minutes, the garden is back to normal, and the gazebo is quiet and sleepy; although a perceptive visitor will see some pieces of a dead munchkin buried in a compost heap under a pile of splinters. Gazebos eliminate waste rapidly; their healthy, quick digestion process helps in the efficient production of mulch. This is one reason gazebos are sought out as garden caretakers.

The adventurers move on toward the wizard's house, minus one party member. They have no mage of their own now, but should they have the bad luck to alert the wizard to their presence (which they probably will, given how his house is booby-trapped – setting off alarms will be inevitable even without the added problem of a noisy and bizarre gardening accident) they do have other options. Wizards might be subtle and quick to anger, but they are also vulnerable to being stabbed in the back by well-wielded knives. I'm sure the assassin in the adventuring party will realize this should it become necessary.

GRADUATION DAY ARRIVED; OF course, I was invited, and of course, I attended. Lydia now has a bachelor's degree in philosophy. She also has a bachelor's degree in accounting, courtesy of her double major, so of course she actually has a job waiting for her.

Taking the job entails moving to Portland. She had interned there in late November through December and lived with her father for the duration of the internship. Internships are a solid way to land a job offer, especially when the internship in question is obtained through family connections. It was a smart decision on her part. So was taking her father's suggestion to declare a second major.

"You will stay in touch, won't you?" I ask. "Send me email." Since her father gave her a brand new computer as a graduation present, she gave me her old one. I am now the proud owner of a used computer setup. *Magister* and I have something on which to use the floppy disk we got in the mail from AOL a few weeks ago. And no, I'm not just hoping to create my own AOL account so that I can hear from Lydia after she moves. Although that factors in.

"Of course, I will."

I don't want to get my hopes up. I strongly suspect she won't.

It's probably for the best.

It doesn't hurt. No, really, it doesn't. It never does, provided, of course, you have no heart to be broken in the first place.

I HAVE A CULINARY experiment going on. It's called "*poule au pot* for the completely lazy cook."

Authentic *poule au pot* recipes all rely on an awful lot of frying and fussing. The ingredients have to be fried in butter or olive oil before being simmered on a stove in a large roasting pan, just long enough to cook all the way through but not so long that the meat falls off the bone and the contents become soup, then transferred in the roasting pan to the oven so that the cooked meat cooks even longer, which means frequent basting to ensure the meat doesn't dry out and become tough. Then everything has to be removed and set aside while the broth is reduced into gravy. The result is delicious, but very time-consuming and labor-intensive; also, it practically orders arteries to harden ("Toughen up! We know you can take more butter! Wimps!") and I think the ingredients would taste almost as good if they were simply boiled into a stew.

The only way to prove my hypothesis correct, of course, is to test it, so I have a frying chicken and a small ham boiling in a stockpot with some wine and *herbes de Provence* added to the water. In a couple more hours I'll add the carrots, leeks, celery, mushrooms, and potatoes. All the vegetable ingredients will be tied into pretty little bundles or sectioned off in cheesecloth bags, just like in the original recipe, so the presentation shouldn't suffer too much. The dish will be ready in time for supper.

Another, even lazier version of *poule au pot*, also one I invented, involves simmering everything in a crock pot in a base of homemade gravy. I'll try that on a day when we both have to work and so won't be home until after nine.

Shortcuts are not cheats. They're creative variations.

They let me do things like dance with *Magister* while I'm cooking dinner.

This afternoon, I presented him with a mix tape I'd made earlier in the day. I used to make mix tapes a lot when I was a teenager, but that was when I had a stereo of my own and a library of records, cassettes, and compact discs. I left those behind in one of my moves. However, public libraries have extensive music collections of their own, and *Magister* has his small stereo in the living room, and blank cassette tapes aren't very expensive, so I decided to make him a present. The music is mostly classical. There are a couple of New Age pieces on it, though, and some pop songs – one a Bryan Ferry song that reminded me of him, a couple of Moody Blues pieces, and a few others, most of them from the early to mid-seventies. They seemed to fit.

Magister found the latter selections amusing.

"You do realize these were hits when I was young, don't you? Was that deliberate on your part?" He smiled at me when he said that. "Trying to make me feel old?"

"Bah. You're not old." I hadn't thought of that while I picked the songs. For the most part, I don't usually think about his age. I'm aware that there are two decades, an entire generation, between us, of course, and I can't say that I see him as a peer, exactly, but neither do I think of him as an "older man," let alone as old. He's just himself. "I thought they suited us."

And so, we're dancing, like twin planets in search of a sun, slowly orbiting the chest that sits more or less in the center of the living room. Then the Jefferson Starship song that I put on the tape starts playing, and I catch my breath.

"They're singing about Thelema, aren't they?" I ask. "Or at least about sex magick."

"Entirely possible."

I stop our rotation to sway in place with him. I'm listening to the lyrics, and for some reason, I have a hard time moving my feet or otherwise dancing when I'm concentrating hard on the music or the lyrics to which I dance. This is probably why I don't dance often. "They are. The song isn't just a metaphor. The singers are ascending through love and sex. It's about Thelemic sex magick. It's got to be. Oh, my *erastes*. This needs to be our song."

"Hmm. It does seem to suit us, doesn't it? All right. We'll have a song." He smiles. "I suppose if we're going to do something traditional and sentimental like having an official song for our relationship, we might as well use one that references Aleister Crowley. However obliquely."

We sway together, memorizing each other's faces with our lips and fingers as we do so.

"I think it's time for a dip," he says. "It wouldn't be a romantic slow dance without a dip, now, would it?" Seconds later, I'm leaning back, giggling, with my head suspended above the floor. When he pulls me back up, our mouths meet briefly. And then I feel his teeth on my neck, biting slowly but firmly; my knees give in as the sweet, inexorable spasm grips me between my legs. I tremble in place, braced only by his arms, tossed by orgasmic pleasure; a tree in wind.

Within a few short moments, we're both on the floor, seeking each other, and finding.

"I love being able to cry with you if I cry," I say, as I get the buttons of his shirt open, and he works at the zipper on my pants. "Did you know I never used to cry much, until you somehow got me to do it? I don't even know if it was the pain. I've been hurt before, after all – it goes along with being bullied in school. It wasn't the same. Somehow you find ways to get under my skin. But if I'm going to cry, I want to do it in your arms. It feels good when you hold me. Your holding me when I cry feels good even when you were the one who made me cry. It makes the crying itself feel good. Isn't that weird?"

I feel him smile against me as he buries his face in my shoulder, planting sharp little kisses along my neck and chest. Little kisses, little bites that make me gasp. "It's supposed to feel good, *eromene*," he murmurs. "Otherwise, there wouldn't be much point."

His silvering hair is soft and fragrant when I kiss the crown of his head. When I concentrate, I can feel a slight glow, and I bask in warmth.

Our naked bodies embrace each other, melting into each other, trying to forget that they are two instead of one. He pushes my legs apart and drives himself into me deeply, making me cry out. It hurts; it feels good. I want more.

The lyrics break through the heat of my passion again for a few moments, because one word that I'm sure I used to be very familiar with is now unfamiliar to me, and I find that distracting and can't let it rest. "My love?"

"Yes, *eromene*?" Of course, he isn't stopping; he doesn't have my distraction-by-nitpicking problem. His focus, as always, is unbreakable. The way he's doing what he's doing almost makes me forget what I wanted to ask him.

"What does it mean when... when the lead singer is... singing *'Allez?'* I... I haven't studied French since... I was... in lower school. Oh. Oh, my. That... I like that..."

"Good angle? You like that, do you? I'll have to do more of it. Like this?" He smiles down at me. I have no idea how he can keep talking so calmly while he is pushing into me like that. He isn't even breaking his rhythm.

Meanwhile, I'm groaning hoarsely, bucking my hips, desperately impaling myself on him.

He pins me down with one hard rocking of his pelvis and resettling of his weight, making me cry out from a bizarre combination of frustration and pleasure. I can't move anymore, although I try anyway. "Ask me nicely, now. Your voice sounds so sweet when you beg."

"Please. Don't stop. Please, more, my love, please, I'll do anything for you..."

"Yes. You will." He leans down to cover my mouth with his as he thrusts, taking my jaw in one hand and holding me in place. His kiss enters me, insinuating, stealing my breath away. I gasp in sudden weakness and dizziness. "And I will always love and cherish you for it, among many other things about you. I think later tonight we'll see what else you'll do for me if I ask. Oh. Loosely translated, it means 'let's go,' or 'come with me.' *Allez*, beloved," he murmurs in my ear, as he grabs my calves and pushes my thighs higher to drive himself into me even more deeply. "*Allez... Allez...*"

With every thrust, he wrings a sharper cry from me.

When we are both spent, I find myself gazing at his naked body, how it glows in the square of golden afternoon sunlight that we are lying in. If I wanted to look away, I couldn't, but I don't want to. The glow is warm, as warm as inner light. My own body lies next to his, and my arm, next to his arm, is white stone, reflecting sun. We are alabaster statues in a temple, illuminated by warmth.

I whisper, "I love you more than words can say."

"That's what making love is for." He covers my mouth with his. He strokes my forehead; his fingers feel like velvet against my skin. We have more to tell each other, so much more, that will not fit into words. Some of it needs to be told now, sharply and sweetly, but of course, there is still so much more to making love after that. A lifetime of telling would not be enough to tell it all.

Oh, my *Erastes*.

WE'RE SNUGGLED ON THE couch going through *Magister's* latest haul of in-dependently published newsletters and small-press BDSM periodicals. The air conditioner is going full blast, and the couch is right in front of it; on a miserably hot day like today, this is the only way to stay comfortable. I'm getting a crash course in scene etiquette and traditions. From what I've seen so far, I don't think I want to get involved, but *Magister* thought it would be a good idea for me to at least be familiar with my own subculture, which seems sensible enough. There are, at any rate, worse ways to spend a muggy August morning.

There is apparently a bandanna for every kink that exists – at least, for every common and relatable kink. Somehow, I don't see too many people advertising a fondness for inflatable doll worship, or for sex with luggage, or for necrophilia.

Wearing a scarf or some other prominent accessory on the left side indicates a preference for doing, while wearing the same article on the right side of the body indicates a desire to have the same action done to you. There doesn't appear to be much mixing and matching. The convention also doesn't seem to be strictly limited to gay bars anymore, although that's where it originated. Now I know why he tied the black silk scarf onto my right wrist when he gave it to me. Black is for edge play, pain, and extremes in general. Extreme. That would be us.

"I must admit, I find some of these paraphilias baffling, but *de gustibus non est disputandem*. I wonder what a tie-dyed scarf would indicate?" I ask him.

"An LSD fetish?"

I elbow him in the ribs and go back to reading.

And grimace.

"Good grief, this is sexist," I complain. "Where are the women who play the top? Are we really that rare?"

"Hardly. Professionally, for instance, the vast majority of female sex workers who cater to kink are dominatrixes – which makes sense, if you think about it. It takes a lot of trust simply to submit to someone you know. Submitting to a client whom you've never even met before getting sent out by an escort agency? That takes a rare and special kind of nerve. And unfortunately, sexual assault is a very real hazard of sex work, and women who do sex work are disproportionately at risk. Add to that the general perception that people who play the bottom do so because they want to be abused, and – well. Professional submissives of both sexes receive very high client fees as a result, about twice as much as dominatrixes do, because dominatrixes are so much more common. In the scene, meanwhile? It depends on where you live and what group you belong to. Most of the groups I know of in the Midwest do indeed cater to male dominants and female submissives, when the couples are of both sexes. I'm not sure why. It might be because we live in a conservative part of the country, and there's some unresolved tension regarding gender roles. Move west to California and you'll find it more common for groups to be predominantly comprised of dominant women and submissive men, if they aren't single-sex pairings. Dominant men like me are as scarce as hen's teeth in San Francisco, at least, those of us who also happen to be heterosexual."

I make a sour face. "That's lopsided, too."

"You might like one group I heard of that is based out of Los Angeles. It was founded by a married couple that happens to lead a Wiccan coven. They're also, independently of their spiritual roles, both BDSM switches. Dominance and submission, sadism and masochism – the full axis. Between Beltane and Samhain, the half of the pagan year ruled by the Goddess, the wife is the High Priestess of their coven and has dominance over her husband. Between Samhain and Beltane, the half of the year that is associated with the Horned God, Consort of the Goddess, her husband is dominant and is the High Priest of the coven. Mind you, I don't think there's any deliberate overlap between their domestic lifestyle, and what they do in the coven – oh, yes, they're lifestylers, too, their roles aren't limited to play that goes on in the bedroom, they actually live as Mistress and slave or Master and slave in the rest of their domestic life as well, depending on what time of year it is; it just worked out that whichever of them is currently dominant also happens to take the active leadership role in religious ritual, probably because the polarity affects their energy. The BDSM group that they are the public face for, meanwhile, has a higher-than-usual incidence of switches, and among the less switchable members of the group, the number of male dominants and female dominants is roughly equal."

"That does sound nice," I say. Nice is an understatement. It's the sort of arrangement I would probably find ideal for my own life if only I could swing it, if I ever felt a need for something resembling a social life. "Why can't all groups be like that?"

"I don't know."

"Why are the switches brushed off in so many other instances? Most of what I read assumes that a person must be one thing or another: dominant or submissive, sadistic or masochistic, no playing both sides of the fence or you're not serious or you don't know who you are. It's like being bi, only worse, to everybody else – I've told you how lesbians won't accept that I like men, and straight people don't like that I want women, right? What am I, chopped liver?"

"You, dear one, are not chopped liver." He turns my head around so that he can reach my lips with his and gives me a kiss that starts out warm and eventually sears me down to my toes. "Alas, I have no easy answer for you as to why so much of the subculture does not like to acknowledge its switch hitters. It does seem rather odd, especially given that arrangements like ours, where one partner plays the submissive to a more experienced dominant to learn the art, are fairly common, although the majority of those relationships do not also involve a magickal apprenticeship such as the one we have. I think perhaps many people are uncomfortable with grey areas. Ambiguity can be challenging."

I still don't think I would find a home in the scene. I find it surprising that he was so active in it when he was younger, but then, he doesn't have the advantage of extreme flexibility that I have – his switchability seems to be limited at best. Learning by being done to wasn't an option for him. He doesn't talk about his experiences much, but I'm getting the impression that while he might have had a fair share of women in his bed years ago (it was, after all, the 1970s when he came of age) he played the role of voyeuristic wallflower more often than not if the setting was a public one. Every time I try to imagine him getting involved in a public scene in a nightclub or at a play party, my mind trips up on the image. He's so intensely private.

"So 'zines like this are how other pervects communicate with each other and try to meet up, if there are no actual social groups or support groups in a given city?" I ask. "It's like looking at the bastard child of an amateur press literary magazine and a mail-order bride catalog, with Hustler acting as the drunken fairy godfather at the naming ceremony."

"Pretty much," he agrees. "If you live in a major metropolis, where the BDSM scenes are large and active and extremely diverse, there's little need to communicate via pen pal lists and periodicals. If you live in a small town, or even a mid-sized city like ours in a conservative part of the country, finding folk of like mind, if that is important to you, gets rather more difficult. It's a common enough kink, in its milder expressions anyway, so finding a romantic partner to handcuff to the bed or give you the occasional spanking probably won't pose too many problems, but if you want to socialize with birds of your feather, or find someone to play with who is more hardcore, it gets problematic."

"Hence the various ways to use the mail to meet other people."

"Yes."

I glance down. "Well, the personals speak for themselves. I could see how someone who lived out in East Oshkosh would want to advertise availability in a magazine, because spontaneously meeting someone compatible in East Oshkosh would be rather unlikely. Though not impossible. I seem to recall bumping into someone randomly in a bookstore." I smile. "I could also see where going through one of these magazines would be like consulting a cookbook for food preparation ideas – the bondage illustrations in particular. I can just imagine someone pinning one of the pictures up to use as a pattern while trussing their partner up with rope. So that's useful. I really like this one picture, by the way, the one where the woman has her girlfriend tied up to a tree – it's very artistically done. Also very romantic. You can see by the way they're looking at each other that they love each other very much. The photographer must have had fun doing that particular shoot. You know, I bet my first ex-girlfriend would have wanted to see this."

"Down, girl," he says, with a grin. "I don't want drool on my periodicals."

"Then distract me or move the periodicals out of my way. And you're drooling, too. You've been poking me in the back for some time, now."

He proceeds to go about distracting me. As it transpires, I am easily distracted.

Mud squishes under our shoes as we walk along the path that overlooks the river gorge. It's not exactly a narrow path, but wet fallen leaves and slippery rocks make careless walking treacherous, and there is a steep slide downhill that, at best, would end in a close encounter with jabbing underbrush, at worst, in an involuntary bath in rapids that have been swollen with autumn rain; so we're taking this section of trail at a slow and careful pace. The earlier part of the trail was gently sloped, even paved in parts, and led to a rather nice overlook from where we could see the waterfall, or, if we preferred to walk just a little farther, a wide cave mouth; it's a popular part of the park to visit, though, even on wet, chilly days in late fall, so we're pushing on. I'm glad this is a day we both have off, because it means we can take our time. There are rocks and trees in this park that have graffiti carved into them from the nineteenth and even the eighteenth centuries, left by wandering trappers, soldiers, and settlers; looking for their carved signatures and initials is half the fun of walking this trail.

After a particularly rugged section that has me wishing for a walking stick, he looks around, sees something on his right, and veers off onto what I would be tempted to call a goat track, except I'm pretty sure, given the crushed beer can that I can see in the scrub brush, it was made by teenagers, not goats.

He looks over his shoulder and beckons. "This way," he says, and I do my best to tiptoe in mud and wet leaves without stumbling. He's more sure-footed than I am; he has to stop every few minutes to wait for me to catch up to him.

Eventually, we are perched side by side on a large, moss-covered log, overlooking a gully that leads down to the river.

It's a long way down.

"Excellent. We have a good view of the river, and we're just exposed enough to the mist that we'll stay in touch with the dampness. A little further on is a cave passage that would also have worked well for my purposes, but it's on the path, and while it's unlikely anybody will be coming this way, given the weather, I didn't want to risk a chance of being interrupted. This is better. I thought we'd work on channeling the elements. Sit facing me, please."

I rotate gingerly until I am straddling the log. It seems a stable enough position. More or less. He's in the same position himself, and he seems comfortable enough.

"You'll probably find this particular lesson rather enjoyable," he says, and smiles. "It involves a lot of kissing."

He's right. I like the sound of it already.

"Attend. I am sure you have noticed, by now, that quite aside from any questions of technique or style, there is a qualitative difference between certain of my kisses. It's because I sometimes channel different types of elemental energy for different desired effects. When working with Air, for instance, I've generally done so to take a very small amount of yours away from you. I do that to intensify certain physical reactions you have while we're making love, also because I happen to greatly enjoy it when you start swooning in my arms. You look cute when you do that. I'm not going to demonstrate it right now, because we're perched on a log over a steeply inclining slope and a ravine. Earth, on the other hand? Earth is another matter. This is Earth when channeled through a kiss."

He takes my face between his palms and leans in toward me and covers my lips with his. Instantly I feel a hungry, desperate stirring of desire that starts between my legs and works its way up me, caressing my flesh, murmuring to me of things to come. At the same time, I feel blissfully secure; the leather-clad hands that hold my face still are my rock, my anchor, my home.

"There," he says, as he slowly pulls away from me. "We are both grounded. I've just pulled the element of Earth through you, using you as a channel, and into myself. Some of that Earth energy actually came directly from you, from your body, although most of it came from the soil and trees and rocks around us. Did you feel how it flowed?"

I reflect on his words, but ultimately, I have to shake my head. No, I was too busy noticing how wonderful it felt to be kissed.

He can be very distracting that way.

He smiles. "Well. We'll just have to try again. This time, pay attention to the energy, not just to what the energy does to you. I know you are capable of this. There have been times when I had you on the receiving end of my riding crop, and I could swear a part of your consciousness was sitting on the side, taking notes. This situation is no different. I am going to kiss you and use you to channel Earth again. Attend."

Our lips connect once more, and by some Herculean effort, I manage to hold a bit of myself apart so that I can trace the energy flow. This time I feel it. He's pulling it up from the ground, through the soles of my dangling feet, and blending it with my *ch'i*. Once more, I feel the bliss of absolute security in his hands.

"Better," he says at last. "I think you got it that time; and that is good, because now I want you to show me that you can do the same thing. Practice on me. I think we'll be going back to this element often, in the days to come – since your personal energy is predominantly Fire, you have a bit of a hard time with patience, which can be a dangerous flaw when you are the one in control. You need to be the anchor of stability when you are dominant. Earthing your own desire is a skill you need to have, and you need to be able to do it easily. Channel Earth through me now, please." He smiles again. "Take all the time you need. It's Earth, after all. Earth does not need to be rushed."

Well.

When I lean into him, concentrating on his energy, I notice mostly his warmth, and a tightly reined passion that I desperately want to release, but that's Fire. I'm looking for Earth. I focus instead on his body, on the delicate bones of his face, the salt and pepper of his hair; the log underneath us asserts itself, so I weave in my awareness of the wood and the moss and imagine us growing roots that sink deep into the soil. There is a sweetness about him, a sweetness I want to taste, and I open him gently; our tongues dart around each other as I take him in.

I pull back.

"A reasonably good first attempt. We'll be working more with Earth over the next few weeks. An important thing to keep in mind, by the way: you cannot create something from nothing. You cannot bring out and work with what is not there. So, in a sense, you can rest assured that although you are dealing with the emotions and needs of another person when you kiss in this manner, you won't be forcing yourself on your partner. If what you seek is not there, you simply won't get a response. You'll wear yourself out for nothing.

"The flip side of that, however, is that most people do have strong emotions, many of which are repressed for whatever reason, and the reason is often a good one. Toying with emotions can be quite dangerous, and you can expect it to backfire on you eventually if you make a habit of it. It's unethical to play with the emotions of other people for your amusement. Be careful who you use as a living channel, and don't do it without a good reason.

"Now. Let me demonstrate Fire. You're very familiar with this energy, of course, as with others, especially given that Fire is your natural element, but not under these circumstances, and it's important to have Fire under conscious control. Unrestrained Fire can scorch. The first step toward controlling any element is knowing it."

He seizes my chin with his hand and pulls me toward him, crushing my body against him with his other arm. The chill of November vanishes. His kiss ignites me; I have *become* Fire. I want to have him here, on this log, now. Now. All I have to do is throw on a little more tinder. I want to feel his skin under my hands, his body writhing beneath mine, and I feed him my desire, tearing at the buttons of his coat with my free arm. It's too warm for coats, anyway. There, under his shirt, there is a place that likes being teased. It's mine now. His mouth, too, is mine. I will drink in this passion that he keeps buried deep inside. I know how to reach it, and I want it, all of it.

He gasps. Oh, sweet and delicious, that gasp. I pull him closer and nudge myself onto his lap so that our pelvises touch, my legs straddling his. Only a little more.

Come to me, lightning.

His face between my hands. His body writhing, arching. He moans into me. Oh, how sweet is the taste of that moan.

This time I am the one to break contact.

He chuckles under his breath when his head collapses onto my shoulder. "I think it's safe to say that since you were able to not only detect my working from the very start, but also completely take it over, with fine control, you already thoroughly understand how to use the element of Fire. I asked for that one, didn't I?" He coughs and clears his throat. "I'm going to have to catch my breath before we go on. I'm a bit drained."

I smirk.

We sit in place, leaning into each other, heads on each other's shoulders, listening to each other breathe, holding each other. A wet breeze begins to stir. Eventually, I notice that it's getting cold and drizzly, and I press closer for warmth, feeling the strong, steady current of his being pulse against me.

It's amazing the things you learn to notice when your voice is stilled.

"There. Now that I can focus again, I think it's time to channel Water through you. This should be interesting – not that I haven't done it before, but this will be the first time you're aware of it as such. Believe it or not, you're very easy to use as a Water channel, because, quite independently of compass corners, Water is your polar opposite. Water opposes Fire; Earth opposes Air. Anyone who has strong tendencies toward one element will have a buried side, corresponding to what Jung called the Shadow, in which their opposite element predominates. You burn with a white-hot Fire, but you have hidden Watery depths. They are profound and dark, to match your brightly burning flames. Any power that great is very easily manipulated by someone who knows how to do it." He smiles, and his smile is like velvet and midnight. "I happen to very much like stirring your waters and plumbing your depths. You probably knew that."

I think I noticed that some time ago, yes.

He reaches out for me with one hand, stroking the bottom of my jaw with a gloved finger. I shudder. Already I can feel it, and he hasn't even taken possession of my mouth yet. "Come here," he murmurs. "Come to me, now."

I swallow past the lump in my throat and lean forward into the kiss. I couldn't resist if I tried.

Our lips meet.

Drowning. Melting. Disintegrating, disintegrating. I'm dissolving into him. All I feel is my desire, which will kill me with ecstasy; and him, overwhelming, hard as granite on the outside, sharp as steel, and yet warm and soft and comforting beneath the surface, a blanket, a hearth fire. In this is everything I ever wanted or needed, and it caresses me softly, holding me in warmth and sweetness. My body is reduced to atoms, spinning dizzily, falling apart. From a far distance, I can tell that I'm trembling as I collapse against him, and then even that awareness is gone on a flood of drunken bliss. His lips are all over my face, tenderly kissing my cheeks, my eyelids, my hair. Every kiss leaves blossoms in its wake.

"Mine?" he whispers, caressing me softly on one cheek.

I nod speechlessly. Yours, yours, all yours, forever yours.

His lips meet mine again. I moan into him, nearly in tears from happiness. When his hand plays at the back of my neck, tracing a faint circle before seizing me gently and holding me in place near the place my birthday necklace usually sits when I wear it, a faint cry escapes me. He kisses me there, too.

I feel his lips against my ear. "*Mine*," he whispers, and I press closer to him. His.

"Come for me."

My body convulses, and a hoarse cry starts to escape me before he covers my mouth with his hand. Muffled, my cries go on, until at last he releases me and pulls his face away from mine, and I sag, exhausted.

I feel a chuckle begin to rumble in his chest. "There. I think we're even now."

"We are *not* even," I mutter, before I remember that I'm not supposed to be talking. "Not even close."

He smiles as he puts his finger against my lips. "I've had practice. Speaking of which, did you follow any of that closely enough to try working it yourself?"

I shake my head. No. How could I possibly trace an energy path, when I was busy being drunk?

"Ah. Well, then. We'll just have to keep trying this until you can trace the energy and follow it when I work with it."

I had a feeling he'd say that.

EVENTUALLY, I MANAGE TO keep a part of myself withheld enough to observe and take note of the flowing current. My knees are jelly, as is the rest of me, both physically and emotionally, but that's all right, it's a good jelly state. Very, very good jelly. I'll just sit here and be jelly for a while, shall I?

Except I can't, because we're doing work. Rats.

"Water is a very useful element to channel through another person. It's not just a way to arouse emotions and encourage surrender; Water is also a healing element. There are far worse ways to encourage healing than through a touch, or a gentle kiss. It's also good for dreams and visions; a well-directed kiss can be transforming. Come to think of it, a touch or a kiss of Fire can heal and transform, too, but Fire is not a gentle element to work with, as I have emphasized from the beginning of your education – Fire is purifying, and its purification sears. Indeed, the root of purify is *pur*, the Greek word for Fire. Water can be dangerous in its seductive power, but it's a much gentler way to encourage healing and transformation than Fire is, provided it does not drown your subject. Now. Try it on me."

I blink at him.

"Beloved one, it is important that you practice this skill and master it before you try using it on another person – especially with the Water element, which can be elusive and tricky. That is why we are here today, by the river rapids: to use its proximity to help you focus and boost your power. I do not think you will hurt me. Aren't you just a little curious about what you might bring out in me? I am." He leans his forehead against mine. The sudden sensation of being touched by his presence is impossibly intimate. "It's all right," he whispers. "I trust you to not shatter me if you hold me."

I take his face between my hands, drawing on the misty air, the river that surges below us. He starts to tremble. "*Se philo,*" he whispers, and closes his eyes.

Then our lips meet.

Deep within, a warm, flowing current pulses. It wants to swell. I am profoundly thirsty, and oh, I'm hungry. Swell the current. Raise the river, bring down the rain, overflow. Overflow your life into my mouth, and my dear love, let me in, let me in. I have never needed anybody so, and here, you need me too, I can taste it in your kiss, in every wave I drink in, I am here, let us float together. I will hold your head above the water. Let us swim in love, rushed along the currents at flood. We will swim in eternal bliss.

You are so vulnerably beautiful, naked in this torrent.

When I break the contact and release his face, I see a drop of blood pooling on his lower lip.

His eyes are astonished when he opens them. "My God," he whispers. "My God. I didn't know that it was like *that* for you."

WE MELT OFF THE log and somehow manage to navigate the hillside paths without stumbling or slipping. The wider part of the trail is a welcome sight, however, and it is with relief that I set my feet upon it. I don't feel tired – quite the opposite, in fact, which is odd – but my joints feel like river water, and my limbs all seem to want to tremble.

When we get back into the car, I find myself reaching for him again. There is something about the warmth that I sense under his coat that lures me. Soon we are unbuttoning each other, seeking each other out with our hands.

Did I ever love, or hunger, before him?

Yes, but not like this.

Our groping hands brush up against each other by accident, and I clasp his in mine, pressing it to my breast. Our eyes meet. He smiles.

"Let lips do what hands do; they pray. Grant thou, lest faith turn to despair."

Two can play at this. It's a famous passage, after all. "Saints do not move, though grant for prayers' sake."

"Then move not, while my prayer's effect I take. Thus from my lips, by yours, my sin is purged."

A flood of bliss. Waters flow back and forth between us, drenching us with desire.

"Then have my lips the sin that they have took," I gasp at last.

"Sin from thy lips? O trespass sweetly urged! Give me my sin again."

We float together on this boundless sea of our own making, caressed by waves, dissolved by tides.

ON THE WAY HOME, he stops the car outside the post office that is on the way. He looks down significantly at the stamped, addressed envelope that rests between us in the well between our seats.

Sighing, I pick up my college application and run out the door with it, to drop it in the mailbox for the next collection.

The rain begins to fall in earnest. By the time I make it back to the car, I am soaked and freezing.

ONCE HOME, WITH THE door shut behind us, he steers me to the bedroom and starts undressing me. Or maybe I started undressing him first. I can't be sure. I do know I desperately want to get our wet clothes out of the way, and he seems to be of the same mind. Our coats and gloves fall to the floor, soon followed by other articles until we are naked, and all our clothing kicked into the corner.

A gust of wind blows rain and sleet against the window.

"God, you're warm," I murmur into his lips when our faces collide. "Feels good. More."

He is smiling as we sink onto the futon to tangle our limbs and bodies together. "Cold?" he asks. "I would have thought you'd have warmed yourself up by now. You've never had problems generating heat."

"I want yours." I run my hand through his hair. His hair is one of the most magnificent things about him. The parts that are still sable really are black, while the increasingly large number of silver strands are a true silver, not grey or white, and it's glorious to feel under my hand: thick and very rich, the sort of hair I could bury my hand in indefinitely. There have been nights when I fell asleep stroking his hair, while he dozed against my shoulder.

"Hmm. I'll consider it. You seem quite warm already."

"I do?"

"*Eromene*, you are an inferno. I don't think you are in any danger of contracting a chill. On the other hand, making sure you stay warm does have a certain appeal, although it might not be a very comfortable sort of warmth for you. I'll have to give this more thought. Right now, though, we still have work to do. This is a much more appropriate place to practice channeling Air through a kiss. We're lying on a futon. It's a safer place to be if one of us passes out than on top of a log over a high ravine."

I look at him wide-eyed. "Is that likely?"

"I won't rule it out. You're a novice, and Air is another element that can be very tricky to work with, so until you get more accomplished at what you are doing, results can be somewhat unpredictable. We are dealing with the original stuff of life. *Psyche*, translated, means not just soul, but also life and breath. The bride of Eros is sometimes depicted as being a butterfly, or as having butterfly wings, further emphasizing that Psyche is the embodiment of life and spirit and showing her link to Air. Meanwhile, further to the north, Odin is seen as the

Father of All because he took the clay being crafted by Loki and breathed life and soul into it. In the beginning is Air... The first few times I started experimenting with it, I wound up giving both myself and my partner a nasty fright. I hadn't known my own strength. In the end, everything turned out all right and nobody was hurt, but – well. She took a long time to regain her consciousness, although her breath came back almost immediately after I stopped kissing her. It certainly *felt* like a long while until she came back, though it was probably only a few very frightening minutes. At any rate, there is a slim chance you might take enough breath away from me when kissing me, or impede my airflow somehow, that I'll start to lose consciousness. I doubt I'd accidentally do the same to you, but on purpose is another matter – come to think of it, putting you on the receiving end of a large working of Air might be a good way to help you get the feel of the element. Something more subtle would be too hard to notice at first. And I do need to replenish all the energy you inadvertently took from me when we were perched on that log. At least, I presume it was inadvertent on your part."

Gulp.

"You shouldn't be nervous. I think I mentioned having done this to you quite often, just not to any dramatic degree. You've always seemed to enjoy it." He smiles. "Immensely."

Oh. I see. He's been using the *Waiting for Godot* method of foreplay.

"Do you trust me?"

I nod. Of course.

"Then I am going to kiss you. This time, I will not hold back." He reaches out for my cheeks and holds me as he covers me with his mouth and body, rolling onto me almost like a heavy bank of clouds.

At first, I don't notice anything unusual. It's a kiss. I bask in the warmth of his lips, the gentle feel of his hands caressing me, fingers stroking lightly along my torso, around my breasts, up and down, circling over and over, pinching and kneading the nerves and meridians he knows so well, playing my strings until I start to sigh and moan. More – so much more, my skin is alive under his fingers, singing, higher and higher, spiraling up until the orgasm seizes me between my legs and up and up my spine and I am screaming into his mouth. Screaming. Gasping. Gasping... Then I notice it. My breath is leaving me faster than I can replace it. *He's eating my air*. My life. But I can't stop coming or crying out, any more than I can stop him from sucking the wind out of me.

If I am going to die tonight, I will die of pleasure.

There are worse ways to die.

Eventually, my screams become moans, then mewing noises, and then I feel my limbs shaking uncontrollably. Dizzy. I think I'm going to be sick. Still coming, despite it all. That can't be humanly possible.

Blackness.

"FIVE MINUTES. I SUPPOSE it could have been worse."

The alarm clock winks at us from its place on top of a pile of books on the floor.

"Glurg," I mutter articulately into his arm.

He wraps himself around me more tightly; I sigh happily. "Did you manage to trace the path of the wind that I was raising and drawing out of you? I would prefer to not do that again tonight. The five minutes I just spent were a little too long for my liking."

No, I nod.

"I think we'll save further intensive work with this element for another time. You seem too tired to focus."

I nod again.

He lets go of me briefly to get up off the futon and walk a couple of steps to the window. "It's a bit close in here. That can't be helping," he says, lifting the window sash. Icy, wet wind begins to blow into the room.

It actually feels good.

He crouches down to sit on the floor, his naked back propped against the bookcase that takes up space on that wall, and beckons me to him with his arm.

Somehow, I manage to drag myself off the futon to cuddle up against him. I suspect he was testing me to see if I needed to be carried.

The late afternoon sky darkens to dusk as we gaze at the cemetery through the open window. Rain and sleet continue to fall, and every now and then the wind will swell, blowing damply against our faces. One gust lingers, cold and sharp and wet, but somehow managing to feel like a caress, despite its biting cold; it's as if the wind loves me. It tickles under my chin in an eddy before slowly quieting.

"Air is your element, isn't it?"

"Yes."

We rest together in companionable silence, gazing out at the bare, wind-swept trees, the sleet driven against the windowpane.

"Can kisses of Air do anything besides take breath away?" I eventually ask.

"Of course. You can breathe life into someone else if that person is receptive." He cups my face. "Very useful, for instance, when someone's energy is too low to allow play to continue, but both of you want to keep going anyway."

The warmth of his kiss makes me sigh with delight.

Outside, the snow is falling, a dizzying ballet of large flakes on a stage of white. All is snow. Nothing else exists.

"You first," I say. It's become traditional for him to open his Yuletide presents first, but it's also become traditional for me to importune him into doing so; not that he particularly needs encouragement, but he thinks I'm cute when I wheedle. I give him my best wide-eyed, eager look and lean into him. "Please? Pretty please?"

"With sugar on it?"

"What else would you like on it?"

He smiles. "Depending on what 'it' is, I'd like a number of different things. Have you given yourself to me as a present, perhaps?"

"Oh, love. You ask that every year. My answer is still the same, too: I gave myself to you a long time ago, *Erastes*."

Our lips meet, followed by our bodies.

"I'll unwrap you later," he says at last, a bit breathlessly. "I like to save the best present for last. Let's see what else you put under the tree this year."

He reaches for the largest of the three packages I arranged by the tiny little tree. "It feels squishy, and it's as light as air. Hmm. I see dark fabric. It's black. And if I unfold it, it's... a silk shirt. That's a fine silk, too."

I got lucky at the thrift store. Very lucky.

"I like you in silk."

"You do, don't you?" he muses. "I'll have to wear this tonight."

The thought of that silk against my bare flesh is enough to send chills up and down my spine. "Yes, please," I gasp. The evening suddenly seems too distant.

"This one's heavy. What on earth did you put in here, a rock?" Underneath the wrapping is a box, which he opens. "Oh. You did give me a rock. I'm sure you had your reasons."

I can't help but laugh. His puzzled expression is priceless. "It's not just a rock. Try lifting it out of the box."

It's a pity there is no morning sun pouring through the east window.

"My word. A geode. A magnificent one, at that. That's beautiful. I'll keep it here for now. I can't wait to see what happens when it catches the light. All right, let's see what this last one is. It looks like a book. I wonder what's inside?" He slides his finger under the wrapping paper. He's very careful about the way he unwraps his presents. "A reproduction of a calligraphed, illuminated Song of Solomon. English translation on the right-side pages. Oh. Thank you. That is exquisite. How did you –"

"I saw it and grabbed it before anyone else could notice that it was there, the same way I did your new silk shirt," I reply. The geode was on display at a scientific supply store, and it was by far the most expensive of my purchases. The painfully high price may have been why it had been on display for months, in my line of sight every time I walked past the store in the downtown mall. The shirt and the book, on the other hand, were pure secondhand serendipity. "I want to read it to you. May I?"

"Read me love poetry? I would never turn that down, *eromene*. Now. Your turn."

There's a pile of presents this year. I suspect he's been buying things and setting them aside as Yule presents for months.

I decide to go for the books first – there are books, of course; whenever we give each other presents, books are likely to be involved, one way or another. It's an interesting (and *large*) assortment: the complete works of C. G. Jung, in translation; a book on dreams by James Hillman; a Red Cross textbook on advanced first aid; several practical handbooks on BDSM that, in my mind, I am already classifying as "cookbooks."

Knowing that there is always method to his madness, I ask, "These all go together, don't they? No red herring in this batch, since these are gifts, not assigned reading?"

"Correct. Some of them address various ways to handle the body of a submissive; the other books are to help you study how to handle a soul that is, however temporarily, in your care. When a person surrenders his or her person to you, you hold far more than just a body. You hold a bundle of needs and longings, hopes and fears. You are a bringer of catharsis, either through agony or ecstasy, or a mixture of the two; you can give release, healing, catalysis, and transformation. In a way you are a kind of priest, because you act as psychopomp, leading your partner into the realm of the underworld and back again. Handle this role with reverence. The human soul deserves no less."

I bow my head in acknowledgment.

The next package is a small one. It's probably jewelry; I might as well get it over with. Hoping that he didn't spend a fortune on it, I remove the wrapping and open the box.

"An ouroboros," I whisper. "It's perfect."

I turn the pendant over and over in my hands, marveling at the fine detailing of the individual scales and segments.

"The same silversmith that made your whip made the pendant," he says. "I commissioned him to do it."

"It's beautiful. Should I – or do you want to – "

Smiling, he lifts the pendant out of my hands; the chain falls down and dangles. When he loops it around my neck, the pendant hangs between my breasts.

Two other presents are made of leather and velvet: a set of lined manacles, and a riding crop; both will no doubt be broken in soon enough, one way or another.

"When you are a full-time college student again, these will probably be well out of your price range. Consider them an investment," he says.

"Which one of us gets to break in the crop?"

"You do."

I do? I remind myself that there are several uses for a riding crop, most of which do not involve inflicting pain, but this is still an unexpected pleasure. We're going to have an interesting discussion soon.

The last present is clothing: a black velvet teddy with matching opera-length gloves.

"One would suspect that you like velvet in the same way that I like silk," I murmur.

"One would be correct in their suspicions."

"I think I'll wear these tonight. They'll go well with your new silk shirt. And then we will go well together. We do go well together, don't we?"

"Yes," he sighs. "Very much so."

Neither of us mentions the other Christmas present that I received: a letter of acceptance from the university that I applied to in November through the early decision process.

It's only an hour away to the north. It's an easy commute for him. I'll be living in a dorm room during the week and staying with him in our apartment on the weekends.

Part of me wants to burst with pride and happiness. The other part looks out the window at the falling snow and shivers with cold.

AFTER SOME CABERNET SAUVIGNON to wash down our celebratory dinner (spinach leaf and pomegranate seed salad, with freshly chopped mushrooms; green bean casserole, heavy on the mushrooms; beef and mushroom stroganoff, also heavy on the mushrooms. We went a little overboard on buying mushrooms this week, so it's been mushroom this and mushroom that. Fresh mushrooms are best eaten while they're actually *fresh*) we decided that it was time to take a bath.

Both of us having wiry, bony frames means we fit easily in a bathtub together, and his bathtub is ideal for this. It's a gigantic old-fashioned claw-footed tub with a reclining back and deep sides. We aren't even slightly squashed.

"I am the Rose of Sharon, and the lily of the valleys. As the lily among thorns, so is my love among the daughters. As the apple tree among the trees of the wood, so is my beloved among the sons. I sat down under his shadow with great delight, and his fruit was sweet to my taste."

I put the book down behind me on the little table we use to hold folded towels and take his face in my hand to bend his mouth to mine. He moans.

Sweet fruit.

"How am I doing with Water?" I ask at last, when we come up for air. "Is my finesse getting any better?"

Still gasping, he opens his eyes. "Yes, I believe so. Although it probably doesn't hurt that we're in a bath."

I smile, reach for the book again, and go back to reading.

"My beloved spake, and said unto me, Rise up, my love, my fair one, and come away. For lo, the winter is past, the rain is over and gone; the flowers appear on the earth; the time of the singing of birds is come, and the voice of the turtle is heard in our land; the fig tree putteth forth her green figs, and the vines and the tender grape give a good smell. Arise, my love, my fair one, and come away. O my dove, that art in the clefts of the rock, in the secret places of the stairs, let me see thy countenance, let me hear thy voice; for sweet is thy voice, and thy countenance is comely."

My hands are shaking. I put the book back onto the towels and go back to the sweetness and delight of kissing his mouth. Floating. Falling. Drowning.

"My Beloved is mine, and I am His," I gasp.

Sweetness ravishes me as he takes my mouth with his lips. His hands close about my wrists.

Eventually, we relocate to the bedroom. There are some things the bathtub is too small for, even with our frames being slight.

THE FILM VERSION OF *The Princess Bride* must be one of the best Valentine's Day movie selections ever. It's interesting to watch again, after having experienced a sexual awakening, and while being held tightly in the arms of the man who caused that awakening. The Dread Pirate Westley/Roberts doesn't just look like Errol Flynn anymore. I wouldn't put the film's perversion quotient as high as that in the Addams Family movies, but a lot of the scenes could be framed with an alternative meaning.

"Princess Buttercup looks fetching blindfolded, bound, and with a knife held to her throat," I observe.

"Down, girl."

I chuckle and snuggle closer to Magister. He's not in much of a position to make comments about the direction of my attention, if my power of observation is at all reliable. Although he did tell me at one point that his arousal comes more from watching my own aroused state, under conditions like these, than it does from watching characters in movies, however pretty the characters might be; which is odd, but probably no odder than anything else about us.

He's certainly not doing much to calm down my state of arousal, judging from what he's doing to my breasts, which is more evidence that he's not being serious with his advice, although what he is doing is distracting enough that I'm having a hard time paying attention to the movie. Good thing I've seen it countless times already. His hands are more interesting right now anyway.

When he starts kissing me along my neck and ears, and one of his hands makes its way lower, I stop paying attention to the movie entirely.

At some point he lets me know that the credits are running, and maybe we would have more room to pursue certain activities if we did them in bed.

That sounds agreeable.

WRESTLING. STRAINING. THE AGE-OLD dance of bodies seeking, and finding, what they want in each other. Kisses that taste like wine and chocolate. Skin slick with desire and sweat. He thrusts into me; I cry out for more. Sandalwood from the scented candles blends with oils of frankincense and spikenard and cedar, and the musk of our passion.

I look down, seeing his skin golden in the flickering candlelight. My hands are on his wrists.

He looks good like that.

"*Erastes?*"

"Yes?"

"I think we should use my Yule presents again tonight."

"That seems reasonable," he says, a smile playing about his lips. "And you probably should get more practice, on general principle if nothing else."

"Practice?" I dive down and hiss in his ear. "I think there's more to this than practice. Don't you?"

He lets out a low chuckle. "Perhaps."

"Is that all I'm going to get out of you?" I murmur, as I reach behind the futon for the manacles and start fastening them on his wrists and ankles. I like seeing him stretched out like that; it makes his wiry muscles stand out nicely. Very nicely. I start imagining what else might make him look good.

"Most likely."

"You're being obstinate tonight."

He grins.

"All right, then. If that's how you want to play it, I can go along with it. We'll see if I can't get a more definite answer out of you." It's hard to keep my face deadpan when my every instinct is trying to get me to burst out laughing, but I manage heroically.

Although I didn't have to interrupt our activity to fasten his wrist manacles to the chains at the sides of the futon, I had to lift myself off him briefly when I was securing his ankles; I could go back to what I was doing, but I opt for pleasuring him with my mouth, because I know he likes it, and I want to see how long I can tease this out. The sounds he starts making gratify me immensely. I make a mental note to use my teeth on his intimate areas more often.

"So. Only perhaps?" I murmur. "Are you sure?"

"Yes," he gasps.

"Yes, what? Yes, maybe is your final answer, or yes, you actually want me to dominate you tonight?"

"Yes, I want you, *eromene*."

"On top? As I am now?"

"As you are."

"Oh, good," I say, and lift myself so that I can mount him. "I was hoping so. I was getting tired of waiting to feel your cock inside me again. You don't mind if I stop what I'm doing with my teeth to take advantage of you, do you? Dear God. That feels good. *Yes*."

Riding him, I summon Fire through my hands as I stroke his arms and his chest, reaching into him for his heat. He cries out, and bucks underneath me. So beautifully taut. I lean down to kiss him.

"I think you are looking for my submission, not just my passion, *eromene*," he rasps. "Try Water instead. My surrender does not generally flow without a little elemental nudge from you. If I didn't feel so much love for you, I doubt there would even be any. It's never been there before with anyone else."

Oh. Right.

I focus on the watery things in the room when I kiss him again: the sweat on his body, the wetness of my desire, the pulsing of his blood. He starts to shudder beneath me, showing a telltale sign of Water's influence taking effect. I feel him mentally dissolving.

"Need you," he moans, and I can't tell whose need is greater, his or mine.

He strains toward me. I can see his throbbing veins. They need to be kissed. I run my lips along them, worshiping the current of his life with my mouth.

His moans become hoarse cries.

I want to drink them in, too.

I lower my lips to his neck again and kiss my way up to his mouth. Sweet, sweet moans. More, I want more. He shakes underneath me. When my fingers brush his nipple, he pants. He's always been so sensitive there.

Now?

"I want to hurt you. May I?"

He thinks for a few seconds – which astonishes me, when I'm under the influence of Water I don't have the presence of mind to think, but perhaps he is not as strongly affected as I am – and then answers, "Very well. Let's see what comes of it."

His lips are soft, and they seem to tingle when I lick them. I squeeze my fingers together as I bite down on his lower lip. He is the fruit of the Tree of Life, and ripe enough to burst.

Sweet, forbidden fruit in my mouth and under my hand, a promise of delectation to come.

"Stop. Enough. Stop, *eromene.*"

I have to fight myself to get myself to let go. I'm going to find that disturbing later when I think about it.

"I don't think I like to be hurt, not even by you. I'm sorry. There are some things I cannot give you. I love you; I love you in a way I have loved no one else. I love you so deeply that it frightens me. I wish my love for you would help me feed all your appetites, but I can't do it. That is why you tried to get me to surrender to pain, isn't it?"

A lump builds in my throat.

"I wish we could be everything to each other when making love, too, *eromene*. Believe me when I say that."

"I want you forever," I sob. "I was hoping... I was hoping... if only neither of us would have to go hungry... I want you to be mine. I want to be yours. I *am* yours. I don't want to lose you. I want to spend my life with you."

"I know."

I shake with tears. It's not fair.

"I can't comfort you in my arms unless you let me out of the shackles," he says gently.

I nod miserably and get to work.

Later, in the darkness, after the candles have been blown out and the toys put away, he cradles my body against his, stroking my hair and whispering to me. I feel the Earth he is channeling with his presence, and cling to him.

This time he is the one to bind our wrists together with the black scarf. "Don't think of the future," he murmurs, "think of the present. I am here. We have each other now. Let now be our eternity. We do have this, beloved." He strokes my wrist, bound to his, and a small sigh escapes him. "We are bound to each other, bound as tightly as our wrists are bound by this bit of silk cloth. Focus on that and let me hold you. Here. Rest on my heart. Listen to it beat. You are on the verge of nodding off, aren't you? Hush, then. Let it happen now. *Hypnotte, eromene, hypnotte...*"

Ensorcelled by words, I eventually succumb to sleep in his embrace.

KETHER

WE HEAD NORTH ON the interstate. The radio is on, playing something classical, but neither of us is really listening. He keeps his eyes on the road; I look out the window without paying much attention to what I'm seeing. We don't talk, nor do we brush hands like we usually do when we're in the car. I'm afraid I'll start to weep if I so much as open my mouth.

Or worse, that I'll make him weep.

MIDSUMMER EVE.

We drove to one of the massive suburban parks that circle the larger metropolitan area to the north like a long emerald necklace. Like any other park, it's closed to the public after dark, and patrolled, which is why he parked the car in a parking lot about a half a mile away from the park entrance we accessed, and why we've been walking in shadows to our destination, a formation of three hundred-million-year-old ledges and boulders that overlook a lake.

When we reach them, I look up in awe. The boulders are huge – some of the rocks are the size of small houses. They're dwarfed by the ledges themselves, which soar above the trees.

He says quietly, "This used to be an ocean bed. These sandstone ledges used to be mud and silt; when the ocean dried up, the stone was lashed by wind until the boulders and ledges you see here were made. The rock formations, made of conglomerate sandstone, a soft and brittle rock if ever there was one, then somehow managed to survive multiple ice ages, and glaciers three miles high and as wide as the continent they covered, glaciers that flattened the terrain and left not just till behind when they melted, but also deep grooves in the earth, and a series of massive lakes. These rocks and ledges remained through it all. It puts a certain perspective on things, doesn't it? *Eromene*, are you certain you want to do this?"

"Yes."

"What we do will be permanent. These are not just vows. We are binding our souls together."

"My *Erastes*, our souls are already bound."

"They will be more so, after this."

I don't see how that could even be possible. How could the two of us be more knotted and interwoven than we already are? I smile and swallow past the lump in my throat. "I accept. This is what I want, my love. I think it's what I've always wanted. I'm tired of running. I thought we had this discussion."

"We need to be certain. There will be no undoing what we do. Not in this life, nor in what is to come. It will be forever. You are certain, then, that this is your Will?"

"Yes."

He falls silent for a moment. "It is mine, too. For a number of reasons, I do not think this is sensible or logical on our part, nor do I think it even remotely wise, but it does feel right, and inevitable, and I believe that, not common sense or rationality, is what operates here, and what aligns our Wills. And may all that Is witness our intent. Well, then. Let us move on."

We begin to pick our way uphill, weaving our way through stone and trees, finding a path that will take us to the top. It's a good thing the waning moon is still a few days away from being new. The ground looks treacherous.

Eventually, we scramble to a high spot and find a good place to lay down the blanket. It's surrounded by just enough scrub brush and sapling trees that we don't stand out in silhouette to the casual eye, so if there is a park ranger or a police officer on patrol, we probably won't be spotted; meanwhile, our location is just exposed enough to the air that when we look up, we get a good view of the

moon's crescent, and what stars we can see through ambient light. We're too close
to the city to see much more than the brightest heavenly bodies.

My book bag has been temporarily converted into a picnic carrier. After the
blanket come the teacups, which are from a Japanese tea set and hold about half
as much liquid as their Western equivalents, and have the virtue of being sturdier
than the antique shot glasses we use for drinking absinthe when we're at home,
or any other kinds of receptacles made from glass; a box of sugar cubes; a slotted
silver spoon; and our bottle of homemade absinthe, which after two years still
has several shots left in it, because we only bring it out for our magickal workings
which rely on heightened concentration and awareness – guided visualizations,
dream work, scrying, seeking conversations with our higher Selves.

And now, performing a *Hieros Gamos*. Our personal circumstances couldn't
be more in conflict with what we are about to do. Our souls, however, disagree
with our personal circumstances.

I think we could have skipped the spoon, the sugar cubes, and the fancy
teacups, and just made do with a thermos with some absinthe and simple syrup
mixed into it, but he likes the quasi-ceremonial trappings of absinthe served the
Victorian way. It must be the romantic in him.

Silently, I watch him put a sugar cube onto the spoon and pour absinthe over it,
letting the resulting mixture drip into one of the teacups. The dripping becomes
a pouring as the sugar cube eventually dissolves.

"There," he says, "that's yours," then repeats the process.

When he is done, he lifts his cup, and we drink to each other.

I cast the circle myself when we have both drained the cups. It's more practical
this way; we're outside, in a public park, and all the trappings he'd be using if he
was the one setting it up would have been cumbersome. Now that my magickal
training has been completed, I am no longer under silence, but I keep my silence
anyway. It's still how I focus my energy.

I walk slowly, stopping at each cardinal point as I invoke the elements; when I
call Air from the east, a slight breeze kicks up, bringing a welcome chill to the hot
summer night.

Fireflies dance in the distance.

Heat lightning flashes.

He reaches for me, and I ground the energy through him, palm to palm, lip to lip, feeling the ancient sediments of the ledge holding us fast. We are two, in the process of becoming one: man to woman, Shakta to Shakti, heaven to earth, priest to priest, god to goddess. Soul to soul, self to self.

Will to Will.

Our hands begin unfastening each other's clothing. It doesn't take long; soon we are naked to each other and to the flaring night sky, our flesh warm and electric as we move over each other, caressing all the places we know so well in each other and never tire of rediscovering.

He kneels and covers my genitals with his mouth, flicking me with his tongue. I gasp but manage to avoid making any actual noise. Just. Even after four and a half years of practicing silence in a cast circle, it seems almost more than I can bear to keep my voice inside myself.

His tongue is so sweet, so gentle.

Eventually, my climax overtakes me; my knees collapse, and I find myself trembling against him, grinding my pelvis into his mouth and tongue, held up only by the strength in his arms. A strangled noise escapes me.

When I open my eyes and look down, I see him smiling one of his rare softer smiles.

He lets me down slowly – it's the only way I can move at all, short of falling onto the ground, my knees are still shaking so hard that they don't support my weight – and onto his lap. I almost cry out as I feel myself impaled on him, and instinctively start to writhe back and forth, my breath hot against his shoulder.

"Hush. Stop," he whispers. "Or it will be over before we've begun to weave our souls. Focus on me. Breathe with me. Focus your energy on mine and *be still* while I braid. Don't move."

His lips are as hot as fire when they meet mine. Our tongues brush against each other; lightning travels up my spine as he reaches into me with his breath and pulls, and despite myself, I find myself moaning and rocking my hips against him.

He tightens his grasp on my hips and pushes me down further so that I can no longer ride him. He's in me so deep. I hang on edge, keening, as my body burns.

A wry smile pulls at one corner of his mouth. "I know the temptation is very great to only concentrate on the sex. Believe me, I am quite tempted, myself. Please. Focus on me instead. Meditate until we are both in trance. I need your cooperation in this, or I won't be able to perform my own role in the work we do. You're... starting to get very distracting."

I listen for his breathing pattern, breathe in deeply, hold it, exhale. Repeat.

Eventually, my own howling need seems to not so much die down as fade into the background and become unimportant. I listen to his breath and feel my own breath start to synchronize itself with his. I pay mindful attention. My hips still seem to be trying to rock of their own accord, but no longer urgently or quickly. He punctuates his breath with kisses; every time his lips touch mine, a little current of lightning tickles up and down my spine. Mostly, though, we just breathe in and out.

Wind swirls around us. The sky flickers with light.

At some point in this sighing of wind, the absinthe lucidity comes into our minds, enfolding us with green fairy wings; we look into each other's eyes, and in one accord, our mouths meet once more. I reach with my breath for the core of his being as he breathes me in, and soon we are burning in fire, sailing in stars, free of our bodies, rising into the multifoliate rose of the heavens as we dissolve into each other; we dance in flame, our passion a starburst in the darkness, witnessed by all the stars of the cosmos. God and goddess, we love.

We explode as one, we cry out as one, we burn together and are One.

MY BOOKS ARE CRAMMED into milk crates as full as the milk crates can be packed. I had to sacrifice some of my crates because we couldn't fit all the crates into the back seat and trunk of the car in one trip without leaving behind my suitcase and bedding, so all the books got double and triple stacked. I can always steal more milk

crates. Free modular bookcases, available behind cafeterias and convenience stores in the wee hours of the morning, if you're quick about it and keep yourself covered.

He's keeping the computer Lydia gave me. There's no room for it in the car. Besides, I won't have any need for a PC of my own if I have access to the campus computer lab, nor will I need to use the AOL account to access the internet on campus.

A large shopping bag sits on the floor, with a new pillow in it, a couple of towels, and a twin-size bed-in-a-bag with striped sheets and pillowcases and a dark paisley print comforter inside it, all from the department store in the mall we visited earlier today. The home goods section was nearly picked clean; I was lucky to find something that I liked. This time of year, there are a lot of college students getting dorm furnishings.

Another shopping bag is stuffed full of cheap white cotton undershirts from the men's department. There are enough disposable shirts in there to cover my back for two months before I will need to buy more, if my back still needs protective coverings by then. It probably won't, but it never hurts to be prepared.

I can fit most of the rest of my possessions in a single large suitcase, which I bought from the same department store where I found the bed linens. My regular clothing barely takes up half the space; my winter coat fills up the other half. There's plenty of room in among the clothing to fit the rest of my belongings, most of which are presents Erastes has given me over the years we've been together: The brocade fabric and trim from various Yule present wrappings that I eventually sewed into an altar cloth – not that I've ever bothered setting up my own altar, but someday, I might. A deck of tarot cards that look like they were inspired by Alphonse Mucha. Crowley's Thoth deck. A large gazing ball made of obsidian. An ornate jewelry box containing the ouroboros pendant, the opal choker, my earrings, and some other trinkets he gave me because he said they reminded him of me.

One of the photos Lydia took of the two of us the day she had me pose for her in the cemetery is stuffed inside a book. I dithered over whether to take any of the pictures, but ultimately, I decided that I wanted the option to look at his face, some time in the indefinite future. He's keeping most of them, though, including the framed photo.

The manacles go into the suitcase, then the steel-tipped scourge and the riding crop. I would have the other riding crop as well, the one that was his before we met each other, that over the years I covered with my bite marks and various bodily fluids, but he wants to keep that to remember me by, although he'll never use it again. A few other sex toys that are mine by default, because they can't be used on anyone else now that they've been inside me, go in as well.

All that's left is the red-handled cane. I never did find out what wood it's made of, but whatever it is, it's incredibly sturdy, given the heavy use it's seen. I place the cane on top, diagonally, and start to zip the suitcase, but then decide it would be safer to just carry the cane separately. I don't want to risk breaking it.

The tears start flowing when I zip the case shut.

I'm still crying when he comes into the bedroom. I must have gotten loud. I was trying to keep my sobbing quiet. I don't want to burden him with this, not when he's hurting, too. We're trying to handle this rationally. That our attempt isn't working is irrelevant.

I didn't want this to happen. I didn't want our last night together to be spent in tears.

He puts his arms around me gingerly, and I cry into his shoulder.

WE HAVE ABOUT A month and a half left before I go off to college. Usually, the heat and stickiness make the summer drag, for me, while I wilt miserably and think of cooler days to come, but now the summer is moving too quickly. The days and nights can't be long enough. Of course, the only way to make them long enough would be to stop time altogether.

We had the blinds drawn all day to keep out the sunlight. Too much extra heat. It's been an unusually hot summer, so far. The air conditioner helps combat the humidity, but it's not up to keeping the apartment cool. Today the heat was so oppressive that the extra floor fan didn't even help circulate the air well enough to the bedroom; we wound up dragging our pillows into the living room, along with a couple of sheets, and tonight will be spent on an air mattress. Moving the futon into the cooler part of the apartment seemed like too much work.

We'll inflate the air mattress when we're ready to sleep. We're not ready yet.

We writhe together on the couch to the drone of the air conditioner, our skin covered with sweat. He has me pinned by my arms, and the things he's doing to my neck with his tongue and teeth are wringing cries of desperation out of me. I try to reach him with my pelvis, to drive him into me, but he's maddeningly out of my range. I have to settle for pushing against him.

He rubs up against me, hard with desire, letting me feel his length without actually entering me. I whimper from frustration.

"Did you like that?" he whispers.

"Yes."

"More?"

"Yes. Please, yes."

Another rocking movement that makes me cry out.

"Do you want my cock inside you?"

"Yes, dear God, yes..."

"Hmm. I think I'll make you wait a while. You're very pleasing this way."

A small groan escapes my lips, and he chuckles softly.

"Perhaps you do need a little more attention than I've been giving you," he whispers into my ear, putting my wrists together into one hand while he reaches down with his other hand to stroke the wet spot between my legs. His fingers enter me, one by one, with slow and practiced teasing; I arch, desperately trying to get him further in.

"More. Please. Don't stop."

He continues to whisper into my ear, maddening me.

"More. *Please.*"

"You're so beautiful like this," he says, a wistful tone creeping into his voice. "This moment should last forever. I want to remember you exactly like this. Look at me now, beloved. Your eyes are so lovely when you're hungry." And he slowly pulls out his hand, leaving me empty and gasping.

"Please, I want you," I cry out, "please, my *Erastes*."

"Don't worry. I'm not going to leave you perpetually hanging. After all, that would be cruel, wouldn't it? I promise I will give you your release – in a short while. Get up and drape yourself over the couch arm, please."

Now he's smiling. After all these years, I know what that means. For that matter, even in the early part of the relationship, I knew what it meant when he started grinning like a Cheshire cat.

He opens the living room chest, releasing scents of saffron and sandalwood and cedar into the air, and rummages. Out of the corner of my eye, I can see he's pulled out the red-handled cane.

"It's been a while since I've used this one on you," he muses. "Did you miss it?"

I briefly consider not dignifying that with an answer, but I give the matter some thought, and after a few moments I surprise myself by saying, "Yes." It's one of the wickedest implements of destruction in our apartment, and yes, I've missed feeling it against my skin these past few months. Go figure.

"We'll have to make up for lost time, then. Don't move."

The wood bites into me hard, making me cry out.

And again.

"I love you," I cry, when the third blow lands, burning like fire. "I love you, I love you, I love you." Over and over, with every harsh stroke. It becomes both a mantra against the pain and a plea for more. "I love you..."

Eventually, the blows stop, and he's behind me, leaning into me, kissing tears off my cheeks and sweat off my neck, reaching around me to tease my labia and clit with his fingers. It doesn't take long for him to finish me off; his own need is unrelieved, however, and mine is, as usual, quickly resummoned. "I love you," I scream as he plunges inside me, and then we are pumping and bucking against each other until we are both screaming.

He collapses on top of my back. "*Se philo, eromene. Se philo.*"

I sigh into the sofa cushion, crumpling my face into the fabric, and reach for his hands.

WE'VE PASSED THROUGH THE suburbs of our own city and through a no man's land of industrial parks and towns that might count as suburbs. Now we're reaching the outskirts of the city where I'll be attending college. The music on the radio has mostly become static. I don't know when this happened. I haven't been paying attention.

He notices the poor reception and turns the radio off. Static hurts his ears.

Neither of us felt like listening to music anyway.

I glance out the window again, seeing the peculiarly golden glow of summer on the verge of turning into autumn. It's too sunny and beautiful. The only appropriate weather for today would be dismal, rainy, and cold.

"We need to talk."

I look up from the Gene Wolfe book I've been devouring. Gene Wolfe has been my latest obsession; he tells deceptively simple stories that you only realize near the end you didn't understand at all, so you need to read them a second time, and then a third, and maybe on the fourth or fifth reading you'll have an idea of what he was trying to imply between the lines.

"Yes, *Erastes?*"

"We will be parted from each other after you move into your dorm room."

"That does seem likely since I can't bilocate."

"No. You misunderstand me." He takes a deep breath. "We've talked about this before; I can't be everything you need. That will never change. I couldn't help but notice, when we watched *Sirens* last night, how you looked at Giddy throughout the video, especially when the other women teased her or put her in distress; nor could I ignore your tears after the end of the movie, despite your efforts to hide them. You don't need to hide things from me, by the way. You never did. That you still try to keep some deeply held feelings to yourself is a bad sign. That was ultimately what made me do some hard thinking. But quite aside from the trust issue, there are still things you need that I can never provide for you. I can never be a woman, for one thing; I can submit to you, but I can't enjoy the pain you need to inflict; I can't give you the variety you need, because I can't share you..."

"How do you know that if you haven't even tried?"

"Spoken by someone who has told me she has never once felt jealousy, so monogamy never seemed worth her trouble. This is a rift between us that I don't think can be bridged. Please believe me when I say jealousy is excruciatingly painful. It makes me afraid to lose you when I get jealous. What if you meet a woman who meets your needs better than I do? What if something I say as a result of my jealousy angers you, or pushes you away? You're only twenty-five. You have your entire life ahead of you still. By settling down with me, you give up your chances to live life on your own terms."

"No."

"Look me in the eye and tell me you won't miss the chance to be with other women. Or to be with anybody capable of going more extremely into sensation play and submission than I am. I'm still astonished that you could get as far with me as you did, but you need more. Why did you initially ask to be not just my lover, but also my apprentice? Was it to tie yourself to me forever and use almost nothing of what I taught you?"

"But I have been using it with you, haven't I? Some of it? Anyway, it's a bit late to think of that now. Our souls are married. Permanently."

"Our fortunes, however, are not. Beloved, I am a dead end for you. You will resent that, eventually. We need to part ways after I drop you off at college. I can't keep you."

No. No. No, no, no, no, no, no, *no*

A LUMP BEGINS TO build in my throat. I swallow it. Hard.

HE LOOKS AT ME incredulously. "Are you sure about this?"

"I want a piece of our relationship that will last forever. You say we can't have each other. At least leave me with scars I can look at and run my hands over."

"Ordinarily I'd save that for the aftermath of a collaring or a legal marriage, you know," he says quietly. "Marking you in preparation for severing our partnership seems almost sacrilegious."

"We wed our souls this Midsummer." I've been saying that in protest a lot these past few days, albeit mostly to myself.

"Yes. And we are parting so that my soul will not swallow yours."

I hold out the whip in silence, imploring him with my eyes.

Eventually, he sighs and takes it from my hand. "Are you sure you wouldn't rather have me do something a little less physically traumatic? Perhaps have me carve something pretty on you with a blade, to make it look more artistic? Some intertwining roses and vines, possibly? If I cut deep enough and pull your flesh apart just a little as I do it, there should be some keloid tissue formed. A cautery pen would also work for that, if I had one; I'm not sure I could obtain one on short notice, especially not without medical credentials, but I could put some feelers out."

"Then it would be decoration. I don't want just decoration. I want a part of us that I can keep."

"*Eromene.* This is going to have serious consequences. I'm going to have to work hard to keep you out of the hospital after I'm done. And after we separate, I won't be around to clean and dress your wounds as they heal."

"I think I can perform first aid on myself."

"I'm half tempted to let you put the marks on yourself, too," he mutters.

"Will I have to?"

He gives me a sharp look. "That was uncalled for, *Eromene*."

"I'm sorry..."

"Forgiven. And no, *do not* do it to yourself. It will cause less damage for me to do the deed since I have a more experienced hand. Well. You seem determined, and it's your body to modify as you see fit. I wish the occasion was a happier one, though, and I wish you were choosing a method that wouldn't require as much aftercare. I don't like this... Take off your clothes. They're in the way. Let's get you in better lighting, too, so I can see what I'm doing."

A few moments later, I'm standing in a patch of sunlight as he runs his hands over my body. This must be what it feels like to be sculptor's clay.

"Your buttocks and thighs are the only part of you that have an ample subcutaneous fat layer," he murmurs, kneeling down to look. "They'd probably be the safest place to mark, although whipping you hard there would make it nearly impossible for you to sit down or otherwise put your weight on the area for weeks, which will be impractical for you. Hmm. You might already have a few scars from the last time I used the whip end of your scourge on you; there are some interesting pale lines here."

"They might be stretch marks. I did gain some weight since moving in with you."

"You may be right about that."

He kisses my legs and runs his hands along them, up and down.

"I want to wear them close to my heart," I whisper. "It's the part of me that will miss you the most when we're separated."

"In that we are equal," he sighs. "Oh, my beloved." He stands up and puts his arms around me. I lean against his shoulder; we sway in place, unwilling to relinquish each other.

He is the first to pull away.

"It will have to be on your upper back. Using the whip on your breasts would be an extremely bad idea. I'm going to assume you prefer your nipples to remain attached to your body."

Well. Yes.

"And I think you'd better lie on top of the chest and hold on tightly," he says. "Even if I only hit you once. If I hit you more than once, I'll need to get some ropes to secure you and give you something to strain against. Did you only want one blow, since we're only doing this to leave marks? Or should I keep going?"

"Have we ever stopped at just one of anything?" I ask wryly, arranging myself as best as I can on the chest.

"It will be interesting to see whether or not you safeword before I risk flaying your back to ribbons," he muses. "I can't believe that after several years with me, you have still never used your safeword, except for the one time, which probably shouldn't count because you forgot it before you could actually use it... All right. We'll do that, then. When you lose control of your body, though, I'm going to have to restrain you, provided you don't beg me to stop, first. If I make you scream uncontrollably, that will need to be addressed, as well. I'd rather not get a knock on the door from the police. It is unlikely that any police officers called to the scene would understand or sympathize with the nuances of our situation. If I must gag you, repeatedly opening and closing your hand will be your safeword, and I *will* be watching carefully for it. Brace yourself."

The first lash lands. I feel my flesh rip apart in a blaze of agony. It matches the pain in my heart.

I will love you forever, I think, as I start to cry.

WE PULL OFF THE interstate and drive along a road that winds through a large public botanical garden, and then up a hill. This is the same route we took when we went to hear the symphony orchestra and chorus perform Wagner. The university that gave me a free ride happens to sit across the street from the concert hall, and

from the art museum grounds where Erastes and I embraced on the lawn and talked
about why we had no future together despite wanting to belong to each other forever.
It was sound reasoning that neither of us wanted to heed.

I will no longer wake up by his side each morning, my wrist bound to his. Instead,
I will be walking past my memories every day on my way to classes. I have no idea if
they will seem a blessing, in my exile, or a torment. No doubt they will be a mixture
of both, just like everything else about this relationship; only without him delivering
it, the torment will no longer be sweet.

My back starts itching again. I resist the temptation to scratch.

He helps me move the suitcase and books into my new dorm room. I have
a single. It's air-conditioned. All the rooms in this dormitory are singles, cli-
mate-controlled, and grouped in suites around a kitchenette, bathroom, and den
to mimic apartments. In my experience, bedrooms in apartments are not the size
of walk-in closets, the way the dorm rooms seem to be, but I hadn't expected
much when I listed this dormitory building, an ugly mid-story concrete tower
that sits on a far corner of the campus, as my top choice of residence hall – all that
mattered to me was privacy. I've lived on my own for too long to want to endure
having a roommate again, not that my past roommates ever wanted to endure me,
anyway; and the prettier, less cramped dorms on the north side of campus all have
shared rooms.

The building seems oddly deserted right now. Either there is a lull in activity, or
everybody is in an orientation meeting that I neglected to find out about. Maybe
they're eating lunch.

He puts down my last overstuffed crate of books as I fuss with my new bed
coverings. I am still fussing when he gently pushes me aside and makes my bed
for me.

There is nothing more to carry or settle.

Our eyes meet.

Silence.

And then his arms reach for me, and I know nothing more. "Please," I whisper, afraid to trust my voice, because I know I'll start crying again if I speak louder. "Let me have you one last time. I don't want to let you go yet. I can't let you go yet..."

Our lips meet. We fumble at each other's clothes with shaking hands. Eventually, he has me down to nothing but my protective cotton undershirt, and I've somehow got his clothing off. I want to be completely naked next to him, skin to skin, but of course, that isn't a good idea with my injuries. So much awkwardness, now. We, who know each other so well and who have shared so great an intimacy for years that we know each other's bodies like we know our own, are reduced to this clumsiness. I want even this to last forever.

Of course, it won't.

He is gentle when he takes me; neither of us has the heart for more. Our hands reach and grope, confused, around each other's wrists. "Hold my hands," I rasp, and we clutch each other tightly as if sending the energy of our passion to each other through our palms could somehow preserve us from endings. We try to be slow; but when he kisses me, I feel the flood well up within me and I can no longer hold myself back; we roll together, and I am riding on top of him, hard and fast and hungry. Orgasms pound through me in waves. I feel him straining underneath me, coming with me; and then it is done, and I fall into him, and the sobs shake me until we are both covered with my tears.

I'm not the only one crying.

We cling to each other. Afternoon sunlight lands on our skin, taunting us.

The sun eventually sinks lower, and we are left in shadow.

"I CANNOT STAY HERE forever," he tells me gently. "As much as I would like to."

Of course, he can't.

"Look at me, beloved. This is important. I have one last request, and it will probably be the worst one I ever ask of you. Do you promise to follow it?"

"Yes. For you, anything," I reply, choking back tears.

"Very well. I ask you to be brave for me. It is bad enough for me that I will never be with you again, but the thought of hurting you like this is horrible; I wish it could be avoided, but it can't. It was with your future happiness in mind that I made the decision to separate. I need to know that someday you will be happy again, and that I haven't completely shattered you. Please. Live and be brave. Until you can do that for yourself, at least do it for me."

I nod miserably.

"I need to hear it from your mouth, *eromene*."

"I promise to live. I'll be brave," I whisper, my throat swelling with more tears. I'm sure they won't be the last I shed tonight.

"Good. Thinking about you happy and whole in the future will give me the strength that I need to endure this." He sighs. "I am proud of you. I will always be proud of you. I will always love you. And if you do not let me go now, I may never be able to leave, and we both know I must."

I bite my lip.

"Goodbye, my beloved."

He gets up from my narrow bed. It only takes him three steps to leave the room. He closes the door behind him, leaving me in twilit darkness.

I am alone.

I bury my face in my pillow and start to cry again.

It was good that I arrived on campus during freshman orientation before classes started. I had originally meant to attend orientation, despite technically being a sophomore, because I figured that the orientation would have useful information for transfer students as well.

That never happened.

After Erastes closed the door behind him, I continued crying into my pillow until I had no more energy for it. I cried myself to sleep that night without ever leaving my room. Later I woke up to use the bathroom – I think the clock in the lounge might have said one in the morning, but I wasn't paying attention – tears running down my face and into my throat; when I was done, I stumbled, still crying, back to my room, and continued to sob into my pillow until exhaustion overtook me again.

Morning came. With morning came yet more tears.

Oh, it wasn't constant, at least, not entirely. At various points, I was able to quiet myself down enough to take care of a few mundane details of everyday life. At one point I unpacked my suitcase – removing the gifts Erastes had given me and finding places on the dresser and on the hutch over the desk to store them was another exercise in torment, but I got through it, also through the unpacking and restacking of the books, which included all the books he had given me, and there were a lot of them – and I nearly panicked over having forgotten to buy basic toiletries such as toothpaste and soap, because I had no money on me; until I saw that in a corner of the suitcase, Erastes had packed my scented shampoo and conditioner, also a bottle of chlorhexidine that came with a notecard on which he had scribbled POUR ON BACK AFTER SHOWERING. USE FOR ONE WEEK ONLY. USE ONLY SOAP AND WATER TO WASH THEREAFTER. DISCONTINUE ANTISEPTIC WASH IF IRRITATING TO SKIN. (SEEK MEDICAL ATTENTION IF YOU DEVELOP A FEVER OR IF YOUR URINE TURNS BROWN) in permanent marker, along with several tubes of antibiotic ointment for my upper back and some other personal care necessities from our bathroom, and a new toothbrush and toothpaste, wrapping all the items neatly in zip-sealed plastic bags. Of course, this, too, was an occasion for tears, but I got everything packed and stored, and after a while, I was settled in.

Later that morning I noticed that I was thirsty, and when I emerged from my room to get water from the sink in the kitchenette, I found that I was also hungry, and I realized that I hadn't eaten in two days, so I looked at my campus map and found the dining hall nearest me and the time lunch would be served in it. I even managed to get there on time and to eat my food without bawling in public and causing a scene.

At some point, I must have picked up an orientation packet and checked in. I don't remember doing it. Nor do I remember enrolling in classes, or talking to the financial aid office about getting a student loan large enough to pay for the books and other incidentals my grants did not cover, or introducing myself to the resident advisor on my hall – which was a hall of upperclassmen and had no other transfer students, so I was the only one living on my floor for the first few days until the official beginning of the academic year – but I'm sure I did all of those things at some point.

One thing I do remember clearly is showering unassisted for the first time in the suite's bathroom. For the past couple of weeks, I hadn't had to worry about the practicalities involved – Erastes had washed my back for me with a sponge, while I sat soaking in a bath in a sort of tea made with comfrey, calendula, chamomile, and lavender that he'd boiled in a stock pot with salt to add to the bathwater, and then after bathing me, he'd applied the antibiotic ointment to the wounds he'd made. I didn't have that luxury anymore. For the most part, they had stopped bleeding and oozing, having reached the scabby, itchy stage of healing, but whenever they got exposed to water for a long enough period, they opened up again in a few places, and I really didn't want the lacerations to get infected, because that would mean I'd have to get professional medical help, which would mean having to explain how they got there in the first place. Bandaging was difficult, which was why Erastes had bought me armfuls of disposable cotton undershirts to protect my healing flesh (not to mention my clothing, in case I bled) but I still had to apply the ointment myself, which proved problematic. Eventually, I got used to doing it, just as I got used to the stinging sensation the shower inflicted on me until all of them were closed completely and scar tissue began to form. But that first shower hurt. The only thing good about it was the heat. I had a peculiar chill that had settled in my bones, completely unrelated to my actual body temperature.

For the most part, though, I wasn't paying close attention to these little details of settling in, so I don't remember much else about them.

I couldn't stop crying that first week. After a while it became terrifying, at least, it terrified me, because aside from the things Erastes did to me, almost nothing before this had reduced me to tears easily. But there I was, weeping randomly and completely uncontrollably, in my room, or walking down the sidewalk on my way to meet with my faculty advisor, or washing myself in the shower. Once it started, it took hold of me until I was nearly senseless with misery. The more I tried to get myself under control, the worse things got.

After several days of this, I had swallowed so much snot from crying that I made myself sick, and after I vomited, I looked down into the toilet bowl and saw blood. For a few frightening seconds, I thought I was dying of internal bleeding; then my common sense returned, and I realized I'd merely cried for so long that I'd made my throat and esophagus raw, hence the blood.

AFTER THAT MY WEEPY tendencies quieted down somewhat – something about looking at my bloody vomit and sputum shocked me into stillness – and from then on, instead of spending my days drowning myself in my own tears, I spent them in numbness.

I went to classes – I'd changed my major from philosophy to English, because from what I had seen in my last academic institution, new English instructors were hired far more frequently than new philosophy instructors, and I liked the idea of being hired in my field after graduation, rather than going back to telesales – and I did the course assignments. I couldn't really call it work. It was child's play compared to the four years of private tutoring I'd had before reentering college full-time.

When not in classes, I existed. I ate meals. I read books in the campus library. I auditioned for a concert choir and was given a place in the alto section. It was a way to stay busy.

From time to time, I would be doing homework in my dorm room; and I would stare at the white paint on the cinder blocks of my bare walls, and rage would overtake me. Like Heloise before me, I did not like being shut in a glorified convent cell, unable to be with my lover and soulmate, unable to do anything but meditate and study. Unlike Heloise, I was not a nun, so I could have found a new partner for my bed had I been interested, but I was not interested. I only wanted one person, and he was forbidden to me.

I wondered if he was spending his days and nights longing for me the way I longed for him. When things were quiet at the reference desk, did he, too, stop what he was doing, whatever it was, and stare off into the distance, reaching for our conjoined souls automatically with his thoughts, then pulling back because reestablishing contact with me was inappropriate? Was he tempted to walk into my dreams? Did his memories pluck at him, the way they did at me, begging to be touched? Of course, there was no way of knowing for certain. And that was the hell of it: The one person in all the world, who I desperately needed for advice on how best to handle this agony of separation, to hold me when I found myself crying, to explain to me what I was going through ("Is it harder to get over the end of a romantic relationship if you were sexually submissive to your ex-lover? What if you were the dominant partner in the relationship? Does the power exchange make a difference? Is it harder on submissives than it is on dominants, or not? What if you've also conducted a ritual that bound your souls together forever to the point where your lives in the future, whatever form they may take, will be latticed together like the double helix of a DNA strand, so closely and tightly that no matter how far apart you are, you can never be distant, but you are forbidden to reach out for the link in this lifetime? Is it normal for that to feel like torture? And how can I go on without you?" No answer), who could let me know when the pain might finally be easier to bear, or failing that, who might simply ease my torment by being there and holding me through my ordeal, was gone. I was utterly alone.

And I was ill.

It started with a chronic, nagging headache, exhaustion, a chill, and a bit of queasiness; I figured I had caught the flu.

However, instead of clearing up after a week or two, it got worse. I started to get migraines every day. Sometimes my headaches made me see strange things: flashing lights, or things moving in the corner of my vision that I could never quite focus on.

Time began to move strangely for me. When I was in the throes of an agonizing headache, time moved all too slowly; but then afterwards, sometimes, I would pass out from the pain, and that made time seem to skip disconcertingly. Time itself simply felt weird. Alien. I can't describe it.

Meanwhile, my back, which eventually lost its itchy scabs for a mass of scar tissue, would periodically clench up so tightly that it hurt to move (I forced myself to stretch, anyway, when that happened, fearing that if I didn't make myself move, I might never move properly again).

I got sick when I thought about food, even though I always felt hungry. I began to live on a diet of peanut butter sandwiches, rice, and oatmeal, with the occasional glass of milk or fruit juice, because that was all I could force myself to eat.

I was always tired. I wanted to spend all my free time in bed, but once in bed, I could not sleep. The headaches and the pain in my tense muscles kept me awake. The best I could manage was to practice my Zen meditation. I knew how to meditate through pain. I'd had years of practice, after all.

Then there was the cold. I was always cold; it seemed I would never know warmth again, even on mild, sunny autumn days. The cold was in the marrow of my bones. I could not rid myself of it. I shivered at night, and at dawn, my shuddering flesh would wake me up if I'd somehow managed to fall asleep. It was worst at dawn. Wrapping myself up in my comforter did nothing to thaw me.

When the chest pains started, I finally forced myself to go to the campus health clinic, after having avoided it for fear of what would happen when I had to remove or lift my shirt for a stethoscope; the less said about what happened when that inevitability was reached, the better. Suffice it to say that the conversation was embarrassing, unpleasant, and involved a few white lies on my part, because I didn't think the truth would be very well received.

The doctor tried various prescriptions to ease the headaches, including antidepressants on the grounds that I was certainly exhibiting chronic misery, and my other symptoms seemed consistent with the sort of psychosomatic bizarreness that sometimes accompanies clinical depression, but the best he was able to do was turn the pain in my head down to a dull roar.

Meanwhile, the pain in my chest never got eased at all. At least I seemed to be in no danger of dying, given my normal heartbeat, and the lack of any indication that there was something actually wrong with my heart or lungs, although nothing the doctor did seemed to be of very much help, either. So much for the depression theory; or maybe antidepressants simply couldn't help the form of melancholy that had settled into me, seeping into the very fibers of my body.

THE SNOW STARTED FALLING *sometime shortly after Thanksgiving. Winter break would come after finals; I would need to make arrangements to board over the holidays. I knew some dorms would remain open, for the sake of the large number of international students who attended the university, and other students who, like me, either could not travel home during the winter break or had nowhere to go, but I didn't know if my dorm was one of the ones that would stay open, or if I would need to move temporarily into another room. If I did need to relocate, I hoped I would not need to share a double with another student.*

It wouldn't be fair to the other student to have to put up with my company.

I paused by the concert hall on my way back from classes (all of which were on the north side of campus; the south side was mostly for practical subjects in the sciences, mathematics, and engineering, subjects that I had little interest in studying). I did this often. Every time I passed it, I felt stabbed by memories, but I could never help myself – I had to go there. It was one of the few solid pieces of my past that I could still access. I don't know if I can fully convey how disorienting it is to be cut off from everything that was once your everyday existence, let alone to go through it once in your late teens, then to have to undergo the process again a few years later. It makes memory itself seem unreal. Having a piece of my past that I could see and touch kept me from disintegrating.

And so, I tried to go to the concert hall every day; once there, I would sit on the steps, and hug my arms, and if what I was wearing allowed it, run my hands over the lumps of scar tissue on my upper back, wishing it was not my own skin that I was caressing.

Today was not a day that I could stuff my hands under my shirt and run my fingers across the skin of my back, bundled as I was against the cold, so I settled for holding myself by the arms.

A faint leitmotif of memory in my ears sang to me of love, death, and transcendence.

My head was pounding again. Nearly three months of excruciating headaches, now. My joints were hurting, as well. My chest was in pain. Everything hurt. I was so tired that the mere thought of walking the rest of the way to my dorm room made me tremble. I wondered if that would be my lot for the rest of my life.

I wondered what it would be like to fall asleep on the steps, and never wake up. Dying of cold exposure was supposed to be one of the more peaceful ways to die, or so I'd read at some point.

The wind came gusting out of nowhere, landing on my face full on and drawing tears from my eyes.

"Damn you," I muttered. "I can't do it, but I can at least think about it, can't I?"

And then I wept. Again.

THE COUNSELOR'S OFFICE WAS decorated in Contemporary Inoffensive Ugh. Or something like that. I doubt that there ever was such a style, officially, but I can't think of a better description for cheap pastel office furniture, framed posters with "inspirational" messages and faded, bland reproductions of Impressionistic art, fake flowers and ferns made from silk and wire, and institutional wall-to-wall carpeting. In all fairness, the counselor probably found the university-provided décor as uninspiring as I did.

There was also a teddy bear in the corner, holding a Valentine's heart.

I hated Valentine's Day that year.

"So. You're experiencing chronic pain, and you recently had a breakup with your romantic partner?" the counselor asked.

"The doctor at the campus health center thought I ought to try talking to you," I replied. My reply was probably not a very nice one, I am sorry to say; I have never liked going to counselors for "talk therapy." The thought of swallowing a live frog is more appealing to me than the prospect of spilling out my guts to a total stranger. It's a form of therapy that often seems to do wonders for other people, and I have nothing against it in the abstract, but personally, I'd just as soon avoid it. Why should the intimate details of my life be anybody's business but my own? "Erastes – my former Magister – and I separated when I started college this fall. The migraines and soreness and exhaustion started shortly after that. I've been on antidepressants for the past few months, and they haven't really been doing much good. My head nearly always hurts. It's not a matter of how many times a week I get headaches, or even how many times a day; it's a matter of how much my head hurts at any given time. I've also stopped having periods. I think I've had maybe one period since September. No, I'm not pregnant."

"Erastes, that's an unusual name. How pretty. Your... what?"

Here it comes, I thought to myself; well, either the counselor's head will explode, or it won't. I began to understand the reason why the duties of a student of magick are to know, to dare, to will, and, especially around the uninitiated, to be silent.

"My Magister. It might be easier to call him my former Master, but it wouldn't be strictly accurate, because it was a little more complicated than that. We had a temporary arrangement, or what was initially supposed to be temporary, anyway, meant for instructional purposes. I wasn't bound to him, at least not in any deeply subservient way; I was magically and sexually apprenticed to him for four and a half years, and yes, I submitted to him and followed his instructions when he gave them, but it was for the sake of learning, not for a full enslavement, and even that apprenticeship was something separate from the way our souls eventually bound themselves together. Wed themselves. This is so hard to describe to someone who's never been in that kind of situation. It wasn't originally going to be a romantic relationship – sexual, yes, of course, I thought it would be easier to learn how to do

certain things, such as how to use riding crops, if I had those things done to me first;
also, I wanted him – God, I wanted him – but falling in love? We never meant to
fall in love, because we didn't originally think we were meant to last together, and
maybe we were right about that. Teachers and students aren't supposed to fall in
love, anyway. It can make the dynamics of the relationship awkward. But we did.
We fell in love."

"Wait, he was your high school teacher?"

"No, no, I was twenty when I first met him. I went to a Catholic high school,
anyway. The classes there were mostly taught by nuns and priests. They aren't
allowed to date anybody."

"So, is he a professor here? Were you in one of his classes? Was that how you met?"

"No. He's not that kind of teacher. He doesn't live in this city, by the way. He's not
connected to the university. He works for a public library. Somewhere else."

It had been long enough, at least, that simply saying the words aloud did not
trigger another attack of tears. I had finally reverted to my old habit of never crying.
It was just as well; crying seemed to make my head hurt more.

"And I'm always in pain, now. Headaches. I get these terrible migraines. Chest
pains. My bones are so cold that they hurt. My muscles ache. My shoulders always
hurt, no matter what I do to stretch them – of course, that might be due to scar tissue
from where the whip landed, we got a little overzealous the last time we used it,
although it was nothing that put me in the emergency room, thank heavens, that
would have been awkward. He was very careful. He left nothing that would require
skin grafts."

He could have sutured the wounds he'd made, and removed them just before
driving me to college, but that would have involved needles, and of course, I'd wanted
to avoid needles, even if they were being used in a place where I could not see how
they were being used. I probably should have allowed him to stitch me. In the end,
though, the bleeding stopped before I lost a dangerous amount of blood, and my flesh
managed to heal on its own.

The counselor's face had, if I recall correctly, turned an interesting shade of
white. Perhaps I am misremembering; I am trying to recollect a minor incident

that occurred a long time ago, and the mind can play tricks with memory. Still, I remember milk-white skin, and a hint of sweat, which would be odd, because the room was not hot.

After a long pause, the counselor finally asked, her voice shaking, "You say he was your teacher. Was there a significant age difference between the two of you?"

"Oh. Yes. Yes, there was. He was about twenty years my elder. I don't see why that would be important, though."

"He sounds a bit predatory."

"Actually, I made the first move." And the second, and the third.

Ice was beginning to settle into my voice. I should have known where this conversation would go.

"I see." Another long pause. "How is your relationship with your father?"

"Nonexistent, like my relationship with my mother. And no, my father and my ex have nothing in common, except for both being older than I am, and both being good teachers. This is not about my father. This was never about my father. If it was my father I wanted, I would have chased after my father the way Anais Nin did – and that is a really disgusting image, so I would prefer not to dwell on it. Ew. Yuck."

What on earth did this counselor learn in college, anyway? Was she fed on a steady diet of Freud or something? Freud's theories of the Oedipus complex and the Elektra complex were debunked ages ago.

Eventually, the school counselor sent me out of the office with an assignment to write down some affirmations, and list qualities that I found good about myself, to "boost my self-esteem."

Apparently, I was suffering from "low self-esteem."

WELL, I HAD NOTHING better to do.

I sat on my bed with a pen and a sheet of notebook paper and started to write down personal qualities I considered to be mine, that I liked enough about myself to list them as positive attributes: Intelligence. Courage. Grit. Devotion. Curiosity.

Insight. Conviction. Resilience. Imagination. Taste. Independence. Self-discipline. Focus. Drive. Strength of will.

All these things, I realized as I wrote them down, came with memories; all of them had been qualities Erastes had praised and cultivated. I remembered studying in libraries, or at home, writing essays, and proving points no matter how hard I was pressed to defend them. I remembered holding myself silent and still through bloody canings that would make most people scream, and even harsher things that almost nobody could bear without first being restrained, things that probably stretched the limit of human possibility. I remembered snow evaporating into fog around my naked body. I remembered my first awful cooking experiments; I remembered doing tai ch'i in the living room, side by side with Erastes, and thought to myself that I ought to take it up again because I was rusty and would need a good deal of practice to get the forms back into my muscle memory.

I remembered lying against him in bed, sated and sleepy, wrist tethered to his, as we whispered to each other how much we loved each other; me whispering in English, he usually whispering in Homeric Greek. It took so much to get him to talk in English when he had something emotional to say, but what he said was usually clear no matter how he said it, or in what language.

Remembering hurt me, of course. It did not, however, make me cry.

I could handle this. I was used to pain.

I decided I had no self-esteem problems; also no need for counseling. Such a hard decision to make, almost as difficult as a decision to wear boots when walking in snow.

BY THE TIME SPRING *arrived, my headaches were finally under control. The campus doctor had found an old-school, "non-preferred" ergot-derived medication that, if taken daily, seemed to be an effective form of migraine prevention for me, although there were still a few days when I could not stave off the dizziness and roar of oncoming pain in my head, and on those days I resorted to hitting a bottle of*

strong narcotics that he had finally broken down and prescribed for me. I wondered why it took him so long to prescribe them. Was he afraid I would grow addicted? If so, it was just as well that he didn't know about the shopping bag full of "flower arrangement" poppies that I bought at the craft store in the nearest mall, and how they made a halfway palatable tea if I added enough honey to feed a hungry bear, and which I only drank if I was starting to hallucinate from pain or if I was on the verge of vomiting from it.

I started to force myself to do more therapeutic stretching and range-of-motion exercises to limber up my too-taut shoulders. I found the exercises in the campus library, in a book on sports medicine. I wished I'd been doing them earlier. I also started getting more mindful of other ways to loosen up the scar tissue to avoid being stuck with constricted arm movement for the rest of my life. My motion was already constricted, of course, but I didn't want to risk it getting worse. Several times a day, I would massage camphor and menthol ointment into the tissue, hard enough that I had to grit my teeth when I did it. The scar tissue felt little or no pain; the muscles underneath it were another matter. It would have been even better had I a friend or a lover to do the massaging for me, or failing that, a heavy flogger to use to massage my muscles, but all I had then was myself, and the only flogger I had was the one that had created the scar tissue in the first place, which would have done me little good.

The chest pains and chills never went away. They were easier to endure when I wasn't constantly fighting migraines, though, so eventually I got used to them.

I continued to do well in my classes without actually expending any effort to do so. Part of me was relieved, while the other part was disappointed. I was used to more intellectual challenge; I had grown spoiled under Erastes when he was my Magister. *Hopefully, the upcoming year would provide a little more opportunity to test my worth. On a wall bulletin board in the building that housed the English department, I'd seen an advertisement for a study abroad opportunity at an institute in Oxford for the study of medieval and Renaissance humanities, and upon finding out that my financial aid package could be used for study abroad, I had sent in an application. My year abroad would begin in August.*

IT WAS AROUND THE time of my twenty-sixth birthday that I made the decision that I was ready to rejoin the human race.

I had managed to secure a house-sitting job for the duration of the summer, so provided I found somewhere to store my books and miscellanea after that situation ended, I had no need to worry about the logistics of studying abroad, at least not regarding my worldly belongings; meanwhile, my bank account was slowly starting to fill from a part-time evening job that I had taken with the symphony. It involved using the telephone. Unlike my other telemarketing jobs, though, the people I called to renew lapsed subscriptions or to solicit donations were mostly happy to take the call, even when they had no money to spare, which in itself was a pleasant surprise – but even better, working for the symphony meant I got free tickets. They weren't seats in the best parts of the concert hall, but still, they meant I could attend performances every other weekend or so for free. I thought I could get used to that.

I was even able to attend concerts in that building and enjoy them for their own sake without being consumed by the memory of the first concert I'd ever heard there, and the man I'd sat next to throughout the performance.

I was returning from the calling room and was about to make for the elevator that would carry me to the floor my dorm room was on when my attention was distracted by the smell of fresh pizza. I hadn't had time to eat much before I had to go to work, and that had been a few hours ago. I started trying to identify toppings by smell. Pepperoni, I thought, and onions. Mushrooms? There were probably green peppers on there, too, and whatever cheese was used, there was a lot of it. Just thinking about it made my mouth water.

Then I heard a voice say, "Roll for initiative."

Given that I was living on the geek side of campus, the chances of my stumbling into a campaign in progress in my own residence hall were pretty high – I'd probably passed the gamers before, come to think of it, but was too wrapped up in my angst to take notice. I wondered what game they were playing. I also wondered if I could spare ten dollars or so to order myself a pizza when I got back to my room. By now my stomach was growling.

I wandered over in the general direction of the gamers.

"Oh, no! No way. I don't believe it."

"What did you roll?"

"Three."

"Uh-oh. Attempt at stealth failed miserably there. Well, we'll see. Maybe the balrog will have a bad stumble or something."

"An Elven thief against a balrog? How could things get any worse?"

The die hit the table again, three times in succession, making a clattering sound.

"I'm doomed!"

"Well, Kiera's doomed, anyway. Probably. Sorry."

"Hah. He likes being doomed by dungeon masters," one of the other gamers piped up.

Really.

My stomach picked that moment to growl exceptionally loudly. To this day, I have no idea if it was the pizza that it was growling for, or something else, but whatever triggered it, it was apparently loud enough to be heard, as I found myself invited over to help finish off the pizza.

"Is this a closed group, or do you have room for any other players?" I asked between bites.

It is a truth universally acknowledged that every all-male group of role-playing gamers must be in want of a tall, redheaded female geek, especially if the female geek in question plays the game the group is playing and expresses interest in joining the campaign.

"His character just got killed. You want to play an NPC tonight, and roll up a character of your own later? His backup character's an illusionist. That makes us magic-heavy; we could really use another thief."

They weren't going to ask the new female player to take on the role of Nurse Cleric? I felt an urge to pinch myself, although I successfully resisted it.

"I'd love to!"

I sat down next to the guy who had been playing the now-deceased thief, squeezing myself in between him and another one of the players and reaching for another slice of pizza. It felt strange to be associating with so many people at once in a purely social setting, but the strangeness wasn't a bad strangeness. It was more like using forgotten muscles or speaking in a language I hadn't used for a long time.

"So," I asked him sotto voce, *"what's this I heard about your liking to be doomed by dungeon masters?"*

"I like playing in dungeons," he replied.

I remember thinking that he sounded like he was chirping when he said it. And indeed, there was something birdlike about him. We were both seated, so I couldn't be certain, but from what I could see, he was shorter than me by a head, and less bony than I was. Somewhere between slight and average build, then. His hair was an uncertain shade somewhere between blonde and light brown, and rumpled, like feathers in need of preening. I couldn't quite tell what color his eyes were behind his round wire rims, the lenses were so thick, maybe blue, maybe grey, but the glasses made him look owlish, in a cartoon character sort of way.

It made me wonder if there were any owls anywhere that chirped. Did the fluffy little spotted owls on the northwest coast make little chirping noises? No, wait, they didn't chirp, they whooped, I remembered. They also looked less like little fluffy feather balls and more like owls when they reached adulthood. No matter. He reminded me of one of them anyway.

"Especially if there are whips and chains involved!" one of the other players added.

The former Elven thief didn't even blush. Apparently, his private life wasn't a secret – and he was perfectly okay with that.

"Tell me more," I said. "I'm intrigued."

That was how I wound up going out on my first date in almost a year.

With the person who would eventually become my slave.

WE SPENT THE EARLIER part of the evening at a small English-style pub, drinking ale, eating food that tasted much better than British food was supposed to taste (which was heartening to me, given that I would soon be living in England and thus unable to escape British food) and listening to a folk singer perform Irish tunes. By the time the performer's set was over, we had finished our dinner and decided to make our exit.

It was dark when we emerged. A warm rain was falling; it had been raining off and on all day. Up here, April showers arrive late in the month. I usually like walking in the rain, but I had decided to wear my velvet tunic blouse to impress my date, and I didn't want to get it wet, so I had him get the car, and ran for the passenger door when he opened it for me.

We're driving to his house now to pick up a toothbrush, change of clothes, that sort of thing, which he forgot to throw into the car when he left the house to pick me up – he actually lives at home with his parents rather than on campus, because they are local and it helps him save on expenses, although he's planning on moving into an apartment or a dorm room if he gets an assistantship next year when he upgrades from undergraduate to graduate student. I've been running over ideas in my mind as I sit in the car and watch the rain patter the windows. I still haven't figured out what to do with him.

The easiest thing to do would be to just ask him what he likes, but until recently, we were in a crowded restaurant, and I felt awkward asking certain questions in a relatively public place. So, tell me, how do you feel about vibrators stuck in intimate places? Do you think being penetrated by one would enhance a whipping session, or detract from one? How about afterward? I'm sure the other diners would have loved accidentally hearing pieces of that conversation.

So I kept my questions to myself, and I'm mulling over possibilities right now, instead.

It's funny. I finally have an opportunity to indulge my appetites with a partner who seems more than willing to go along with them, and I'm utterly petrified. I have a form of stage fright. I have to perform; the performance will only have an audience of one person, but I only have one chance to impress him. It has me shaking in my shoes.

I fidget with the black scarf on my wrist. It's on my left wrist, now. I've had the scarf there for several weeks. It seemed to make more sense to wear it on the left side of my body than on my right, all things considered, but I still wear it. I feel naked without it.

Touching it reassures me and gives me a feeling of strength.

We pull into the driveway. The rain is now coming down in sheets. Wordless, I listen to the drumming of the rain on the roof and windows, the whapping of the windshield wipers, the Enya tape my date has playing on the car stereo.

"I'll be back in just a minute," he says as he opens the door and starts to climb out. "I can't believe I forgot my clothes. Probably nerves. This. Um. I should probably tell you. I talk big, but. Um. It's my first time."

Oh. This could either be very good, or very bad, depending. "Are you sure it's me you want?"

"Yes. Absolutely. I've done a lot of independent study on the subject over the past few years, you know. Also, in a weird sort of way, you're cute." He stares at me, with a gaze that could pierce my very soul. "I know what I want. I might lack experience, I'm definitely nervous, but I do know what I want."

Feral hunger pulls at my lips. "This is your first lesson, then," I growl, grabbing him by the arm and yanking him back into the car, seizing him by the fluff of his hair.

The rain on his lips is sweet, but not as sweet as his moan. I wonder what else about him is sweet.

He stands before me, naked. I did the undressing myself, kissing his flesh all over as I removed each article of clothing. I'd read in an interrogation manual that women feel more helpless when they are forced to strip themselves, whereas men feel more out of control when they are stripped by their interrogators. The kissing was my own idea. He looked like he needed it. Also, kissing is what one does with adorable things.

I hope he has condoms. The last time I bought any was years ago, because I was on birth control pills until Erastes and I parted, and I hadn't anticipated needing birth control again any time soon. I really ought to buy condoms of my own. Even if I go back on the pill, latex is good protection against diseases, and I can't count on my partners always having barrier protection of their own at hand. At any rate, although my periods are ridiculously unpredictable and infrequent when I'm not using artificial hormones to regulate them, there still exists a possibility of getting pregnant, and I don't want to get pregnant from the first time I have sex after a long period of abstinence, especially when my lover is someone I only recently met and barely know. I should have asked about the condoms ahead of time. Rather like I should have asked my soon-to-be-lover what his sexual fantasies consisted of, ahead of time.

Oh, well. Something will work out, one way or another.

At least I remembered to close the blinds and curtains before taking away his clothes. The light from the streetlamp across the parking lot wasn't sufficient for me to see by, so I have my cheap little table lamp on, and the window covered, instead. I didn't want to give any passers-by a free show. Admittedly, at this time of night, there aren't many pedestrians, and what few there are would be unlikely to see much, given that my room is on the sixth floor of the dorm, but better safe than sorry.

Naked, he looks more birdlike than ever. He has such small bones.

"Turn around," I whisper, my voice threatening to shake. "I want to see what you look like from behind."

He rotates.

Very nice. His posterior has an interesting pear shape to it that suggests the extra padding he has there might make heavy-impact play easier on his flesh.

Dear God, I can't help myself, he's so sweet in my arms. I wrap them around his chest, leaning him back against me, bend down, and bury my face in his neck, biting him until he shivers and moans; so I bite more, and harder.

"I hope you don't mind if I dispense with the more traditional forms of foreplay," I say softly in his ear, trailing one of my hands up to caress and pinch a nipple. "I'm not really in the mood to fumble my way to various bases with you while reclining horizontally on the bed or in the back seat of a car. I had a few ideas for your skin before I found out you were still a virgin. Would you rather I make an effort to be more romantic and conventional about your first time?"

"This isn't romantic?"

Slightly astonished, I laugh. Maybe what I'm about to do to him *is* romantic. It's all about perspective, after all, isn't it?

"You'll have to bend over and grab the mattress. I have manacles, but there's nowhere on the bed to shackle them to. There wouldn't be much point in getting them out just yet. Can you hold still? We don't have much space in here – if you get too frisky, it could get a bit problematic."

"I don't know."

I should have known that. Nerves, I have too many nerves, and they're all jittery.

"We'll just play it by ear, then."

I look up to the top of my bookcase, where I've been keeping my implements of pleasure and destruction, trying to decide what would be best to use. Cane? No, too nasty. Scourge? Way too nasty, also, it has a reach that's even longer than that of the cane.

And then a realization hits me. I snicker as I reach for my riding crop.

"What's so funny?"

"Heh. You know the old saying, 'There isn't enough room in here to swing a cat?' That's what."

And then I lay into him.

He whoops like a startled owl. He actually *whoops*.

So adorable.

"ARE YOU READY TO try pleasing me another way?" I murmur. I think I'm going to burn up. He doesn't seem to be in much of a waiting mood, either, going by how hard he is.

He nods frantically.

His welts look beautiful in the lamplight, almost delicate.

I use one hand to hold him by his hair as I grab a wrist with my other. "Unbutton me. I want you to play with my breasts."

Underneath the velvet tunic, I am bare; I've never had breasts large enough to need a bra for support. That bothered me when I was a teenager, but when I stopped trying to wear bras, I realized that being relatively flat was a good thing. I hate bras.

I don't take my top off once he's unbuttoned it. I'm not quite ready to explain my back yet.

I gasp when he wraps his mouth around one of my nipples. If he hasn't had much experience, he makes up for it with natural talent. I have his pinned hand on my other breast, and he's finding some interesting things to do with it, as well. This, of course, inspires other ideas, and I pull his wrist down until I have his fingers at my waistband.

"Off," I gasp. "Take them off."

He begins to fumble.

"Do you – do you need help?"

"I think I've got it," he mutters. "Sorry. Blew my dexterity roll."

I hadn't expected to be reduced to giggles so easily. I hope I'm not killing the mood for him. "You'll get a chance to re-roll again in a few seconds," I reply, and move his hand to the appropriate place, gasping when I put one of his fingers inside me. "Oh. Success. That was at least a thirteen, and you have an easy target. Keep doing that. I like that. Good."

"More?"

"*Yes,*" I cry out, and groan when he slides another finger inside me next to the one I guided. "Like that. That's what I want. Oh. Did you – did you pack any condoms when you packed your bag? I forgot to buy them before we went out."

"Got it covered."

"Good. Get one. I'm going to have you. Now."

The nice thing about small rooms is that he doesn't have to go far to get what he needs, and it only takes seconds for him to be within my reach again. I grab him by his member and pull him to me. He gasps. It sounds like a gasp of pleasure, even though what I just did had to have hurt. I should explore this at more length when I'm not quite so desperate.

And then, when I start to unroll the condom and slide it onto him, he comes. It isn't self-contained, either, although he manages to avoid my tunic. Mostly what misses the inside of the condom lands on the comforter.

"Goodness," I say at last.

"Sorry."

He's cute when he's sheepish. Then again, I don't think there's been a moment tonight when he hasn't been cute. If he was any cuter, I'd want to keep him as a pet.

I smile and stroke his cheek. "We have plenty of time. Come here. There are a couple more things I want to try." I kiss him, summoning Fire, as I put his fingers back where he'd had them before. His skin burns, now; he starts to shake. "Let's start with your mouth, shall we? I liked what your tongue did with my breast. It needs to go somewhere else. Down, please. I'm not done yet."

He moans almost as much as I do.

SUNRISE ARRIVED SOME TIME ago; by the time my west-facing window showed light, the sky had already gone from rose to gold. We watch the approach of the morning through the slats of my blinds. Despite the blinds being closed and the curtains drawn, and the rising sun being on the other side of the building, the light manages to creep onto my bed, anyway. At least it's not direct light. I've never liked being woken up by sunbeams glaring into my eyes.

I deflowered my virgin between the middle of the night and the breaking of the dawn. Neither of us was in a particular hurry to finish.

It feels good to have someone in my bed.

My chest pain is gone – bizarrely, blessedly gone. For the first time in months, it no longer hurts to breathe or to be aware of the beating of my heart. I'm also warm for the first time in what feels like forever. How puzzling.

He kisses me. I lean into him.

"I've never actually – you were my first submissive. I hope I gave you what you wanted. Was I – was that what you wanted? Since it was also your first time? Ever? I hope I made you happy."

"Critical success," he quips.

The sky begins to brighten. Although I can't hear anything through the glass of the window, I imagine hearing birdsong.

AFTERWORD:
Book Structure, the Kabbalah, and the Tree of Life

This novel is the first part of a trilogy and is structured on the Kabbalah, in part because my protagonist's mentor follows the path laid out by the Hermetic Order of the Golden Dawn, with a good sprinkling of Thelema tossed in, and both those orders, I am sorry to say, appropriated the Kabbalah for its own purposes, although I would like to iterate that the reality of Edwardian era cultural appropriation of course does not render the Golden Dawn path invalid for those who believe in it and follow it. Nor does it invalidate Thelemic magick for those who feel called to follow that path. I do have some rather strong and unflattering opinions about Aleister Crowley, the creator of Thelema, but they aren't relevant for the purposes of my book's plot, or for this discussion.

Entire books have been written about the Kabbalah, both the original medieval Jewish form and the culturally appropriated Golden Dawn version. There is no way I could possibly explain the entire spiritual system in one brief afterword. I might as well define the universe and give three examples, or narrate the history of the Roman Empire in a page (briefly, concisely, and specifically!) The reader who is curious about all things Kabbalistic could do worse than to consult Wikipedia. See it as a starting point, not as a final destination.

For further reading, if you are exploring the Hermetic Order of the Golden Dawn's interpretation of the Kabbalah, look for books written by Israel Regardie. If you want to investigate the intersection of the teachings of the Kabbalah with Western ceremonial magick and chaos magick, meanwhile, try Donald Michael Kraig. (On the other hand, if you would prefer to stick to the original stuff, reference the books my protagonist reads in the *Hod* chapter).

I used the Tree of Life to structure and determine the plot of *Ancilla*, with most of the book chapters themed on the Sephiroth as my protagonist ascends the tree toward Heaven, right to the point where she falls from the heavens and hits the ground. The spheres are put in order from bottom to top to reflect the fact that my protagonist, like her mentor, is on a left-hand path of ascent, searching for gnosis and apotheosis through self-perfection. She follows the "lightning path" between spheres exactly, from bottom to top, as she searches for her Self.

Here, then, are the meanings and traditional associations of the chapter titles. The sphere for each chapter determined each chapter's theme. I primarily use the Golden Dawn interpretations in *Ancilla*, rather than the traditional Kabbalistic interpretations. My protagonist's mentor and lover is not Jewish; he is Golden Dawn. Since he is the teacher in this book, his perspective is what is used to interpret the Sephiroth.

On we go.

There are three main parts of the Tree of Life. Usually, despite being tree parts, they are referred to as the three pillars of the Temple of Solomon, but I am going to try to stick with the tree analogy for the sake of simplicity, so I ask the reader to picture a tree with three trunks, which is not uncommon for birches. It also sometimes happens when a tree has been coppiced to produce canes.

Imagine, then, a coppiced pomegranate tree that grows in a sheltered garden. It has three trunks. You are standing bolt upright, with your back against the middle trunk. The middle trunk is the main trunk, the trunk of balance.

There are also two other trunks. The one on your left, Boaz, channels qualities ascribed to severity; the other, Jachin, the one on your right, qualities ascribed to mercy. Boaz is traditionally considered to be the feminine trunk, and its function is to set limitations, defining the *terminus*, the borders, parameters, and demarcation of a person's life. Jachin, the masculine trunk, pushes limits and overcomes when necessary.

People who follow the ways of the Hermetic Order of the Golden Dawn attempt to align themselves with the gender-neutral trunk of balance while also receiving the sap and nutrients (the wisdom) from the other trunks, so that no part of their Self starves and withers from neglect. Too much limitation is no way to grow. A total lack of boundaries, on the other hand, is indulgence and chaos, and can potentially result in violation of the Self, or the Selves of other people.

Plot twist: This tree is rooted in Heaven and grows upside down.

Most people who study Kabbalah hope to pull wisdom down the trunks from the Tree's divine roots. To climb the Tree of Life in an attempt to reach the roots and pass the gates of the eternal Garden involves a quest for the forbidden fruit of gnosis.

Malkuth (the tenth sphere) is the physical realm, the manifestation, the Kingdom. It is the furthest sphere from Kether, which is the heavenly root of the tree; nevertheless, it is still part of the tree and thus has its own spiritual qualities. Malkuth gives tangible form to all the other Emanations (spheres, fruits) on the Tree of Life. It is the sphere of Ishim, souls of fire, the lowest rank of angels – angels who are like human beings. (Or, as the original members of the Hermetic Order of the Golden Dawn phrased it, angels who are like men. Most of the original members of that order were men. And the eighteenth and nineteenth-century Freemasons, who the Hermetic Order of the Golden Dawn borrowed this appropriated interpretation of the Kabbalah from, were *all* men. The Ishim were angels who were "like men." Fancy that). Malkuth is part of the middle trunk.

Yesod (the ninth sphere) is associated with pathways and roads, and with moonlight. Yesod pulls the sap of divine energy from on high so that the rest of the Tree may receive. Yesod is transitional. For this reason, I decided to make that chapter stream-of-consciousness, as if my protagonist was finding herself a path in a forest at night, lit by shifting moonbeams. Yesod is the sphere of Cherubim. Yesod is also part of the middle trunk.

Hod (the eighth sphere) is generally associated with plans laid out, with research; traditionally, this sphere is also associated with prayer, worship, and submission to God. And with splendor and glory. *And* with passion and music. That's quite a lot of ground to cover. In this chapter, I used Hod for plans and schematics, but also for a terrible pun, because I couldn't resist the urge. In fact, my hod is full of puns. Hod is the sphere of the Bene Elohim, the Sons. That excuses my dad jokes. Hod is on the trunk of severity.

Netzach (the seventh sphere) is the sphere of victory over obstacles. It is the juggernaut that knocks down and smashes everything in its path. In medieval Jewish tradition, this was the sphere of kindness, but it was a kindness that was preceded by a prelude of harshness. This was all about the concept of "cruel to be kind." It is a catharsis that removes heaps of dead and decaying debris, and there is nothing gentle about catharsis. Despite being on a masculine trunk, it's also the sphere associated with Venus, which is one reason my protagonist's close encounter with her "inner goddess" referenced Inanna/Ishtar, who was the goddess of love and war in ancient Mesopotamia. Use the words "inner goddess" around me at your own risk, especially if you couple that phrase with some nonsense about cheerleaders and pompoms. I will take your fifty tropes, turn them upside down, and shake them violently until loose change falls out of their pockets. Netzach is the sphere of the Elohim, the Godly Beings. Netzach is on the trunk of mercy.

Tiphareth (the sixth sphere) is the sphere of balance, beauty, peace, and harmony. It is the center of the Tree of Life. If you were a nightingale sitting in the middle, singing a song, you would be in Tiphareth. Tiphareth is also where meditations and life lessons can get a little weird, making it the perfect sphere for a protagonist who is tripping balls as a result of an initiation ritual that worked perfectly well for its purpose but gave her the psychic equivalent of a bad sports injury. Tiphareth is the sphere of the Malachim, the angelic messengers. Tiphareth is of course on the middle trunk.

Gevurah (the fifth sphere) is the sphere of harshness, severity, justice, and raw power; it is where strength is found by standing firm in the face of fear and adversity. Gevurah is the sphere of the Seraphim, the burning ones. Gevurah is on the trunk of severity.

Chesed (the fourth sphere) is the sphere of gentleness, mercy, love, charity, and grace. It is the sphere of the Hashmallim, the softly glowing, amber ones. Chesed is on the trunk of mercy.

Binah (the third sphere) is the sphere of intuitive understanding, self-aware-ness, womanly power, gestating motherhood, and the divine feminine: Isis, As-tarte, Diana, Hekate, Demeter, Kali, Cybele, Mother Mary, and Sophia. It has been described as a "hall of mirrors." The fun thing about a hall of mirrors, of course, is that the mirrors can reflect, but they can also cause the person in the hall to get disoriented and lose their way. Binah is also associated with the color black, reflecting the fact that maternal power is sometimes nurturing, like fertile earth, and sometimes terrible, like the dark of night. It is the sphere of the Erelim, the brave ones. Binah defines Boaz. Binah is on the trunk of severity.

Chokmah (the second sphere) is the sphere of divine wisdom and masculinity, of the soul, of fatherhood, and of flashes of wisdom that strike like lightning bolts. It is the beginning of creativity; it is holy fear and holy love. It is the face of that greatness that causes the human mind to gibber and turn to mush. It is the sphere of the Ophanim. Yes, those are the creepy angels that look like wheels within wheels, covered with eyes, and act like giant flying saucers or chariots. This seemed like a good place to return my protagonist to the beginning of her studies. Chokmah defines Jachin. Chokmah is on the trunk of mercy.

Kether (the first and topmost sphere) is the sphere of divine glory. It is the root of the Tree of Life; it is pure consciousness. It is the Crown. It is beyond ordinary human comprehension. Oh, and according to Aleister Crowley, it is also Death. (Go figure). It is the sphere of the Hayot Ha Kodesh, the holy living ones. Kether is central.

My protagonist does not master the lessons taught by Kether. She is not ready.

The next book in this trilogy, *Soror Mystica*, will be structured on the alchem-ical process.

ONE FINAL STRUCTURAL NOTE, this time on names: *Logos* is the idea, the incep-tion; it is reason, order, form, and meaning; it is word made reality. The pure or ideal form of something defines the phenomenal forms that reflect the ideal. *Logos*

is a running theme in *Ancilla*, and to bestow or claim a name or a label is an act of power. In keeping with the book's focus on self-determination, self-definition, self-perfection, and chosen destiny, I have therefore chosen to avoid labels and proper nouns for the duration of the book, except when using them is completely unavoidable.

If named at all, characters get use-names based on function. Those "names" are subject to change. For instance, my protagonist's mentor starts out as *Magister*, but once he becomes more of a lover to her and less of a teacher, he becomes *Erastes*. My characters ascend or not as they see fit, as I write. I do not impose their evolutionary paths on them. I give them their structure, but they have their own Wills, and only they know their own Names.

APPENDIX: GREEK, LATIN, AND THE TRANSLATIONS THEREOF

Occasionally, "Magister" is overcome by his emotions, at which point he retreats into speaking Homeric Greek. It's a dead language that almost nobody knows, so in his perception, it's safer for him to use when he utters things that expose his vulnerabilities and passions. I've included a rough translation. It's rough because my Greek grammar is terrible. I never studied the language; I cobbled together "Magister's" utterances with the help of Google Translate and an online Liddell and Scott dictionary.

First, two words of classical Latin (ground that I find far more comfortable and familiar):

Magister – teacher, tutor. Ironically, most teachers of this sort in ancient Rome were slaves.

Ancilla – This one's complicated. In ancient Rome, an *ancilla* was an enslaved handmaiden to the lady of a large house. The word got frequent use in medieval times because nuns saw themselves as servants of God and the church, married to Christ; in the Latin translations of the New Testament, Mary called herself an *ancilla* of the Lord when Gabriel announced her pregnancy to her. Heloise called herself Abelard's *ancilla* in one of her more famous letters to him, so naturally I couldn't leave the word alone! In modern times, an *ancilla* can refer to an appendage, an aid to learning, or a helper.

On to the Greek. *Literae humaniores* scholars who read this book were probably screaming over my mistakes.

Erastes – Lover. There is a strong implication that the lover is dominant.

Eromene – Beloved. The understanding is that the beloved is the submissive or passive partner. This word has, furthermore, been feminized from its originally masculine form, *eromenos*.

Se agapo – I love you (unconditionally, absolutely).

Se philo – I love you (deeply, as a friend, affectionately).

S'ero – I love you (passionately, lustily); I desire you.

Livomai pou se pligosa – I'm sorry this hurt you.

Sinkhorese me – I regret this/I'm sorry.

Enupniazomai – Sleep and heal/have healing dreams.

Gnothi sauton – Know thyself. This one's famous. You've probably heard of it.

Hypnotte – Fall asleep. (This is a command).

Anapnei – You can breathe. More literally: You are not unable to breathe. You are not *not* breathing.

Anastaso – Revive; come back to life; don't die. (This is a command. It is also, of course, a plea).

Reviews and Praise for Ancilla (First Edition)

PROFESSIONAL/LITERARY REVIEWS:

"It is nearly impossible to put a genre on *Ancilla*, and I don't honestly mind... Sera Maddox Drake purposely chooses not to give names to the two main protagonists, and instead refers to 'Ancilla' and 'Magister.' From the beginning, we're told that this relationship between the two of them is purely educational and temporary, as the best way to learn is by doing. And yet by the last third of the book, I was still (pleasantly) surprised with where we leave Ancilla... If you're not interested in magic and philosophy being sandwiched in between some of the ***hottest*** scenes I've read in recent years, this book may not be for you... I'll certainly be pulling it back out from time to time, and recommend it to open-minded readers with a craving for a more truthful, consensual relationship. Loved it!" *-Hannah Gonzalez, Reedsy Discovery*

"Drake's erotic saga is full of graphic sex, detailed BDSM scenarios, and intricate tutorials on occult sex lore ("A lot of it is Thelemic sex magick, with an eye to gnosis through ecstasy and self-perfection, but a good part of the practicum comes from Siberian and Finnish shamanism"). The prose sounds rather academic at times, but at its best it conveys the charged thrill of BDSM and the sense of intimacy and release that flows from Ancilla's voluntary surrender to sexual torment: "'I love you,' I cry, when the third blow lands, burning like fire....Eventually, the blows stop, and he's behind me, leaning into me, kissing tears off my cheeks and sweat off my neck." BDSM afficionados will love it... A richly imagined, lurid love story that's not for the faint of heart. (Our verdict: Get it!)" - *The Kirkus Review*

"The narrative unfolds as a symbolic initiation, blending dreamlike interiors and ritual chambers with the protagonist's quest for sovereignty over her body and spirit, culminating in a series of explicit, boundary-pushing scenes that serve as both acts of submission and avenues for transcendence... Drake's beautiful prose and dense symbolism will challenge you to think about profound questions about the body, mind, and spirit, particularly in the context of queerness and ritual mysticism. *Ancilla: Master, Teach Me* might be psychologically disturbing for some, sexually exciting for others, and intellectually stimulating; it is deft and balanced." - Meg McKinnon, *The Book Commentary*

"The story's queerness, chronic pain, and spiritual urgency pulse beneath every ritual and philosophical exchange. At its heart, this is a novel that asks not just what we're willing to suffer for truth, but who we must become to survive it... Uncompromising, dense, and erotically charged." - *Book View Review*

"A singular tale, braided with blood, mystery, and intellect, that dares to fuse the sacred and the profane." - *The Prairies Book Review*

"The academic setting, imbued with mysticism, offers an enchanting backdrop that is well-penned with atmospheric descriptions that match and enhance the emotional mood of each scene. The story's honest, raw exploration of themes like identity, acceptance, and resilience, especially through the lens of bisexuality and neurodivergence, will certainly resonate with diverse readers everywhere. Overall, *Ancilla* is a refreshingly unique narrative that celebrates love, magic, and the courage to start anew, and it's a read I'd certainly recommend." - *K. C. Finn, Readers' Favorite*

"Sera Maddox Drake leads readers through each tantalizing scene while revealing a character with a unique realness. With its raw emotion and penetrating dive into the protagonist's mind, readers may think, 'Surely, this must be a memoir and not a work of fiction.' Readers who are new to this genre will amass a great deal of knowledge as they absorb the main character's diary-type entries. This isn't my first read of this type of work, but I discovered many new things about the novel's subject material... The protagonist is led through lessons that provide opportunities for self-discovery, and I have never felt such a fully involved love story radiating off every page with any other book of this nature. Readers who are ready to absorb and are not prone to triggers will truly enjoy *Ancilla*." - *Courtnee Turner Hoyle, Readers' Favorite*

"Kinky and thought-provoking in equal measure, *Ancilla* is part erotic drama and part coming-of-age tale beautifully woven together to craft an absorbing narrative. If sizzling romances are your jam, this is the book for you. Additionally, readers of literary fiction who love stimulating stories with philosophical and emotional themes at play will also find plenty to love about this novel. Sera Maddox Drake's storytelling style is refreshingly unique and authentic. As a reader, it may take you a few pages to get into the narrative, but once you do, you will find yourself deeply invested in these characters and their fates. The master/slave dynamic between the narrator and the Magister felt genuine and believable. That's because the author adds so much emotional depth to the characters to go along with the intoxicating lovemaking scenes. I very much enjoyed the book and recommend it to adult romance readers." - *Pikasho Deka, Readers' Favorite*

"Sera Maddox Drake's *Ancilla* is sure to appeal to a subset of readers, namely, those with a more-than-casual interest in BDSM and other aspects of the occult." – *Michael Howard for IndieReader*

GOODREADS INFLUENCERS AND AMAZON READERS:

"This is erotica done well... This novel has incredibly well-written HOT scenes. It's not overly graphic, but it is ALL there. At times uncomfortable, at times gut-wrenching, the D/s relationship between Ancilla and her Magister had me enthralled. There is a section where the two use elements in a power exchange that had me breathless (with envy!) The eroticism in this book keeps you in a dream-like state... It starts off slow with the expo but the moment Ancilla meets Magister you'll be floating. I was. If only Magister could be my teacher!... If you enjoy well-written erotica and clever references to artistic and literary works, I highly recommend." – *R.A. Volt, author of "The Bookstore," The Whore, and Hard Ride, via Goodreads*

"I rarely read romance because of the toxic nature of the protagonists often involved, and the way Sera has depicted a D/s relationship here is an amazing achievement... The characters have supernatural powers, but these are shown subtly and do not become cliched... Even if you don't read the BDSM scenes (pay attention to the warnings, particularly the Netzach and Gevurah chapters - these are intense) you can still appreciate the book for its literary content... I can't wait for the sequel." – *Rachael Adam, author of* Sangre De Toro, *via Goodreads*

"*Normal People* meets *Fifty Shades*... Like the titular character of this book, *Ancilla* is a complex, captivating read... The novel follows Ancilla and Magister through several years of their relationship, blurring timelines and combining philosophy with emotional scenes of romance, heartbreak, and passion... It is spicy but highly intellectual. It is as much an academic novel as it is erotica." – *Em, via Goodreads*

"The intimacy is scorching hot, but the story is so much more than that. The writing is poetic and beautiful. If you are looking for an erotic book for the only erotism, this is not the book for you. It is a deep story for adults, and one that will stick with you long after you close the book or swipe the last page." - *author Mae Camp, via Goodreads*

"Magister is soft-spoken, a bookworm, and a gamer. He's also one of the best-written men I've ever read of in my life." - *Shreya North, via Goodreads*

"A work of art" - *Mikkel, via Goodreads*

"This is so much more than just an erotica book... The characters stick with you, especially Ancilla, who is trying to figure out who she is, and Magister, who is maybe the kindest dom I've read in any book. It's not just all about the steamy scenes, which are definitely there and don't hold back, but there's also a lot of big questions about power, trust, and finding yourself... If you want something that's smart, sexy, a little weird, and super honest, I'd say pick this up. It gets under your skin and I keep thinking about it days later. Totally recommend for open-minded readers who want more than just the usual romance story." - *author Micki Mirello, via Goodreads*

"The book is a gorgeous beginning to a literary experience that appreciates inner reflection and emotional attachment. It will appeal to both young and adult readers who like character-driven plots." - *Rahman Ibrahim, via Goodreads*

"Drake's richly symbolic language and mystical references create a surreal, ritualistic atmosphere that demands intellectual engagement. The protagonist's internal struggles—her queerness, her need for safety, and her spiritual hunger—resonate deeply, making her journey both personal and universal. Ancilla is a dense, provocative work that refuses to separate the physical from the divine, offering a radical meditation on how suffering and surrender can lead to ultimate freedom and understanding." - *Christian Sia, via Goodreads*

"So much thought and research went into this book and it reads that way on every page. The characters are thought out and full of depth and the storyline is amazing... This is the opposite of Fifty Shades and the likes. Drake is highly successful in creating a truthful, consensual relationship between Ancilla and Magister while being true to more realistic BDSM play. Drake humanizes the characters in a beautifully written manner." - *Ariel Cash, via Goodreads*

"Ancilla tore through my expectations like a riotous spell, weaving rust-belt grit and forbidden yearning into a blazing tapestry of self-discovery and desire... Sera Maddox Drake's prose is both razor-sharp and sonorous, a defiant anthem for outsiders who crave transcendence, and those who dare to insist, 'Take me,' will find in Ancilla a transformative spell that lingers long after the final incantation." - *Justin Goldston, via Goodreads*

"Ancilla is unlike anything I've read before! The story was raw, sensual, and deeply emotional. What begins as a BDSM romance quickly deepens into something more spiritual and psychological. The dynamic between Ancilla and Magister is intense. The writing is both literary and intimate, blending coming-of-age, romance, and mysticism in a way that feels truly original. I was drawn into the main character's journey right away, and the chemistry between the characters is electric." - *author Kayla Cunningham, via Goodreads*

"I didn't know what to expect when I ventured into this novel, but I am glad I ventured... For those who appreciate more literary/academic erotica, this will absolutely appeal... I find it difficult to categorize this novel under any single label. What is not difficult is enjoying this book... It starts slow with a long exposition, but hold on because once the main characters meet the story gets magical fast, and keeps you fully engaged. I devoured it in three reading nights and fell in love with Magister, the character who is Ancilla's 'Master.' Their relationship, and the chemistry between them, the longing soul-mate connection they have, is indeed "magickal…" The erotic scenes in this novel are beautifully written - not overwrought, but neither are they 'closed door.' At times brutal, at other times hauntingly sweet, I wanted to crawl into the book and live some of those scenes. Alas, I could not. But the magickal elements almost (almost!) made me think I might… If you want to read a book that is dripping with sensuality and brutality and the aching torment of a human soul longing for completion with its other half… read this. It won't fit neatly into your head, but it will surprise, burrow, and then linger in your being. I'm glad I picked it up." – *Dill Iester, via Amazon*

WATTPAD:

"Beautiful and incredibly detailed…some of the hottest, kinkiest, and most passionate sex scenes, even with the scenes that aren't technically sex…This book and its very slow-burn, artistic style might not be what the average smut reader is looking for, but I would recommend it to any literature geek looking for something adult, in every sense of the word." – *HappyCoati for The Gloria Regale Awards*

"People will remember it after some time due to its amazing plot…The perfect story for the perfect genre." – *_aishimyy_ for The Gold and Pearl Awards*

"Have you ever had a dream about a tall, handsome man with an accent? Have you ever fantasized about a man who could satisfy a woman mentally and physically while also cooking chocolate chip cookies? If so, then this book is for you. And for anyone who believes that men who read are attractive... Even though I enjoy books about bad boys, I must say that we need more men like him in books... This character is not like the ones you see in today's mainstream romance novels; he is a complex character who immediately captures your heart... He is the type of character who gets into your head, alters your brain chemistry, and raises your fucking expectations... Never settle for less when you can have a Magister." – *gremlinsbookstash for The Hot and Bothered Mini Awards*

"While it plays on adult themes, it is written in a mature manner that many people would enjoy... The author did portray great emotions in their characters, putting us inside their heads so we felt all..." – *SSears90 for The Lilac Awards*

"I love the concept of this story! It was done nicely and I appreciated all the different elements woven into it." – *AthenePersephone9 for Phoenix Awards*

"The portrayal of a BDSM practitioner who is well-educated, respectful, and enjoys intellectual pursuits adds a layer of complexity to the stereotype... Magister is a complex and intriguing character. His intellectual pursuits, quiet confidence, and experience in BDSM create a multifaceted personality... The dynamic between him and the narrator is intriguing, with... a power exchange that is both consensual and emotionally charged. The portrayal avoids cliches and explores the emotional and intellectual aspects of BDSM alongside the physical." – *The Grand Masquerade of Writing Awards hosted by TaeTaeGinger*

"The characters are realistic, complex, artistic, and beautifully encapsulate the 'slow-burn' factor of this book... Very out-of-the-box plot... It is simple, not too hard to understand, yet complex and unique in its own way. Both the protagonists are a mystery. Actually, scratch that, the entire plot is a mystery, and it feels like the layers are peeled off moment by moment as we delve deeper into the plot and understand this uniquely crafted erotic magical realism romance while the characters discover magic, sexuality, and their own identity." – *The ELPIDA Awards*

"A rare find indeed... The story hooks the readers right from the prologue itself." – *sungielxver for The Brumous Awards*

"I cannot start this review without expressing how deliciously dark and magical it was... I have read erotica in the past, but nothing could have prepared me for the intense character chemistry that walks the tightrope between consent, dominance, submission, trust, respect, and communication... I wasn't prepared for this book, not because it was strong, but because of how well-executed the themes were..." – *Saramitra for The Cloud Awards*

"Extremely interesting plot with well-described fantastical elements as well as established characters." – *arrowgig for The Watch Awards*

"I loved the character introduction... The development is strongly built... The story is original... A perfect book." – *sugararmy07, for Realistic Fantasies Awards*

"This book takes readers on such a wonderful journey... The magickal elements were interesting and worked into the story well... It was clear how Ancilla's past affects her and it was wonderful to see her grow and come out of her shell. I absolutely loved that the characters being neurodivergent wasn't their defining personality trait... I could easily see it from their interactions and how they react to things, as well as Ancilla's tangents when discussing things and Magister's info dumping. I also loved how nerdy they both are! The characters are definitely relatable... Overall, this story is very well crafted and thought out. It's clear a lot of research went into the development... The spicy scenes were described well and the magickal elements made it unique and interesting... I don't usually read the whole book for my reviews, however, I simply couldn't help myself and I had to read the whole thing!" – *Holly (lantea) for Primrose Reviews*

"The story possesses such uniqueness that I believe I've never encountered one quite like it before... From the meticulous detail to the vivid descriptiveness, even the minutiae that one might overlook are crafted perfectly by the author... The storytelling is exceptional, worthy of a chef's kiss." – *Emily's Blunt Reviews*

About the Author

Sera Maddox Drake fell to Earth several eons ago and skulked around doing odd jobs (trilobite herding, quantum particle illumination, stromatolite swaddling, mayhem instigation, dragon impersonation, peirazomancy, data entry) until they found an opportunity to write a book. Alternately, they find it both impossible and bizarre to draft an author bio that humble-brags about published writing, literary connections, experience, etc when there is nothing to put on the page, other than "*Ancilla* is my first book. It will be part of a trilogy, and I am self-publishing it, and the two sequels, under a pseudonym. I have some other stuff, as well. Also self-published, also published under my pen name. No, still no Fragile Major Awards at this time."

They live in one of the many rectangle-shaped states in Flyover Country with their spouse, children, and pets.

This bio is much too strange to have been written by a chatbot, but if you need further verification that *Ancilla* was written by a living person, the author has an online presence:

https://seramaddoxdrake.com

Social Media Links Further Proving That the Author Is Not A Frakking Toaster

FACEBOOK – https://facebook.com/sera.maddox.drake

BLUESKY – https://bsky.app/profile/seramaddoxdrake.bsky.social

INSTAGRAM – https://instagram.com/seradrakethebookwyrm

PINTEREST – https://pinterest.com/SeraDraketheBookwyrm

MEDIUM – https://medium.com/@seramaddoxdrake

But don't look on TikTok. The author has a severe nano allergy to pixels and avoids TikTok to avoid triggering theirself.

NOBODY IS THIRSTIER THAN A SELF-PUBLISHED AUTHOR. If you liked this book, please leave a glowing review somewhere.

OTHER BOOKS

Morsels: Tales of Love and Passion

An Author Shout Recommended Read
2025 Passionate Plume Finalist, Erotic Fiction (Short)

Need a bite?

A stripper gets caught in the act of impersonating a goddess... A beauty is loved by a beast... A painter makes her work come to life... literally. But there is a price to pay... Two Sapphic edge-players put the pieces of a flower arrangement to unusual uses on their first date... Here are some short stories that might satisfy you. Some are sweet. Some are savory. But be forewarned: some of these amuse-bouches are as spicy as ghost peppers. They are marked accordingly.

Explicit. 18+ only.

"Sera Drake showcases impressive range, moving seamlessly from dark, Grimm-esque fairy tale retellings to contemporary tales of BDSM and magical realism... A highly recommended collection for open-minded readers looking for something beyond the conventional." - Champion (Amazon)

"I loved the subtle aura of this book, the way the stories built up slowly, peaked, and faded, leaving me pondering, and I liked that the characters and vocabulary were not vulgar. I loved how the stories were arranged so that each story was better than the last." Ann Linus for Readers' Favorite

Excavations

An Author Shout Honorable Mention
Favorite, 2024 Amby Awards (Poetry)

These my offerings,
tiny and fragile, they must take root
in stubborn soil. Fertilize them.
Give them shape. Twisted they may grow,
but their trunks must be strong.
They must reach through the night.
They must be of their ground...

Excavations is a collection of poetry. Some of it is structured; some of it is free verse. Many of these poems are archaeological artifacts. The old material has been examined, arranged, and prepared for display. What does not shine is still pleasing to the eye.

FIVE STAR REVIEWS:

"Why we love poetry" – Dylan (Amazon)

"It's the kind of book you don't just read once—you sit with it, come back to it, and notice new layers each time. A great pick for anyone who loves poetry that isn't afraid to dig deep." (CLP, Amazon)

www.ingramcontent.com/pod-product-compliance
Lightning Source LLC
Chambersburg PA
CBHW061522050726
47503CB00015B/2385